The Fragrance of Her Name

MARCIA LYNN McCLURE

Published by Distractions Ink
P.O. Box 15971
Rio Rancho, NM 87174

Published by Distractions Ink
©Copyright 2013 by M. Meyers
A.K.A. Marcia Lynn McClure
Cover Photography by ©Valua Vitaly/Dreamstime.com, ©Jaren
Wicklund/Dreamstime.com
and ©Kalinn/Dreamstime.com
Cover Design and Interior Graphics by Sandy Ann Allred/Timeless Allure

First Printed Edition: August 2004
Second Printed Edition: June 2009
Third Printed Edition: January 2013

McClure, Marcia Lynn, 1965—
The Fragrance of her Name: a novel/by Marcia Lynn McClure.

ISBN: 9780982192177

Library of Congress Control Number: 2009905393

Printed in the United States of America

This story was inspired in part by an angel that I know,
And for that I dedicate it to her—

To my beautiful Conne Mara…
For standing beautiful, strong, a beacon of hope,
For your perfect beauty of spirit and person,
And for the beauty of your friendship to me.
You are beauty!

I once lived an adventure with another beloved one,
And that experience became an indispensable part of this story.
For the memory of that adventure, and for her essential
contributions, I likewise dedicate this story to—

My beloved little sister, Luanna…
For the ground we trod in Franklin,
For that "regal" path in Memphis,
For our unforgettable adventures in history!
I love you!

CHAPTER ONE

Lauryn Dawn Kensington had been eight years old when first she'd met the Captain, eight years old only by mere hours. Nana later told her granddaughter that Lauryn had met the Captain long before—on the day of her birth in August of 1901. But it was when she was eight that Lauryn truly and officially met him—her eighth birthday.

It had been a hot, very humid day just like any other in the small southern town of Franklin. The blossoms of the wisteria, and their beloved fragrance, had long departed with the summer breezes, not to be enjoyed until the next spring. It was the scent of roses that traveled in through the open windows of Connemara House now, and Lauryn's eighth birthday celebration wasn't scheduled to begin until later in the evening when her father returned home from work at the office. And so, when little Lauryn Kensington found herself anxiously impatient, it had been her Nana that suggested an activity to pass the time.

"Why don't you run along up to the attic, darlin'? Your daddy used to love rummagin' through those old trunks and such up there when he was just your age. Run along, Lauryn honey. I think it's time you found…what you need to," Nana encouraged, smiling as if she had cached some great secret knowledge.

Lauryn thought that it seemed an odd thing to send a granddaughter off to the dusty old attic in search of a means of battling boredom. But she did as she was told and wandered up the great main staircase of Connemara House, pausing rather nervously before the attic door. She'd been in the attic only twice before and remembered it both times as being dark, musty, and stiflingly hot. But that day, as she pushed against the heavy oak door, Lauryn found it gave way far more easily

1

than expected and that sunlight streamed into the dark place from the dusty windows, giving the room quite a feeling of comfort and safety. Still, as an anxious child, she looked about tentatively as she entered.

Almost immediately, Lauryn's anxieties began to vanish. All around her was every manner of antique and sentimental treasure. The old oval standing mirror that had been an anniversary gift from one of her great-uncles to one of her great-aunts stood in one corner. She'd heard tell of it. And there it was! Tangible testimony that it truly existed.

Nearby were the old dress forms used to make the Vicksman girls' dresses, back when Lauryn's mama was planning her coming out in the '90s—back when the ramifications of the war between the states were still all too fresh in everyone's mind. Yes, even at her tender age, Lauryn was familiar with that long-ago war, and its results.

There were other things in the attic as well—an open crate with her mother's dolls lying in it, their small porcelain faces weathered from play and love, the old grandfather clock that was put to rest after Great-Grandfather O'Halleran died during the war. Boxes and boxes littered the floor filled with letters. Her Nana kept every one she had ever received. Great-Grandmother O'Halleran's oak rocker and the grand old music box were there as well.

The music box had always intrigued Lauryn. It had belonged to one of her great-aunts, the one so tragically lost during the war with the North. Lauryn went to this treasure in particular. Sitting down on the floor before it, she cautiously lifted the large lid to reveal the workings within. Carefully, she cranked the handle on the outer side of the box and watched as the small gears churned out the familiar tune. Lauryn suspected her fascination with the music box was why it now was hidden away protectively, and somewhat forgotten, in the attic. She had driven her mother nearly insane playing it the year she was five. It fascinated her to think of the young woman who had owned it and the tragedy that befell her. It had been mystical to sit quietly with the music box before her and imagine a young woman from long ago sitting with the very same box, working the crank and listening to the beautifully haunting tune.

Lauryn's great-aunt, Lauralynn O'Halleran Masterson, had been a fantastic beauty, it was said. The painting of her downstairs in the front parlor was confirmation of the rumor. Her hair, and she had been well known for it, was her crowning glory. It was the color of spun honey and butter. Her voice was like a meadowlark's in the quiet of summer and her eyes as deep a green as the rolling hills of Ireland. It was also said that her young husband had given her this music box, which had been crafted solely for her, as his wedding present to his beautiful bride. It played a tune that was familiar to Lauryn only as being heard from the box itself. She'd never heard it anywhere else. Lauryn loved the box. She had forgotten how much she loved it until that moment. Reverently, she closed its lid and stood looking at her surroundings once more.

"Oh, the trunks!" Lauryn gasped, excitedly. "The trunks!" Trunk upon trunk upon trunk was strewn hither and thither, dust-covered and holding so many secrets that Lauryn's young mind could not begin to imagine them all. Her mind immediately began to race about, enumerating the mystical items that might be cached away within the rectangular bellies of the wood and leather devises of intrigue. What magic there must be stored in them! What legends and histories!

The warm southern sun streamed through the attic window and seemed to shine upon one specific trunk that stood in a nearby corner. As Lauryn approached it, it seemed singled out among the rest. First and foremost, and odd in itself, was the fact that there lay upon its weathered self not one hint of dust. Furthermore, it looked as if it had been lovingly polished very recently. In fact, as Lauryn moved closer to the rather small, oval-topped trunk, she could smell the almond oil that her Nana sometimes used to buff her own furniture.

Then, as she stood before the trunk and put out her hand to lift the latch, Lauryn fancied she heard her name being called, and with it the faint yet familiar fragrance of wisteria. But the wisteria blossoms had been gone from the trees and vines of Connemara for months. Surely she only imagined both her name being called and the fragrance. The fragrance dissipated almost instantly, and since she did not further imagine her name being whispered on the air, Lauryn shrugged in a child's manner and returned her attention to the trunk resting on the floor before her.

Carefully, her small hands lifted the latch, and the young girl peered in excitedly as if it promised to reveal hidden treasures to her. Again Lauryn fancied the scent of wisteria filling her nostrils for a moment as she pushed the lid to the trunk back and lifted out the yellowing and brittle paper cover that lay within. *I must really be missing my beloved wisteria today*, she thought as she set the crumbly, ancient paper on the floor next to her. When she looked back to the trunk, something on the inside panel of the lid caught her attention. A name. Indeed, her name! Great-Aunt Lauralynn's!

Lauralynn was printed in fading gold lettering in the lower right corner of the trunk lid. How exhilarating! An ancient case befitted with the name so similar to Lauryn's own. It was obvious to her, even at her young age, that the woman who had owned the music box had owned this trunk as well. *Great-Aunt Lauralynn's very treasures*, she thought— things to imagine being owned by the lovely face on the painting downstairs. Running her hand over the smooth texture of once-white lace that was the first treasure, she again inhaled deeply the faint scent of the wisteria blossom.

"It's a weddin' dress," the child whispered to herself, even before she carefully removed the garment from its protector. Holding it up to admire the fine tatting of the lace, the tucks, and the embroidered lavender wisteria blossoms that embellished the bodice of the gown, Lauryn knew what it was. As she struggled to completely deprive the trunk of its yards of yellowing fabric, she muttered, "This one wore big hoops if ever I did see one that did!" Then, gently placing the treasured dress on top of the previously removed paper, she looked to see what other romantically nostalgic spoils were within.

A sampler came next, cross-stitched to perfection, on yellowing linen. The brilliant green and lavender colors of the threads, however, seemed as vibrant as the day it was finished. Holding it up in the sunlight, Lauryn read aloud, *"Brandon and Lauralynn Masterson wed August 16, 1863."*

"Lauralynn," Lauryn whispered, reading the sweetly familiar name once more. "Lauralynn and Brandon." Setting the sampler aside, she reached again into the trunk, withdrawing an aged doll with a china head and cloth body. The paint of the doll's face was chipped and somehow made Lauryn sad. Setting it aside, she withdrew a tintype. It was small and dark, but at once all else that may or may not have been in the trunk seemed of no interest to Lauryn. As she gazed, mesmerized at the image before her, a great warmness began to wash over her being. An unusual melancholy nearly overwhelmed her youthful heart as she peered into the faces of complete strangers that seemed, somehow, as familiar as the people she lived with.

"Lauralynn and Brandon," Lauryn whispered to herself as her tiny fingers traced the figures in the likeness. "Your weddin' portrait." For it was obvious that the woman in the type, the woman from the painting downstairs, wore the very dress, hooped as was the fashion of the time, that Lauryn first had removed from the trunk. The man wore the uniform of a soldier. "You were beautiful," Lauryn whispered, gazing intently at the young woman's face. "And such a handsome soldier. Yankee at that." And it was true. Brandon, Lauralynn's husband, was tall, dark-haired, and as handsome as any prince in the fairy tales Lauryn's mother read to her at night—even if his uniform was of Yankee origin. "What a scandal that must've caused!" she exclaimed to herself.

At that very moment, the air in the attic seemed to refresh itself. There came a breeze that danced through the room although the windows were closed. From behind her came a voice—no more than a whisper at first—and in the next instant Lauryn felt a calming, comfortable, unseen presence.

"If I turn around and look at you…will you be there?" Lauryn whispered. Knowing full well how silly it would sound if anyone from downstairs were to enter the attic in search of her and find her talking to the breezes, Lauryn paused, only half expecting an answer. Of course there wouldn't be an answer. She would've seen or heard anyone enter the attic. But when an answer did come, she sat frozen, her eyes intent on, but blind to, the tintype in her hands.

"I will," came the voice. It was a man's voice, deep and commanding, yet oddly reassuring. Still Lauryn feared to turn and look back, but not because she feared seeing ghosts. There had always been stories of ghosts roaming the house and grounds of Connemara. Some said they were the spirits of vengeful slaves that had once worked the fields nearby. Others said they were soldiers who had died in battle in those same fields or had been brought to Connemara to be tended to during the Battle of Franklin. And still others claimed that the ghost of a Union soldier had been seen, walking the grounds as if in search of something. Therefore, ghosts were not a new idea to Lauryn.

All the same, she could not turn to speak to him and simply asked, "Are you Brandon?"

"I am," came the answer.

"I…I'm gonna look at you now, Mr. Brandon. That I am, sir," the young girl muttered. Slowly she turned where she knelt before the trunk to see standing just behind her, as if he'd just walked into the room, Captain Brandon Carmichael Masterson. He stood there—really stood there with her—looking as if he'd stepped directly out of the dingy tintype she held in her hand and into a world of color in 1909.

⅋

Ten years! It had been ten years since Lauryn had first ventured into the attic and met the Captain. And now she was on the train back to Franklin, back to her beloved Connemara and back to the Captain. How she'd missed him while she'd been gone! After all, he had been her dearest companion for the past decade. She had missed him desperately while she and Nana had been in New Orleans for the past year.

"Nana?" Lauryn whispered to her grandmother. The elderly woman's eyes were closed, her tiny hands folded neatly in her lap. "Are you sleepin', Nana?" Lauryn asked once more. Her grandmother appeared to be resting, head propped comfortably on the lacy pillow tucked against the seat back.

Reaching over and tenderly brushing a loose strand of snowy-white hair from her grandmother's forehead, Lauryn smiled. What a beauty her Nana was! *There is nothing so beautiful as an aged woman*, she thought. The wisdom that shone from her bright eyes, the unmatched comfort that came from her nurturing words and embraces gave to each snowy-haired matron the essence of an angel. And Lauryn's grandmother, Virginia Anne Kensington, was the most beautiful of all.

Long ago, Lauryn had come to realize the mischievous little woman was often quite wide awake and coherent even though she appeared to be sleeping. Yes, Lauryn's grandmother was no less than an expert at playing possum. This time, however, slumber had gotten the better of Virginia Kensington, and she was truly asleep. Lauryn sighed contentedly as she propped her elbow upon the armrest of her own seat. She placed her chin on her fist and gazed out the window as the train passed through the scenic countryside.

The steady rumble of the train traveling along the track provided a soothing accompaniment to her thoughts and fancies. The trees were not decked in various shades of tree-green as they would be come spring, but their late wintry state was beautiful in its own right. Lonely, leafless branches reached toward the clear blue, promising skies. Birds fluttered here and there, and small grayish-brown squirrels scurried about in the once-green meadow grasses. The promise of spring was quite evident—if one simply took the time to notice.

Sighing heavily, Lauryn caught sight of herself in the glass of the train window. Her brows were nicely arched and perfectly accented her hazel-green eyes. A small, rather heart-shaped mouth and high cheekbones were the only features of her face Lauryn found acceptable. She inwardly thanked the heavens for those satisfactory attributes. Her teeth were straight and white as pearls, and she assumed that made her smile something to be thankful for. Her figure was pleasingly well proportioned, and although she was not many inches above five feet, she could be considered of average height.

But her hair! The mass of brown, thick, wavy locks was her greatest frustration. It was a rather unusual shade of brown, like cinnamon and nutmeg sifted together. The problem was the seemingly blessed curl that let it hang in full, perfectly formed ringlets. It was impossible to get the thick mass of tresses to stay in any sort of style true to the times. When her hair was down, she reminded herself of some wild, untamed woman raised in the jungle. She did indeed keep it long, for cutting it short would have given her the appearance of wearing springs on her head! Consequently, when in public, Lauryn forever had to pull back the dark, wavy mane or deal with the surprised, disapproving stares of all mankind.

Finally admitting herself shallow in pointless musing, Lauryn thought, *Perhaps there are those who are all the more beautiful than I am. But still, there are those who are less attractive.* This was how she always managed to find peace with her seemingly common appearance. With one final sigh, Lauryn returned to her pondering on other of life's factualities.

It had been over three-quarters of a year since she and Nana left Franklin, Lauryn reflected. It seemed hard to imagine they had been gone so long. It had been a glorious year in many ways, yet horrific in so many, many others. The war had ended. The world could be thankful for that. Yet the influenza had taken a massive quantity of human life. More people were taken by disease than men lost in the war. It seemed unfathomable to Lauryn that she should have been spared by the influenza's merciless, murderous rampage. Then she realized it had been nearly six months since the influenza struck and took her father.

Lauryn's mother had sent word that she and Nana were not to return home, as her father had fallen ill. It was a mere six days later that they received word of his death. She and Nana were not even able to attend the funeral. Her younger brother, Patrick, had contracted the disease, and they were advised not to travel. Nana was heartbroken that she could not attend her son's wake to say her last good-byes. It was nearly unbearable for Lauryn as well. She missed her father! What would home be without him? She wondered if it would even seem like home. Her father's presence dominated their home; his love permeated every inch of it. A part of her was frightened at life without him. And yet she was beginning to heal. The past months away from home had forced her to heal.

Lauryn closed her eyes and tried to dispel the visions of the evils that had devastated the world—the evil of war and the sickness of influenza. Oh, how she missed her mother and siblings, her friends in Franklin! The train could not arrive in Tennessee quickly enough for her.

She dreamily imagined her beloved Connemara House. She was so glad her Great-Grandfather O'Halleran had named it after the place of his birth, a little-known region in Ireland. It couldn't have been more beautifully named. It was exciting to anticipate that in a few months spring would be nurturing the tiny buds of the prolific wisteria vines and trees that covered the grounds at Connemara so that…ahhh! Lauryn could almost smell them, almost feel the fragrant lavender blossoms that hung heavy on the vines. Inhaling deeply, eyes still closed, she tried to envision what the house had looked like the spring before she left.

The wisteria was beautiful that spring! Even with the war raging abroad, even with the ever-oppressive anticipation of good news or bad that prevailed upon everyone at home, the wisteria at Connemara was beautiful like a promise that God had not forsaken the world. Lauryn loved to watch the long clusters of blossoms dance softly with the breezes among the green of the vine's leaves, spilling out their gently intoxicating scent. It seemed to be the pure perfume of heaven.

And, yes, her family—the loved ones of her heart. How wonderful it would be to see everyone! They were the spirited souls that made Connemara a piece of heaven. Lauryn had missed them all! And her father. She opened her eyes to dispel the vision of him, concentrating on those who remained.

She imagined her mother kneading bread dough and then busily cleaning up the kitchen while it was set to rise. Patrick would be waiting, very impatiently, for Nana and Lauryn's return. There would be someone else to assist him in setting up his toy soldiers and shoot them down with pebbles to imitate the terrible war that had raged overseas. Who? None other than Lauryn. It was a certainty that elder brother Sean was too busy with his wife, Melinda, and new baby, Junie, to find a moment to entertain his wee boy sibling. Over the past long months, Patrick's letters had pleaded with Lauryn to return, for he had not one worthy playmate—no one whose aim with a pebble were as deadly to a small tin soldier as his older sister's. And how absolutely wonderful it was to now have a small niece to spoil and love! She could just imagine the wonderful scent of the new baby's head and soft fuzzy hair. Yes, the new baby would be especially fun to greet.

And Penny, her dearest friend! Penny McGovern would have returned from her time away as well. Letters just weren't the same as giggling face-to-face. Lauryn thought of the days she and Penny had spent playing on the grounds of Connemara. She smiled, remembering their pretended romances with Henry, the ancient statue that stood weathered and worn just outside the gate that led to the family cemetery. In her mind's eye, Lauryn could still picture the way Penny demonstrated how to properly kiss a boy using Henry's granite lips as proxy. Lauryn cleared her throat, realizing she had giggled out loud. Yes, it would be fabulous to see Penny again.

However, of all the people she'd missed, it was the Captain Lauryn was most excited to see. It had been nearly intolerable to be parted from him for so long—and yet almost a peaceful respite for her mind. Would he visit her immediately? she wondered. Would he wait until she had been home for several hours or days? She could not wait to see him! How she hoped he would not tarry in seeking her out. Even now she could imagine him, standing before her—his countenance so uncommonly handsome, his eyes searching hers familiarly, his uniform as inspiring as that day he'd first donned it before going off to war so long ago.

Closing her eyes once more, Lauryn sensed a smile spread across her face and a comforting warmness fill her body at the thought of him. How she longed for his company. And it was only natural that her mind then wandered back to the first time she met him, so very long ago—when her child's heart was pure and open to believing all that it needed to believe.

&

"Speak to me, sir! 'Cause y'all'r givin' me a fit of the shivers worse than I ever had 'em before!" the young Lauryn ventured as she stared in awe at the manly apparition standing before her. Instantly, she felt reassured when the man hunkered down to meet her face-to-face, an enchanting grin spreading across his features. My! He was handsome!

"No need to be scared of me, little one. We already know each other," the man said.

"I have to say it, sir…I never in my life remember meetin' up with you! And I'm sure that I would if I had," Lauryn told him.

His chuckle was like deep, rich honey and warm summer bees buzzing, and Lauryn liked it. "Well, now, maybe I was a little soon in saying that we know each other. I know you, anyway. I remember the day your mama had you, the day you sat up and took notice of the world, and I know today's your eighth birthday. And I believe if you think about it very hard, you can tell me what you've learned about me by rummaging through that trunk this afternoon."

Lauryn loved a challenge or a game, and this seemed to be both to her at that moment. "I know your name is Brandon. And I know your wife's name is very close to my own…Lauralynn. I think this here is y'all's weddin' portrait, and I think you're as handsome as she is beautiful. I think that there near-bolt of fabric was her weddin' gown, and I think—by the manner of your uniform, sir—that you were a Yankee!"

Again the gentle laughter. "You're a smart girl, all right, Miss Lauryn. And I knew you would be. Anything else?"

She may have been only eight years old, but Lauryn had a very discerning mind, and as she looked at the man and at the likeness in her hand and at the well cared for trunk, she said, "Y'all'r a ghost. And ghosts only come back to see the livin' if they're in some kinda trouble or havin' a worry." She wrinkled her tender brow for a moment thoughtfully and then continued. "I've seen Miss Lauralynn's paintin' in the library, but I never knew her story exactly. Only that it was tragical. Never thought 'bout askin'...before now. But I think...I think tragedy must be with you too. And I think that's why you roam around the grounds here searchin'. Are you lookin' for Miss Lauralynn, sir?"

The man smiled, though his eyes showed a deep, sorrowful pain. "I am, miss. I am. And you're the one to help find her. I've been waiting until you were old enough to understand, and I think you are. I'm Captain Brandon Masterson," he said, standing. "Brand to my friends. And I'll be here whenever you need me, Miss Lauryn. And I hope that someday you'll be willing and able to help me find my Laura...my sweet Lauralynn. Now, go on down to your grandmother. She's got a story to tell. And after your party tonight, you and I will have a talk, okay?"

"Yes, sir!" Lauryn exclaimed, jumping to her feet and starting for the attic door. "Oh, wait! I've got to tidy up the trunk!" she said, coming back to stand by it.

"Oh, you leave that to me, sweetheart. You leave that to me," the ghost mumbled. And even at a young age, Lauryn understood a person's—a spirit's—need for privacy, and she left the room, closing the attic door behind her.

"Nana? Where are you?" she called as she dashed down the stairs of Connemara House.

ॐ

"Lauralynn was my older sister, child," Lauryn's Nana told her as she sat in the rocking chair on the front porch that day, staring out at the beautiful greens of summer. "She was ten years old when I was born, and I was only eight—just your age today—when I saw her last. The war was comin' to an end...but now, let me start before that, darlin'. Long before."

Lauryn settled herself at her grandmother's feet, crossed her legs, folded her hands in her lap, and looked up anxiously at the wise woman.

11

As the fragrant summer breeze swept across her face, Lauryn Kensington began to learn of the dark tragedy that had veiled her family for over fifty years.

"Go on, Nana. Go on. It's hours and hours before Daddy comes home for my party. Tell me the whole story. No matter how long it is!"

Virginia Kensington drew a deep breath and began again. "My daddy, your great-granddaddy, was—"

"Kiel McCrea O'Halleran!" Lauryn interrupted proudly.

Nana smiled. "That's right, sweet pea." Nana reached down and caressed Lauryn's cheek lovingly. "He came to Tennessee in 1835 from Connemara, Ireland. He was twenty-two years old, highly educated, and had enough money to buy this land and build Connemara House. He was Franklin's finest doctor, you know, angel."

"I do know it, Nana," Lauryn giggled.

"Then I'm tellin' things you know already." Nana paused and brushed a stray curl from Lauryn's cheek. "My daddy was Kiel, my mama was Erynn Shayla Keenan, and they were married in 1835 when Mama was sixteen years old. Their first baby was my oldest brother Ethan. Then came Erynn, then William, then Sean, then Lauralynn, then...then baby John. My sister Lauralynn was ten years old when Mama finally had me, and I was the last. Lauralynn was my perfect, beautiful big sister, and I thought the sun and moon and the stars in the heavens danced to her will. Oh, she was the most beautiful girl in Franklin, and nobody would argue it. We all called her Laura.

"Well, the summer that Laura was fourteen, Daddy went to Knoxville and hired up a couple of young men to help out around the grounds. Daddy didn't own slaves. He only hired on folks, no matter their color, and paid them wages. Daddy was an Irishman, and he'd seen how people treated the Irish, and he didn't think it was right. He didn't think slavery was right either."

"He was a wise man," Lauryn interrupted.

"Yes, he was, angel," Nana chuckled. "Consequently, we had a hard time hirin' local boys to come and work. And all the other black folk...well, most were still slaves. So Daddy hired two nice boys from over in Knoxville to help him out. Daddy knew a couple of families over there that had boys they wanted workin' for the summer. One of them boys was Brandon Masterson. We called him Brand." Nana smiled. "I guess Brand had been givin' his folks nothin' but fits with his antics and pranks, and they felt he needed to be developin' his work skills. Needed hard work to settle him down a bit. So they sent him down here with Daddy. Oh, he was a handsome one, that Brand." Lauryn smiled and nodded, and her Nana winked at her. "But I guess you'd be knowin' that yourself by now."

Lauryn nodded delightedly, and Nana sighed as she continued.

"It was love at first sight, Brand and Lauralynn. No one had ever seen the like of it! But they were young. Brand was only seventeen, and Lauralynn was just fourteen. Still, that summer everyone knew they were meant to be together. And then…then the war started. And Brand signed up Union. East Tennessee was more Union than Confederate, you remember hearin'."

Lauryn nodded, though she hadn't really remembered owning the knowledge before that moment.

"Lauralynn was heartbroken to watch him go. We all were. But Lauralynn and Brand were true lovers. At first, letters arrived a couple of times a week from Brand, and Lauralynn wrote every day. Then the battle lines were more strictly drawn, and Brand would usually send messages through other people or through couriers. I don't know how he did it, but Lauralynn never had cause to wonder whether or not her soldier was thinkin' on her every moment.

"Then, that second year of the war, Brand got wounded and was sent home for a time. Mama took Laura over to Knoxville to visit him, and while he was recoverin', Daddy let them get married—in August of '63. It wasn't hardly more than a year later that we lost Daddy and Laura…and then dear Brand." Her grandmother paused, reflectively.

But Lauryn couldn't abide her stopping midstory and begged, "Great-Granddaddy and Lauralynn? And Brand? The same year?"

"Yes. And Daddy and Laura were lost on the very same *day*, sweetheart," came her Nana's quiet answer. "You've heard so much about the Battle of Franklin." Lauryn nodded as her grandmother continued. "How it was fought right here on these very streets! And in the fields around us! Connemara House was used to patch up the wounded or let them lie down while they died. Anyhow, Brand was off fightin' elsewhere, but the battle that raged here…well, the horrible part of it all, sweetheart, is that none of us really know what happened to Laura."

Lauryn's brow puckered into a deep frown. "What do you mean, Nana? How could y'all not know what happened to her?"

Nana wiped a single tear from her cheek daintily with her handkerchief. "November 30, 1864. Everythin' was chaos. Purely chaos. Men were bein' hauled into the house by the wagonload, it seemed. They couldn't fit another poor soul into that big house just out of town that they were usin' as a hospital. So…they were bringin' them here. Mama and Daddy and me and Sean were helpin' as much as we could. But I was so young, and Sean had lost an arm in the war and was home, but still sufferin' and weak. We did what we could, but we could hear the guns and the yellin'. The noise of the battle was so loud! And then Daddy went out to help some men bring in a soldier who had been shot just outside on our front lawn…and a stray ball hit Daddy square in the left shoulder. Mama nearly lost her mind when Daddy came staggerin' in, but she stayed strong and tended to him calmly. The man who had been hurt was still outside, and there were balls flyin' about and Yankees everywhere. And Laura had such a helpin' nature. She ran out to help the man, and…and she was shot. The ball hit her low in her tummy. It was horrible! At the same moment that Sean was helpin' Laura into the house, the Yankees surged forward a bit and tried to storm us! Our boys were fightin' them off, but it frightened Daddy, and he told us all to hide. Sometimes I think that because he was hurt, maybe his mind wasn't just where it should have been. He hid Mama and Sean and me in the secret crawlspace under the stairs—you know the one you children play in?"

Lauryn nodded, knowing that the crawlspace would never seem the same to her again.

"And Daddy said he would take care of Laura," Nana continued. "Mama argued with him…told him that he and Laura both needed carin' for. But he said he knew where they'd be safe, and he shut us in. I'll never forget bein' huddled up in that hidin' closet, listenin' to those wounded men cry out for help…the men that were still in Connemara House when the Yankees tried to get in."

Lauryn wiped the tears from her cheeks and shivered herself as her grandmother trembled at the memory.

"Can't imagine why a little girl of eight would have to see such things, sweet pea," her grandmother whispered, wiping her own tears. After a moment, Nana began again. "Anyway…when things finally quieted down and Sean said we could come out of the hidin' closet…Daddy was sittin' in the parlor, starin' out the window like he'd just come home from seein' a patient and was restin' his feet. He…he was dead. Another ball had hit him in the forehead. And…and we never did find Laura."

"But…but where was she, Nana?" Lauryn asked. What could her grandmother possibly mean? How could she not be found?

Nana's tears ran profusely down her cheeks, and she dabbed at them frantically. "We couldn't find her, darlin'. We looked everywhere…asked everyone. But no one had seen her. No one knew where Daddy had taken her…where she had gone or wandered off to. No one. Ever." Nana wiped daintily at her nose. "Mama never quit lookin' for her. On her deathbed, she called out for her…apologizin' for havin' lost her."

"And…and what of Brand?" Lauryn ventured.

"Brand came walkin' down the street one day soon after the war had ended. He was sick, weakened, and…and I think he knew. I remember when Mama told him, he dropped to his knees and cried like I had never seen any man cry. I'd seen men cry when they were gettin' their legs sawed off, and they didn't sound as anguished and in such agony as our dear Brand was. I think he died of a broken heart. He was dead within the week. The doctors said things had been damaged inside his body…and that his makin' the trip back to Connemara had been too much for him. But…but I think his heart broke right in two." Nana paused for a moment, wiping her tears again with her now sodden handkerchief. "He loved her so, you see. We buried him in the family cemetery, leavin' a space for Lauralynn just next to him," she sniffled.

Lauryn brushed the tears from her own cheeks. "He…he's still lookin' for her, Nana," she offered.

"I figured as much," her grandmother whispered. "His last words livin' were, 'I won't rest until I rest with Lauralynn.'"

Then through her tears of heartache, Lauryn asked, "Why me, Nana? Why did *I* see him? Was I the first?"

Lauryn's grandmother reached down and gathered her small granddaughter into her lap, hugging her tightly and smoothing her hair. "Why you? I don't know. I think…I just don't know. And were you the first to see him? No. I saw him too. Once. A long time ago."

Lauryn smiled up at her grandmother. "You did?"

"Yes, sugar. He and I met out by the gazebo when I was sixteen. 'Are you lookin' for my sister, Mr. Brand?' I asked him. He nodded and smiled at me, and he was gone."

"He…he talked to me, Nana," Lauryn whispered. "You…you believe me, don't you?"

Again her grandmother's tears were profuse as she nodded. "Oh, I do believe you, Lauryn. And I know you'll figure it all out one day. All this time none of us have been able to…but you will. I know it!"

&

Lauryn opened her eyes and looked out the train window, wiping at her tears with her sleeve. The story her Nana had told her that day had been the stuff of nightmares. Lauryn, like everyone else, had always felt that Lauralynn's father, in trying to protect his daughter, had hidden her away and had died himself before being able to tell anyone where. Lauralynn's family had searched and searched for her, but she could not be found. Never could she be found. And Brand had died so tragically. Mere weeks later, Yankee soldiers arrived, forcing Great-Grandmother O'Halleran and her children to leave Connemara House, claiming their safety was threatened since the area had been ravaged by the battle.

And so, the remaining members of the O'Halleran family were loaded into a wagon and taken away, nevertheless, to find that their destination was the home of Brand's family in Knoxville. Lauryn's Great-Grandmother O'Halleran slipped into a deep melancholy and severe illness for many weeks. But Brand's mother cared for her, nursing her back to health. Still, Nana said that her mother had never been the same.

Brand's parents made the trip back to Franklin with the O'Halleran family when they returned to Connemara that following spring. They were awestruck when they saw that, although Connemara House itself was in a horrible state of disrepair, the wisteria bloomed vibrant and renewed. Still, for the rest of her life, Erynn O'Halleran was certain that her daughter Lauralynn Masterson had died somewhere hidden away and waiting for help that never came. And it haunted her until her own death a year or two after her great-granddaughter Lauryn was born.

It had been an incredible amount of information and emotion for an eight-year-old girl to take in. But somehow, that day on the porch with her grandmother, Lauryn did understand it. All of it. Most of all, she had an uncanny understanding of the pain and devastation that Captain Brand must be haunted with—for her young heart had a unique capacity to love with such intensity that she did indeed understand his pain. And with it came her own pain. From that day forward, Lauryn Kensington had her own stabbing heartache. She felt a loss of her own, of sorts. For it was hard for her to live her life in constant merriment without her heart aching for her precious Captain and his lost lady.

Lauryn thought then of the nearly ten years she'd spent searching for her beautiful, lost great-aunt. As a child, she'd obsessed about the mystery so much initially that she'd nearly caused her own mother great illness with worry for her daughter. Every day she'd search the springhouse, the smokehouse, the gardens, the root cellar, and Connemara House. When she could find no clues there, she would search the ground for depressions or mounds that might be an unmarked grave. It was the very day she turned twelve and her mother had fainted upon finding Lauryn digging an enormous hole near the family cemetery in search of, as Lauryn had put it, "the bones of the Captain's lost heart" that Lauryn decided she must be more discreet in her search. Her mother had worried herself into a state of illness, and Lauryn knew that she must be considerate of her mother's health and well-being.

Often young Lauryn would go to her great-grandfather's grave in the family cemetery and talk to him, hoping that he could communicate with her from beyond the way the Captain did. But the Captain explained that Kiel O'Halleran lived completely in the arms of heaven and that she must rely on her own wits and his help to find Laura.

Still, for all the searching and wondering, the Captain had returned Lauryn's gift of helping him with friendly companionship that was unlike any other. Always he was there to talk with her, to listen to her, to play games with her. All the children at school assumed Lauryn was an eccentric with an imaginary friend, for no one else could see the

Captain as she and he played hide-and-go-seek or talked for hours sitting under the wisteria-veiled gazebo.

The Captain had been Lauryn's best friend—even more so, in some ways, than was Penny McGovern—and she had missed him the past months while living in New Orleans. Lauryn had wondered at first whether perhaps the Captain could follow her to New Orleans. But he had told her that he could not. He was bound to Connemara House as long as Lauralynn was lost. And yet he encouraged her to leave, telling her that she needed to be away from him, to live life without the constant reminder that he was unable to be at rest. She had missed him sorely, longed for their talks and sleuthing adventures, and missed his stories, his voice, and the piercing blue of his eyes.

Did she love him? Lauryn wondered at that moment. She had wondered that many times before. But today it was different. For the first time in most of her life, she had been separated from the Captain. And she wondered, *Do I love him?* Of course she loved him! More than almost anyone! But loving him didn't mean she was *in* love with him. Yes, she loved him. But his heart belonged to Lauralynn, and hers belonged to…no one.

In fact, as much as Lauryn loved the Captain, as much as she desired to help him find Laura and his peace, she was lonely. It hadn't been so noticeable when she was a child. But as she grew and matured, she began to realize that, if all went well as she wished, someday the Captain would be at rest and she—she would be alone.

In her adolescence, Lauryn had begun to wonder what would become of her. Who would she love? Would anyone love her? And as ever, after her parents had consoled and encouraged, there was the Captain to soothe her worries. And always, he promised her happiness. She did not know how or if he could guarantee it, but she believed him.

She believed in her dreams as well, her dreams of finding the perfect man—that is, the man perfect for her. A handsome, rugged, strong man who would adore her the way the Captain did Laura. A man of intelligence and wit. A man who would desire to protect and keep her to himself. Often she spoke to the Captain of her "perfect man," and he would always smile and encourage her dreaming. But there was one day, one afternoon in particular, that something happened—something that threw Lauryn's very soul into a whirl as far as her future and her dreams were concerned. Never had Lauryn been able to decide if that particular moment with the Captain, that revelation, had been a profoundly good thing or a destructive thing to her dreams.

৵

"Now tell me again," the Captain teased Lauryn as she demonstrated to him her progress in the crossover step while they waltzed in her bedroom one dreary winter's afternoon. "This perfect man you're always talking about—what's he like?"

Lauryn closed her eyes and sighed dreamily. "Perfect!" she sighed. "Yet…at the same time, not so perfect."

"How so?" the Captain asked as they continued to dance.

"Well, he looks perfect, of course. Handsome and tall, just like you. Eyes that could burn a hole right through you when he's angry…or melt your very soul with enchantment when he's passionate."

The Captain raised his eyebrows in a rather surprised expression.

"Oh, go on with you," Lauryn scolded. "Passion is a good thing. And you know what I mean."

"Are you meaning to tell me that you plan to kiss this man at some point?" he teased.

"Of course! Are you insane? Kissin' is the moment when two souls are most met," Lauryn sighed.

"Really?" the Captain chuckled.

"I'll continue with my description now," Lauryn stated, ignoring his teasing manner. "Dark hair, strong jaw—I can almost see him if I close my eyes." Lauryn closed her eyes for a moment and once again tried to picture her dream of the man she would love. But as always the vision was just beyond her mind's eye, forever elusive.

"What else?" the Captain asked, and Lauryn opened her eyes again, smiling at him.

Inhaling deeply, she looked past him dreamily and continued. "He'll always, *always* kiss me when he wants to or when I want him to…no matter who's lookin'."

"Is he a scoundrel then?"

"Somewhat. All interestin' men are, you know, Captain," Lauryn giggled. "He'll cause me to feel safe, be witty and able to make me laugh, champion me when I need him to, comfort me when I'm in despair. He'll never, never let me run away when I'm upset or in tears when we have our tiffs. Always he'll come after me."

"You make him sound like a slobbering pup!" the Captain asserted.

"Oh no! Never. But he will love me. And if he cares for me and loves me, he'll care what I think and what I feel. He'll be interested in my opinions—rare quality in a man, from what I've seen of the world. He'll be perfect! Perfectly *imperfect*, you understand."

"And what will you offer, my girl?" he justifiably inquired.

"Me? I'll be a slave to my love for him…to his love for me. I'll care for his needs and his household…and our children! I'll love him as much when I'm eighty as I did the day I met him. More even than that! I'll make certain to converse with him, to listen to his concerns, to nurture his mind and interests when I can. I'll make him laugh when he needs to…and even when he doesn't. I'll love him with everythin' that I am—so deeply that nothin' on earth could possibly match it!" Lauryn smiled up at the Captain as he halted their waltz.

He smiled back briefly, and then his smile faded as he spoke. "I can tell you, Lauryn…that there will be such a man for you."

"Now you sound like my daddy, Captain. But I know that even you can't promise me such a blessin' as a man like the one I dream of," Lauryn told him, reaching up and patting his cheek affectionately.

"But I can, Lauryn." The Captain's face was serious, and there traveled through Lauryn's body a sudden disconcerting chill as he spoke. "There is such a man alive on the earth—already a man, though you're still a girl. And…and you were born for him…as he was for you. Just as Laura and I were born for each other. The bond between you and him was fastened long before time was counted. Your love, infinite in perfection, existed before."

"Surely you do not profess reincarnation to me, my Captain," Lauryn mumbled, confused and rather frightened somehow.

"No. Each soul has one worldly existence. One. And in waiting its turn, often relationships are formed before birth that stretch out from beyond and bind people. It's why you must, and will, recognize him when he enters your life. Maybe not in that first instant. It may be gradual. But…you'll know him. For those souls, few though they may be, that have been bound before…never find complete happiness if they do not find each other here. Likewise, as it is with Laura and me, despair can imprison them if they are lost on the way back. For where is paradise if not with those you love more than your own life?"

"Where is he?" Lauryn asked, for she knew that the Captain always spoke the truth. "When will I…how will I know him?"

The Captain cupped her cheek gently in his hand. "Never fear, my girl. You'll find him. Or he'll find you. Now, no more worrying about it. Let's have one last waltz. You really have improved on your crossover step."

"But—" Lauryn started to argue as he began their dance.

"I can tell you nothing more, Lauryn. I've said all that I can. Just know that you will not be lonely in life after you have reunited my love and me."

Then the Captain began to waltz more determinedly and yet more slowly. Lauryn had the feeling of weightlessness somehow as if she were suddenly lifted into a dream. And in that moment, the Captain's face changed. Simultaneously her surroundings seemed to alter, appearing softened and fuzzy. But it was the Captain who held her attention—for she no longer danced in the Captain's arms. Or did she? Before her, dancing with her, and yet not, was another man. Definitely a full-grown man, a great deal taller than the Captain. But his face was clouded, as if a thick fog danced between them. And it seemed as if he said her name, though she could not hear him. As she tried to see him, tried to further discern his appearance through the veil of fog about her, she could sense her name being spoken from his lips. And strangely, her young lips desired suddenly to receive kisses from this hidden mouth that endeavored to speak her name. And it *was* her name that echoed in her mind as it fell silently from his lips. In the next moment, the fog had cleared; the dream was gone. And so was the Captain.

"Captain?" Lauryn called. But he had vanished, leaving her trembling and confused—leaving her lonely and longing for…something…someone.

CHAPTER TWO

"Ladies and gentlemen" the porter announced, "we're carryin' a load of convalescin' soldiers with us today, and the good doctor who's tendin' them has asked me to inquire—are any of you ladies willin' to give him a hand in the wounded car?"

Leaving her reminiscences, Lauryn's hand rose immediately in volunteering. She smiled as she looked to her Nana, now suddenly wide awake, to see her waiving a dainty hanky at the porter.

"We'd be more than willin' to help out, sir," Nana assured him. But as Lauryn helped her Nana to her feet, she was very disappointed to see that only one other woman in their particular passenger car had volunteered. The eyes of the other contributing woman met Lauryn's, and she smiled, raising her eyebrows in disapproval as she too looked about at the other passengers. No doubt the lingering memory of the danger of the influenza scared them. So many people had forfeited compassion for fear over the past year.

"Good thing all the fine soldiers that fought and *died* for our freedom weren't as uppity as most of us southerners seem to be," the woman stated quite loudly as Lauryn and her Nana followed the porter out of their car.

The train car with the convalescing men in it was stiflingly hot—so many men lying or sitting about in such cramped, uncomfortable quarters. And it was hardly more than a glorified boxcar to boot. The door was open, allowing fresh air to enter the car and revealing the passing landscape. A makeshift fence of sorts had been rigged across the open door to allow for the men's safety. At a glance, Lauryn discerned that these men were not recently wounded as she had expected. These were men who had been convalescing somewhere else for a long, long time.

"Ladies! Bless you!" a man in a white doctor's coat greeted as he approached them. "Our poor boys need waterin' and just plain carin' for, and I can't keep up with it any longer on my own. I'm Doctor Nelson," he announced, offering his hand to Nana, she being the obvious matron of the group and thereby deserving the first respect.

"Virginia Kensington," Nana answered, smiling at him. "We're glad to serve these valiant men however we can."

"Lauryn Kensington," Lauryn told him as he shook her hand.

"Betty Anne Wilson," the third woman offered as he then took her hand.

"Ladies, y'all are angels. Sent from heaven, and that's all there is about it!" The doctor did indeed look tired, and Lauryn felt a pang in her heart, sympathy for a good man. "If…if you could just talk to a few of them. Listen to their stories, give them a sip of water now and again. These boys have been laid up in New Orleans for near to a month, and they're gettin' itchy to get on with whatever life-livin' they can."

"Where are they bound, Dr. Nelson, and why move them at all if they're not fully healed?" Nana asked in a hushed voice.

"Well, to be honest," the doctor explained, dropping his voice to a whisper, "these boys…they need to be home. All our boys do, of course. But home will heal the wounds these boys are carryin' far better than any medicine I ever could administer. We call them the 'blue boys' down in New Orleans. Home and family—best medicine there is for what's keepin' these boys down. And, well, the flu is still lingerin' down there, as you ladies well know. Much worse than farther up. And…these young men are weak, and I don't want them dyin' from some insipid disease when they've struggled so hard to survive this long. New Orleans is still too infectious with the weather warmin' soon. I'm takin' them further up where it's still a bit cooler and the regional conditions are maybe a bit less conducive to breedin' influenza!" he answered.

"Blue boys," Lauryn mumbled, looking around the car.

"New Orleans in winter would be bad on a soul in despair," Nana agreed.

The doctor nodded. "New Orleans in any season would be bad on the souls of some of these boys…some bein' from so far up north and all." Then, motioning about him, he urged, "Jump right in, ladies. These boys are starved for feminine attention."

Lauryn watched as her Nana knelt next to a nearby soldier who was laid out on a cot. "Hey there, boy. What's your name?" she asked in her most grandmotherly voice. Tenderly, she caressed his worried-looking brow with her tiny, soft hand.

Immediately the young man's eyes brightened, and he said, "Tommy Vaughn."

"Well now, Tommy…where y'all from?" Nana asked, smiling.

"I guess we just need to follow her lead," Betty Anne said, hiking up her skirt just enough to help her walk toward a soldier who sat in a nearby corner peering forlornly out the boxcar doors.

Since the present end of the car seemed well in hand, Lauryn cast her gaze to the other end. Her attention fell on a soldier who stood leaning on one shoulder against the back wall of the boxcar. His face was hidden in the shadows. A strange feeling flowed through Lauryn, as if she'd just had a warm, sweet glaze drizzled over her whole being. An odd nervous sensation began to kindle within her bosom. Her hands trembled as she moved toward him, zigzagging through the other men lying or sitting here and there in the boxcar. She could not take her eyes from the man, even though his standing position implied he was better healed than most of the men in the car.

Lauryn stopped just behind him. He hadn't seemed to notice her approach. For long moments, she could not bring herself to speak to him. He was facing the shadows, almost intentionally, and she could not see his features. So she stood behind this "blue boy," studying his unusual height, the broadness of his shoulders, and the dark shade of his hair, hanging well below his collar, indicating he had not seen a barber in some time. For all her usual ability to rattle on endlessly in sometimes meaningless conversation, she could not decide how to speak or what to say to approach him. She simply stood at his back, trying to find the courage and words to speak to this recovering soldier. But even without having seen his face, even without having spoken to him, something in her soul was drawn to him. She remained still, waiting for the moment when courage would overtake her fear and she could speak. She startled rather violently when he unexpectedly spoke first.

"I knew you'd come to me," he muttered. She heard him even though he spoke quietly. "All this time, I knew somehow you'd find me."

This stranger's voice was tranquilizing. Deep, somewhat rasping, and yet, for all his convalescing appearance, the voice was strong but tainted with despair. The surprise of hearing him speak such words struck Lauryn dumber still. His next utterance nearly caused her heart to stop!

"Give me your hand, Laura," he said. Lauryn closed her eyes and shook her head in unbelief at what she had heard. Had he actually spoken her name? No! Not *her* name—but a name almost as familiar. Lauryn's astonished thoughts were interrupted as he repeated, "Your hand. Please! I need you now."

Ever so tentatively, for she knew not what else to do, Lauryn reached up, placing her small left hand at his left shoulder. The soldier reached up with his left hand and took hers, bringing it to his side in a tight grip. His touch! The touch of this faceless stranger was undeniably and instantly invigorating! And when he pulled her hand to his lips, kissing the back of it tenderly, Lauryn could not avoid bumping against his back, her knees nearly buckling beneath her. The soldier clasped her hand tightly between both of his and then turned to look at her. "Your hand is oddly warm today," he muttered, and Lauryn saw, for the first time, the face of the soldier to whom she had been so irrevocably drawn.

At that moment, Lauryn knew she had never met this man before. A brief second before she had wondered if perhaps this were an old school chum she simply had failed to recognize. Now she knew that was not true. She would have remembered such a face. The man who stood before her boasted a jawline any man would envy. It was squared, powerful, and blessed with an ever-so-slight cleft chin. His nose was not large and not small but just the right size for his face. But his eyes! His eyes! One eye was heavily bandaged, the other had a lighter gauze covering it, and Lauryn's heart nearly bled for the disappointment of not being able to see his eyes. The eyes of a man were the first attribute she usually noticed—the first thing she found to be attractive or not— the way she hoped to read a man's integrity. Further, she realized this man could not see her. Even had she known him, how would he have known to use a name so close, so familiar to her own?

"I...I haven't forsaken you, Laura," he whispered, a frown puckering his brow and causing his mouth to curve downward. "I...I haven't been able to get home. I...I...you *are* oddly warm. Your hand...I can feel it so...so definitely. As if you were...and yet the fragrance lingers, faint as it may be."

Lauryn had to speak to him. He had obviously confused her with someone else. "Sir, I—" she began.

The stranger gasped, released her hand, and demanded angrily, "Who are you? What kind of trick is this?"

"Sir, I assure you...I'm only here to help. My name is Lauryn Kensington. I'm bound for my home in Franklin, and I only—" she stammered.

"Kensington? Franklin?" he mumbled, seeming confused. Then much to her dismay, he began tugging at the lighter patch that protected one eye.

"Sir, please! I meant you no harm! I only wanted..." Lauryn began, tears unexpectedly filling her eyes and threatening to spill.

"What's the matter over there?" Doctor Nelson called from the other end of the car.

"Lauryn? Honey? Are you all right?" Nana inquired. Lauryn glanced over her shoulder to see Nana making her way toward her.

"I'm afraid I've upset him somehow! I...I didn't mean to," Lauryn explained.

"Captain! You leave the patch on that eye! You have another three weeks, at least, before it's supposed to come off. Brant! Do you hear me?" Doctor Nelson shouted.

"Brant?" Lauryn breathed, looking back to the soldier in time to see him succeed in tearing the bandage from his eye.

Lauryn gasped as she saw his eye. Though he shaded it with his hand against light from the open car door and there was deep bruising caused from an injury, his eye was fascinating, fascinating in its depth of blue and fascinating in its familiarity—the Captain's very eye color!

"Brant?" she whispered in disbelief.

The color of his eye was the only resemblance the man bore to the Captain, but it was frighteningly familiar to her. And his name—Brant?

27

It was nearly the Captain's very name! And yet he was completely different from the Captain—far more handsome! Larger, brooding, angry.

Before Lauryn could fathom anything else, the soldier reached out. Taking her chin firmly in one hand, he growled, "Who are you?" The demand was neither gentle nor congenial.

"Brant! Unhand that girl this minute!" Doctor Nelson snapped as he quickly walked toward them, tripping over one poor convalescing soul.

"I...I told you. My name is Lauryn Kensington. I'm only on my way home. I...I didn't mean to upset you, sir. Truly." Lauryn's eyes filled with tears.

Bending toward her, the soldier closed his eye. Placing his face close to her neck, he inhaled deeply. "That fragrance. Why did I sense it before? It's gone now."

"I...I'm sorry if I offend you, sir. I truly only wanted—"

But she was interrupted as the man suddenly pulled her protectively against his body, wrapping her in his arms as Doctor Nelson and Lauryn's Nana reached them.

"Now, boy, you let that girl go. She didn't come in here to be assaulted by some delirious man," Doctor Nelson coaxed quietly but firmly.

"It'll be fine, Doctor," Nana said calmly. "I believe I know this young man."

Lauryn felt the man's possessive hold loosen at her grandmother's words. "Who are you?" he asked. "Everything is cloudy still...and I don't recognize your voice."

"I'm Virginia, Brant," Nana explained. "Virginia Anne O'Halleran Kensington. I'm Laura's sister and young Lauryn's grandmother. We met in Vermont once when you were just a boy. Do you remember?"

Lauryn looked up into the searching, clouded eye of the man who held her. Her heart beat erratically as she felt a sudden, instant, and overwhelming attraction to the man. She wanted to embrace him, soothe him. For Pete's sake, she wanted to kiss him! What had come over her? She couldn't begin to understand. He seemed so lost, so helpless and desperate, and at the same time the most powerful man she'd ever met.

Looking down into Lauryn's face, the soldier spoke to her Nana. "Lauralynn's niece?" he asked.

"Her grandniece. Yes, Brant," Nana soothed softly.

"The one who sees the Captain?" he asked.

"What? Nana…who is he? I…" Lauryn began.

The soldier looked searchingly at her again, but Lauryn could not tell for certain whether he could in fact see her.

He took her chin firmly in one hand, his thumb traveling caressively and rather intimately over her soft lips as he whispered, "Who am I? I'm Brant Masterson. Brandon Masterson's grandnephew."

The next moment surely was a hallucination. A dream purely! Surely it was. There was no way on earth that what Lauryn sensed happening could, indeed, be happening! For she felt the moist tenderness of the soldier's lips caress her own in the softest, rather saddest of kisses. Yet even for the tenderness of it—even for the sorrowful, regretful mood of it—still it thrilled her beyond anything she had experienced in her entire life! The sensation of his lips meeting with hers, however brief, was almost unendurably perfect.

Then he pressed his unshaven cheek to her own soft one and whispered quietly into her ear, "The only person alive who understands exactly what you're looking for."

This revelation, coupled with the mighty reaction sent through Lauryn's body by his fleeting kiss, was too much for her senses, and she felt the soldier's arms tighten around her protectively as consciousness was lost to her.

Lauryn seemed to be swimming in a black dream—a dream of sound void of light and vision. She could discern voices—the doctor's as he spoke to her grandmother and then ordered the soldier to set Lauryn down softly. She heard Nana's as she soothed the two worried men, Betty's as she approached, inquiring about what had happened. And she could hear his voice, Brant's, as he argued with the doctor about replacing his bandages.

The biting stench of the smelling salts caused Lauryn to cough. She opened her eyes to find that her head rested on Betty Anne's lap. Nana leaned over her with concern showing in her face. Dr. Nelson labored to replace Brant Masterson's eye bandages as he sat in an attitude of defeat, leaning back against the boxcar's inner wall.

"Nana?" Lauryn whispered.

"Are you all right, darlin'?" her grandmother asked. Lauryn nodded reassuringly as her grandmother smiled down at her and helped her to sit up.

"Nana…he's…he's—" Lauryn stammered, pointing to the soldier that now was on the receiving end of a lecture from Dr. Nelson.

"He's Brant Masterson. And he's obviously had a bad time overseas."

Lauryn simply continued to stare at the man who ran his fingers through his dark hair in discouragement.

"I met him when he was a boy," Nana confessed quietly. "His aunt contacted me once upon a time, concerned for his well-bein'." Lauryn looked to her Nana as the older woman lowered her voice. "It seems…he was somewhat haunted by the past."

"I am sorry, Miss Kensington," Dr. Nelson apologized, returning to the two women and offering a hand to Lauryn to help her to stand. "Are you all right? I mean, truly?"

"Yes. I'm fine," Lauryn answered, though her attention was completely arrested by the slumped shoulders of the defeated-looking Brant Masterson.

Following Lauryn's gaze, Dr. Nelson whispered, "He's a very frustrated young man. But strong. Very strong. And I'm encouraged about his sight. I do worry about leavin' him off at Memphis alone though. I hope he didn't upset you too much, Miss Kensington."

"Alone?" Nana and Lauryn asked simultaneously.

"Well…yes," Dr. Nelson stammered. "Apparently there was some difficulty, and his family will be over a week late in gettin' there to meet him. I've arranged for someone to help care for him. This will infuriate him when I tell him. He's an independent little devil."

"You can't just leave him off in Memphis!" Lauryn exclaimed. "With strangers?"

"Of course not," Nana stated. "I'll telephone his family myself, and the boy can come home with us to Franklin."

"Oh my, no, ma'am," the Doctor protested. "He needs a world of assistance still and—"

"We're related…by marriage way back," Nana interrupted. "We're nearer to family than some strangers in Memphis."

"It's highly unheard of to just leave off a man somewhere when prior arrangements have been made and…" the doctor began to argue. Then he looked at the soldier still sitting and looking so very beaten. Returning his attention to Nana, he finished, "Still…it's the most life I've seen in the boy since he staggered off the ship."

Lauryn looked to where Brant sat. There was an air about him of being utterly conquered. It was heartbreaking. The conversation between her grandmother and the doctor concerning the man's fate faded from her mind. Lauryn found herself being propelled toward the soldier; her feet seemed to suddenly have a will of their own.

"A woman's step is so much lighter than a man's," Brant muttered. "But I can still hear it." He rose to his feet and turned toward her. Lauryn's heart ached brutally for the lack of being able to see his eyes. "I'm sorry if I frightened you, Miss Kensington," he spoke. "I…I…"

"I understand," Lauryn finished. "It was quite a shock to me as well." She noted the way his shoulders sagged. "Please, sit back down. You need your rest, I'm sure."

He sat, without argument. Lauryn sat next to him and studied him intently. He was far more interesting and attractive, even with his bandaged eyes, than any other man she had ever met. A pang of guilty disloyalty pricked at her heart as she thought of the Captain waiting back home in Franklin—the man she'd thought no other could compare to, until now. Her thoughts of the Captain led her to the reality of the knowledge owned by the man that sat next to her.

"You know then that I…that I…" she found herself stammering awkwardly in a hushed voice.

"That you see him," he stated without pause.

Lauryn inhaled deeply, afraid to confide her greatest secret to anyone, let alone a stranger. "I do," she whispered. It was inconceivable to her. All these years—all these years that the Captain had been wandering in search of Lauralynn, all the years that she had kept her secret about her spirit friend—someone outside the family had known?

"What scent does he carry?" the man at her side asked. It seemed a very odd question. In fact, it was so incredibly odd that it threw Lauryn's thoughts into a jumble.

"Scent?" she asked.

"Yes. When he appears to you. How…how do you first know he's there?"

"He…he appears. I sense him coming. He appears. We talk and—"

"You mean *you* talk," he corrected her.

"No. I mean *we* talk. Together. Converse. As you and I are now."

Whatever was the matter with her? She was telling her deepest secret, details of it, to this stranger! This man whom she'd been kissed by, deliciously kissed by, but with whom she had no acquaintance otherwise. Had she lost her mind completely?

But then Brant Masterson turned his face toward her quickly, as if he wanted to look at her, as if he were, at last, surprised by what she was saying.

"You hear his voice?" He seemed angry and disturbed.

"Of course. He has been with me since I was eight. We're great friends."

He must think her an utter lunatic! There she sat calmly confessing relationships with ghosts. And yet he looked away again, unsurprised, his lips curled downward in a frown. His silence was irritating. She had offered him a part of her most cherished secret, and now he was silent?

"Why?" she asked simply.

He didn't answer for some time. Then raising his face and laying his head back against the car, he said, "She can't talk to me."

"What? Who? What do you mean?"

"All she can say to me that I can hear is her name. *Lauralynn. Laura.* It's how I know she is coming to me. It brings with it a familiar perfume—a scent with the only sound of her voice that I hear. It's…it's the fragrance of her name."

Lauryn sat dumbfounded! For as many years as she had been a friend with the Captain, had this man been haunted too? Was Brant Masterson telling her that he knew Lauralynn?

"You…you know Lauralynn?" she asked in an astonished whisper.

He made some sort of a sound similar to the beginning of a chuckle. "Of course! What? Do you think you're the only person in this mess that sees ghosts?"

"All your life?" she asked.

"For as long as I can remember. I was…oh, three or four when I first remember her clearly though. She's more of a feeling before that."

Lauryn put a hand to her forehead to try and soothe the confusion in her mind. Lauralynn could appear to this man but not to her own husband, who was searching so desperately for her? It didn't make any sense. No sense at all.

"You mean no one ever told you that I know her?" Brant asked.

Lauryn shook her head, as a gesture of assuring him that no one ever had.

"If you're nodding or shaking your head, sweetheart, keep in mind…I can't hear your brain rattling," he growled resentfully. Lauryn looked at him angrily, only then remembering that he was sightless. Of course he couldn't hear her head nodding.

"No one ever told me about you," she told him humbly.

He was angrily silent for a moment. Then sighing heavily, he mumbled, "I suppose no one would've ever told me about you either if they hadn't thought I was going insane."

"I'd be insane if I couldn't talk to the Captain," Lauryn muttered out loud to herself.

"You call him that?" Brant asked. His voice was so affecting to her senses that a tickle ran down her spine, causing her to shiver. Its deep intonation seemed to vibrate through her soul. "Captain?"

"I do," Lauryn admitted.

Then she began to study him again. The man couldn't see her, so why not take the opportunity to look at him? She studied the lines of his face, the strength of his jaw, the texture of his hair, which was the darkest shade of brown, not quite black, but almost. His shoulders were incredibly broad, his arms very muscular, and his hands very masculine. Nothing was pampered or manicured about them. They visually told the tale of a hard-working man, even considering the weeks he had been unable to labor because of his loss of sight. Lauryn noted the large scar that ran diagonally over the back of his right hand, noted the calluses on his palms. The breadth of his chest nearly matched that of his shoulders! The shirt he wore bordered on being too small, for it was stretched to its limits, revealing a very well-sculpted torso beneath. Brant Masterson was, undeniably, magnificent to look at. And Lauryn fully appreciated the opportunity to study him so without his knowledge.

"And…and he talks to you?" he asked again, interrupting her thoughts. Brant shook his head as if he couldn't believe it. "You actually hear his voice and hold conversations with him?"

"Yes," is all Lauryn could say, for somehow she felt devious for studying him so intimately without his knowledge and guilt-ridden for the blessing of the Captain's friendship.

"I met your grandmother when I was younger," Brant began. "I was fourteen. And incredibly frustrated with the fact that I couldn't help Laura. I flew into a rage at my Aunt Felicity one day, and she…she thought I was losing my mind." He paused for a moment and mumbled, "I wonder now if maybe I was." Shaking his head, he continued. "So my aunt contacted your grandmother, and she came out to Castledale and talked with me. She told me that her little granddaughter, you, knew Brandon…that he wanted you to help him find Lauralynn. I couldn't understand it. If I had Laura and the little granddaughter had Brandon…why couldn't we just tell them where they each were and have it all work out?"

"What *is* the reason?" Lauryn asked. For, indeed, it seemed simple enough an answer.

The man shrugged his massive shoulders in a rather boyish gesture. "She's lost. I asked Laura. I told her where Brand was. She just shook her head and cried, and I don't know how I understood…but I did. I have to find the part of her that was lost here, during her life. For some reason—I can't figure it out—there has to be something else. But until I find out what happened to her—her body—she can't go to him." He shook his head and rubbed at the whiskers on his chin for a moment.

Then, angrily, he seemed to change, to turn on her like a rabid dog. Standing, he barked, "I don't even know you! Why the hell am I talking to you?"

Lauryn stood too, so startled by his sudden change in demeanor that she was immediately provoked to defense. "Because…because it's like you said. I'm the only one alive who understands what you're lookin' for."

"You don't understand anything!" he growled. "You're just a pampered little southern girl who—"

"And you're far too steeped in self-pity to see anyone else's—" she began to argue back at him. His words had hurt her deeply—far more deeply than a stranger's words should have the power to.

"Save your self-righteous lectures for someone who will benefit from them, girl."

His voice was filled with anger. Anger and pain. Lauryn knew that whatever had happened to Brant Masterson in the war, whatever horrible event had left him blind, had also left him worthy of owning resentment and self-pity. But the path was set now.

"All right," was all she could stammer as the tears filled her eyes. "Good day to you, Mr. Masterson." And she turned to leave him.

She was halted, however, as Brant reached out and took her arm. "Hey, Laura—" he began to apologize.

"My name is Lauryn," she spat at him. For some reason she didn't fully understand, Lauryn wanted to be sure he knew the difference between her name and her great-aunt's.

"Lauryn," he corrected himself. "I'm...I'm sorry I was rude to you. I'm just...not the person I used to be."

"Well, that's a conscious choice you've made, Mr. Masterson," Lauryn stated, finding it hard to easily forgive him for his abuse of her emotions. "I have absolutely no doubt that you have endured more...more torture than I can ever imagine. But if you were once a man of character, of manners...you still are. Or else you've chosen not to be. Now, if you'll excuse me," she said, her voice breaking and betraying her emotion. Pulling her arm from his grasp, Lauryn stepped over men and cots, making her way back to the passenger car.

"Miss Kensington!" she heard him call after her. "Lauryn, wait!"

The tears were streaming down her face. Somehow Lauryn felt as if this man she'd known for mere minutes, this stranger, had reached into her chest and taken her heart in his hand, crushing it in the power of his masculine, callused fist. She could not return to him, even to accept an apology! For what would he think of a girl who became so emotional over a stranger's opinions?

"Lauryn? Honey?" she heard her Nana call.

But she rushed on. Reaching the door leading to the passenger car, she fairly burst through it, causing startled passengers to look up curiously. Lauryn noted the many sets of eyebrows that rose, astonished to see a young woman in tears charging toward her seat. Self-consciously, she sat down next to the window that such a short time before had been the object of her reflection. She marveled at the difference in the image looking back at her now. In an hour's time, she'd gone from an innocent, sweet girl looking forward to returning home to family and friends to a young woman who knew sudden and immediate heartache at the hand of a complete stranger.

He knew her! Brant Masterson knew Lauralynn! All these years that Lauryn had been searching for her—trying to find where and when she died so the Captain could rest—all this time, Brant had known her. It was unfathomable, surreal!

"Honey, whatever is the matter?" Nana asked as she took the seat next to her granddaughter. Taking Lauryn's hand, she kissed the back of it tenderly and reached up, smoothing a stray curl from Lauryn's cheek.

For a moment, Lauryn could only shake her head, trying to stop her tears and swallow the lump in her throat. Finally she turned to her Nana and quietly asked, "Why didn't you ever tell me?"

Nana looked away guiltily for a moment. "About a boy who saw Lauralynn?"

Lauryn nodded.

Nana smiled. "Because I feared it would plague you to know that Laura was found…by someone. I feared it would frustrate you to know it…make you unhappy and cause you to see your search for her as pointless."

Lauryn nodded, instantly understanding the wisdom in her grandmother's secrecy. Lauryn knew herself, and it would've indeed plagued her and caused her great unhappiness had she known of Brant and his association with Lauralynn.

"Oh, Brant. You've found us then." Lauryn looked up, having heard her Nana's greeting. Brant stood there, his hand on Dr. Nelson's shoulder.

"Nana," Lauryn whispered as her grandmother motioned for Dr. Nelson to seat Brant directly across from Lauryn. "Don't leave me with him," she pleaded in an even softer whisper as her grandmother stood.

"I've got to…finish makin' the arrangements with Dr. Nelson, Lauryn. If we're to have a guest, there's things I should know," Nana explained. Then, much to Lauryn's astonishment, her Nana, still holding

Lauryn's hand, placed it in Brant's. He held it tightly, signaling that there was no escape this time. He would have his say with her.

"Thank you, Doc," Brant mumbled.

"Y'all be good, Captain," Dr. Nelson warned.

Brant nodded, his frown deepening.

"Nana?" Lauryn pleaded.

"You have a good long talk with Mr. Masterson, honey. It's about time. Don't you think?" And with that, Nana accepted Dr. Nelson's arm and left her granddaughter in the company of the strange and unnervingly attractive Brant Masterson.

Lauryn immediately tried to pull her hand from Brant's grasp. It was completely unsettling the way he held her fingers in both of his hands now, stroking the backs of them lightly with his thumbs. But he held tight, foiling any attempt to escape him without causing a disturbance. Instantly, Lauryn felt her tears begin anew, traveling the still moist path down her cheeks as she looked at the handsome, haunted man before her. He frightened her! The feeling in her bosom, as if she might explode with delight and pain at the same time as she looked at him, frightened her.

"I'm sorry," he said plainly and very sincerely. "I…I'm a brute. I had no right to bite your head off like that. And you're right. I am an ill-mannered, rude…devil. Swearing in front of women—my Aunt Felicity would skin me alive."

"I had no right to place a judgment on you. I—" Lauryn began her own apology.

"Yeah, you did," he interrupted. "You were right too. I let my pride get the better of me…again," he explained. "Blindness forces you to let other people care for you…serve you. And I'm not humble enough to accept it at times. My pride reacts with cruelty."

"You were injured…blinded servin' others. You should allow people the opportunity to show their gratitude by serving you," Lauryn told him, again trying to gently pull her hand from his.

Her thoughts were stalled as he drew her hand toward his face and seemed to inhale deeply as if…as if he were…yes! He was smelling her.

"Good advice," he admitted. "But very difficult to initiate when you're Brant Masterson." Again he seemed to inhale deeply the scent of her skin. "Do you forgive me then?"

"I don't have any reason…" she began, unable, for some reason, to find more words.

"You owe me an apology in return," he told her as her silence wore on.

"I know. I'm sorry for my judgment. I—"

"Not that. You had every right to treat me badly. I mean an apology for running off so that I could not offer my apology on the spot. Running from a blind man—how heartless."

Lauryn's brow puckered into a hurt and ashamed frown until she saw the grin spread across his handsome face. He was teasing her. Yet his making light of his injury was painful as well.

"I'm sorry," she whispered softly.

Then to her surprise, Brant kissed the back of her hand lightly before releasing it and straightening his posture.

"Now, all apologies aside…what's he like?" he asked bluntly.

"Who?" Lauryn asked in return. For the first time in years, her mind was void where the word *he* was concerned.

"Your Captain," Brant chuckled. "What's he like?"

"Oh!" Lauryn exclaimed, rather embarrassed that she hadn't instantly known to whom Brant was referring. "He's…he's wonderful. And miserable without his lady."

"He's haunted in his own right," Brant mumbled, his enticing grin fading as his head fell defeatedly back against the seat. "I know the feeling. Being haunted."

Yes, haunted! And Lauryn could not begin to fathom the frustration and pain that would've been heaped upon her if she had only been able to see the Captain, never to hear his voice in conversation—only to see him sad and alone and begging for her help the way it seemed Brant saw Lauralynn.

"Before I'd see her…" Brant paused and put a hand to one of the bandages at his eyes. "When I could see her, I'd hear her name, like a whisper on the wind, and a sweet fragrance of some flower would wash over me. It was so strong…like nectar that you could breathe in. *Lauralynn* is all I've ever heard of her voice."

"And you know everythin'? The stories? The reason…" Lauryn prodded. She was curious, suddenly. Did he know something she did not? Something that would help her, help them find Laura? *Could it be?*

she wondered suddenly. Had she found, in Brant, the help she'd needed, the help they'd both needed to end the mystery?

"No. Not everything. I know she's lost. I know that she was married to Brand Masterson, my grandfather's brother. I know that she died during the Battle of Franklin and that she was never found. I know the stories from my Aunt Felicity and your grandmother—and from Laura nodding yes and no to questions I have asked her. And now…" His voice became deeper and angry. "Now I'll have no way to communicate with her." He reached up and began tugging on the bandages at his eyes. His anger had returned, his frustration full-fledged.

"You mustn't!" Lauryn scolded, taking his hands in her own. "The doctor is obviously hopeful that your sight may be saved. And you must follow his instruction. You must not lose hope or damage your sight further because of frustration."

"Sweet thing," he mumbled, the slightest of wistful grins capturing his mouth again, "I have been blind for near to four months. They have operated on me now…given my father false hope. False hope helps no one."

"But…but you saw *me*," Lauryn reminded him, trying to ignore the thrill that traveled through her at the thought of his sudden kiss in the boxcar.

"I saw you as if you were standing in a thick fog, Miss Kensington. Enough to know where to reach to molest you…not enough to know whether or not you resemble your great-aunt."

Lauryn was disappointed. Deeply. She had thought he had seen her more clearly and that her familiarity of spirit had prompted him to kiss her. And yet she had hoped the opposite. She knew that she did not want this man's attention simply because she resembled his fragrant lady ghost. But for the first time since she was eight years old, Lauryn silently wished she did bear some resemblance to the lost lady, Lauralynn.

"Well, do not be too disappointed, Mr. Masterson. I don't look like her," she mumbled. "And you far from molested me, sir."

"My Aunt Felicity would disagree," he told her flatly. "I…I awkwardly beg your forgiveness for that as well." His apology sounded less than sincere.

"Because your aunt would expect it of you?" Lauryn asked him.

"Exactly."

"Then I refuse it," she stated. "Now, back to our previous subject. I wonder, does Lauralynn—"

"You refuse it?" he exclaimed, leaning toward her suddenly. "You can't refuse that apology."

"I can too. And I do."

"But it's…it's rude. And after the way you scolded me for being rude. Anyway, I thought southern girls were always the epitome of propriety." The expression about his mouth was that of being completely taken back.

"It's not rude. What's rude is to apologize when you don't mean it. Now, do you want me to talk to you about our special…acquaintances or not?"

Brant sighed with relief and shook his head, actually grinning again. "Yes…if you can keep from being so rude. And besides," he added, lowering his voice, "you're right. I withdraw my apology for molesting you. It was the first time I've felt like a real man in over four months. Come to think of it, I don't think I've ever had a woman faint from one of my kisses. I guess there's hope for me yet."

Lauryn blushed and looked about to see if any of the passengers were eavesdropping. He was oddly incorrigible, this handsome, haunted, wounded soldier.

"Very well," Lauryn began, feeling completely unsettled and yet somewhat triumphant in helping him avoid another outburst like the one in the boxcar. "What do you know?"

Lauryn found it hard to concentrate on the subject of the Captain and Lauralynn, however. Brant's presence seemed to dominate every sense she owned.

"I told you," he reminded her. "She died; he died. It was tragic and an unsolvable mystery."

"Oh, you have to know more than that. I could learn that much from the family Bible."

He sighed in irritation before speaking. "Laura loves her husband. She is lost and wandering without him."

"How does she appear?" Lauryn asked. "What's she wearin'?"

Brant shrugged his shoulders as if his answer were inconsequential. "A dress, true to the times, blue…soaked with bright red blood at her stomach."

"What?" Lauryn gasped in horrified astonishment.

"It was a wound to her abdomen. Wasn't it?

"Well, yes. But…" Lauryn was distracted, imagining the horror of a young child having to be haunted by a ghost soaked in blood.

"And she wears a gold locket and two rings," he added as if it were no strange thing to be haunted by such an apparition. He spoke as if he weren't in the least disturbed about Lauralynn's appearance. Of course, he'd had over twenty years to get used to the sight of her that way. "Is your Captain still in uniform?" he asked.

"Um…yes," Lauryn stumbled, still overwhelmed by Brant's description of Lauralynn.

There was silence between them then. Each seemed to be lost in thoughts of their ghostly counterparts.

At last, it was Brant who spoke first. "How will I help her when I can't see her anymore, Lauryn?"

At that moment Lauryn, finally, sensed the true depth of Brant's pain. Not only was he blinded, unable to see the world, unable to be fully self-reliant, but his only method of communication with Lauralynn, his own lost lady, was gone.

"How are you feelin', Brant dear?" Nana asked upon returning at that moment with Dr. Nelson.

"I'm fine," he assured her. "It wasn't me that got assaulted in the wounded car." Smiling, he said, "I'd wink at you teasingly, Miss Lauryn Kensington…if I could."

Dr. Nelson and Nana both chuckled with amusement. But Lauryn was not amused. She understood now how devastating his injury had been to his soul.

Nana settled herself in the seat next to Brant. "Well, my sweet soldier boy," she began, "it's all settled. You're comin' home with Lauryn and me to Connemara House until your dear brother can come for you." Nana patted Brant's hand maternally, but his smile faded.

"I thought Parker was meeting me in Memphis, Dr. Nelson," Brant said. Lauryn saw his hands tighten into fists at his sides.

"There's…there's been some sort of delay, Brant. He can't come for another week or so," Dr. Nelson explained.

"So strap the two Florence Nightingales with the invalid, is that it?" Brant mumbled.

Lauryn was shocked as her Nana slapped the man softly on the mouth. "That's enough of that, Brant Masterson!" she scolded. "We'll have none of that self-pity from you. Do you hear me?"

Brant shook his head. "You're determined to leave me off with these compassionate ladies then, Doc?" Brant reworded his question, teasingly. Nana's soft slap had obviously had its desired effect, for Brant had indeed brightened.

"Your sight will be restored, Brant," the doctor told him. "You've wasted near to all your patience, my boy…and I understand. But you treat these women the way you ought to. You hear?"

Brant nodded, turning his face toward the window as if everything in him yearned to see out to the passing landscape. Lauryn was sure everything did.

"Yeah. I hear you," Brant mumbled. "In that case, if I'm off to Franklin, I'm tired. Think I'll sit right here and doze a bit. You'll pardon me, won't you, ladies?"

Lauryn could see that his jaw was clenched in annoyance. She suspected it took every ounce of self-control he could muster not to fly into a rage at being passed about like a homeless puppy.

"That's fine, Brant," Dr. Nelson assured him. "You do need the rest." Looking to Nana, Dr. Nelson winked and added, "I'll be back to check on y'all later."

"Thank you, Doctor," Nana said, and the man took his leave.

Lauryn's discomfort increased. It was impossible to tell if Brant were sleeping or not since his eyes were bandaged. So, for long moments, she and her grandmother simply watched the passing landscape. Soon the sun had set, and Nana seemed to think a little private conversation was safe enough, considering that Brant hadn't moved a muscle in over thirty minutes.

"Well, my peach," she began in a near whisper, "if this hasn't been the grandest adventure either of us has ever had on a train…I don't know what is!"

"Undeniably," Lauryn agreed.

Lauryn watched then, amused to see her grandmother look over to Brant and start visually investigating him.

"My! He is a handsome one," Nana exclaimed quietly.

"Hush, Nana! He'll hear you." Lauryn was delightfully astonished at her grandmother's brazen appraisal of Brant.

"Well, he is, june bug. Look at the size of him! Broadest shoulders I ever did see on a man." Nana smiled, adding, "And since he's fast asleep…I can size him up all I want to."

"He makes me nervous," Lauryn whispered.

"Darlin', I suspect he makes every woman nervous."

"No, Nana," Lauryn stammered. "I mean…he makes me uncomfortably nervous."

"That's 'cause he's a man, pumpkin. You're used to boys. Men are different. And this one…" Nana paused, touching Brant's shoulder lightly. "This one is unique." Then an impish twinkle flickered in the old woman's eyes. "And to think…he's already kissed you!"

Instantly, Lauryn's face went crimson. "Nana! He's…he's a complete stranger."

"Many a great story starts with a handsome stranger, my darlin'."

Brant Masterson struggled to regulate his breathing so he appeared to be completely asleep. The women's light, complimentary discussion was the most soothing, interesting event he'd experienced in months. It was hard for him not to smile at the discomfort of his new acquaintance, Miss Lauryn Kensington. Somehow he delighted in the knowledge that he unnerved her. And she had given him hope—hope that perhaps not all had been lost to him when his sight was taken. She obviously knew a great deal more than he did about Lauralynn and Brandon Masterson. Briefly, he thought of the feel of her body in his arms when he had embraced her and the soft innocence of her lips when he'd kissed her— the comfort it had unknowingly given him. Yes. Maybe this girl, this bloodline of Laura, could help him find his lost lady.

CHAPTER THREE

Lauryn awoke with a start when the conductor announced the train was nearing Franklin. She didn't even remember dropping off to sleep. Her attention immediately went to Brant, who remained seated directly before her, his bandaged eyes seeming to be looking directly at her. It was odd, the way she could feel him staring at her when she knew he could not.

"At last," Nana sighed, sleepily. "My sitter is completely numb from sittin' so long."

"Hush, Nana. For Pete's sake." Lauryn scolded in a whisper, noting the amused grin that spread across the handsome face of their companion.

Nana chuckled delightedly as the train began to slow. Turning to Brant, she asked, "Well, my boy…are you ready for the adventure awaitin' on you at Connemara House?"

"Yes, ma'am," he answered. "And I do apologize beforehand for being such a burden to you."

It was a difficult apology for him to make, Lauryn knew. Humility wasn't the easiest virtue for the man to express, from what she'd gathered of him so far.

"We'll have none of that, Brant," Nana told him. "You know we're completely delighted to have you with us." She patted his knee reassuringly and rose as the train halted before the Franklin station.

Lauryn stood as well, stretching slightly to ease the stiffness in her back. But as Brant stood, the train gave one final lurch, and Brant lost his balance, falling forward and knocking Lauryn back into her seat. As he caught himself awkwardly with the armrests at either side of her, his forehead met with her own in a painful collision, and she heard him swear under his breath. He righted himself almost immediately, and Lauryn knew by the tight expression on his mouth that his temper was barely restrained.

"I'm sorry," she heard herself apologize unnecessarily.

He shook his head, assuring her that her apology was indeed unnecessary, before he held a hand toward her, a gesture indicating he would help her to her feet. Tentatively she accepted his offer, and he did pull her securely to a standing position once more. Again, his touch was unsettling. Lauryn was thankful she had put her gloves on so he could not feel the nervous heat of her hand.

"I'll get the porter," Nana informed them, looking around for assistance. "You get Brant off the train and into the waitin' arms of our family."

Lauryn was horrified at her grandmother's suggestion. Surely Nana did not intend to leave her alone with Brant. She opened her mouth to argue but paused, looking to the injured man and realizing that it would only serve to further upset him if there were any indication she was uncomfortable with him. No doubt he would incorrectly attribute her discomfort to his blindness and not the fact that he was simply an intimidating presence.

So inhaling deeply a breath of courage, Lauryn reached out and took his hand, saying, "This way, Mr. Masterson. If you please."

Brant drew a long breath as well, attempting to gain calming humility, and stepped forward. Once he stood behind her in the aisle of the passenger car, however, Lauryn was startled at the goose bumps that broke over her when his hand released her own, traveling rather caressively up her arm and across her back, finally resting at her shoulder. It would indeed be easier for her to lead him thus, but his touch was startling to her senses.

"Lead on, Florence," he mumbled.

"Nana told you…none of that, Mr. Masterson," Lauryn reminded him. Such sarcasm was going to be thick during the week to come. She had no doubt about it.

"Won't your family be surprised to see me escorting you off the train?" he added in obvious disregard for her reprimand.

"Yes," she agreed, not taking his pity-bait. "We've always wondered about the Captain's family. They'll be ecstatic to have you here."

"Ecstatic?" he mocked.

"Ecstatic," Lauryn assured him. "Especially Patrick."

A thought struck her then. She paused, turning to look at him, reflexively taking his hand in hers when he was forced to drop it from her shoulder. "I may as well warn you. Patrick, my little brother, will be quite tactless in his questionin' you…especially about your service abroad."

"How old is he?" came his unexpectedly interested response.

"Nine," Lauryn answered.

"Don't worry. I was nine once myself, believe it or not. He can ask me anything. I won't take offense. I completely understand."

Lauryn was amazed by the sudden calmness about the man. It was certainly obvious that he didn't know Patrick! Patrick Kensington could exasperate even the most patient of saints. But she was encouraged and in admiring awe that Brant would be so understanding of a young boy's mind.

Lauryn directed Brant's hand to her shoulder once more as she turned and again began leading him out of the train. As she led him down the stairs from the train car, it was indeed Patrick that met her first.

"Lauryn!" the young boy greeted, throwing his arms around his sister's waist and hugging her brutally as she helped Brant down from the last step. "You're home! Finally! Finally! Finally!"

Lauryn couldn't help but smile as she looked down at the tousled blond hair of her baby brother.

"Sean is such an old grouch now that the baby is here!" he rattled on. "He doesn't want to play with anythin' but that danged baby!" Patrick ceased in his prattle suddenly and looked past Lauryn to Brant.

His brown eyes widened with rude curiosity. "Hey, Lauryn…" he began. And even though Lauryn frowned at him and shook her head violently to indicate that he should not speak anything further, he did. "Y'all brought home a blind man with you?"

"Patrick!" Lauryn scolded immediately. But she was startled when she heard a low chuckle coming from Brant as he stood behind her.

"Are you surprised, boy?" Brant asked, smiling. "That your sister should come home dragging me along?"

Patrick answered honestly, "Oh no, sir. It's just like her. She's strange, you know."

"Patrick!" Lauryn scolded in a firm whisper.

But Brant laughed and said, "I know she is."

Lauryn felt her face go crimson with embarrassment. "Patrick...where's Mama?" she demanded. She must escape her little brother before he heaped more humiliation upon her. But no sooner was the thought in the front of Lauryn's mind than it was proven.

"So are you and Lauryn gonna have a baby, mister?" Patrick asked.

"Patrick!" Lauryn fairly screamed. Instantly, Brant was laughing so hard he doubled over, his hands on his knees as he attempted to catch his breath.

"Well?" Patrick said, shrugging. "You must've married him, Lauryn. Why else would you come draggin' him home like this?"

"Patrick! Shut up and go find Mama!" Lauryn told him through clenched teeth.

"All right, Lauryn. All right." Patrick whined. "You don't have to go gettin' your bloomers in a ruffle. And I'm tellin' Mama that you told me to shut up!"

"Patrick," Lauryn growled, stomping her foot on the ground.

"All right, I'm goin'. I'm goin." And she watched, her eyes filled with tears of humiliation as her little brother ran off to seek out their mother.

Brant was standing again and sighed heavily after one final chuckle. "That was the best laugh I've had in months," he sighed.

"Well, I'm glad he amuses you," Lauryn snapped, wiping at the tears on her cheeks.

"Ah, let it go, Miss Kensington. He's just a boy," Brant suggested.

"Yes. And y'all stick together tighter than teeth," she grumbled.

Lauryn had half a mind to leave him standing there with no assistance. That would teach him to find amusement at her discomfort. But he was smiling broader than she'd seen him smile all day, and it warmed her heart. Patrick, in his tactless, improper, boyish way, had brightened the heart of the tortured man. How could she begrudge either one of them that?

"You've got a sharp little tongue in your mouth when you need it, don't you, Miss Kensington?" Brant asked, grinning with amusement.

"If I need it," Lauryn assured him.

Goodness, he was handsome. More than handsome—attractive! Attractive like a magnet attracts ore. And she couldn't look at him any longer, for her discomfort at her own unsettled senses was too strong.

"Gracious!" Lauryn's grandmother exclaimed breathlessly as an older man helped her down from the train. "If this trip hasn't just taken all the sassafras out of me."

"Patrick has run off to find Mama," Lauryn stated.

"Has he now?" Nana asked with a knowing smile. "And just what has that little dickens done to put that tight set to your mouth already, Lauryn?"

"Nothin' to be goin' on about," Lauryn answered, inhaling a deep breath in an effort to calm herself.

Lauryn looked from her Nana to see her mother, Georgia Kensington, approaching. Actually, it was Patrick barreling toward them, yanking mercilessly on his mother's arm to hurry her along.

"See, Mama!" Patrick exclaimed excitedly. "I told you she brung a blind man home. She ain't gonna have a baby though."

"She *isn't* goin' to have a baby," Lauryn's mother corrected, seemingly completely unaffected by the fact that her young son had posed such a question to her daughter and a strange man. "*Ain't* isn't a word, sweet patata."

Lauryn's mother greeted her with a warm and rather needful hug. Then kissing her lovingly on the cheek, she wiped the tears from her own face before looking up into the bandaged face of Brant Masterson.

"Oh, Lauryn!" her mother began. "I've missed you so, it has nearly broken my heart. And who is this fine young man with you on his arm?"

Lauryn inhaled deeply to try and calm her embarrassment and impatience with her family's assumptions. It was apparent that her mother too thought she had surprised them with a nameless lover.

"For cryin' in the bucket!" Nana exclaimed through her laughter. "Do y'all know who this man is?" she asked.

"Yeah, I do," Patrick answered. "It's a blind man that Lauryn's draggin' home."

49

"Patrick, for Pete's sake!" Lauryn's mother exclaimed quietly.

"This dear man before y'all is…Brant Masterson," Nana announced.

"What?" Georgia gasped.

"Who?" Patrick asked.

Nana shook her head, delighted with the boy. "Brant Masterson. He's grandnephew to our own Captain Masterson."

"And y'all just picked him up somewhere and brung him home?" Patrick asked, walking around Brant and looking him up and down.

"Mother!" Lauryn exclaimed. "Would you please settle him down?"

Brant chuckled, however, and slightly squeezed Lauryn's shoulder encouragingly where his hand still rested for direction.

"You're one big boy, mister," Patrick noted, whistling afterward for effect. "You a soldier?"

"Yes, sir," Brant answered. "And I figure you and I will have plenty of time to talk. You can ask me all the questions you want."

"Really?" Patrick squealed. "Did you hear that, Mama?"

"I heard it, Patrick," Georgia sighed. "Now, you settle down. I want to hear how this all came to be."

"Your daughter here has just got bad luck, Mrs. Kensington," Brant answered.

Georgia reached out and took Brant's hand in greeting. "Well, may I say that it is a pleasure to meet you, Mr. Masterson."

"Brant's goin' to stay on at Connemara for a week or so," Nana explained, "'til his family can get down from Vermont to get him home."

Immediately Brant began to apologize. "I…I'm really sorry for the inconvenience, Mrs. Kensington. I was against it, but Mrs. Kensington here is a very persistent woman."

Georgia giggled. "Oh, don't I know it, Mr. Masterson. And to save confusion, you call me Georgia. All righty?"

"Yes, ma'am," Brant agreed.

"Besides," Georgia continued, "we wouldn't have it any other way!" Lauryn's mother looked from one of the travelers to the other, each in turn. "Y'all look completely tuckered out. I think it's time we got on home."

Lauryn felt her mood brighten a bit at the thought of home. And yet it was only her mother and Patrick who were there waiting for them at the station. Her father…her father would never meet her again—not in this life, anyway. But Connemara House waited. There was comfort in that. And the Captain. Lauryn could not wait to tell the Captain everything that had transpired that day. She smiled, thinking how ironic it was to be gone for nearly a year and all that she wanted to tell the Captain of her adventure was of the events of the past few hours.

℞

"So," Patrick began, hardly letting Brant sit himself completely down in the seat of the auto before beginning to pop out questions, "you got hurt in the war, huh?"

"I did," Brant answered simply.

"Patrick," Lauryn's mother warned gently from the driver's seat of the auto, "everyone is very tired. I'm sure that Mr. Masterson would like a few moments of peace before you start in pickin' his brain."

"Yes, ma'am," Patrick mumbled obediently, if not resentfully. The disappointed boy slunk down in his seat.

"And besides," Georgia continued, "I have my own questions."

Brant smiled as he settled in his seat next to Patrick. So did Lauryn and her grandmother. Lauryn was beginning to think that maybe a family, even one other than his own, would do this man, so injured in body and soul, a bit more good than she expected. And maybe a man, stranger though he may be, would do her family, who had suffered such a great loss in their father's death, the same good. Lauryn realized that, had the appearance of Brant not caused such interest, had he not arrived with her and her grandmother, the scene at the station would've been quite different—most likely wrought with tears and sadness.

"How did y'all meet? Lands sakes! I mean, it's amazin'!" Georgia began.

"On the train. Just today," Nana answered. "It was no accident, I'm certain. I've no doubt that somebody intended it."

"Mr. Masterson," Georgia began another question.

"Brant, ma'am," Brant corrected her.

Georgia smiled. "Brant." Then she began again. "Where were you bound? Were you as astonished as I am now to find out who these two ladies were?"

51

"Yes, ma'am," Brant answered. "I was heading for Memphis to meet my brother, and then these two angels of mercy came into the wounded car. And we just sort of…bumped into each other."

Lauryn felt she were in a dream. As she sat, so completely fatigued, listening to Brant and her mother converse, she could not quite believe she was in a realm of reality. It seemed too strange, to simply meet Brant on a train as she had and have him here, in their auto on the way to Connemara.

Patrick wriggled, miserably confined in the back seat.

Lauryn put her arm around his shoulders and whispered, "Don't you worry, Patrick. Mr. Masterson will have plenty of time this week for you."

Patrick sighed heavily and squeezed Lauryn's hand. "I'm awful glad you're home, Lauryn," he whispered in return. "And I'm glad you brung a blind soldier with you too."

Lauryn smiled. Yes, she was home. As they drove along the streets of Franklin, she breathed in the familiar air, gazed at the familiar buildings in town, and felt whole once again. There was something about home that was comforting, secure, loved.

"So you're stayin' with us for only a week?" Lauryn's attention was drawn back to the conversation by her mother's disappointed exclamation. "That's hardly long enough to have sit-down supper." Georgia's disappointment was obvious. "And besides, between Sean and Patrick, won't any of us women have one minute of your leftover attention."

"Sean, ma'am?" Brant asked.

"Sean. Lauryn's older brother," Georgia explained. "He and his wife, Mindy, and my adorable grandbaby live a few doors down from Connemara House. He's been home near to a year. Got the flu overseas and made it through, thank heaven."

"Is the baby just too cute, Mama?" Lauryn asked. The thought of a baby nearby caused her heart to flutter with delight. Her own little niece to dote on!

"Well, of course!" Georgia exclaimed. "What kind of a silly question is that?"

"I take it that you like babies, Miss Kensington?" Brant chuckled. It was obvious he'd noticed the thrill in her voice, as well.

"Does Lauryn like babies?" Patrick exclaimed as if it were the most ridiculous question he'd ever heard uttered. "Why do you think I thought y'all was married and gonna have one, mister?"

Again Brant chuckled, and Lauryn's face turned crimson as her grandmother giggled as well. Reaching over, Lauryn pinched Patrick's knee in retaliation.

"Ouch! Mama! Lauryn pinched me!" the child tattled.

"That's enough! Patrick, you shouldn't say such things. And Lauryn...quit pinchin' your brother."

Brant was still enjoying a chuckle when Lauryn looked over to him. Though he tried to restrain it out of respect for their mother's reprimand, it was obvious that he was deeply amused.

If the train ride had seemed long, the mere five miles home from the station seemed even longer. Lauryn's mother continued to pop out questions to Brant, and Patrick continued to be completely tactless in his interruptions. Several times, Nana reached back from the front seat and patted Lauryn reassuringly on the knee. But all Lauryn wanted was escape. She kept wondering why Patrick was sitting between her and Brant. And it bothered her that he was—which also bothered her, because why did she care?

At long last, they reached Connemara House, and a sweetly familiar warmth and calmness sifted over Lauryn's tired mind and body. There it was, lights beckoning from the windows. Mindy, a baby in her arms, peered out anxiously through the large window in the parlor, and Sean stood against one column on the porch, waiting on his own terms.

"Nana!" Sean exclaimed, helping the elderly woman from the auto and hugging her tenderly. "You look even more beautiful than the day you left."

"Oh, go on with you, boy," Nana giggled, kissing his cheek affectionately. "Where's that great-grandbaby of mine?" And she toddled off toward the house, seeming to forget everything else. Lauryn smiled to herself. That was another thing she adored about the elderly— the way they were drawn to little ones and the way the little ones seemed to recognize the great worth of their old folks.

Lauryn stepped out of the car and into Sean's warm embrace as well. "My, my, my!" he whispered. "Haven't we all but blossomed?"

Lauryn shook her head. Sean was the sarcastic member of the family. "You haven't changed an ounce, I see," she told him as he kissed her cheek.

"I'm serious, Lauryn!" he assured her. "You're so grown up and pretty that I can't believe you didn't come home on the arm of a man." Sean stopped his teasing when Brant stepped awkwardly out of the car with Georgia's assistance.

"But she did, Sean," Patrick corrected. "A blind soldier!"

Lauryn buried her face miserably in her hands even though she heard Brant chuckle.

"Well, how do you do, sir?" Sean greeted, raising his eyebrows daringly in Lauryn's direction as he took Brant's hand and gave it a firm shake.

"Well enough, sir," Brant answered, smiling.

"You up and married a soldier already, Lauryn?" Sean asked.

"Mother!" Lauryn whined.

"Sean!" Georgia scolded.

"I see you and young Patrick here know how to properly tease a sister," Brant chuckled.

"We try our best to make her life as miserable as we possibly can," Sean affirmed, smiling at his sister and pinching her cheek affectionately.

Brant chuckled and placed his hand on Lauryn's shoulder. Again his touch thrilled her, but somehow, she felt the need to escape into the loving embrace of Connemara House.

"Well, let's get this mob in the house, Mama," Sean ordered. "Mindy's beside herself with waitin' to show Junie to Lauryn and Nana."

As Lauryn walked toward Connemara's front entrance, she marveled at the ancient, winterly barren vines that covered the columns and most walls of the house. In a matter of a few months, they would be heavy with green leaves and their flowers' heavenly perfume. She couldn't wait! The wisteria was something she'd adored, treasured, cherished since she could remember. And when she entered the house, Brant at her heels, she sighed, brushing tears of joy from her cheeks. Home! At last! It had been far too long.

"Lauryn!" Mindy exclaimed. She held her baby safely propped on one hip, but she threw her free arm around Lauryn and hugged her tightly. "I'm so glad y'all are home." Then, looking past Lauryn and up to Brant, she added, "And who's this dashin' young man with you?"

"He's a blind soldier that Lauryn drug home. Only they ain't…isn't married or havin' a baby," Patrick explained.

"Hello," Mindy greeted, taking Brant's hand. "I'm Mindy Kensington, Sean's wife."

"It's a pleasure, Mrs. Kensington," Brant greeted. "I'm Brant Masterson."

Immediately the color drained from Mindy's face. "The Captain?" she whispered.

"Oh no," Georgia assured her startled daughter-in-law. "This is a relative of the Captain's. His grandnephew."

Mindy sighed with relief. "Oh. For a minute there I thought I was…" She stopped and swallowed, trying to regain her composure. "Well, it's a pleasure to have you here, Mr. Masterson."

Brant nodded, still grinning, obviously very amused by all that had transpired with Lauryn's family.

"Just look at this little angel!" Nana exclaimed, taking the baby from Mindy's maternal possession.

Lauryn's eyes brightened. Sean's baby, his own daughter! And she was indeed an angel. Her eyes were green, her curly hair as dark as night. It was very apparent who her father was.

"Hey there, Junie baby," Lauryn cooed, holding her hands out toward the baby. Junie, being but eight months old, paused, shyly looking toward her mother for encouragement.

"It's okay, Junie. That's your Auntie Lauryn," Mindy assured her.

"Don't you want to come to your auntie, Junie?" Lauryn coaxed. And in the next moment, the adorable child stretched her arms out toward Lauryn. Lauryn's heart swelled as she propped Junie up comfortably on her hip and studied her intently.

"Aren't you a pretty girl?" Lauryn asked. Junie smiled and nodded, and everyone, except Brant, laughed.

Suddenly, anxiety washed over Lauryn as Junie looked up to Brant, his eyes bandaged, his hair long and rather unkempt. Lauryn was so afraid Junie would be frightened by Brant's appearance that she found herself to be, once again, struck mute. What could she say to assure the child without making Brant uncomfortable?

"That's Mr. Masterson," Mindy told the baby. "He's come for a visit, I gather."

Amazingly, Junie held her arms up toward Brant, wanting him to take her.

"There now, Mr. Masterson. Junie wants to make friends with you," Mindy told him.

"What?" Brant asked as Junie began tugging at his shirt.

"She wants you to hold her," Sean explained.

"Me?" Brant questioned.

"Come on now, sir," Sean said, taking Junie from Lauryn and handing her to Brant.

Brant took the child in his arms, awkwardly at first. But after a moment, he had her neatly arranged, cradling her against his chest with his arms.

"Owee," the baby cooed, touching the bandages on Brant's eyes.

"Yes. Owee," Brant mumbled. And Lauryn was delighted when Junie then planted a slobbery kiss on Brant's cheek and threw her arms around his neck in a warm baby hug. Then she turned and held her arms out to Lauryn once more. She took her and lovingly kissed the top of the sweet-smelling little head.

"She is a beauty, Sean," Lauryn complimented her brother.

"I know. She takes after her mother," Sean agreed, hugging his wife.

"What is wrong with all of y'all?" Patrick exclaimed suddenly. "We have here, in our very own house, a blind soldier! And all anyone can think about is how cute Junie is!"

"Patrick," Georgia scolded again, "go out and feed your dogs. This minute!" she added when Patrick paused.

"You and me," Patrick told Brant in a hushed voice, "we'll have our time later."

Brant smiled. "We will," he assured the boy. Once Patrick had left, Brant spoke once more. "I...I don't mean to seem rude or ungrateful to all of you," he stammered, "but...but there's things a man needs to tend to and—"

"Say no more, sir," Sean said, placing a hand on Brant's shoulder. "Lauryn will be glad to take you to the water closet."

"Sean," Lauryn whined.

Brant chuckled, and so did Sean. "Follow me, sir. I'm not one to leave a fellow soldier in need."

Once the men were out of hearing distance, Georgia and Mindy immediately began casting out a string of questions directed at Lauryn and her grandmother.

"For Pete's sake, Lauryn!" Mindy exclaimed in a whisper. "How in the world did you end up bringin' home such a fine man as that? A relative of your Captain, no less?"

"We met on the train," Lauryn answered simply.

"Today? Y'all just met him today?" she asked, astonished. Lauryn nodded. "And he's blind. How sad," Mindy mumbled sympathetically.

"He'll be with us a week," Nana explained. "His brother, who I do need to try to telephone, will be out here in a week. As far as his family knows right now, Brant's on his way to Memphis. I need to let them know we've kidnapped him."

"I'll need to freshen the sheets up in the guestroom," Georgia mumbled to herself, "and get a fire goin'. We don't want him to catch cold." Then looking to Lauryn, her eyes filled with tears. "Oh, my sweet, darlin' daughter. How I have missed you!"

Lauryn returned her mother's loving embrace. "I'm so sorry I wasn't here when Daddy…" Lauryn began. But she couldn't speak another solitary word, for the pain was so deeply stabbing at her heart.

"I know, honey," Georgia whispered. "But you let it all go now. We can't be a house of bawlin' women with this new man here who so desperately needs encouragement. Now can we?"

Lauryn released her mother and inwardly recognized that Brant's coming home with her and Nana may have been just what her own mother needed for now—a welcome adventure, someone to dote over and care for, something to ease her thoughts of loss.

"Now, you run along upstairs, Lauryn," her mother encouraged. "I'm certain you're needin' to get out of those travelin' clothes. You too, Nana."

"In good time," Nana said, taking a seat near the fire with Junie on her lap.

However, without another moment's pause, Lauryn was up the stairs and in her room. Closing the door behind her, she nearly burst into tears again at the familiarity of the room. Her own bed draped in the quilts stitched by her grandmother's gentle hands. Her window, the window with the seat that overlooked the wisteria-drenched gazebo. It was heavenly! Her wardrobe, her vanity, her books and other treasured things placed lovingly on the wall shelf. And there was the overwhelming feeling of anxious anticipation at seeing her dearest friend.

"Captain?" she called softly. "I'm home!"

It wasn't even an entire instant before he was there, standing before her, his arms outstretched, beckoning her to embrace him.

"Oh, Captain," she sighed as she threw herself into his familiar embrace, "how I have missed you!"

"And how you've changed," the Captain chuckled. "All grown up, my little Lauryn."

Lauryn lingered in his embrace, savoring the familiar scent of his clothes—that soothing scent of wool mingled with the fragrance of burning cedar. It was always the same, so warm and comforting. Ever since she had met the Captain, she'd loved the smell that accompanied him. Oddly however, it wasn't until this very moment that Lauryn even realized she had. It wasn't until she had returned home from being away so long that she had actually identified what the aroma about him was—the comforting scent of a well-worn, woolen uniform that had spent many a long, cold night around a campfire.

"And bringing home strangers too," the Captain added playfully.

"He's no stranger," Lauryn giggled, looking up into the mischievous eyes of the Captain. "Not to you. He's your blood kin."

"And almost as handsome as me, I might add," the Captain chuckled. "Now, you sit here and tell me the tale of this Brant Masterson."

Lauryn paused, uncertain whether she should tell him everything about Brant. Should she tell him that Brant had spent his life with Lauralynn, all the while the Captain was being miserable without her?

"He sees Lauralynn," she blurted out, surprising herself. "He's known her since he was a child."

Immediately, the Captain's face paled, his grin disappeared, and an overpowering sadness seemed to envelop his countenance. Instantly,

Lauryn regretted this should be the first thing she told him after returning from being away so long.

"The way I appear to you?" he asked.

"Yes…and no," Lauryn answered. "He sees her…but she can't talk to him."

The Captain sighed heavily, the sigh of defeat. Lauryn scolded herself again for blurting out the information she had. And why, she wondered, had she chosen to tell the Captain about this instead of simply how she met Brant and how she felt about it?

"But don't you see, Captain?" she pleaded. "This is what we've been needin'! It must be meant that he should enter our lives. Because…somehow I know this will help us find Lauralynn."

"But why would she be there…with my family? Instead of here where…where…with her own?" the Captain asked.

Lauryn shrugged and again tried to encourage her dear friend. "I haven't had a chance to talk to him about it all," she began. "But I know he can help us. I know he can! With Brant's help…we'll find her, Captain. We will!" And she did know it. Something in her soul knew it! Her heart even seemed to beat differently since she'd met Brant. Of course, the fleeting thought breezed through her mind that maybe her heart being lighter had something to do with Brant's handsome features and otherwise overall attractiveness, rather than the knowledge he may hold a secret that would help find Lauralynn.

Quickly, however, Lauryn shook her head to dispel the notion. No! Brant had been a gift from heaven to help her heal the Captain.

The Captain reached out and caressed Lauryn's cheek adoringly. Smiling, he whispered, "I've missed you, you little runt."

"Well, I'm home now. And more determined than ever." Lauryn smiled at him.

"And what about your trip to New Orleans?" the Captain asked. "What grand adventures did you have?"

Lauryn could only shrug her shoulders once more and shake her head. "None. None more wonderful than today's!"

"What?" the Captain gasped, exaggerating his astonishment. "No handsome young man endeavored to steal your heart? No returned soldier tried to woo you into his arms?"

"Not really," Lauryn answered honestly. "None of them…of the men I met were…none of them were *him*."

The Captain chuckled once more. "You mean none of them were Mr. Perfectly Imperfect? This dream man you've invented? Or do you mean none of them were this Brant Masterson?"

Playfully Lauryn glared at him for a moment. How dare he tease her about her dream man! And how dare he tease her about this stranger that now sheltered at Connemara. Then she realized something. "Either one," she told him.

He smiled with understanding. "Well, you'll have a lot you'll want to talk to your family about. And no doubt you do need your rest. And so, my girl, I'm off." The Captain bowed respectfully, kissing Lauryn's cheek as he'd done since she was a little girl. "Good night."

"Now? You're leavin' now?" Lauryn exclaimed. She didn't want him to leave! She'd been away for nearly a year. She had missed him desperately. She had longed for conversation with him. And yet somehow the feeling of wanting him to linger began to be overshadowed by fatigue. "I guess…I guess…I should go down with the family. And sleep will do me some good too. But when will we talk? First thing in the mornin'?"

The Captain shrugged. "We'll see. Your mother has had a bad few months, peach. She needs you. My life…my existence hasn't changed. I have no news to report. But you…you've had such adventures. And your mother needs you."

"Brant will help us, Captain," Lauryn whispered with conviction. "I know it!"

"Then I'm certain of it too." The Captain kissed her cheek once more.

"Good night," Lauryn sighed as he disappeared, leaving only the faint aroma of worn wool and cedar.

Once she'd freshened up and tidied her mane of wavy hair, Lauryn returned to the parlor. She found everyone, including Brant, sitting around the hearth enjoying light conversation. Brant sat to the right of her grandmother, Nana's hand resting reassuringly on the young man's knee. Baby Junie was crawling around on the carpet giggling as Patrick pretended to chase her about. For all of Patrick's whining about Junie getting all of Sean's attention, it was obvious Junie's young uncle adored her. Mindy sat elegantly on the floor next to Sean. Lauryn's mother looked up from her seat near the hearth, smiling as she caught sight of Lauryn entering the room.

"There you are, my angel," Georgia chimed. "Do you feel quite refreshed?" She winked at her daughter. No doubt Lauryn's mother knew to whom she'd been talking.

"I do," Lauryn answered with a nod and a pleased smile. "And yet I'm tuckered out."

"I imagine you are," Mindy sympathized. Then nodding toward Brant, she added, "Mr. Masterson has just been tellin' us all about his family's orchards and cattle up in Vermont."

"Oh! I bet it's cold up there this time of year," Georgia exclaimed.

"Yes, ma'am," Brant confirmed. And somehow the tone of his voice caused a delightful shiver to travel through Lauryn. It was so deeply smooth and rich. She felt that if she just opened her mouth, she would taste the honey of it. "And I'm certain it surprises you to be told that I miss it," Brant added.

"Not at all, Brant," Georgia assured him. "The south, beautiful as it is, can get very…stiflin' at times. I remember when Lauryn's daddy and I went up to New York State one autumn. That cool, crisp air was very revitalizin'."

"I've telephoned Brant's family, Lauryn," Nana said quietly. "They're relieved to know he's here with friends instead of with strangers." Lauryn nodded, thinking it odd that Nana should see no difference in the people at Connemara and other sets of complete strangers that might have met Brant in Memphis. "His brother, Parker, will be here to strip him from us Thursday next," Nana explained.

"By which time you all should be quite ready to have your home to be your own again," Brant added, smiling. He covered his mouth, trying to hide a yawn.

"Mother, I'm certain Mr. Masterson is worn out," Lauryn suggested. Suddenly, she felt overly concerned with his health. He needed rest. And he certainly wouldn't find any in conversing in the parlor with the lot of Kensingtons.

"Of course. Oh my! How selfish of us, Brant," Georgia exclaimed. "You certainly need your rest."

"I'm fine, ma'am," Brant responded.

"Don't you lie to me, young man!" Georgia scolded playfully. "You come along. Lauryn and I will get you settled in for the night."

Brant inhaled deeply, and Lauryn couldn't quite be sure, but it seemed that he blushed. "Um…if you just show me the way, Mrs. Kensington…I'm sure I can manage."

Georgia stood up. She walked very determinedly to Brant, took his hand, and tugged on it so he stood. Then she looked directly into his face and shook her index finger at him. "Now, you listen here," she began. "You are a guest in this house. More than that, you're family. I won't have you feelin' like you're just company. Lauryn and I will take you up now, and you'll do darn well what I say!"

Brant smiled and chuckled slightly. "Yes, ma'am."

"Now, say good night to everyone, Brant," Georgia ordered as though Brant were merely Patrick's same age instead of a grown man.

"Good night, Mrs. Kensington, Mindy, Sean, Patrick, Junie," Brant obeyed, chuckling.

"Lauryn, bring Brant upstairs, will you?" Even Lauryn smiled at her mother's bossiness. She was very entertaining to watch when she was bossing—the typical southern woman who would not have anyone feeling uncomfortable in her home.

"Yes, Mama," Lauryn giggled, taking Brant's hand and placing it on her shoulder. She tried to ignore the warmth of his touch, the power in his grasp, as she, leading Brant, followed her mother upstairs.

"Now, I've got the fire goin' in there, Brant, but it should die down soon enough," Georgia rambled as they climbed the stairs. "And there's an extra quilt at the foot of your bed. Sean lugged your bag up, and since I didn't find a stitch in it resemblin' nightclothes, I figure you'll be sleepin' bare as you were born."

"Mother!" Lauryn gasped. Her family had no tact whatsoever. None.

"Yes, ma'am," Brant chuckled.

"You went through his things, Mama?" Lauryn scolded. Still, her mouth dropped open, and she looked at Brant, surprised and a little delighted at the thought of his being so willing to do without nightclothes.

"I figured I'd just lay things out for him. Wasn't that what I should've done, Brant?"

"Yes, ma'am," Brant agreed. "But just in case of an emergency, ma'am…maybe it will ease your daughter's mind to know that I do sleep in my…my…" he stammered.

"Your underwear?" Georgia finished. Lauryn wanted to crawl into a hole! How embarrassing the entire conversation must have been to Brant.

"Exactly," the tired man confirmed.

"You see, Lauryn? Nothin' at all to worry about. Now, this will be your room, Brant." Georgia opened the door to the guestroom, and Lauryn stepped inside, Brant following her lead. "Like I said, there's an extra quilt, and I put a pitcher of water on the nightstand in case you need it. And, oh! I've brought up Grandpa Kensington's old chamber pot. I thought that might come in handy, being that you're not familiar with the house yet."

Lauryn shook her head and dropped her face into her hands. What was wrong with her family? Couldn't they leave Brant any shred of dignity?

"I appreciate your thoughtfulness, ma'am," Brant told her, sincerely grateful. "You seem to have thought of everything. This room is warm and comfortable, and I'm done in, I will admit it."

"Well, we'll leave you to get ready then. But I always, always, always tuck my children in at night, Brant." Georgia went to the bed and turned back the covers. "So I will be in to tell you 'sweet dreams' as well."

"I'll look forward to it," he said, smiling. Lauryn led him to the bed, and his hand dropped from her shoulder, indicating he no longer needed her assistance.

"Good night, Mr. Masterson," Lauryn told him.

"Good night, Miss Kensington. Mrs. Kensington," Brant mumbled.

"Lauryn and Georgia, Brant," Lauryn's mother corrected.

"Yes, ma'am." Brant chuckled and shook his head, obviously delighted with Lauryn's mother. Lauryn felt a pang of disappointment pinch her heart. She had not managed to impress him the way her mother had. She took one last look at him, standing there appearing rather helpless next to the bed. Then she left with her mother.

"Now I want you in bed too. You look like the devil!" Lauryn's mother told her.

"Well, thank you," Lauryn giggled.

"You know what I mean. Now, tomorrow we are gonna have some time to talk, me and you. How I've missed you, my sugar plum." Again Georgia embraced her daughter. It was the kind of hug that speaks of need, love, loss, and relief, and Lauryn was glad again that she was home.

As tired as she was, as filled to throbbing as her head was with trying to sort out the events of the day, Lauryn could not seem to fall asleep. She listened as the clock struck eleven and then midnight. She thought about calling for the Captain. He would keep her company. But somehow she could not keep her thoughts from turning to Brant. Was he warm? Dreaming good things? What did he know that might help her to find Lauralynn? Did he need anything? Her mind was completely busy with worry and concern and curiosity about him. And she knew— she knew that she would not be able to rest until she'd checked in on him, until she'd made certain he was comfortable in a place so strange to him.

How thankful she was when the door opened silently, that the hinges of the guestroom door didn't squeak like Patrick's door did. Of course, the guestroom door wasn't slammed shut and flung open with the strength of the Titans every five minutes like Patrick's was.

Silently Lauryn walked to Brant's bed. The fire had died down, but its embers glowed warmly enough to provide sufficient light for viewing a sleeping person. The room felt chilled, however, and Lauryn was disturbed when she approached Brant to see him lying on his back, hands tucked beneath his head and quilts pushed down nearly to his waist. She wondered for a moment—was she disturbed because Brant might be chilled with a lack of quilts covering his torso, or was she disturbed because the sight of him bare from the waist up was very…disturbing?

For Pete's sake, she thought. His shoulders were nearly as broad as the small bed was wide. His upper arms were as thick as some of the tree limbs on the old maple, and even relaxed and sleeping, the muscles of his chest were solid and perfectly sculpted. Realizing she was far too intrigued with studying him thus, Lauryn knew it would definitely be the wise thing to adjust his quilts—to keep him warm, of course. So carefully, so as not to wake him, Lauryn began to pull his coverings up over his stomach.

She was startled when his hand rose suddenly and caught her wrist. For a long moment, she didn't say anything. His hand slid from her wrist to clasp her hand loosely.

"Laura?" he whispered. For a moment, Lauryn's mind considered remaining silent, in order to see what else he would say if he indeed assumed she was Lauralynn. Quickly she reconsidered, however, realizing she might not want to know for some reason.

"No. It's me," she whispered in response.

"Oh," he grumbled, immediately releasing her hand and tugging the covers up himself. He tucked the hems of his sheet and quilt over his chest, folding his arms across its broad expanse. Lauryn felt awkward. It was obvious he was self-conscious, uncomfortable with her being there.

"Do you have everythin' you need?" she ventured. How she hoped, prayed, that he wouldn't inquire as to what she was doing sneaking into his room at such a late hour.

"You mean, in this room…to help me to sleep comfortably?" he asked. Lauryn understood all too well his implication. There was an undertone of bitterness in his voice, and she was certain he was thinking of his loss of sight. Had he been lying awake as she had? Had he, however, been lamenting his condition? His dependent situation?

"Are you warm enough?" she stammered.

"Yeah," he mumbled.

"Well, then," she said quietly, turning to leave, "I'll just—"

"How old were you?" he asked unexpectedly.

"How old was I?" Lauryn wasn't sure what he meant.

"When you first saw him…your Captain? How old were you? I can't remember what age you told me you were." Brant sat up in his bed, tucking the covers around his waist and folding his arms across his chest again. He looked expectant, as if he were ready for a lengthy conversation. And suddenly Lauryn was exhilarated by the prospect of spending time alone with him, in the dead of night, in intimate, verbal correspondence.

"I was eight," she answered. "It was my eighth birthday…the day I first met him."

"That's right," he mumbled. He seemed pensive about her answer. "I was about four maybe and in the attic playing with my wooden soldiers. A breeze blew through, and…and there was this…this fragrance…heavy, sweet, intoxicating. I turned, and there she stood."

"I was in the attic too!" Lauryn exclaimed in a hushed voice, for her mother and Nana slept in rooms just across the hall. "I was looking through Lauralynn's trunk and—"

"Her trunk? You've seen her things?" Brant interrupted. "Touched them?" He was alert, wildly interested. Lauryn's excitement was growing as well. Brant had been on that train for a reason. Call it fate or divine intervention, but she knew it to be true. And now, after such a long day, after such a long journey, they were beginning—beginning to share information about the greatest mystery to ever evade solving in both of their families.

"Her weddin' dress is in there. And a tintype of her and the Captain," Lauryn offered.

Brant smiled and repeated, "Her weddin' dress?" He had mimicked Lauryn's accent, and now she felt ashamed of it.

"Her wedd*ing* dress, I meant to say," she corrected herself humbly.

"No, no, Miss Kensington. Don't you change the way you speak," he told her. "It's cute and sweet. It's you." Lauryn didn't know what to say. It was hard to respond to such a compliment—if it were a compliment. Brant patted his bed at his side. "Sit down. Let's sort it out."

Lauryn's excitement over the prospect of gleaning information from Brant overcame her shyness at sitting at the foot of his bed, both of them scarcely dressed for visiting. She plopped down, ready to fire questions at him.

"Did she scare you at first?" she asked.

"A bit. She looked very lost and frightened, and there were the stains at her abdomen. But she was so beautiful and sweet and smelled so good that I wasn't afraid for long." Brant grinned a bit and asked, "And you? Did he scare you?"

"No. Not really," Lauryn answered. "He was kind, and he bent down to look me in the eye. And I knew who he was already because I'd seen his likeness in the tintype." It seemed natural that it should be her turn to ask something. "How did you communicate with her if she couldn't talk to you?"

Brant shrugged. "I watched her lips, or she made gestures." He paused for a moment before going on. "She was always, always there when I needed her. She'd sit with me during the night if I were anxious. She'd stroke my hair and teach me songs to play on the piano."

Lauryn looked away from Brant to the dying embers of the fire. "The Captain has been my best friend too. He taught me so much...helped me feel confident. Like I could accomplish things. But..." Lauryn stammered.

"But you've failed him," Brant finished for her. It wasn't a cruel remark; it was how she felt. And it was, no doubt, how he felt.

"But I can't fail him. I can't," Lauryn whispered.

"You won't." Brant turned his face toward the hearth as well. "I'll...I'll help you as much as I can while I'm here. I don't know what I have to offer. Maybe the more we talk...maybe there's something I know that you don't. Something that will help you." He shook his head, discouraged, and added, "Maybe."

Reflexively Lauryn reached out and placed her hand comfortingly over his. "I'm positive you do know somethin'. Why else would we have met today?"

"Why else indeed," Brant mumbled, forcing an agreeing nod and simultaneously pulling his hand away from Lauryn's.

How sweet she is, this little girl from the southern town of Franklin, Tennessee, Brant thought. How eternally, and somewhat naively, hopeful. If he'd met her as a sighted man, before the war...but there was no use in thinking of what ifs. He would help her all he could. He would help her because he realized it was up to Lauryn to help Laura now. He'd faced the reality for some time that, when he returned home, he would no longer be able to converse with Laura. Along with his sight, he'd lost his only means of communicating with Lauralynn. He could do nothing more to comfort her or help her to be found. That knowledge had eaten at his soul more fiercely than the actual loss of his sight most times. He couldn't bear the thought of Laura wandering lost and alone forever.

But maybe heaven still cared for Brant Masterson. It had sent this sweet girl, Lauryn, to mend the past, sent her to fix what Brant wasn't capable of fixing anymore, thereby giving him some sort of peace. Still, her touch was too friendly, too enjoyable, and Brant knew he must look like an escapee from an asylum. He hadn't been to a barber in months, hadn't been able to labor very hard physically or participate in much of any other activity to keep his body strong and healthy. And it was far too disconcerting to have people touching him when he couldn't see the expression on their faces. He imagined Lauryn grimaced each time she saw his unkempt appearance.

Still, he determined at that very moment to spend his week at the fabled Connemara House talking with Lauryn Kensington. He'd spend it trying to help her solve the puzzle of Laura's disappearance. Maybe then there would be something to feel good about, something that proved his worth in the world.

Lauryn clutched her hands together uncomfortably. Her mother had always warned her that not everyone was at ease with affection or friendly gestures that involved physical contact. Even the slightest hint of intimacy unnerved some. But it bothered Lauryn greatly that Brant seemed so against receiving her sympathy or friendship. She wanted him to trust her, to talk to her, to let her help him. But she also realized it must be incredibly difficult for him to accept those things from anyone, especially someone as recent to his acquaintance as Lauryn. No doubt he'd been quite independent before the injury to his eyes. She knew that she must be patient and strong. She mustn't let his moodiness or his being irritated deter her from discovering everything he knew about Lauralynn.

"So tomorrow, when you're a bit more rested…" Lauryn ventured.

"I'll tell you everything about her that I know now. And you don't need to wait until tomorrow to ask me." He turned his face in her direction once more and seemed to be waiting for her to begin her questioning.

Lauryn was completely undone! Where to begin? It was impossible to know what might be important. "Tell me again—what is she wearing?" she asked, finally.

Brant nodded. He didn't seem the least bit surprised by her inquiry. "A blue dress, white sleeves, a gold locket on a black ribbon around her neck. It has a little likeness of Brandon in it." He paused and seemed to be searching his memory for more details. "A wedding band and an amethyst ring on the other hand. Simple shoes, but…"

"Yes?" Lauryn prodded when he stopped.

"The hem of her skirt," he continued. "I never thought about it before. It's stained. Mud maybe. A dark stain—yeah, mud, I guess."

"Is she very beautiful?" Lauryn asked in a whisper. "I mean, still?"

"Hell yes!" Brant exclaimed. Then he seemed to remember the presence of a lady and corrected himself. "Sorry," he mumbled. "Yes. She's beautiful. She hasn't changed at all in over fifty years, I suppose—as beautiful as the day she died."

Lauryn smiled, rather oddly amused by his swearing in her presence and delighted that he should feel so inclined to apologize. But somehow it bothered Lauryn that Brant should be so adamant about Laura's beauty—so determined about its foreverness. Lauryn had seen paintings and old photographs of Lauralynn, and—well, she must admit it to herself—her great-aunt was beautiful.

Suddenly Lauryn felt very tired. Her mind couldn't think clearly at such a late hour, and she stood up from the bed. "You'll talk to me some more tomorrow?" she asked.

She half expected him to growl, *No!* But he nodded instead.

"Good night then, Mr. Masterson."

"Good night, Lauryn," he mumbled. "And thank you for your concern about my comfort," he added just before she opened his door to leave.

"You're welcome." And somehow sleep did come to her then. Once Lauryn was warm in her bed, she found her mind at ease, calm and able to rest. It wasn't until the birds in the trees outside her bedroom window began their morning song rehearsal that she awoke again.

CHAPTER FOUR

"And over here," Lauryn explained as she carefully led Brant toward the aged building, "is the old springhouse."

Brant had seemed very interested when Nana had suggested after breakfast that morning that Lauryn take him on a tour of the house and grounds of Connemara. Lauryn was very thankful that Patrick was off somewhere playing with a friend. His endless questioning and babbling at Brant had completely interfered with the endless questioning and babbling that Lauryn had planned to fire at him.

"Careful," she warned, leading him cautiously. "It's a little downhill right here." As always, an odd anxiety rose in Lauryn as they approached the ancient springhouse. "The O'Hallerans used this water for everythin' until my Paw Paw, my Grandpa Kensington, had the well dug," she explained. She wondered again why this place made her uncomfortable. The springhouse was a small building built over a natural spring. A little watermill and pond were on one outside wall. Steps leading through a short doorway at the adjoining wall led down into the spring water inside, where a brick shelf walkway, built level with the base of the springhouse, made it possible to enter without going for a swim. There were windows, although barred, down low near the water to let in the sun and illuminate the room. Still, in Lauryn's mind, it was as plain and unnerving a place as there ever was.

"You don't like this place much, I take it," Brant remarked.

Lauryn looked at him, surprised that he should have been able to sense her discomfort. "No. I don't. It's always made me nervous. It's a bit better in spring and summer when the flowers are bloomin' all around. But on an average day...I don't care for it."

"Why?" he asked.

"Well, for one thing, I guess it just made my stomach turn to come out here and see dead mice and things floatin' around in the water. Yeck! To think folks used to drink out of here. There are always, always rats runnin' around in there too. And in the summer, it's a perfect place for skunks and everythin' else to hide. I can't tell you how many dead animals my brother Sean has fished out of this water! He, by the way, loves this place, I might add." Lauryn shrugged. "Otherwise...I don't know. I just don't like it. For years, when I was younger, I used to think that maybe this is where Lauralynn was lost. But when I finally got up enough courage to go in there and look around, I'm sure it wasn't. It would've been too easy a place to be found."

"And besides, she's not wet."

"What?" Lauryn asked, momentarily puzzled by his comment.

"When I see her," Brant explained, "she's not wet. It seems like she'd be drenched and dripping in pond water if she'd drowned or died and fallen in there."

Lauryn shivered at the vision created in her mind to accompany Brant's description. Again she was amazed at how nonchalantly he talked about being haunted. And yet somehow it comforted her to know she needn't feel guilty for not having the courage to go swimming in that horrible place looking for Laura's bones.

"Well," Brant sighed, squeezing Lauryn's shoulder, signaling he'd heard enough about the springhouse, "I think we can safely scratch this place off our list of where to look for a skeleton."

Lauryn looked at him quickly. "I can't believe how matter-of-factly you talk about it."

"It's what we're looking for, isn't it?" he reminded her.

"Well, yes, but it seems so...so irreverent the way you put it."

"I don't mean for it to. It's just that...we know where Laura is, Miss Kensington. She's back in Castledale, Vermont, waiting for help. What we're looking for is just what remains of the shell that housed her while she was here."

He was right. Lauryn knew that. But it still seemed disrespectful to her way of thinking. Maybe that was one of the massive differences between a man's perception and a woman's.

"What else is out here that I can't see?" Brant asked.

"Well, back over this way are the servants' quarters," Lauryn offered, leading him away from the springhouse and toward another building some distance from it.

"You mean the slaves' quarters'," Brant corrected.

"No. I mean the servants' quarters," Lauryn repeated. "My great-granddaddy didn't think slavery was right. For one thing, he was Irish and had seen the way the Irish were treated. But mostly he simply recognized that people were people no matter what color their skin was."

"Wise man. Especially for his time."

"Yes. And he endured great ridicule and tribulation at times because of it. The family employed servants. Granted, most were black, but at least they were free men and paid an honest wage. So…this is what remains of the servants' house." Lauryn reached out and pushed at the old door that led to the first floor of the small house. Stepping in, she startled and let out a squeal as a rat scurried across her path.

"I loathe rodents," she mumbled. She stepped farther in, and Brant followed. "As you can see, it's a very nice house—plenty of privacy and fireplaces enough to warm it well." Then she realized what she had said. Of course he couldn't see it all! "Forgive me," she began to apologize.

"Don't be apologizing all the time for coining a phrase, Miss Kensington," he grumbled. "I suppose it'd be stupid to ask you if you searched in here."

"I did," Lauryn affirmed. "Everywhere. I had even heard tales of there bein' a secret hidin' place in here like there was in Connemara House. But I never could find it. I knocked on every wall and stomped on every floorboard from center to circumference. No luck."

"It sounds like you've been very thorough over the years," Brant noted as they left the servants' house.

"Oh yes. I've crawled under the gazebo and endured the seven thousand and eighty-two spiders under there. Believe me when I tell you…*that*, if nothin' else, should be testimony of my dedication."

"I imagine that it is," he chuckled.

"I've knocked on every wooden panel in the house, roamed around in that dark, damp, stinky old basement until I was sick to my stomach. I've wandered for hours along the creek bed, sat in the attic for days sortin' through the old trunks. But my mama nearly had apoplexy when she caught me diggin' a hole out by Henry near the old cemetery lookin' for bones and such when I was twelve."

Brant burst into laughter suddenly.

"What?" Lauryn asked, smiling herself, for his amusement was quite amusing.

"And you think I'm irreverent?" he chuckled. "What made you decide to dig then and there anyway? And who's Henry?"

Lauryn shrugged. "Oh, Henry's our statue. He's pretty beat up these days. He's been out there by the cemetery since the war. Actually, he never was finished. I think he was forgotten durin' the fightin' and…just never got finished. And why did I dig out there by him? Well, I was angry that day." Lauryn explained further, "Really frustrated with tryin' to find Laura and not bein' able to. So I told the Captain that I was goin' to find her if I had to dig up every foot of ground at Connemara! But Mama foiled my plans."

Brant chuckled again, and Lauryn couldn't help but smile, pleased that she had caused him to do so.

"So where's the old cemetery?" he asked. "Is it the one where the Captain is buried? And is Henry sculpted after a real person? Someone in the family?"

"The cemetery is over just south of the house, and the Captain is buried there. And Henry…well, my friend Penny and I named him that. I don't know who he was gonna be. My great-grandmother's brother was chiselin' away at him. Penny and I just called him Henry whenever…"

"Whenever what?" Brant prodded, curiously.

"Whenever we were outside playin'," Lauryn stammered. She had no desire to go into further detail about Henry. Henry was a secret she shared with only Penny—though she suspected the Captain knew that Henry had been the proxy for whatever boy Lauryn and her friend dreamed about kissing when they were girls. "We'll go to where the Captain was buried next."

Lauryn led Brant there in silence, and Brant said nothing as well. It was as if they both were pondering the significance of where they were about to go and who was laid to rest there. And who wasn't.

Brant let go of Lauryn's hand and hunkered down in front of the tombstone. Reaching out until his fingers met with the granite of the marker, he ran a thumb over his great-uncle's name.

"I smell…flowers," Brant mumbled.

"Pansies," Lauryn explained, reaching down and pinching a large violet-and-yellow–faced winter blossom. "My great-grandmother planted them at his grave, and they've bloomed year-round ever since. They've just kept reseeding themselves for fifty years. And they are unusually fragrant." Taking Brant's hand, she placed the bloom in his grasp.

He caressed its petals roughly with his fingers, drawing it to his nose and inhaling deeply of its fragrance. Then he nodded and released the wasted flower to the ground in front of the tombstone. "Is there a marker?" he asked in a hushed tone.

"You mean…for Lauralynn?" Lauryn whispered. She felt, again, an overwhelming sympathy for the man who had so recently lost his sight. How desperately she wished he could see the beauty of the cemetery, the marker that lay next to the Captain's headstone—wished he could drink in the vision of the white arbor, engulfed in wisteria vines, arching protectively over the two grave markers. In the spring, the wisteria that covered the arbor lattice would bloom, along with all the rest at Connemara, creating a perfect loveliness as it complemented the perpetual, and somewhat miraculous, profusion of pansies that grew on the Captain's grave.

"Yes," she answered quietly. "There's a marker just next to the Captain's…with her name and that she was…was lost."

Brant inhaled deeply and was pensive for a moment.

"You know," he began, "it was so strange to be a child when I met her and then to grow up into a man…and she stayed so young. One day I was ten; the next, it seemed, I was twenty…twenty-one…twenty-two. But she was still the same. Never aging. Always young and beautiful."

"Did…did it change your perception of her?" Lauryn asked. "Your growin' up and her not?" Her heart was hammering with a sort of anxiety that was becoming all too familiar, yet stranger than anything she'd ever known. Even though she had known this man less than twenty-four hours, his opinions and his thoughts were incredibly important to her. "I mean…did your feelings change toward her?"

Brant smiled and stood straight, still facing the tombstone. "I suppose so. When I was small, it was like she was a big sister. And then as I got older and, you know…" he stammered. "You know what I mean. I began viewing women differently in general. I suppose I was sweet on her in a way."

Lauryn tried to ignore the heat rising to her face—the heat of jealousy. Jealousy, for pity's sake! And over a ghost! And what right did she even have to be jealous? How ridiculous it was.

"But then," he continued, "I grew into a man, and…and she seems like a young girl to me now."

Lauryn gritted her teeth in irritation. At the time of her disappearance, her death, Lauralynn was the same age Lauryn was at that very moment. If Brant considered Lauralynn a young girl, then he must most certainly consider Lauryn one too! Suddenly she felt small, inexperienced, and immature. His next question caught her off-guard because she was so preoccupied with her anxieties.

"What about you and the Captain? Was it about the same? Or did you always perceive him as you do now?" He turned toward her then, genuinely curious.

Lauryn shrugged her shoulders, and a lump of thick embarrassment at her youthfulness stuck in her throat, rendering her unable to answer for a moment. But then swallowing hard, she said, "He…he was mostly like an uncle to me, a good friend—the best. I think my infatuation with him was over…long ago. I realized that his heart was elsewhere, and all I ever wanted was for someone to…" She stopped abruptly, having almost revealed too much.

"Someone to what?" he urged.

She paused, trying to think of an answer to give him without telling him the complete truth.

"Go on. What?"

"Just…just…" she stammered.

"Someone to love you like he loves her?" he finished.

"Well, yes," she admitted.

Brant shook his head. "Not me," he grumbled, turning back to the tombstone. "I never want to be wandering around after I'm dead, alone and in agony."

"So you'd rather wander around alone and in agony while you're livin'?" Lauryn scolded. She didn't like when people made love sound so miserable. Love was a beautiful thing—something to dream of having, something to make life worth living. She couldn't understand why some people only saw the pain. And yet this man—again she thought how different his relationship with Lauralynn was from hers with the Captain. She had been lucky. He hadn't.

"I suppose you think I'm a heartless devil," he mumbled.

"No. I think you're an injured soldier returned from the horrors of war, and you've forgotten that love and loved ones are the very reason you went."

He grinned then. "Not one to mince words, are you, Miss Kensington?"

"Not with certain subjects," she admitted.

"Well, good thing I rub you the wrong way. You wouldn't want to condemn yourself to wandering around after a blind man for eternity." He chuckled, but Lauryn was furious.

"If you weren't blind and could see it comin', I'd slap you smack across your face!" She was angry with him. It was time to get over his self-pity, his defeated attitude, and get on with his life. She was losing patience as well. However could she find out everything he might know to help her find Lauralynn if he were forever being distracted by his own pain?

"Well, why don't you do it?" he growled at her. "Don't treat me any different because I'm—"

And his words were halted as Lauryn did indeed slap him soundly—soundly but far less forcefully than she could have. He stood before her, mouth gaping open, stunned into silence.

"Now that I have your attention," she began, rather horrified at her own actions, "if you're gonna help me find your lost lady, then you're gonna have to quit thinkin' about yourself. There are others, even those who came home from the war, with much worse injuries and challenges in their lives than yours."

He still looked more surprised than angry. "Admittedly," he mumbled. "You better say your piece, or I know I'll never have mine."

Was he implying that she talked too much? It didn't matter. She was going to say what she must, else she'd always regret not doing so.

"Fine!" she began. "Be thankful you didn't lose your sight and your arms. Be glad you're healthy otherwise, that you didn't die a horrible death from the mustard gasses. Be glad your eyes didn't get poked right out altogether! At least you still have hope."

"How would you like to be saddled with me for the rest of your life?" he interrupted angrily. "I'm going home, and my family—"

"No one will be saddled with you. And your family's pain won't be a grain of sand compared with what it would've been had you been lost."

"Would you, Miss *Love-Is-So-Wonderful*," Brant mocked, imitating her soft, southern accent, "would you want to go through life with me? Like this? Would you go through eternity?"

"If I were in love with you, it wouldn't matter." It was out of her mouth before she could stop it. She had said something, out loud, that had been lurking in the corner of her mind since the moment she'd approached him on the train—that there was something about him that whispered to her soul and the loving part of her heart. "And besides, you won't be blind for eternity," she added in an effort to distract him from her first remark.

"How do you know?"

Lauryn was relieved that Brant had chosen to address whether blindness remained an affliction in the afterlife, as opposed to the fact that she had mentioned love again.

"Ever hear anyone tell of seein' a blind ghost?" she asked plainly.

He smiled and shook his head, his mood obviously having been lightened by her positiveness.

"And besides," she continued, "I asked the Captain once if people still carried their afflictions and deformities with them, and he said they don't when they're at peace."

"What if I don't die peacefully? What if I'm lost like Laura?"

"Then I'll find you." Lauryn dropped her gaze to the ground, embarrassed at making such a promise to a man who was nearly a complete stranger. And she wondered how much merit it would hold anyway, considering how long it was taking her to find Lauralynn.

"I think you just did," he mumbled. Lauryn looked to him once more. He was again turned away from her, but there was a peacefulness, a profound humility to the set of his mouth. And something in Lauryn bloomed suddenly. Like a butterfly that had just taken to the breeze, her heart fluttered, and she felt that her adventures in life were only just beginning.

༄

Brant was very quiet for the remainder of the morning. He seemed pensive, thoughtfully withdrawn. It wasn't until Sean, Mindy, and Junie arrived at Connemara later that he appeared to be aware of something other than the echoing thoughts of his own mind.

Sean and Brant talked for hours about the war, politics, the economy, automobiles, and other such subjects that interest men. Even after supper they visited. There seemed to be a lot in common between them, and although Georgia smiled, delighted to see both men enjoying each other, Nana smiled understandingly each time her eyes met Lauryn's. Yes, Nana understood Lauryn's envy over Sean's ability to capture Brant's attention so completely and for such a long period of time.

But when evening had settled and Sean and his family had left Connemara for their own home, it was Lauryn that Brant asked to help him upstairs so he could retire. He accepted Georgia's and Nana's affectionate kisses on each of his cheeks and Patrick's friendly handshake, bidding them a kind and grateful good night.

"Have you got everythin' you'll be needin' for the night?" Lauryn asked.

"I do," he assured her, beginning to unbutton his shirt even though she still stood in his presence.

"Well, then…I guess I'll be leavin' you to your rest," Lauryn stammered.

"Too tired for ghost stories tonight?" he asked.

"Never," she assured him, excitedly, her mood lifting.

Brant didn't bother to rebutton his shirt—simply let it hang open as he sat down on his bed obviously ready for discussion. Lauryn went to the chair that sat in the opposite corner and pushed it over to the bed so that she could sit just across from him. She was feeling more comfortable with him. After all, she'd known him for an entire day.

"Laura's lost," Brant began. "She's not wet; she's not hurt anywhere else but her stomach."

Lauryn nodded, acknowledging that these were facts known to them both now.

"She's still wearing her jewelry…"

"So it wasn't thievin' Yankees that found her," Lauryn finished for him.

"That's what I think." He was thoughtful for a moment. "Why the fragrance though?" he asked, mostly to himself. "I've never been able to figure that out."

Lauryn shrugged and simultaneously offered, "Perfume?"

"I don't think so, though it is perfumey." Brant seemed pensive again and then added, "Oh well." He moved on. "Mud stains at the hem of her dress. Was it raining that day?"

"Nana never mentioned it, but we could ask her specifically." Lauryn could feel the excitement rising in her bosom. Brant would help her. She knew he would! Something in his mind, in his memory, was the key.

"She weeps when she thinks of Brand…but also when I mention her family. She's mournful over someone else," Brant suggested.

"Her father maybe? Or just being separated from them?"

Brant nodded. "Maybe."

"What else?" Lauryn prodded.

"Sometimes…though actually not in recent years," he began, "she would be holding a little cup, maybe a teacup. But she hasn't had that in her hand for years and years."

"A little teacup? A child's teacup?" Lauryn was puzzled by this bit of information.

"Maybe," Brant mumbled.

Lauryn was intrigued. Why would Laura be holding a teacup? "Was it a child's teacup? Or maybe a demitasse?"

Brant smiled and shook his head. "Hell, I wouldn't know! That's girl stuff." He quickly mumbled an apologetic, "Sorry," for having sworn in her presence. Lauryn smiled, amused and again unconvinced of the sincerity of his apology. "I hadn't thought of that little cup in years. How strange. I can see it clear as ever in my mind's eye now," he seemed to think out loud.

"It must be important," Lauryn assured him excitedly. "Go on. What kinds of things would she talk about…try to make you understand, I mean?"

Brant shrugged. "It's hard to know where her giving me every clue she could ends…and where our friendship begins." He lay back, stretching his legs out on the bed and tucking his hands behind his head. As his shirt fell open, revealing the well-defined lines of his chest and ribcage, Lauryn reminded herself that he was obviously a returning soldier used to being in the company of men only. Still, she gave him no modesty reprimand and simply tried to avert her gaze. This was difficult, however, because the revealed section of his body was quite impressive. And to one so inexperienced in such sights as Lauryn was, it was still unnerving.

"Just tell me anythin'," she urged. "There might be things that don't seem important to you…that might be significant for me to know."

Brant nodded and thought for a moment. "She has always wanted me to come here…to Connemara," he mentioned. "When I was younger, I'd say, 'Someday I'll go to Connemara, Laura,' and she would cheer up and nod frantically. She always wanted me here."

"To look for her?" Lauryn asked.

"It's the obvious answer. Maybe to make absolutely certain that Brandon was safe. She knew he was searching for her because I'd told her about you. But she really is quite selfless, and I know she worries for him."

He yawned, and Lauryn knew he needed his rest.

"You're tired. We can talk more tomorrow," she said. She hoped he would assure her that he was fine and ask her to stay. There was so much to be unraveled—and so little time.

But instead he nodded and said, "Yep. Maybe my mind will be less foggy in the morning." Then, much to Lauryn's surprise, he sat up, stripped off his shirt completely, and fumbled with it until it hung haphazardly on the bedpost. "I like mornings. But I notice that you down here in the south are more night people. I can't keep up." He smiled, and Lauryn stood, replacing the chair in case he should get up in the night and it would be in his way.

"Hot days, cooler nights, I suppose," she muttered. "Good night then, Brant."

"Good night, Lauryn." And it was done.

It wasn't until Lauryn returned to her own bedroom and found the Captain pacing anxiously back and forth across the room that she even realized she hadn't spoken to him all day.

"Oh, Captain!" she began to apologize. "I'm so sorry! It's just that—"

The Captain nodded, smiled understandingly, and interrupted, "Does he know anything that will help you?"

Lauryn shrugged. "I'm sure he does. He told me several things tonight that I think must be pertinent. I just have to sort it out, and…and…I'm afraid it will still take some time, Captain."

She could see the disappointment on his face, although he smiled and reached out, taking her hand in his. "I know. I just…I've no right to be impatient but—"

"You have every right to be impatient!" Lauryn exclaimed. "And my bein' gone for so long was pretty selfish."

"No," the Captain argued firmly. "You must have a life too, Lauryn. A life of your own. That is one of the reasons this frustrates me so…watching you waste your life because of me."

Lauryn smiled and threw herself into the Captain's warm embrace. "That's nonsense, and you know it. What fun would my life have been up to now without my best beau?" she teased, trying to find the lightheartedness that she seemed to be losing.

The Captain chuckled and patted Lauryn affectionately on the back as he returned her hug. "Well, you're older now, sweetheart. It's time you had a real beau…one that is still alive." He embraced her for a moment longer and then, releasing her, reminded, "His time here is very short, Lauryn. I want you to make the most of it. Do you understand what I mean?"

"Yes," Lauryn assured him.

"Don't worry about me," he demanded. "I'm here and there all the time. Spend your time with him. Understand?"

"I will," she agreed, and tried not to feel guilty for the pure delight she felt at the prospect of carrying out the Captain's order. "And don't worry," she added. "I'll pick his brain raw. I'll find her…for you. I promise."

The Captain shook his head, seeming amused. "Don't pick it too raw, angel. And…and spend some time enjoying yourself. Don't be afraid to—"

"I am enjoyin' myself," she interrupted. She didn't want him to say anything further. She didn't want him to add any further hope to the beautiful dreams of owning Brant Masterson that were already lurking in the corners of her mind.

The Captain smiled in understanding. "I see," he mumbled. "Good night, sweetheart." Then putting his hand to Lauryn's cheek and cupping it affectionately, he vanished.

Lauryn sighed, heavily. Her mind was a messy cupboard of wondering and confusion. The Captain was right. Brant would only be at Connemara a few more days. She must get every morsel of information she could from him. And with the short time given her in his presence, she would let her heart soak up every ounce of the perfect dream he was.

Amazingly, sleep came quickly to Lauryn that night, and her last thought before drifting off to slumber was, *I hope Brant is warm enough.*

ᘒ

"So…is it as bad as everyone says?" Patrick asked as he sat near the creek with Brant.

Brant smiled. He could well remember when war seemed like an exciting adventure to him too. But that was before he knew the reality of it.

"Yep," he answered the small boy. "It's worse."

"But…when you're fightin', you feel good 'cause you're doin' the right thing. You know you have to do it to protect your home," Patrick begged.

Brant remembered too how important it was to know that war was necessary sometimes, that it was a righteous cause, that it was done to protect everything a man held dear.

"That's right. It's what keeps you going." Brant could hear the pebbles Patrick was tossing hit the water's surface. "You have to remember why you went."

"I'd go," Patrick stated. "I'd go for my family…for Connemara."

"Yep. That's why I went," Brant confirmed.

"Did you have a girl at home when you left?" Patrick asked.

Brant chuckled. He liked the way this boy's mind worked. And Brant did notice the similarity between Patrick's way of thinking and Lauryn's.

"Not when I left. I had a girl before, but…she wasn't right for me," Brant confessed.

"Was she pretty?"

"Yep. Very pretty."

"Was she as pretty as my sister?"

Patrick's question wasn't meant to be cruel. It was honest. The boy obviously didn't spend his time noticing that Brant was sightless and couldn't see Lauryn. And suddenly it bothered Brant all the more that he indeed was not able to see her. Surely a girl with Lauryn Kensington's inquisitive mind, sweet voice, and compassion would be attractive physically as well.

"Oh, I highly doubt that she was as pretty as your sister, Patrick," Brant told the boy. Then a thought struck him. "What does your sister look like?"

"Oh," Patrick chuckled. "I plum forgot you were blind." Another pebble made a splash in the creek. "Well, it's hard for me to say. She is my sister and all and…"

"I won't tell her if you say anything nice about her," Brant assured the boy, completely amused at his full understanding of the boy's need to irritate his sister mercilessly and never to be caught being nice.

"Well…lots of men think she is *really* pretty—beautiful, in fact. She thinks she's ugly, and I just let her go on thinkin' it." Brant chuckled as the boy continued. "She's always in a pickle. But what does she look like? Hmmm, let's see. She's got brown hair, a nice smile, good teeth, small ears, and her nose ain't too big. Does that help at all?"

Smiling, Brant nodded his assurance. "Thank you, Patrick. And I won't tell Lauryn you said anything nice about her."

"Whew!" Patrick exclaimed. "Now, back to the war. Tell me some real messy stuff! Some stuff that will give me bad, bad dreams!"

Brant laughed. The boy was great fun! "All right. But don't you go waking up in the night with nightmares and get me in trouble with your mama."

"I won't! I won't! I swear it!" Patrick promised excitedly.

So Brant granted Patrick's wishes of curiosity and adventure, but not too graphically. And he was glad for the boy's company. It brightened his spirit. Still, he kept wishing that Lauryn would return from whatever errand her mother had sent her on so they could continue their conversations.

ɞ

It was night before Lauryn was able to steal Brant away, trap him in his bedroom, and "pick his brain" again. Something delighted in her as she watched him getting ready to retire. She was enchanted by his habitual ritual of unbuttoning his shirt but not removing it right away. She wondered whether this had always been his habit. Or did he simply leave it on longer because she was in the room?

"Why hasn't your brother ever enlisted in your search?" Brant asked as he ran his fingers through his hair and sat down on his bed. Lauryn was sitting in a chair across from him the way she had the prior two nights.

Sakes alive! she thought. If Brant Masterson weren't the handsomest man ever born on earth, well then, she couldn't imagine who was.

"You…you mean Sean?" she stammered, trying to redirect her attention from his attractive form back to his question.

"Yeah."

Lauryn sighed heavily. "Sean thinks I'm an idiot," she stated.

Brant laughed, and it was captivating to see him do it. His smile was incredible.

"He does not," he chuckled.

"He does so," Lauryn assured him. "He's been tellin' me that since I was in diapers. He always calls me the 'mad ghost girl' and shakes his head."

"He has to tease you. He's your brother." Brant seemed to understand all too well the male need to irritate his female siblings.

"Isn't there anythin' else?" Lauryn pleaded. "Somethin' else you know?" In her heart, she knew she was pleading for information to give herself more time in his presence. But she tried to rationalize it by quietly whispering, in her mind, that the mystery simply needed solving.

Brant frowned, discouraged as always. "I can't think of…there's the smell about her, the little cup, the stains on her dress, the locket, her

85

rings. She taught me to play the piano. She'd hold my head in her lap at night and stroke my hair until I fell asleep. She'd play games with me…games that none of my friends knew. A couple of times Lauralynn even had me playing tea party with a bunch of my sisters' old dolls. If I didn't catch hell…heck for that, I never caught it for anything." He cleared his throat and added, "Sorry about the 'hell.'"

Lauryn bit her lip, barely stifling a delighted giggle. Her mother would be horrified if she knew that her daughter found a man's habit of swearing attractive in a way.

"You played tea party?" Lauryn asked. The soft laughter in her voice was not restrainable.

"Yes, I played tea party." he grumbled. "Didn't you ever play tea party?"

He was blushing! She was certain of it. Yes, Brant Masterson was blushing!

"Well, yes, I did play tea party, Mr. Masterson," Lauryn admitted. "But…but that would be a little more expected. Don't you think?"

"Yeah, yeah, yeah." He shook his head. "Let's go on to something else."

But something tickled Lauryn's brain. "Don't you find it just the least bit odd that she would want you to play tea party?"

"I was a little boy. I'm sure she was just finding ways to try to amuse me," he answered.

"But you said she played games with you, other games. Sisters—and Laura was a sister—sisters know how much little boys loathe playin' things like tea party. Why would she want you to?"

"Sisters also like to humiliate their brothers," he growled.

"Did…did she still have the cup when y'all played tea party?" Lauryn found it completely odd that Laura would nurture such a thing with young Brant. It had to have meaning.

"At first," he mumbled. "But, now that I think of it, it was when the teacup stopped coming with her that she stopped trying to get me to play that."

Suddenly, Lauryn couldn't contain herself any longer. As serious as the situation was, as desperate as she was to find Laura for the Captain, the vision in her mind of Brant Masterson playing tea party with a bunch of his sisters' dolls and a ghost woman was too much. She erupted into delighted laughter, unable to stop even to catch a good breath.

"Laugh it up, sugar," Brant growled. "Who knows what kind of damage that did to me? I'll probably turn out to be a lunatic."

Still, Lauryn couldn't stop laughing. "It's…it's just too cute to imagine and not laugh a little!"

"A little?" But she heard the slight chuckle in his voice. Then he stood up and, shaking his head, began to unfasten his trousers.

"What are you doin'?" Lauryn nearly gasped.

"Going to bed," he stated. "So, unless you're planning on jumping in with me…"

Lauryn stood up with indignation. His threatening to undress in front of her was completely improper! Outrageous and intolerable! But his final remark—the implication he made—was just plain hedonistic.

"I'm sorry if my laughin' offended you, but that gives you no right to—" she began to scold.

"Your laughing didn't offend me. And don't act so shocked." He chuckled. Looking up into his bandaged eyes, she was mesmerized by the movement of his mouth as he spoke. "And don't try to tell me that your brothers never dropped their drawers in front of you before."

"Patrick is a child," she reminded him. "And as for Sean…he's a heathen! And he's my brother anyway."

"Well, if it will make you feel better, Miss Kensington…go ahead," Brant suggested. A deliciously devilish smile spread across his face.

"Go ahead and what?" Lauryn asked.

"Go ahead and strip down yourself."

Lauryn gasped. "Why, you…" she began to reprimand.

But his smile faded, and the corners of his mouth turned down in a frown. "What harm would it do? It's not like I can see you now. Is it?" he growled.

There it was—that defiant, defeated self-loathing that Lauryn had begun to recognize as Brant's last line of defense. Whenever things got too comfortable, whenever he began to smile or feel better, he called upon it. Her heart ached for him, and yet, if he continued to be beaten, his life would never be full.

And so she made her decision.

"You're right, of course," she whispered. Then, pulling one of her hands from his grasp, she reached up, touching his face tenderly. He turned his face from her, uncomfortable with her touch. "I could strip down buck naked right now, and it wouldn't even be improper, would it?"

"Don't be ridiculous," he growled again. She noticed the heightened red in his face. "Of course it would."

"But you're standin' here in just your trousers, ain't you?" she asked him.

"I'm wearing my underwear too," he grumbled.

"So that means it's all as proper as proper can be."

"Better not let your mama hear you saying *ain't*, sugar." His voice was odd, the intonation of it different than any Lauryn had heard him use before. "And of course it's not proper. Am I going to spend every minute here apologizing to you for one thing or the other?" he asked angrily.

"I suppose that's up to you, isn't it?" She looked at him—the sad expression on his mouth, the way his broad shoulders slumped in the manner of having been conquered. "Do you know what you need, Mr. Masterson?" she asked.

"A sound slap across the face again?" he chuckled.

"Maybe," she agreed. "But I think it's what Sean needed when he came home from the war all broken and sad."

"And sighted," Brant added.

Then, before she could think of the absolute brazenness of what she was doing, Lauryn moved forward and, slipping her arms around and under his own, embraced him warmly. She felt his chest rise as he inhaled deeply, uncomfortable and uncertain how to respond.

"My mama says everyone on this green earth should have at least two hugs a day. It does more than any medicine ever could," she whispered. At the same time, she wished she hadn't been so bold, because the feel of his body next to hers, the smoothness and scent of his skin against her cheek, was completely appealing to her senses.

It wasn't like she hadn't been this close to him before. Why, just two days before on the train, he'd been the one to take her tightly in his arms. Of course that had been quite different. He'd been fully clothed, for one thing.

"Your mama's right," he mumbled. He patted her rather platonically on the back and did not return her embrace, but did not push her away either. And she knew it was enough—all he could take. But he had received it. He had not erupted in fury. He had needed a hug. It was as simple as that.

"Now," he said, "a couple of things have happened here tonight…that need to be addressed."

Lauryn stepped back from him and waited for his scolding.

"Those bein'…" she prodded.

"Well," he began, "number one, I've acted inappropriately in a house that I'm a guest in—offended my hostess's daughter. I'll apologize to your mother tomorrow if you think I should."

Lauryn smiled. "I've had one or two of your apologies, sir. I think it's best we just keep that one to ourselves."

He smiled. "All right. Now, number two, I've confessed my having played tea party—with dolls, mind you—as a boy. I'd appreciate it if that too never left this room."

Lauryn smiled. "All right. I agree."

"Now, third," he began, "I'm going to bed." He began to fiddle with his trousers button again. "So just in case you don't want anything else going on in here that needs to be a secret…"

Lauryn didn't allow him to finish. She simply turned and fled the room. His warm chuckle followed, and she smiled, pleased that she could lighten his heavy burdens at least for a moment.

"He's fabulous, you know," Lauryn sighed as she entered her room and saw the Captain standing in the corner waiting for her.

"I know," the Captain agreed. "It's in the bloodline."

Lauryn forced a smile. "He'll be here only a week, Captain. And when he leaves…"

"He'll have broken your heart already," the Captain finished.

Lauryn tried to stop the tears that were pooling in her eyes. She nodded.

"It will be all right, peach," the Captain told her as he walked to her and took her in his protective embrace. "You'll see. You'll solve this confounded mystery, and…and everything will be all right."

"It will. It will," Lauryn whispered, trying to convince herself. She fanned her emotionally heated face with one dainty hand and sniffled, trying to regain her composure. "It's just the drama of it all, right? Just the fact that he's a soldier, and you know how I hurt for all of them. Don't you?"

"Yes, Lauryn. I do know," was all the comfort the Captain would give her.

"And…and he called me *sugar*," she confided. "And…and I adored it!" She again fanned her blushing face and tried to regulate her breathing. "He'll be the end of me, Captain. The very end."

The Captain only smiled. "Oh, I very much doubt that, sweetheart."

CHAPTER FIVE

The remaining days Brant would be at Connemara began slipping by faster than Lauryn wanted to acknowledge. Each day, for the few moments she could steal him away to herself, Lauryn talked with Brant about Lauralynn. They reviewed the elements they had a sure knowledge of again and again, going over every detail of her appearance, every fact she had communicated to Brant about the day she disappeared.

Still, it was difficult. If it weren't Patrick wanting Brant's complete attention, it was Sean or her mother or even Nana. And when she was able to get him away for a short time, Lauryn found her innermost desires were to talk to him of nearly anything else but the problem binding them together.

As ever, the Captain was the calming force in Lauryn's life. Ever encouraging, ever sympathetic, he helped her to stay relaxed and hopeful in her moments of near despair. Since meeting Brant, Lauryn felt the pressure to find Laura all the more. Now there was not only the Captain to save but also Brant. It was often obvious that Brant's greatest discouragement came from his realization that he would no longer be able to help find Laura. If his knowledge didn't help Lauryn to find her, he could not see himself being of any worth to his beautiful, lost spirit friend.

The days seemed long and yet not long enough. Lauryn knew she was learning things from Brant that were vital to her success. She knew it! But it frustrated her that she could not fit the pieces together and solve the puzzle. Those were trying days for Lauryn Kensington in so many ways.

One afternoon, when Lauryn was finally able to steal Brant away from Patrick long enough to get a word in, Brant related again the story of his meeting Lauralynn. As always, they spoke of the things Lauralynn told him through gestures and of her appearance. Over and over that day, they discussed her appearance, for it felt significant to both of them. The presence of the tiny cup Laura carried with her for years was especially intriguing to Lauryn. What was its significance? And why, confound it all, couldn't Lauralynn be heard? What was the perfumed fragrance Brant smelled in her presence? Why could he hear her name but nothing else?

All these things and more were discussed and pondered each time Lauryn and Brant were together—always the same questions and always the same answers. The monotony of it was exasperating. Therefore, the conversation would often turn to less frustrating subjects to give their tired brains a rest.

Brant asked many questions about Lauryn's family, and Lauryn learned Brant's family worked a vast apple orchard in Vermont and raised cattle. Brant's mother died when he was quite young. That knowledge gave Lauryn greater insight into why Laura appeared to Brant much earlier than the Captain appeared to her. Brant needed Lauralynn as she needed him. Brant's older sisters, April and Rose, were married with young families. His older brother, Parker, still a bachelor, lived with his father, helping with the orchards and cattle.

Frequently Lauryn felt guilty when she consciously realized she very much enjoyed talking with Brant about things other than Lauralynn and her tragedy. Often an extreme nervousness washed over her when her heart began to swell as she looked at Brant, as she watched him. Every time his arm brushed her own or he laughed at something she said, an overwhelming delight rose within her. After all, she told herself, what woman wouldn't enjoy the attention of such a handsome, wonderful man?

She marked her attraction to Brant in her mental ledger as simple female vanity. She tried to ignore the accelerated beat of her heart whenever he smiled at her or laid his hand on her shoulder to be led somewhere—until one particular afternoon when Lauryn bested Patrick in the battle for Brant's attention.

It was four days before Brant's brother was to arrive to take him home when something happened that was far too astonishing for Lauryn to shrug away. Something spoke to Lauryn's soul, reminding her that Brant Masterson would not soon be gone from her heart. Long after he left to return to Vermont, Lauryn knew there would be an unsoothable emptiness within her—a brokenheartedness like she'd never imagined.

Earlier in the day, Lauryn and Brant had been sitting in the parlor discussing Lauralynn and what could be done. She learned that Brant too was growing weary of the endless discussion with no resolution. Both were becoming frustrated, and it was beginning to seem intolerable.

But that afternoon, as they sat across from each other discussing the mystery, Brant sighed in frustration and slumped back in his chair.

"What's wrong?" Lauryn asked. As he reached up and began rubbing his temples with one hand, she became more concerned. "Are you all right?"

Brant nodded and then unexpectedly changed the subject, as well as his mood. "It's…" Instantly he was angry—seething, in fact. Lauryn sensed it, not only in the tone of his voice but by the stiffness of his lips. His jaw clenched in frustration.

"It's what?" she asked.

"It's…it's frustrating!"

"Yes, I know," Lauryn sighed. She knew how overwhelming the situation with the Captain and Lauralynn was—all too well. "It seems, at times, that it will never end and that—"

"Not that," he interrupted impatiently. "Blindness. It's frustrating."

Lauryn struggled to swallow the lump of sympathy that rose in her throat. What could be said? What kind of response could she make that wouldn't sound ridiculous and cliché? She had assumed he referred to their task at hand—finding Lauralynn. It hadn't occurred to her that he was referring to his injury. She felt quite naive for not understanding what, at that moment, was his true frustration.

Unpredictably he asked, "What do I look like?" Lauryn was silent for a moment, too stunned by his question and sudden change in demeanor to answer. "I can't even remember myself," he continued. "I can see my family, my friends. In my mind, I can see them. But I can't look into my imagination's mirror and see myself. And I have no doubt that I look like a scroungy old dog at best." He bowed his head and rubbed his temples in frustration again. "And what about you?" he asked. "What do you look like, Lauryn Kensington?"

Lauryn was taken back. She had not expected such a question and could not fathom how to answer.

"You've...you've seen me," she stammered.

Brant laughed a solitary breath of a laugh. "I have not."

"In the car...on the train. The day we met." Lauryn did not want to try to explain her appearance to him. She could think of nothing else she wanted to do less! And although she knew he had not seen her, even though he had told her himself that she was no more than a shape in a fog, she feigned ignorance.

"Don't avoid answering. I've noticed you have a deplorable habit of avoiding issues that make you uncomfortable." He grinned impishly.

"If I'm so deplorable, find someone else to talk to." With an aching disappointment and throbbing hurt in her bosom, Lauryn stood, intent on leaving him in the parlor to his own ends, but his firm grasp on her arm halted her.

"What do you look like?" Brant asked again, his voice low and serious. As he stood, more of the anger seemed to leave him. "Are you beautiful?"

"Certainly not!" Lauryn answered bluntly. And it was truly her opinion of herself, however far from the truth it may have been. Brant smiled, and as always, Lauryn was entranced.

"You're lying," he whispered. "Tell me. What do you look like?"

"I...I don't look like anyone else in my ancestry, if that's what you're askin'." There it was, thick in her veins! That unfounded jealousy that was beginning to burn within her at times. "I don't have any of Laura's beauty. I look nothin' like her."

"I didn't ask you if you looked like her," he growled. "I asked what *you* look like!" He raised a hand and ran it through her wavy, tangled mass of hair. "A brunette. Correct?"

It was a rare experience for Lauryn to have a man touch her so personally. "Yes," she managed to confirm. She could not quit staring at him, studying every visible line of his face. He was perfect!

"Brunette like chocolate?" he prodded.

"No. Like…like maybe nutmeg."

He smiled and toyed with one long lock of her hair. "And this is natural?"

"The preposterous curl? Yes," she nearly spat. How she hated her hair!

Still smiling, he rested his hand on the top of her head. "You're short too."

"Slight of height," she corrected, feeling her mood lighten.

He chuckled. "Short."

Lauryn felt herself smile. This was a friendly sort of banter, bordering on flirtation. Lauryn was delighted by it.

"Thin or chubby?" Brant asked.

"Fat," she assured him.

He laughed. "Liar. That much I felt on the train." He chuckled when she gasped at his brazenness. "Nicely…curved." Again Lauryn gasped, even though she was completely thrilled by his roguish remarks, and again he chuckled. "So…a short, curvy, naturally curly, nutmeg-haired one. That's you." His smile faded, and his hand dropped, releasing the long curl of her hair he had been toying with. "So be it," he mumbled. "My imagination will have to do the rest."

"No," Lauryn whispered. She didn't want Brant Masterson seeing her in his mind's eye in any way as Laura's likeness. Her hair may be different, but would he still imagine her face as Laura's? For the first time in ten years, Lauryn didn't want to be compared to her late great-aunt. Before she could think to stop her actions, she took his hands and placed them, one on each side of her face.

Lauryn had seen others without sight feel the faces of people. She'd watched them trace the curves and lines of faces so their imaginations might conjure a familiar image in their darkened minds.

Brant did not pause. Closing her eyes, Lauryn tried to remain calm as his fingertips slowly caressed her temples, traveled lingeringly over her eyelids, brushed her lashes, traced her brow. It was questionable, according to propriety, for Lauryn to allow him to touch her so intimately. She well knew it. Yet her heart raced madly with each caressive pass his thumb made across her lips. As her own imagination began to dwell on the kiss he'd taken from her in the train car, she opened her eyes once more to try and dispel the memory. This only served to make matters worse. Immediately, her attention was drawn to his mouth—to the tiny, oddly attractive scar just under his bottom lip. Lauryn was momentarily distracted as the right corner of his mouth twitched slightly, almost too slightly to notice.

She wanted to be with Brant longer—know him better—feel his kiss again. Such thoughts and emotions were too strong to be comfortable. She pulled away suddenly, stepping back and out of his easy reach.

Brant smiled, seeming to understand her discomfort, and said, "I was right. Very beautiful."

Lauryn could not help but smile at his charm. "A true charmer, I see."

"An honest charmer," he replied.

His grin was roguish, beguiling. Lauryn couldn't stop the admiring sigh that escaped her bosom. "A charmer nonetheless."

He was silent a moment then—a long moment—moments. Then he mumbled, "Let me smell you."

"What?" Lauryn gasped in a whisper. It seemed an absurd request.

"Come on," Brant coaxed, reaching for her hand and pulling her closer again. "Haven't you ever noticed that everyone has a distinct smell, a scent of their own…unique to each individual?"

"No. Not…not really," she stammered as his face moved toward hers. The fact that she'd mentioned the Captain's individual scent was completely chased from her mind. She was entirely dominated by Brant's presence and manner.

"That's because you can see. If you couldn't see, you'd learn to smell better." Brant chuckled. "I mean, you'd learn to use your sense of smell better."

"Very amusing." Yet it had been a clever remark. That she must admit.

"I'm serious," he insisted. "Here. Close your eyes."

Lauryn sighed and disobeyed.

He was wise, however. He reached up with his thumbs, brushing her eyelids closed. "Now…smell me."

"Oh, for pity's sake, Brant!" Lauryn whined, opening her eyes and pulling her face from his grasp. "Don't be ridiculous."

"I'm not," he growled. Then she saw the hurt expression of his mouth and brows. How heartless she must seem to him! His sense of smell had, no doubt, been greatly heightened to help compensate for the loss of his vision. Her reaction must seem rather mocking and ignorant to him. Yet she did not want him to sense her pity for him either.

"Fine!" she snapped. "I'll smell you. But first assure me that you bathed this mornin'."

Brant grinned, obviously amused.

"And are you certain your parents named you Brant? I'm beginnin' to wonder if it weren't *Brat* instead!"

"Nope. I'm certain it was Brant. And yes, I did bathe this morning," he confirmed. "But you have to close your eyes or it won't be the same."

"Very well, Mr. Masterson," Lauryn closed her eyes. She was determined to please him, but when he took her face between his hands and drew it close to his neck, her eyes popped open. She wanted to *see* him as well! As he pulled her face nearer to him, the very tip of her nose softly brushing his jaw, she closed her eyes once more.

"It's doesn't work if you don't inhale, Lauryn," Brant chuckled.

So she breathed him in. And she knew her memory would treasure the scent of him forever! Brant was right. The scent of his face, of his neck, was like nothing she had ever sensed. It was purely Brant Masterson. Her mind couldn't even begin to describe it. There were familiar whiffs of scent about him—the residual aroma of soap, a clean shirt dried outside in the sunny breezes. Her mind's eye also envisioned a warm applewood fire crackling within a cozy hearth, the soothing flicker of a candle's flame, sweet honey drizzled on a hot biscuit. In the end, it was simply *Brant*. Brant smelled of comfort, protection, and warmth. A unique scent indeed!

"You see?" Brant asked in a low voice, sending goose bumps erupting over Lauryn's body.

"Yes," she admitted in a nervous whisper.

"So? Can I smell you?" he asked again. He grinned mischievously, and Lauryn wondered how any woman could ever deny him anything. Still, she knew he would find no such magnificent visions in his mind evoked by the fragrance of her flesh.

"Well?" he prodded.

"I…I suppose," she managed to say. "But you will be greatly disappointed if you're expectin' me to bring some lovely fragrance across the breezes to fill your lungs when…"

She was silenced when his hand clamped over her mouth.

"Shhhh," he commanded. "I'm smelling."

Lauryn obeyed, delighted by the powerful, controlling sensation of his hand quieting her. As Brant bent down, inhaling deeply of her hair, she searched her mind frantically to remember if she'd perfumed it that morning. She hadn't! And then when he bent and placed his nose at her neck just above her shoulder, she truly panicked. What soap had she washed her neck with that morning? Had it been the plain, unscented soap her mother provided for regular bathing? Or had it been the lovely spice-scented soap her Nana made and gave as gifts?

Slowly his assessment of her moved upward, caressing the flesh of her neck with his face. His rough whiskers prickled delightfully, and once or twice his lips brushed her skin, feeling almost like a teasing kiss. Lauryn fought to maintain her steady breathing. She had an incredible urge to reach out and run her fingers through his hair! To kiss him straight on the mouth! But she resisted and simply let him finish his lingering appraisal of her.

With a heavy sigh, Brant straightened, his smile fading.

It must've been the unscented soap, Lauryn thought with disappointment.

He rubbed his temples with one hand, frowning.

"I don't smell like…" she began. "I told you that I wouldn't."

"You smell like the best thing a man could ever taste," he mumbled.

Lauryn gasped, astonished at the nearly poetic charm of his words. They were so intimately flattering, so flirtatious. And then she realized the truth. It was merely that—flattery. Lauryn's heart panged with hurt at her mind's interpretation of Brant's remark.

"Givin' false compliments is unbecomin' to anyone, Mr. Masterson." She stood there before him, nearly panting with nervous anxiety and trying to understand his frustration at not having his sight, trying to forgive him for giving such counterfeit tribute to her. She knew what she smelled like. She smelled like soap and linen, Tennessee grass and garden soil. But she surely did not smell like something any man would want to taste! Still, she forgave him his cruelty, marveling again at how completely sincere he had sounded.

She was startled when Brant reached out and rather brutally wove his fingers through her hair, pulling her face close to his. "It was not a false compliment! I don't give false compliments! It was the truth. Self-pity over the fact that you do not like your own appearance does not become you, Lauryn."

"And you think self-pity over losin' your sight is becomin' to you?" Lauryn retorted. Before she even finished her retaliation, she regretted it. When she saw the look of self-hatred pass over the visible portions of his face, she was humbled. "I'm sorry," she said, reaching up and taking his face in her hands. "I'm sorry. It's just that you…"

He pulled away, turning from her. "No…you're right. You're right. I'm not who I was before."

"Yes, you are. I'm sure you are! You just…"

"No. I'm…I'm lost somehow."

Lauryn stood before him as a look of dejection crossed his face and he sat on the sofa. She desperately wanted to help him, to help him help himself. "Your brother will be here soon. I'm certain that will give you strength."

"Yes. It will," he mumbled.

But she knew he was unconvinced. He looked so conquered, so miserable! Lauryn felt she could not endure. Everything in her that was born to nurture burst forth. Reaching down and taking his face in her hands, she kissed him tenderly on the forehead. Immediately, she scolded herself, horrified at her own actions as he pushed her hands from his face and frowned at her.

"I've had my fill of pity, Lauryn," Brant growled. "I don't want any more of it."

Tears were heavy in Lauryn's eyes as she stared down at him. "You have a lesson to learn, Brant Masterson. There is a world of difference between pity and compassion!" Her voice broke, revealing her emotion as she whispered, "Don't worry. You'll not receive either from me again." And she ran from the room in tears.

Brant squeezed his already closed and useless eyes more tightly shut. He rubbed at his whiskers with one tired hand. Where was he? What was he doing? Never had he struck out so harshly at a woman. Never! And if anything were certain, it was that this girl didn't deserve to be the brunt of his frustration, wrath, and self-loathing.

"You owe her an apology."

Brant straightened and turned toward Sean's voice.

"What?" he asked, startled to find he was not alone in the room.

"Lauryn doesn't deserve that kind of treatment, boy," the man said.

Sighing heavily with great humiliation, Brant answered, "I know it. I know it!"

"Then take care of it. I'm sure it's not like you to treat a woman like that. You want to find yourself, Brant? Then you behave like yourself."

Brant nodded. Then humbly he asked, "Will...will you take me to her, Sean? I obviously couldn't run after her myself." He reached out and found a firm, strong shoulder on which to place his hand, following in silence, humbled to have been so wisely reprimanded. Odd though— he had remembered Sean as being taller.

When they reached the top of the stairs and stood just inside Lauryn's bedroom, Brant heard Lauryn's soft sniffling. Gritting his teeth and angry with himself, he dropped his hand from his escort's shoulder. Stepping into her room, he mumbled, "Lauryn? May I come in?"

"If you've come to apologize, there's no need. I understand that—" Lauryn's tearful voice began.

"Oh, there is need, sugar," Brant interrupted humbly. "I am so sorry. You have shown me nothing but friendship and compassion and hospitality, and I repay you by—"

"Please...I don't want you to apologize," she whispered tearfully.

Brant was reminded that, in the past when he offered her an apology, he gave the excuse that his Aunt Felicity would have expected of him. It was apparent that she thought this apology was offered for the same sort of reason—an apology of good manners only.

"I am sincerely sorry, Lauryn. Please understand, I'm a frustrated man. I...I'm wandering without a direction most of the time. I—"

"How did you get up here by yourself?" she asked suddenly.

Brant was confused. "He led me up here. He—"

"Who?" she asked.

"Your brother Sean." But as Brant thought about it again, the man's voice hadn't really sounded like Sean's. "At least...I supposed it was."

"Sean isn't here. You came in alone," Lauryn explained.

Brant stood frozen; the hair on the back of his neck prickled. "But someone led me in here. I…"

"He told you he was my brother?" Lauryn asked.

"No, no. I just assumed. He called me by name and…"

Lauryn shivered as sudden understanding enveloped her. She fairly trembled with the knowledge that someone else in the world had been touched by the Captain!

"I think you've met the Captain for the first time, Brant," Lauryn whispered. The hurt was gone from her voice, she had moved closer to him, and he dared to reach out and find her hand.

And even though it was obviously a profound revelation to him— one that would need consideration—Lauryn fancied it was secondary in importance to him, for he simply repeated his apology. "I'm sorry for my behavior downstairs. All of it."

"All of it?" she asked. She was disappointed somehow.

"Not all of it. Just my…my snapping at you. My lack of gratitude." His hand was warm and strong, and hers seemed so small as he held it. He appeared to take comfort in her touch as well, for he kept softly caressing the back of her hand with his thumb. It was exactly what she had been trying to give him downstairs—comfort.

"Friends?" Brant said at last.

"Yes," Lauryn whispered, squeezing his hand.

"All right then. I'll leave you to your privacy." Then, it appeared, he remembered how dependent he was. "I'll leave you to your privacy as soon as you lead me from it."

"Not now!" Lauryn exclaimed. "Not when you've just met the Captain!"

Brant turned to her again, the realization of what had just transpired seeming to wash over him. "I…I heard his voice. He spoke to me as if—"

"It must seem remarkable to you," Lauryn mused. "You've touched them both, Brant! Do you realize that?" She was quiet for a moment before whispering, "I…I envy you."

"Oh, don't envy me, sweet Lauryn," he told her. "Don't envy me."

"But I do," she confessed. "I know the Captain so well. And knowin' him and knowin' the past, I've always wanted to know Lauralynn. But you…you've met them both."

Brant nodded but was silent. Then he asked, "Where is she, Lauryn? Where could she possibly be that you haven't looked? She couldn't have gone far. There was a battle raging on your front lawn! She couldn't have gone far."

Lauryn was all too aware of the discouragement in him. His voice fairly dripped with it. "I don't know, Brant, but I'm not givin' up." She felt that in him too—the spirit of a man who'd been beaten down and was considering all impossibilities.

He nodded, seeming somewhat strengthened once more. "All right. All right. I won't—"

"Lauryn? Lauryn Kensington?" Lauryn's mother called as she came up the stairs. "There you are!" she exclaimed upon finding her daughter. "You've got company, child! Penny is here!"

"Penny?" Lauryn squealed with delight. "Oh, Brant! Come on." She took his hand and began to pull him along behind her. "You'll adore Penny!" For a moment, Lauryn's mind spoke to her, reminding her that she wouldn't want Brant to adore Penny too much.

"Penny?" Brant asked.

"The dearest friend of my childhood!" Lauryn giggled. "Oh, I bet she's madder than a buzzin' ol' hornet that I haven't come by since she got back."

"Slow down, Lauryn!" her mother warned. "You'll send Brant tumblin' headlong down the stairs."

Brant fared the stairs fine. It wasn't until they reached the bottom and he was safely down that Lauryn dropped his hand, squealed gleefully, and threw her arms around the neck of her dear friend, Penny McGovern.

Penny squealed, and as the two girls stood hugging and giggling, Georgia shook her head, smiling, and said to Brant, "Those two. They're like little eight-year-old girls again when they're together."

Brant grinned, obviously gathering as much just from the squealing and giggling that was going on.

"Penny has been Lauryn's friend...well, since they were babies!" Georgia explained. "And she'll have plenty of questions about Lauryn's tall, handsome soldier."

"I guess you're stuck with me for a while then, Mrs. Kensington," Brant told her.

Georgia smiled and took Brant's hand. "Sweetheart, any woman would be happier than a baby in a candy store to have you to herself for a while."

"And who is this?" Penny asked Lauryn as she caught sight of Brant. Penny's brilliantly green eyes widened with curiosity. Lauryn smiled at her friend, who smoothed her lovely blonde hair back from her face and straightened the collar of her blouse even though it was obvious the stranger before her couldn't see to judge her appearance.

Lauryn pointed to Brant proudly, her heart swelling at the sight of him. "This is Brant Masterson," she said.

Penny walked to Brant, taking his free hand in hers and shaking it firmly. "I'm Penny McGovern, Mr. Masterson," she said. "And I take it that you're Lauryn's souvenir from New Orleans?"

Brant smiled, obviously delighted with Penny's sense of humor. "That would be one way to put it, I guess," he chuckled.

"Unfortunately," Georgia explained, "he's only a temporary souvenir. Isn't that right, Lauryn?"

"Unfortunately," Lauryn agreed with a giggle.

"Temporary?" Penny whined. "Why, Mr. Masterson, are you gonna disappear like a dream or somethin'?"

"Maybe like a nightmare, Miss McGovern," Brant teased.

"Stop that, Brant," Georgia scolded, dropping his hand and playfully slapping the young man on the shoulder. "Now, you children go on into the parlor and have a chat. I'll bring in somethin' warm for you to drink." Georgia turned and left.

Taking Brant's hand, Lauryn led him into the parlor. Brant was quite amused listening to the girls' conversation. They chattered away like two little birds at a velocity that made his head spin. The only uncomfortable part of it was they kept involving him in their conversation. It was obvious that this Penny McGovern was being eaten alive by her curiosity where Brant was concerned. Lauryn simply explained that he was a friend she and her Nana met on the train who was staying at Connemara for a while.

They prattled on. It was amazing! Brant wondered how either one of them actually heard and understood what the other was saying. They spoke of Lauryn's stay in New Orleans, which was very revealing to Brant. He gathered that she did not like the Crescent City. It was dirty and lewd. There was excellent food, and it was wonderfully historic, but too much a big city for the likes of a girl from a small town. Brant liked that. For some reason, it made him like Lauryn even more to know she was an old-fashioned, small-town girl.

Penny had been away to school in Memphis. Her adventures were quite amusing. She seemed the kind of girl bound to stumble into embarrassing situations, and it was quite obvious she possessed a certain confidence where men were concerned that Lauryn pleasingly lacked.

For near to an hour, Brant sat listening or conversing with the two young ladies. It was the most entertainment he'd had for months. But he was somewhat relieved when Sean arrived and found him being verbally accosted by the two young females.

"For Pete's sake, Lauryn!" Sean chuckled upon entering the room. "What are you tryin' to do? Send Brant to the asylum? Y'all will drive him crazy."

"Hush, Sean!" Penny scolded. "Mr. Masterson has adored bein' here with us. Haven't you, Mr. Masterson?"

"Oh, of course," Brant agreed with a smile.

"These girls will turn you soft, boy," Sean argued. "You come along with me. We'll have us some manly conversation."

Brant chuckled as he stood and found Sean's shoulder. Indeed, he realized now that he should never have assumed that it had been Sean who had led him to Lauryn earlier. Sean was much taller, his voice not as deep.

"Come along, Brant," Sean insisted. "We'll leave these two hens to their peckin'."

"Hush your mouth, Sean," Lauryn said. But the girls went back to their giggling and happy conversation. Brant paused in wanting to leave them. He knew that once he was gone, Penny would be popping out questions about him to Lauryn at an even more amazing pace. But what else could he do?

Sean led Brant to the kitchen and to the table. "You have a seat. I'll dig us up somethin' to eat," he said.

"Oh, I've yet to eat something here that tasted like it was dug up," Brant replied.

"I hear you there, Brant." Sean looked in the icebox and found some smoked turkey. "Had my fill of eatin' horse manure when I was over there too."

"So it was the flu that sent you home?" Brant asked.

"Nearly died of it. Don't know how I didn't. So many boys did." Sean placed the turkey on the table and began slicing bread. "Came home to watch Daddy pass away from it. I felt guilty over that. But then Junie was born, and I realized…it was good that I made it."

"Are you past it?" Brant asked. "The war, I mean. Being there?"

Sean looked at the blind man sitting at his mama's kitchen table. His sympathy was profound at that moment, for he understood what Brant meant. Furthermore, he understood that being blind prevented Brant from seeing the beauty he'd fought for. Only another soldier could completely understand.

"No. I don't think you ever get past it. But there's ways that help," he confessed. "The nightmares are the worst for me."

Brant nodded. "Yeah."

"But I'm a lucky cuss. I've got Mindy right there to hold in my arms when they wake me up. Sometimes I can smell it, you know?" Sean asked.

Brant nodded.

"The fire, the guns, the mud."

"The death," Brant added.

"Yep. But don't worry, Brant. The arms of a woman you love…that's your tonic for it."

Brant smiled. It was quite a euphoric cure, he could well imagine.

"Why don't you try it out on Lauryn?" Sean suggested impishly. "Swoop her up in your arms and kiss the devil out of her! You'd be surprised the healin' power that would have. I'm sure it would go a long way for easin' your mind."

"Easing my mind maybe…but not my integrity," Brant chuckled.

Sean chuckled. "I'd love to see the look on her face! She'd probably die right there out of pure rapture!" Sean laughed again, obviously amused at the thought of his sister's surprise.

"I've no doubt she'd die, all right," Brant agreed, smiling. "But I doubt it would be from rapture."

"Well, you don't know Lauryn like I do. And anyhow, not to offend you, boy, but you haven't seen the look on her face when you're in the room."

"What look is that?" Brant asked, curious.

"That look a woman gets on her face when you know she wouldn't deny you anythin'!" Sean answered, lowering his voice.

"She's known me four days, Sean," Brant reminded.

"Four days would be plenty for Lauryn. She can read a man like a book, only faster. It's pretty unsettlin' at times."

"Really?" Brant was interested. He was learning a lot about his young friend from her brother.

"Oh yeah!" Sean assured him. "Lauryn's had her dream lover in mind since she was in diapers, practically. 'He ain't perfect!'" Sean said, attempting to imitate his sister's voice. "'He's perfectly imperfect!'" Sean chuckled. "Boy, if I didn't get tired of hearin' that while she was growin' up."

Brant accepted the sandwich Sean placed in his hand and took a bite. He had been hungry.

"But...and don't you tell her I admitted this, you hear?"

Brant smiled and nodded.

"She's right! She won't be settlin' for any ol' mangy mutt. She'll only be happy with her Mr. Perfectly Imperfect." Sean had obviously taken a bite of his own sandwich. When he spoke next, it was a rather muffled sound as he chewed. "She's a good girl. And she's taken to you, boy."

Brant smiled, knowing that what Sean didn't understand was that Lauryn hoped Brant held the key to easing the pain of Mr. Perfect, the Captain. Of course, she was interested in him, kind to him. She was a compassionate person. And at that moment Brant hoped he could help her, that somehow something he said would help Lauryn to find Laura. He prayed for it.

Once Sean and Brant left the parlor, Penny did indeed begin questioning Lauryn.

"My stars, Lauryn!" she began. "Where? How? He's fabulous! Magnificent! He's too beautiful!"

Lauryn smiled. "On the train home from New Orleans, in the wounded soldiers' car. And I know." Penny shook her head in astonishment as Lauryn continued. "He's the Captain's brother's grandson."

Penny gasped. "Liar!"

"No. It's true." Lauryn had long ago confided in Penny about her relationship with the Captain. But she would keep Brant's secret, his knowing Laura, in her own heart. It wasn't hers to tell. "It is!" Lauryn confirmed.

The girls chattered away for over an hour, Penny asking questions and Lauryn answering them. The conversation did eventually turn to Lauryn's trip to New Orleans and away from Brant. Lauryn was relieved when it did. She felt very possessive about the secrets she and Brant shared—the kiss when they'd first met, their ghostly friendships, their sleuthing.

Later in the day, after Penny left and Sean had gone home, Lauryn was coming down the stairs when her attention was drawn to the melody coming from the piano in the parlor. It was so familiar and yet…yes! The tune, the very same that the music box played, the one in the attic that she'd driven her mother nearly insane with while listening to as a child—the one that haunted her dreams so often. Quietly, she entered the parlor to see Brant sitting at the piano, rather slumped over the keys and playing the familiar melody.

Lauryn listened until Brant seemed to sense her and stopped playing, asking, "Who is it?"

"It's just me," she confessed. "That melody, Brant."

"Yes. I'm sure you know it well," he chuckled.

"Yes. But I've never heard it played. I only…there's a music box in the attic that belonged to Laura. You're playin' its melody. What is it? No one here knows."

Brant turned to her, a frown on his face. "You're just teasing me."

"No. I've always wondered. I hear it in my mind. But…are there words?"

Brant shook his head in disbelief. "It's called 'Sweet Lauralynn.' Those poor Union soldiers used to sing themselves into fits of melancholy with it. I thought for certain you would know it."

"No," Lauryn confirmed, going to sit next to him on the piano bench. "Will you sing it for me?"

He grinned and chuckled. "Of course not. I sound like a dying pigeon when I sing."

"Please, Brant. It's haunted me. All these years I've wondered what it was…if there were words. Brand gave Lauralynn that music box on their weddin' day. Please! It must've meant a great deal to her for him to have given it to her."

Brant shook his head. He'd lost so much of his motivation, so much of his confidence. Lauryn could see more and more that he had been a confident, powerful man before his injury. Like so many young men who had actually been fortunate enough to return from the war, he had been left scarred, wounded far beyond his sight being damaged.

"Oh, please, Brant. I'll owe you a favor if you'll do this one for me," she begged.

Sighing heavily, Brant breathed a defeated chuckled and began to awkwardly play the melody again.

The prelude was absolutely haunting to Lauryn, all the more so as she watched the blind man next to her play it. He'd played it many times before, she knew, enough that he didn't need his sight to play it. His hands played the melody from his soul.

Then, as Brant began to sing the song, Lauryn thought she might melt into a puddle at his feet. His voice, low and rather raspy, boasted pitch that was perfect. He was, in fact, a very gifted vocalist! Something fluttered in Lauryn's bosom—the same something that fluttered when he'd touched her face so intimately earlier that same day.

The words to the song were hauntingly beautiful, all about a soldier pining for the love he left at home when he'd gone to war, about the loneliness of the campfire and longing for his lover's kiss. Every so often the phrase "sweet Lauralynn" was repeated, causing Lauryn to think how perfectly the lyrics paralleled the story in her own family's past.

Lauryn wiped the tears from her cheeks as Brant played the last few notes of the song. "I never knew there were words," she whispered.

"That's probably because it was popular with the Union troops." He chuckled and added, "You little Johnny Reb," under his breath.

His playful teasing caused Lauryn to look at him quickly, realizing again that his brother would be there in just a few days to take him home, to strip him from her life. She felt an overwhelming sense of loss, and reaching out, she covered his hand with her own as it rested on his leg and softly thanked him.

"Thank you, Brant. For that song. For comin' here and..." She reached up, placing her palm against his cheek. To her great astonishment and delight, he took her hand and lingeringly kissed her palm.

"Thank you, Lauryn. For giving me hope," he mumbled.

His kiss tingled in her palm, even after he'd released her hand. She felt the unwanted sting of tears welling in her eyes. She didn't want him to leave—not only because of his help with the mystery of Laura but also because she didn't want *him* to leave.

"You'll write to me, won't you?" he asked unexpectedly. "And let me know if you find anything?"

Lauryn was disappointed about his reason for wanting her to write. "Of course," she promised, feeling let down. She knew she could not ask him to write to her in return, even if she told him she didn't mind if his letters were illegible because he couldn't see when writing them.

"Nothing too personal now," he teased. "My father will be reading my letters to me."

"I'm glad you warned me," she replied teasingly.

He chuckled and began playing something more lively on the piano. "All right then. Let's lighten the atmosphere in here."

Lauryn recognized the type of music he played immediately. "Someone has obviously spent some time in New Orleans," she commented as she watched his hands move over the keys.

"Wasn't much else to do but listen to the music," he admitted.

But Lauryn didn't hear much of the song he played. She was too depressed, too lonely suddenly, knowing he would be gone soon. Why had he been placed before her, entered her life and heart? Merely to help her find Laura? Or to teach her what heartache felt like?

ଛ

Two days passed, days when Lauryn again shared Brant's attention with her mother, grandmother, and brothers. She tried not to feel jealous and resentful. After all, Brant was an interesting man, and he needed reassurance, friendship, and hope from as many sources as possible. Still, she couldn't help her possessive feelings about him. She was certain that somewhere in his memory or knowledge, he held the key to finding Laura. That was why she resented everyone taking his time away from her—because she needed that time if she were going to find Laura. At least she told herself that was the reason for her jealousy and possessiveness.

After supper on Brant's final day alone at Connemara, Lauryn sat with him on the back veranda. The evening was cool and new, and she felt the fresh air would do him good.

"So," Lauryn began, "we know she was wounded, had mud on the bottom of her skirt, that Great-Grandfather hid her, and that she was never found. We know that she must've had a teacup with her, at some point. She can't speak to you, she can't come back here, she—"

"Yeah, yeah, yeah," Brant interrupted. "We've gone over this until my brain hurts, Lauryn."

"I know. But you're leavin' tomorrow," she reminded him.

"Exactly. I've told you everything I can think of. I don't know anymore. So…let's talk about something else."

Lauryn shrugged. She was more than willing to discuss another subject. "All right. Like what?"

Brant paused a moment, and then a mischievous smile spread across his face.

"Tell me about Mr. Perfectly Imperfect," he chuckled.

Instantly, Lauryn was irritated. "I hate Sean," she mumbled.

"Oh, you do not. He's a good brother to you," Brant reminded her.

"He makes my life miserable!" Lauryn argued.

"That's what good brothers are for." He smiled and then repeated, "Now come on. Tell me about this dream lover of yours."

"Dream lover?" Lauryn fairly shrieked. "Sean is simply lucky that he ended up with someone as wonderful as Mindy, because he certainly didn't have his ideal in mind beforehand. He can tease me all he wants! But I won't settle for anythin' less than the perfect man for me."

As Brant sat still grinning, Lauryn was temporarily mortified that she had confided so much in him.

"So…what's he like?" he asked.

"Quit teasin'," she pouted.

"No. I mean it. Tell me about him."

Lauryn looked at Brant, staring at him for a moment and trying not to think that Brant Masterson was closer to being the epitome of her ideal lover than any man she'd ever known existed.

"It's quite a personal thing, Brant," she told him softly.

"For Pete's sake, Lauryn!" Brant was irritated. She knew it by his tone. "You had to lead me to the bathtub the other day. Are you gonna try and tell me that isn't personal?"

For a moment, Lauryn wasn't sure if Brant were sincere or if he'd simply learned to play the "I'm blind" card in his hand. But she knew him well enough, she hoped, to know that he wasn't a weak fool who would use his blindness to manipulate.

"Fine," she sighed. "I'll tell you about him."

Brant sat back in his chair and folded his large arms across his massive chest, waiting for her to speak.

"He's capable of lovin' me," she began. She paused, waiting for some sarcastic remark the like that Sean would spout off. None came, so she continued. "He's strong, determined, compassionate, affectionate, witty, hard-workin'. He'll be a good father, adore children, play with them, and reprimand them with love."

"He sounds like a saint," Brant commented, but not cruelly.

"No. Because he'll have just enough of the devil in him to make life interestin'," Lauryn confessed. "And he'll have faults too. Like…"

"Like leaving his socks on the floor in the parlor?" Brant chuckled.

Lauryn smiled. "Maybe. But I mean…maybe he'll be a little temperamental. Or too antisocial."

"Or completely bald already," Brant offered.

Lauryn giggled. "Maybe."

"Tall, dark, and handsome?" he asked.

"Definitely!" Lauryn confirmed.

"So that's Mr. Perfect."

"No. That's Mr. Perfectly Imperfect."

"I think you're a wise young woman, Lauryn." His compliment seemed very sincere. "People these days don't put enough thought into who and what they want before they jump into an association. That's how you end up unhappy."

"That's my opinion." Lauryn looked at him, suddenly overwhelmed with melancholy. How desperately she was going to miss him! Having known Brant but a week, she'd already formed a fast and furious attachment, a deep attraction to him. It was more than that. Lauryn admitted to herself that she could love him—that, in all honesty, she already did!

❧

"He's leavin' today, you know," Lauryn whispered to the Captain as she sat up in her bed that morning.

"He'll be back." The Captain made the statement all too confidently, which made Lauryn suspicious.

"You're just tryin' to make me feel better, Captain." She smiled at him, touched by his concern. "Why would he come back?"

"For you," the Captain said.

She realized then that the Captain was playing his old game, the one he always played when she was blue. He was forever trying to create hope in dreams coming true for her. And even though Lauryn knew it was a game he played, she brightened, delighted at his compassion.

"He's told me so much about Laura," she began. "I'm sure there's somethin' in what's he's said that's vital! But I can't put my finger on it."

"Let him leave, Lauryn. Say good-bye to the boy," the Captain counseled. "You and I will have plenty of time to sift through what he's told you. Don't try to ease your disappointment about his leaving by jumping over it in your mind. Linger on him."

Lauryn dropped her gaze for a moment and nodded. It was true. She was trying to get him out of her mind already, trying to force herself to think of Laura again. And the Captain was right. She'd abandoned him for almost a year while she'd been in New Orleans with Nana. What difference would one more day make?

"I don't want to say good-bye." She wiped a tear from her cheek. "I think...I think I like him, Captain," she confessed in a whisper. "A great deal!"

The Captain chuckled. "Really? I hadn't noticed," he teased. He began to fade then, his smile gone and a serious expression on his face. "You tell that boy good-bye properly," he ordered.

Lauryn nodded, even though she really had no idea what he meant by "properly." All she did know was that Brant Masterson was going home.

CHAPTER SIX

Parker Masterson, Brant's older brother, was not as tall as Brant. And even though his features were similar—dark hair, strong jawline—he wasn't the uniquely attractive man Brant was. Still, he was pleasant, good-natured, and very polite.

"Looking around," Parker began as he sat in the parlor talking with Lauryn's mother and Nana, "I'd say Brant must've been one happy boy being here with all of you lovely ladies to himself."

"I see that charm runs in the family," Georgia giggled.

"We've simply adored havin' Brant here," Nana sighed. "I can't believe you've come to take him away. Life will seem so mundane now."

"Well," Parker said, lowering his voice, "I hope we can keep his spirits up. I know the doctors in New Orleans were pretty concerned about his being so…"

"Hopeless?" Lauryn offered.

"Yep. That's what worries me." Parker smiled at Lauryn and seemed to study her quickly from head to toe. "I feel sorry for my little brother—leaving you behind."

Lauryn blushed. "Charmers! The lot of you Mastersons," she told him.

Sean appeared in the doorway, holding Brant's traveling bag in one hand. Brant stood just behind him, his hand on Sean's shoulder.

"Well," Sean announced, "if y'all are ready, I'll be drivin' you on back to the station."

Instantly, Lauryn's eyes filled with tears. Glancing to her mother, the tears almost escaped her eyes when she saw that her mother's eyes were moist as well.

Georgia rose and went to Brant, embracing him firmly. "Now, you don't be a stranger, you hear me?" she told him. "You can't just waltz into our lives and leave us all behind, forgettin' about us."

"How could I ever forget you, Mrs. Kensington? You've been an angel who came to my rescue," Brant charmed.

"I'm leavin' before all the sap from this room full of female maples starts runnin' me out," Sean grumbled.

But Lauryn smiled. She knew Sean was a big old softy who was probably having his own anxieties about Brant's leaving. After all, he'd found a friend in Brant too.

Nana was next, tears trickling down her aged cheeks. "My dear, dear boy," she sniffled. "You take care. Keep those spirits high. And you let us hear from you now and then."

"I will," Brant promised. "Thank you for everything, Mrs. Kensington."

"Thank you, my angel," Nana sniffled, embracing him tightly.

"Miss Kensington," Parker addressed Lauryn.

"Yes?" Lauryn's voice cracked as she attempted to hang onto her own composure.

"When you ladies are finished saying your good-byes to my charming brother—he's obviously much more charming than I remember," he added with a wink, "would you please bring him outside?"

"Of course," Lauryn said, smiling.

Parker left the house, with Georgia right behind, reminding him to have a safe trip home. Lauryn was amazed at her ability to withhold her tears.

As her Nana followed Georgia out the door, leaving Lauryn and Brant in the house, she feared her resolve to stay strong would be destroyed.

"Well, Lauryn...shall we say good-bye then?" Brant held his hand out to her, and she moved toward him as though in a dream. He sensed when she was close and reached for her hand. Raising it to his lips, he lingeringly kissed the back of it. As it was every time he touched her, Lauryn's flesh tingled with goose bumps.

"You've done me a world of good, sugar," he said with a peaceful grin. She began to tremble as the heartache in her heightened in agony. "I thank you for that. For bringing me here...for helping Laura."

"So far I've done nothin' to help Laura," Lauryn reminded him. "And we practically kidnapped you from the train, Nana and I. And I don't possibly see what good I could've done your world when—"

Once more his hand covered her mouth, silencing her. He chuckled. "You know...you do tend to ramble when you're unsettled. Always apologizing."

"I'm sorry," Lauryn whispered, a lone tear escaping her eye and trickling down her face. He was so fabulous! *How can life ever be the same?* Lauryn wondered. She looked up into his face, wishing with all her heart that she could see his eyes, read in them exactly what he was feeling.

"Don't be sorry," he said. "I like that about you." He smiled and reached out, caressing her cheek with the back of his hand. He caressed the tearless cheek. Lauryn was thankful for that.

Her thankfulness was short-lived. He reached out, taking her face between his powerful hands. She knew he must have felt the tear on her cheek, though he said nothing about it. What he did say was, "You'll find her for me, won't you? Since I can't anymore? You will find her. Won't you?"

Lauryn felt as if a yoke heavy-laden with bricks had just been placed on her shoulders. She was again reminded that now, not only was her dear Captain dependent on her to save his eternal happiness, but Brant was too.

"I'll...I'll try," was all she could promise as more tears escaped her eyes.

"You'll do it," he whispered as his thumbs brushed the tears from her cheeks. Unexpectedly, he pulled her into his full embrace, hugging her tightly. For a moment, Lauryn thought a dream was about to come true—that he would hold her in his arms forever, never letting her go. When she felt him kiss the top of her head, she thought she might truly die of an odd, blissful heartache.

"Don't go," she begged him in a whisper as her arms encircled his waist, embracing him tightly. "I...I can't do this alone. I...I..."

"You're not alone, Lauryn," he mumbled. "You've got your Captain and your family and..." He stopped talking when she released her embrace and pulled away from him. "You'll be fine."

"You better get goin'," she sniffled. "You'll miss your train." Turning from him, she took his hand and placed it on her shoulder, wiping furiously at her tears. Sean would never let her hear the end of this, crying like a sobbing widow.

"Wait." Brant turned her to face him. Again he took her face in his hands. "Let's end it like we began," he said in a low, beguiling tone. His thumb caressed her lips softly as his head bent toward hers.

Lauryn's heartbeat was so thoroughgoing she feared she might faint in his grasp. As she shared his tender kiss, fabulous exhilaration replaced her dizziness, and she stood firm. His kiss was lingering but sweet—not at all the brutal, hard kiss he'd forced upon her in the train car. Somehow, in the back of her mind, Lauryn thought she favored their first kiss. This one, sweet and soft, exhilarating as it was, meant good-bye.

"Good-bye, sweet, beautiful Lauryn," he mumbled.

"For Pete's sake, Brant!" Patrick whined, charging up the front porch stairs and into the entryway. Rushing forward, he took Brant's hand and began tugging. "Quit slobberin' all over Lauryn or y'all will miss your train!"

Brant chuckled and released Lauryn. "All right, Patrick. All right."

"You stay in here," Patrick told his older sister. "You look as rotten as an ol' cabbage!"

"Thank you, Patrick," Lauryn grumbled.

"Remember, Lauryn," Brant called over his shoulder as he left Connemara House, "nothing too personal in those letters."

"Good-bye," Lauryn whispered, too quietly to be heard. She watched them all drive away in Sean's auto before racing upstairs and throwing herself on her bed to release her heartache through sobbing.

The Captain appeared, as she knew he would, for he would never abandon her. She snuggled into his loving embrace and cried. The ache in her heart and the loneliness in her bosom were unlike anything she had ever felt. She wondered if, in helping the Captain, she would be forced to experience the kind of heartache he felt being separated from

Lauralynn. Had Brant come into her life simply to give her soul an insight into the pain the Captain and Laura felt?

"Will you stay and talk to me awhile?" she asked.

"Of course, pumpkin," he assured her. Even this assurance did not squelch the loss she felt at Brant's leaving. It frightened her all the more to realize that, for the first time since she met the Captain and he became her greatest friend, he could not soothe her worries and sadness. Something was changing in her very soul, and it frightened her.

&

"Well, brother," Parker Masterson began once he'd settled himself across from Brant, "I feel I'm doing you a disservice in taking you away from that house full of lovely women."

Brant smiled, halfheartedly.

"I'm wondering if you'd have been better off there rather than at home with Dad and me."

"Naw, too much pampering makes a man soft," Brant said. "I need some toughening up."

Parker smiled. "That little Lauryn was getting to you, huh?"

"She's something else, isn't she?" Brant chuckled.

"Hell yes!" Parker exclaimed. "Like I said, I'm wondering if you would've been better off staying there with her."

Brant shook his head. "Nope, time to get home." But Brant was wondering the same thing. Lauryn had helped him begin to come out of the darkness his soul had floundered in ever since he'd been wounded. Would he be able to stay in the light without her sweetness to hold him there?

&

Brant sat on the edge of his bed. It was good to be home in familiar surroundings. He'd been gone from it all for a very long time. And he found it easier to find his way around the house he'd grown up in rather than the foreign twists and turns of Connemara. Yet he was unsettled, dissatisfied. Was it still his blindness that made him anxious? Or was it the absence of his sweet, understanding little southern belle back in Tennessee?

One thing he did know was Laura needed him. At any moment, he expected her to appear. At the same time, he felt his heart ache at the thought of her reaction when she saw he was sightless and unable to help her or even comfort her. Then, as if initiated by his thoughts, he caught the first soft whiff of fragrance on the air.

The scent grew stronger and stronger until it nearly saturated the room, urging Brant to speak. "Hello, Laura." In an instant, he felt her tender touch on his knee, and her soft hand clasped his. "I...I'm useless to you now, Laura. I was wounded in the war. I can't see." Immediately, he sensed her distress and began to try to give her hope. "But I've been to Connemara House! And I've met the girl that sees your Brandon. I've told her everything I know, and..." He stopped, thinking he'd heard a voice. Had someone entered the room? "Who's there?" he asked.

Again he heard something, or thought he did. But had he? It sounded like someone, a woman, had spoken his name. It was so nearly inaudible that he was sure it was his imagination. Shaking his head, he dispelled the interruption and began again. "I've told this girl everything, Laura. She's a witty little thing, and I think..." Again he was interrupted by the tiniest of whispers. For a moment, he fancied that perhaps his sanity were in question. Then he felt Laura caress his cheek affectionately and squeeze his hand. And he listened—listened like he'd never listened to anything in his life. He knew that since losing his sight, his sense of hearing had heightened dramatically.

As he listened to the air, he felt goose pimples break over his body as he did indeed hear a young woman's voice whisper, *"Brant."*

"Laura?" he asked.

Then she placed her hand over his mouth to hush him. He felt tears welling in his eyes as he again heard the softest of whispers. *"Yes, Brant. Listen. Listen to me."* He wondered if he had truly heard her or if, rather, she had found a way to speak to his mind. That is what it sounded like—not so much like a voice coming from someone standing before him but like a trick of imagination. He strained his ears again, strained his mind. He tried to filter out the sound of the breeze outside his window, the quiet crackle of the fire. Then he heard her, like the softest, sweetest dream.

"Don't despair," Laura whispered. *"Tell me."*

Brant felt Laura sit down on the bed next to him. "Tell you?" he asked, momentarily forgetting what he'd meant to say.

"*Of Brand and the girl. Tell me,*" came the quiet, dreamlike voice of Lauralynn Masterson.

As the bandages on his eyes soaked up tears that escaped them, Brant told Laura of her beloved Captain, ever searching, ever faithful. He told her of Lauryn and her mother and of Laura's own sister, Virginia. When he'd finished, he felt her sweet kiss on his cheek.

"There's hope, Laura," he told her. "This girl…she gives me hope."

"*Lauryn,*" came the quietest of whispers. And with it, as was the case when Laura spoke her own name, the fragrance accompanying her intensified tenfold.

"Why can I hear you now, Laura? Never before?" Brant asked. "All these years…all this frustration of not being able to talk with you."

"*Your eyes,*" came a soft, barely discernable answer. Brant was beginning to understand that, although he could hear her now, she was still bound by something. He could not hear all of what she spoke, just pieces.

"I've learned to listen better since being blinded," he affirmed.

"*Differently,*" came another whisper. "*Differently.*"

"I'm sorry that I never listened before," Brant apologized.

"*You did,*" Laura told him. "*Differently.*"

Brant nodded. "I told her everything I could think to tell her, Laura," he stated. "I told her about your appearance, things you've helped me to understand. I even told her about the teacup you used to carry."

"*The blood…my dress?*" came the whispering question.

"Yes, everything." Then he asked her something that had always bothered him. "Where is it, Laura? The teacup—why don't you carry it anymore?"

"*Gone,*" she answered.

Brant nodded and, reaching out, embraced her tenderly. "She'll find you, Laura. I know she will." He felt her tiny hands stroke the back of his head lovingly.

"*Help her,*" she whispered. "*…Needs you. I'm lost and I can't.*"

As he comforted his spiritual friend, Brant thought of how differently he would have left Lauryn had he been the powerful, confident, sighted man he'd once been. There would have been no sweet, tearful good-bye in the entryway of Connemara House—no innocent, childlike kiss. Had Brant Masterson been himself that day, Lauryn's mother would've had him thrown out on his hind end for the way he would have kissed that tempting little daughter of hers.

Maybe, he thought as he lay in bed long after Laura left him that night, *Maybe the doctors were right.* Maybe there was hope in regaining his sight, but it was best to prepare for the worst. Then he turned on his side, his last thoughts being of the poor, sweet girl down in Franklin, Tennessee, whom he had left with such a burden to bear alone.

ଝ

Two weeks passed, two weeks that Lauryn spent searching every inch of Connemara for a clue to Laura's whereabouts—two frustrating weeks that yielded nothing! Nothing, that is, except for the horrifying experience of having a spider drop down her blouse when she was digging around under the gazebo. Two weeks of wondering, every moment, about Brant's welfare. Wondering if he were happy. Wondering if he ever gave another thought to Connemara House and its current inhabitants.

Every day Lauryn talked to the Captain, trying to draw strength and comfort from him as she had in the past. But something was different. Something was changing in her. She felt more distant from her dear friend, more helpless and frustrated than ever.

Nearly every day she'd stroll along the streets of Franklin with Penny, reminiscing about their youth, sharing their adventures of the past year. But always she was just short of giving her friend her full attention. Every moment he was there—Brant, lurking about in her mind and heart, distracting her from life.

"You're an ol' grouch," Patrick told Lauryn one afternoon as he came to sit at the kitchen table across from her.

"Now, Patrick," Georgia scolded, "you be nice to your sister. She's got a lot on her mind."

"Well, she doesn't have to be such an ol' stick-in-the-mud all the time," the boy grumbled.

Lauryn forced a smile. She had been quite neglectful of her little brother. And after the way he'd looked forward to her returning too.

"I'm sorry, Patrick," she told him. "I'm sorry. We'll play soldiers later, okay?"

The boy brightened. "Promise?"

Lauryn nodded. "I've promised Penny that I'd go over to her house for games later, but before I go, you and I will have a fine battle."

Patrick sighed contentedly. "In that case, I think I can cheer you up a bit, sissy."

"Really?" Lauryn giggled. "How?"

Reaching down the front of his shirt, Patrick produced an envelope. Immediately Lauryn's heart leaped. "It's a letter—from Brant," the boy explained. "The postman dropped it off just a few minutes ago."

Lauryn snatched the letter from Patrick's hand, not trusting him an inch. No doubt he would use the letter to taunt her mercilessly if she let him have a second's thought.

"Hey! Be nice! It's just a lousy ol' letter," Patrick grumbled. "And remember, Lauryn...you promised!"

"I know, angel," Lauryn said.

"Mama," Patrick whined, "tell her not to call me angel. It's embarrassin'! What if the fellas heard her?"

Lauryn was oblivious to anything in the room, anything in the world save the letter in her hands. Her heart pounded madly as she opened it and read:

Dear Lauryn,
   I hope you can decipher this mess my father calls penmanship...

A letter! Brant had actually sent her a letter! Lauryn pulled the paper to her lips and kissed the document in delight.

"Oh, for Pete's sake, Mama," Patrick whined. "She's kissin' a letter. It's paper, Lauryn. That's all." Unable to tolerate another second of his sister's feminine behavior, Patrick stood up and walked from the room, calling, "Let me know when you've finished readin' that silly thing, Lauryn. I'll set up the men."

Lauryn glanced at her mother to find her eyes sparkling with excitement. "You'll tell me what he says, won't you, sweetheart? How he's holdin' up?"

Lauryn nodded and stood, intent on privacy. Her mother would understand. Once she had put on a sweater, she hurried toward the cemetery to sit at Henry's feet with the fresh breezes of late winter refreshing her senses and began to read the letter once more.

Dear Lauryn,

I hope you can decipher this mess my father calls penmanship, though he assures me his is more legible than mine would be right now.

I hope that everything and everyone at Connemara is well. It's still very cold up here. I had forgotten how much I missed it though. Nothing like a warm fire on a cold night.

Lauryn paused, trying to imagine Brant in Vermont—trying to picture his face, broad shoulders, handsome smile.

Everything is fine with me. I'm hearing things I've never heard before. I hope you understand.

What did he mean? Lauryn wondered. Surely he didn't mean he'd found a way to hear Lauralynn! Lauryn's curiosity was nearly intolerable, and she read on.

Nothing new to tell you though. I hope this finds you with more new knowledge than I've got.

Lauryn sighed, thinking how disappointed he would be in her when she answered his letter and told him that she'd failed them all.

Thank you again, Lauryn, and be sure and thank your family for me, as well—for all your help, compassion, and care. A house full of angels—that's what I've told my family about all of you. And it's true.

Tell Patrick hello for me. And everyone else. Let me know how your adventure is coming along...and I will notify you if anything important comes to me on my end.

Dad says I should close with some sort of mush, like "yours truly." But that doesn't sound like me. So I'll say this—thank you, Lauryn...for tasting so good!

Brant

Lauryn relished the hot, tingling blush that engulfed her at his closing. Even though she knew his very forward ending remark had been for his father's benefit, she relished it. That he would even think of it! That he had kissed her good-bye and that he would imply it to his father. But there was more to the letter. *My dear Miss Kensington*, it began.

> *Being Brant's father, as I am, I could not post this letter without adding my own thanks to you and yours for taking such good care of my son. I think it did him a world of good to spend a week with you all. His spirits are quite lifted, his attitude more positive than when we communicated with him last.*
> *A grateful father thanks you.*
> *Sincerely,*
> *Darnell Masterson*

It was a short letter, but Lauryn was delighted with it. Apparently Brant was somewhat content. And although it was inconceivable to even try to believe, the letter implied Brant could somehow communicate with Lauralynn—perhaps even hear her.

But most importantly, Brant had exerted the effort to write to her. And even though she could not make him happy by writing back and telling him that she was closer to finding Laura, she could write back. After all, it just wasn't proper not to answer a letter.

Tucking the letter safely in the pocket of her sweater, Lauryn returned to the house to fulfill her promise to Patrick. Her mood lightened, she was actually excited about playing soldiers with him! And then it would be off to Penny's house. Penny would lighten her heart even further. After two long weeks, Lauryn was finally able to smile sincerely.

❧

Dearest Brant, the letter began. Brant smiled as his father started reading the letter from Lauryn. He could imagine how long she'd labored over her salutation. He knew her well enough, even after a mere week, to know that she would've taken a great deal more time in penning her letter than he had in dictating his to his father.

"She's got beautiful penmanship, this girl," Brant's father commented. Brant could just imagine his father adjusting his reading glasses and peering down his nose through them trying to read the letter. It was a comforting image to his mind. He wondered, briefly, if his father's hair were any whiter than it had been when he'd left for the war.

"Thank you for letting us all know that you arrived home safely and are well. We have thought of you every moment since you left, wondering about your welfare. Thank your father for his efforts in writing also."

"She's got the 'we' down too," Darnell Masterson chuckled. "What? She thinks I don't know she's wishing you could read your own letters?"

Brant chuckled too. "Come on, Dad. Just read the letter."

"I hope this girl isn't taking me for a fool. I can read between the lines as well as the next man," Darnell stated. Chuckling, he added, "Well...maybe things are just a tad fuzzier."

"I know that you will be wondering how things are coming along where my responsibilities to dear friends are concerned, and I hope you will not abandon me when I tell you that I am still laboring fruitlessly."

"She's very proper," Brant's father commented, pausing again in his reading of Lauryn's letter.

"She knows you're reading it," Brant chuckled. "Believe me. She knows you're reading it."

"How is your family?" Darnell continued. *"We are all well here at Connemara."*

And then the tone of her letter changed—as if she'd forgotten that it wouldn't be just Brant who would be reading it. Refreshingly, the letter began to sound like Lauryn.

> *Everything is uneventful. Patrick is going to have Mama fairly fleeing to the asylum! In cleaning out his pockets yesterday, she found a dead snake and a hardened lump of dog manure! Patrick explained that he was carrying it around just in case Betty Anne Thompson tried to kiss him again.*

Brant and his father both burst into laughter, having to pause from reading the letter until they could breathe regularly once more.

"I like this girl, Brant," Darnell chuckled.

"I know. I do too," Brant confessed.

Darnell continued.

Penny and I have spent hours in the flowerbeds together. Connemara's gardeners of the past were masters! And I'm afraid that our efforts will not do Connemara justice.

Sean and Mindy and the baby are well and happy. Mindy nearly dropped dead when Junie ate a bug last week. Now we all call her Junie-bug. Naturally.

Nana is well enough. A slight touch of something kept her in bed for a few days. But she's up and around fine now.

Everyone sends love and best wishes. I refuse to write what Sean says to tell you—only know that he is still making my life miserable! You would be proud of him.

Please stay warm and healthy and tell your father thank you for writing for you. We all miss you and wish you well.

Yours,
Lauryn

Brant sat back in his chair, sighing contentedly. He missed Connemara and everyone in it. He had begun to find himself there, to regain his strength. And he missed that little chit of a girl, Lauryn—missed her lectures on the evils of self-pity and the wonders of love. She'd taught him a great deal—taught him of emotions, of happiness, of rising above trials. He'd have to go back, someday. Someday. Maybe.

CHAPTER SEVEN

Winter faded. Not that winter was ever severe in Franklin, but the weather did change. The early spring flowers had blossomed, the grasses greened up, the rain lessened. And soon the beautiful wisteria, which was Connemara's fame, began to flourish. By early May, Connemara's wisteria was in full and wondrous bloom.

Lauryn loved the wisteria, even more than she had as a child. Every morning she was glad she had returned home in time to see it, touch it, breathe of its passionate perfume. She swore to herself that, no matter where she ended up on earth, she would always have wisteria. Always!

Brant had written Lauryn at least once every two weeks since he'd returned home. There were several things he'd learned about Laura that he told Lauryn in his letters. For instance, the locket Laura wore around her neck had been a gift from Brand the day he'd left to go to war.

He told her about the weather in Castledale. He told her about his family, of his sisters and their husbands and babies and of Parker, who was courting a young lady named Violet. Brant suspected that it wouldn't be long before his brother proposed marriage to her.

Each time Lauryn received a letter from him, her heart would swell with dreams of his someday returning to her—if not returning to her, specifically, at least to Connemara. But she knew that until she found Laura at Connemara, there would be no reason for him to return.

Lauryn grew to know Brant more thoroughly through his letters, and in ways that she may not otherwise have had the chance to. The stories he told of his family revealed his strong sense of humor. His opinions and thoughts revealed his wisdom. And the way he wrote, rather contentedly, spoke to Lauryn of a man whose soul was healing. And she reveled in the knowledge.

Now, the Captain had, as always, been Lauryn's friend and confidant. But somehow his friendship didn't fill the void in Lauryn's heart left by Brant. Though they talked, as they always had, Lauryn continued to feel a sort of deep emptiness. She still loved the Captain and was still obsessed about helping, because she did love him. But it was Brant who dominated her thoughts and the images in her mind. It was Brant who made her think it was possible to be in love, Brant who filled her dreams and her wishes, Brant who caused her heart to ache, Brant's existence that made it impossible to go through life carefree and calmly as she had before. And so Lauryn went on searching, hoping, dreaming.

ଛ

"My stars, Patrick! You get yourself into more fixes!" Lauryn scolded from her awkward perch in a neighborhood tree one warm spring day in May. "On second thought," she added as her shoe lodged awkwardly between two branches for a moment, "you get *me* into more fixes!" As she struggled to free the boy's ball, a branch seemed to actually reach out and tangle itself in her hair. "Treed like a kitten," she mumbled as she fiddled with the twig to try to free herself.

"And now someone's comin'," Patrick called up from his lookout position on the ground below her.

"Patrick Kensington, I'm gonna have your hide for this!"

"It's a man, Lauryn, and he's gonna see you up in that tree!"

"Not if you keep quiet and let him pass he won't. You hush your mouth and let him pass, you hear me, Patrick?"

"I hear you, Lauryn. I hear you."

Lauryn sighed and rolled her eyes, hoping the stranger would simply pass under the tree and be gone. What a sight she must be! So help her soul, if Patrick ever threw another ball in that tree, she'd let it, and him, rot up there before she'd fetch it for him.

"Hey there, mister," Lauryn heard Patrick call out. "Where y'all headed?"

Lauryn looked down through the dense leaves to see the outline of a man stop directly beneath the tree at her little brother's prompting.

"You little rat," she whispered angrily. Could Patrick have just let the fellow walk on by? No! He had to stop him for a chat! That child couldn't keep his mouth shut if his life depended on it.

She couldn't see the man clearly enough from her perch to identify him. However, when he spoke to her brother, she felt her limbs weaken, her heart begin to race, and it was nearly impossible to breathe. Brant!

"Don't you remember me, boy?" Brant asked Patrick.

"Brant!" Patrick exclaimed. "Hey there, Lauryn!" he shouted, looking up into the tree where Lauryn wanted to hide for the rest of her life. "It's Brant, come back to visit! Come on down. You've gotta see him! He's all better, it looks like!"

Then, to Lauryn's complete humiliation and horror, Brant Masterson stepped beneath the tree and looked up to where she was balanced above him. She couldn't stop the gasp that escaped her at the sight of him—eyes healed and unbandaged and piercing through her own like sapphire bullets. A smile spread quickly across his fatally handsome face as he studied her from head to toe.

So this was Lauryn, Brant thought to himself. He couldn't help but smile, far beyond well pleased. She was wildly pretty, like some small forest sprite or other creature from a fairytale. Her eyes twinkled with the possibility of mischief, and her face was as soft and creamy as a dream. Her size and figure were more than merely pleasing in their proportions, and her hair—her long, nutmeg-brown, ringletted hair— was most assuredly her crowning glory. She had it pulled back into some sort of loose braid, but most of it had escaped here and there and hung enchantingly about her face and shoulders.

In the best efforts of his imagination, Brant had never expected Lauryn to be so perfectly adorable! He would have to be careful on this trip to Connemara. If he were sure of nothing else, he was certain that this adorable brunette could be far too distracting. Look how she'd dominated his thoughts when he was blind. No doubt, his sight restored, he'd find himself all the more tempted toward flirting, wooing, and the like.

"Come on down here and let me get a better look at you," Brant chuckled.

131

Lauryn was mortified! Her cheeks felt like smoldering embers as a deep blush caused her face to burn.

"I...um...I..." she stammered. Her heart was beating so fiercely within her bosom that she could hardly breathe, and she felt her hands, arms, and legs begin to tremble.

"She can't come down. She's stuck up there. That rats' nest she calls hair is all tangled up," Patrick blurted out.

"I'm fine. I just caught my foot..."

But as Brant removed his jacket, handing it to Patrick, and reached up to take hold of a lower limb, it was apparent he intended to climb up after her.

"No, no, no!" Lauryn argued, shaking her head at him and trying frantically to dislodge her foot and free the branch from her hair. "I'm fine. I'll be right down."

Giving no care to pain or possible bleeding of the scalp, Lauryn fairly ripped her hair from the branch that entangled it and simultaneously almost broke her ankle as she tore her foot free from its trap. Brant, smiling, released his grasp on the tree and stood expectantly beneath her.

"I...I'm comin' down just now," she muttered.

"She'll *fall* down," Patrick told Brant. "She can never get down from that tree without almost breakin' her neck."

And sure enough, whether by her own clumsiness or Patrick's curse upon her, Lauryn lost her footing and handhold. Tumbling headlong out of the tree, she knocked Brant down, landing exactly on top of him in the process.

Lauryn's breathing ceased for several moments. There he was, Brant Masterson—smiling up at her, a delighted, amused smile, the cool sapphire of his eyes hypnotizing her. He was so close! She could feel the warmth of his body, feel his breath on her face.

Lauryn Kensington had thought Brant Masterson intriguing, magnetic, and overpoweringly attractive when most of his face was bandaged. But to see him now, his eyes revealed, his face unbruised and so perfect! He was like some mythical god of masculine beauty, some unnatural creation of perfection in a man.

Kiss me, she thought as he reached up and brushed her wild nutmeg locks from her face. And she gasped audibly at the ridiculous statement of her own mind. But even as the right corner of his mouth twitched ever so slightly several times, Lauryn's mind bordered on insanity again. *Kiss me, Brant, and I'll settle that twitch*, she thought. What was the matter with her? Lauryn shook her head slightly, trying to dispel the hex Brant had woven throughout her mind and body. It was only Brant that stood—rather, lay—before her. Brant Masterson, her friend from the train.

"Hello, Lauryn," Brant greeted, grinning devilishly. "I surely didn't expect to find you here."

"Well, we're even then," she tried to tease, "because I certainly didn't expect for you to find me here either."

As she awkwardly tried to stand, since she'd never had to raise herself from lying atop a man before, Brant chuckled lightly.

"Come on now," he said, standing and helping her to her feet. "Let's get a good look at you."

Lauryn felt ill. He wanted a good look at her? Well, it was the last thing she wanted. What a fright she must be. Her hair was, no doubt, like some wild, insane woman's, for she had only braided it loosely back to begin with. And to make matters worse, she'd been climbing about in the branches of a tree. She wondered, for a moment, if perhaps there were a huge, gaping, bleeding patch of her scalp showing as a result of her tearing her hair from the branch. Reaching up self-consciously, she was relieved to discover that she still possessed a full head of hair.

To make matters worse, it was then that she realized she wore the least flattering set of clothes she owned. And beyond that—well, beyond that she did not want to face the look of disappointment on his face when he saw that she wasn't nearly as lovely as she supposedly smelled.

On the other hand, the light of the beautiful day continued to illuminate his appearance perfectly. And he was gorgeous. Gorgeous! It seemed a rather feminine word to be going through her mind, she noted, and yet it's what he was. Absolutely gorgeous! More gorgeous than he had been a moment before.

It was Patrick's intrusive whining that brought Lauryn out of her mesmerized daydreaming. "Lauryn! You left the ball!"

Patrick's disturbance of the moment caused Lauryn's discomfort and embarrassment over her situation to intensify, and she dropped her gaze from Brant.

"For pity's sake, Patrick," she began to scold.

But Brant was up the tree before she could argue and returned in a matter of seconds, having retrieved the ball.

"There you are, boy," Brant chuckled, trading the ball for his jacket and tousling the child's hair. "You go on and leave your sister to me."

"Gladly, Brant," Patrick sighed. "You can have her! She's completely helpless!"

"Now, Patrick," Brant scolded teasingly, "you haven't been giving your sister a rotten time of it since I've been gone, have you?"

Patrick sneered, assuring Brant that he had. "Sorry, Lauryn," the boy mumbled before turning and running off. "I'll tell them up at Connemara that you're here! Nana will bust her corset strings!"

"Patrick!" Lauryn scolded, even though she knew she was wasting her breath.

Brant watched him go and then turned back to Lauryn. She felt like bursting into tears as an amused smile spread across his face again. "So," he said, studying her from head to toe, "this is Lauryn Kensington."

Lauryn winced as the breeze blew a stray strand of hair across her face momentarily. "Pretty disappointin', I suppose."

He only smiled, an amused twinkle sparkling wildly in his gorgeous eyes.

"Forgive me, my boy," came a booming, masculine voice from somewhere behind Lauryn. She turned from Brant to see the most adorable elderly man and woman walking toward them.

"Brant, honey!" the woman chimed. "I just had to have a wee whiff of those lovely lilacs back there. I just *had* to! I couldn't pass up their heavenly beauty. Why, to do so would've been a sin. Just an utter sin!"

"I know, Auntie," Brant chuckled as the charming couple approached. They walked with their arms linked together, and the small woman placed her hands dramatically in Brant's as they arrived.

"And you know that I completely understand your love of nature, Auntie, but Lauryn here was treed like a raccoon and needed some assistance."

Gasping, the elderly woman turned her full attention on Lauryn. "Lauryn?" she breathed in an awed whisper. "So *you're* Lauryn!"

"Yes, ma'am," Lauryn muttered with a slight curtsy. The woman, obviously Brant's aunt, smiled and brushed a stray strand of hair from Lauryn's face.

"Quite a beauty, that one, my boy," the gentleman chuckled, winking at Brant. His blue eyes twinkled, and his voice was raspy and gruff. Lauryn liked it.

"I'm Felicity Jenson, Brant's great-auntie! And this is his great-uncle, Johnny. And I tell you, when Brant said he was coming back to thank your family for all they've done for him, I just up and said, 'Brant, honey, I'm the one to go with you—Johnny and I! We're the ones!'" She giggled girlishly and added, "And here we am!"

Brant's Aunt Felicity was more beautiful than any queen. Her hair was pure white and perfectly smooth in its style. Her eyes were the same blue as Brant's, and she still had a natural pink in her cheeks. Lauryn could guess at her age, she being Brant's great-aunt. Her hands were bony and frail-looking but obviously capable, and she glided rather than walked.

His Uncle Johnny was the classic example of an elderly gentleman—thinning white hair, a kind, grandfatherly smile, and a walking stick with a silver horse's head on top. Lauryn was aware of her momentary pause as she realized they all three stood staring at her expectantly.

"Oh!" she exclaimed in a whisper as she tried to gather her wits about her. "Well, we're so glad to have you. All of you," she added, glancing quickly at Brant. "Mama will be beside herself with excitement."

"Is this Connemara, sweet thing?" Aunt Felicity asked, looking past Lauryn to the house behind her. "I remember it looking quite differently."

"No. It's just down a ways. Connemara House," Lauryn answered as she moved past Brant, signaling they should follow her. The quicker they arrived at Connemara, the quicker she could sneak away and freshen up! And the less time Brant could stare at her with unnerving amusement he wore on his incredibly attractive face.

"Connemara House," Aunt Felicity repeated reverently.

"Well, Miss Lauryn," Uncle Johnny asked, "what do you think of Brant now that he's unbound for all the world to see once more?"

Aunt Felicity reached up and pinched Brant's cheek lovingly. "Isn't he the devil of the handsomest man?"

There was no manner in which Lauryn could give answer without sounding the complete starry-eyed fool. Instead, she inquired of Brant, "You've recovered then? Fully?"

"Yep," he assured her. "My vision is about as good as new."

"That's...that's wonderful," she stammered. For Pete's sake! She'd turned into a squid, all limp and nervous with no backbone whatsoever. It had been one thing to talk with him, look at him when he had been blind and unable to look back. But now! Now—especially since the complete, magnificently attractive magnetism of him was revealed, the way his eyes seemed to drill right into her soul—now Lauryn was entirely a frazzle!

"Surprised to see me, aren't you?" he chuckled, again appraising her from head to toe.

"Yes," Lauryn admitted, smoothing a wild strand of hair from her cheek again.

"Well," Aunt Felicity sang, "let's have it, Lauryn. Let's see Connemara! I've only been here once before...and so many years ago that I hate to tell!"

"Yes, let's," Uncle Johnny added. "You can woo and win the girl later, Brant, my boy. There are people to meet, things to do! Lead on, Miss Kensington."

Lauryn forced another friendly smile and turned to lead the party home. A mere matter of one block was bound to seem like an eternity. Lauryn's legs could hardly propel her body forward. She was so anxious! Her nerves were completely frayed. She kept wondering if she'd torn her skirt anywhere while climbing the tree. She could only pray that she had not, that she still remained completely modest.

"So," she began cordially, "did y'all have a nice trip down?"

"That we did, angel," Aunt Felicity chimed. "The scenery was beautiful. Just beautiful!"

"And the food wasn't too bad," Uncle Johnny added.

"Well, Nana and Mama will be so surprised." Lauryn couldn't believe that Brant hadn't warned them that he was coming.

"Actually, Lauryn," Brant began to confess, "your...um...your Nana and mama know that we're coming. I guess they wanted it to be a surprise to you."

Lauryn stopped dead in her tracks and turned to look at him. He shrugged rather boyishly, and she swallowed the instant irritation she felt with her Nana and mother, saying, "I guess so." Turning, she began to walk even faster.

"I'm certain you can mend that tear right up, Lauryn. Don't worry. I'm sure the skirt can be saved. It's so becoming to you." Again Lauryn stopped, putting her hand to the seat of her skirt to discover with horror that indeed a large tear was gaping open on her right hip.

"Now you've done it, Felicity!" Uncle Johnny scolded. "Go on and ruin all of the boy's fun, why don't you?"

Lauryn looked at Brant, who simply smiled mischievously and winked at her. For pity's sake! He winked at her! Lauryn tried to walk calmly at a pace considerate to the older couple. But by now she was ready to burst into an explosion of tears and humiliation. Furthermore, she was angry. Angry with her mother and Nana for not telling her Brant was returning. Angry at Patrick for throwing his ball up into the tree. Angry at Sean and Mindy for even purchasing the blasted ball for him in the first place!

Finally, they reached the tall iron fences that surrounded Connemara. Lauryn anxiously pushed the front gate open and started up the path to the porch. She paused when, looking back, she realized only Aunt Felicity and Uncle Johnny followed her. Brant stood outside the gate, the color completely drained from his face as if he felt ill. He stood motionless, staring up at the house. No. He was staring at the wisteria! For a moment, Lauryn thought she understood, for Connemara House had long been the talk of Franklin for its beauty in the spring. Everywhere one looked, there were beautiful, fragrant blossoms hanging like large clusters of lavender grapes among miles of green-leafed vines that wound themselves, seemingly, over everything. The front arbor and all the fences were covered in it. The columns of the porches were drenched in it. And the trellises that lined the house on all four sides gave the illusion that the walls of Connemara themselves were actually constructed of wisteria vines and blossoms. A breeze breathed then, whimsically sending the lavender-colored flowers dancing like a million silent bells of heaven.

Wisteria trees were here and there on the surrounding grounds at Connemara as well. The gazebo was adorned in its fragrant flowers, and though it wasn't visible to Brant then, Lauryn wondered at his reaction when he saw that even the old springhouse and servants' house were covered in it. Wisteria trees grew above the old cellar and along the creek down the hill behind Connemara. Even the fences that bordered the family cemetery boasted its loveliness. Wisteria had always been the fame of Connemara House.

"It's...it's awe-inspiring!" Aunt Felicity whispered reverently as she too paused in her admiration. But Brant's expression was different, not so much that of admiring beauty.

"Brant?" Lauryn asked, going to him. "Brant? Are you well?" He looked at her, and yet she wasn't sure that he was seeing her. His eyes seemed oddly glazed over, and a frown puckered his brow.

"That...that scent," he managed to whisper. "Is it the vines?"

"The wisteria?" Lauryn asked. "Yes. It's only in bloom for a little while each year. It's the blossoms you're smellin'." Why did he seem so stunned? Lauryn had always loved the fragrance of the blooms. To her, it was one of the most beautiful of God's creations. Still, Brant looked unsettled. "What is it, Brant?" she asked.

"It's her," he mumbled. "Laura's perfume. It's the fragrance of her name."

Even before he explained, Lauryn understood. For once, a long time ago, the day she had first opened Lauralynn's trunk, she too had recognized the fragrance of wisteria and had associated it with Laura.

"The scent she carries with her when..."

"She loved the wisteria, no doubt," Lauryn offered. "It was even embroidered on her weddin' gown. Do you think it's significant?" she asked, suddenly realizing it might be.

Brant shook his head and seemed to dispel the shocked state he had been in. "I don't know. I don't know," he mumbled. Then forcing a smile, he reached out and took Lauryn's hand in his. "We'll talk about that later. I want to see your Nana and the others." His touch was more stimulating to Lauryn's senses than it had been even before, and she shivered as the goose bumps broke over her.

Still, she worried for Brant. It seemed to have completely unsettled him to discover the wisteria of Connemara, the scent of Lauralynn's spirit. Walking past her and pulling her along with him, they joined his aunt and uncle on the porch.

As all three visitors looked at Lauryn expectantly, she smoothed her wild hair once more and said, "Well...welcome to Connemara!" Opening the front door, the visitors were greeted with squeals of elation as Nana and Lauryn's mother rushed forward.

"Land sakes, you're a handsome one, Brant!" Nana cooed as she threw herself into Brant's willing embrace.

"Mr. and Mrs. Jenson!" Georgia greeted. "Welcome to Connemara."

"Felicity and John, Mrs. Kensington. Please," Uncle Johnny chuckled.

Georgia shrugged delightedly. "And Georgia to y'all!" Nana greeted the elderly couple next while Lauryn's mother gasped at the sight of Brant. "Why, look at you!" Georgia exclaimed. "Oh, Brant! We're so happy to have you back." She hugged him, and Lauryn felt awkward, being the only female in the room that hadn't received a hug. She thought of how different these few moments with Brant had been compared with the last time she stood in the entryway with him. She felt her face go crimson as Brant looked to her then, as if he too were remembering the last moments he'd spent at Connemara.

"If y'all will excuse me a moment," Lauryn stammered, "I need to change out of this skirt."

"Lauryn?" Georgia asked.

"Well, apparently she had a little incident with a tree just before we arrived," Aunt Felicity explained. "But I've told her that I really do think we can mend it."

"Oh, don't you worry about it, Lauryn," Uncle Johnny chuckled. "Brant and I think it's just fine the way it is!" His teasing wink was that of a playful imp.

"Now, you behave, Jonathan," Felicity scolded.

Brant grinned and winked at Lauryn just before she turned from him, her cheeks beet-red, and rushed up the stairs.

Once inside her room, Lauryn couldn't decide whether to burst into tears of humiliation or explode with pure delight. He was fabulous! Brant was more than that. He was magnificent! And he'd come back!

But why? What was his reason? For a moment, Lauryn let herself dream that maybe, just maybe, it had something to do with her. But she knew better than that. He'd come for Lauralynn. He was sighted once more and ready to help Lauryn search. That was all.

And yet her heart raced with hope. Suddenly, thoughts were leaping about in her mind. What if they did succeed in finding Lauralynn? Maybe then Brant would be ready to see beyond his torment to…no. One shouldn't hope for such things. But still, it was there—the secret hope that Brant had come back for more than just to solve the mystery of Laura.

"I told you he'd be back," the Captain said as he suddenly appeared in Lauryn's bedroom.

Lauryn couldn't help her excited squeal as she threw her arms around his neck. "He did! He did! And I don't even care that it's not for me that he came back. As long as he's back." Then she realized the selfishness of her reaction. "And he'll help us, Captain. He will! We'll find her for you."

"I know, angel," the Captain chuckled. "And he's a fine figure of a man."

"He is!" Lauryn clutched her hands to her bosom. "I nearly fainted when I first saw him! Isn't he so handsome? Even more so with his eyes showin'. And his hair trimmed short…" Then she paused as her heart began to pound with nervous anxiety. "I can't…I have to remember why he's here."

"Let your heart tell you why he's here, Lauryn." The Captain seemed sincere, his smile warm and loving.

But it was too dangerous to imagine that there was any other reason Brant had returned than for Laura's sake.

"I'll be fine. And I'll find her for you," she promised.

"Find her for you, Lauryn," the Captain said, and he kissed her cheek and vanished. "Find everything for you," came the final echo of his voice.

That evening at supper, Lauryn tried to concentrate on the conversation among the others. But every time her gaze wandered to Brant sitting across from her, he was looking at her with that familiar amused grin. That was more unnerving than anything. Lauryn realized that, if he hadn't been blind, if he had been able to look at her when he was at Connemara before the way he looked at her now, she never would have felt comfortable enough to talk with him the way she had. His gaze was piercing, as if he knew what she was thinking and feeling each time he looked at her.

"I do remember you, Felicity." Lauryn's attention was drawn back to the conversation as her Nana spoke. "I was young, and even though you had married Johnny before I was in Knoxville, I remember when we buried dear Brand. You were here. I remember how beautiful I thought you were."

Aunt Felicity smiled and dramatically placed a hand to her bosom. "Oh, youth? Where art thou, beauty?" Everyone chuckled at her humor as she folded her napkin before going on. "My dear brother, Brandon. How I adored him. How I adored Laura." Everyone was silent.

"I was at home…healing when they buried him here," Uncle Johnny interjected. "He was a good man."

"After supper, Nana and I will take you out there to visit his restin' place, Felicity," Georgia offered. "No doubt it'll do him good to hear from you."

"Will he hear me?" Felicity asked Lauryn.

Lauryn was uncomfortable. She wasn't comfortable when people who knew about the Captain asked her too many questions about him. Surely this was different. This was a member of his family—his own sister.

"Yes," Lauryn answered.

"I wish I had a ghost," Patrick sighed.

"Maybe you do, my boy," Uncle Johnny suggested.

"Really?" Patrick brightened.

"Heaven forbid!" Georgia mumbled.

"Well, everyone has angels about them, boy, guarding them. Especially little boys with pocketknives hidden in their shoes." Uncle Johnny chuckled and tousled the boy's hair.

"Patrick Kensington!" Georgia scolded. "What're you doin' with a knife hidin' in your shoe?"

"Ah, Mama," Patrick said.

"Tell you what, boy," Uncle Johnny suggested, "if it's all right with your mama, after supper I'll take you out on that front porch and teach you how to put that knife to good use on a whittling stick. What do you say?"

"Mama? It would be good for me to learn," Patrick begged.

Georgia sighed and shook her head. "Very well. But y'all be careful. I knew a boy once that lost a finger a-whittlin' a pencil down."

Lauryn looked across the table to see Brant smiling at her little brother. He seemed pleased enough to be back with them. Surely he wouldn't have come back if he'd expected to be otherwise.

After dinner, Nana and Georgia took Felicity to the cemetery. Uncle Johnny and Patrick were sitting on the front porch steps cutting things up with pocketknives, and Brant sat in the parlor in the big chair near the hearth, staring across the room at Lauryn.

Lauryn squirmed in her seat on the sofa, uncomfortable under his gaze, until finally he said, "I can hear her now."

"What?" Lauryn asked. Surely she hadn't heard him say what she thought she did.

"I can hear her."

CHAPTER EIGHT

"I can hear her...Laura. Not very well and only some things," he explained in a whisper. "But I can hear her."

Lauryn was amazed. His first letter had implied as much, but she had been certain she had misinterpreted.

"Why now and never before?" Lauryn asked.

Brant shrugged. "I think...I think I listened differently when I couldn't see. It's so quiet, her voice. Like a breeze...when you think you're hearing something but you're really not. Only...I do."

"What has she said to you?" Lauryn's curiosity was fast overcoming her discomfort in Brant's handsome presence. "Tell me."

Brant leaned forward and kept his voice very low. "Well, she keeps saying 'my sister'...especially when I ask her about the teacup she doesn't have anymore."

"Nana?" Lauryn asked.

Brant ran his fingers through his hair in frustration. "That's all she'll say. I ask, 'Virginia gave you the cup?' and she asks, 'My sister?' And that's it. Then I tell her Virginia is fine and happy, and she smiles...seems satisfied."

"What else?" Lauryn pressed, her hopes and excitement rising.

Brant shrugged. "She's says your name. Points to me and says, 'Lauryn.' And she holds her skirt and says, 'There's blood here.' I don't know." Brant shook his head in discouragement. "I thought maybe..."

"You thought I'd know what she was tryin' to say right off," Lauryn finished for him.

"And I looked through the Captain's trunk again," he added.

Lauryn sat up straight. "What do you mean?" she asked him.

"The Captain's trunk—the one in our attic. I spent a whole afternoon rummaging through that smelly old thing again."

"You never told me he had a trunk at your house!" Lauryn was a bit irritated. It seemed, somehow, to be important.

"I'm sorry. I...we're looking for Laura, and I never thought...besides," he began to admit, "I had only looked through it once before, and it upset Laura so badly that I thought maybe it wasn't the right thing to do."

Instantly Lauryn was humbled. Brant obviously had a respect for the Captain's personal belongings that she had maybe been lacking where Lauralynn's were concerned.

"I've gone through Laura's trunk over and over," Lauryn confessed.

"Maybe we need to go through it together," Brant suggested.

"It wouldn't bother you?" Lauryn ventured.

"No. Not now. The clock is ticking, Lauryn. Life has to go on—this life and the next." He seemed angry and somewhat resentful for a moment but appeared to force himself to brighten and asked in a very friendly manner, "So how's your friend Penny?"

"Penny?" Lauryn repeated. Why should Brant be interested in Penny or how she was doing?

"Yes," he chuckled. "You remember that I met her when I was here. She's your friend still, isn't' she?"

"Well, of course," Lauryn said. But why should he concern himself? It bothered her. The odd sort of jealousy that she felt in her heart when Brant spoke of Laura so lovingly now rose in her bosom when he asked about Penny. "She's fine."

"And Sean and Mindy and the baby?"

"They're all just dandy," Lauryn told him, realizing he was just making polite conversation.

"That's good to hear," he sighed, leaning back in his chair.

"Did you come back to stay?" Lauryn blurted out. Then realizing how revealing her question had been, she added, "To stay and help me find her?"

He paused, not answering right away. His eyes narrowed as he looked at her, almost suspiciously. "I came back to help you look for her, yes." It was an answer that rather avoided answering. In other words, he wasn't staying, but he had come back for Laura. No one else.

Trying to seem unhurt, Lauryn said, "Good. So…where do we start?" She'd asked herself that same question many times. She'd asked the Captain. And now, again she asked. There was nowhere to search that she hadn't already. Or so she thought.

"Where do you always start?" he asked.

Lauryn smiled, stood, and went to the small table behind the sofa. "The family Bible, of course!"

"Of course!" Brant chuckled.

Lauryn lovingly lifted the Bible and returned to her seat on the sofa.

"Scooch over," Brant ordered as he rose and walked toward her. He sat down next to her and curiously looked at the Bible. "Why do you start here?"

Lauryn shrugged, tingling violently at his being so near to her. "It all started here, didn't it?" He chuckled at her wisdom as she opened the Bible to reveal the handwritten record of the O'Halleran family.

"We begin with my Great-Grandfather O'Halleran," Lauryn sighed. "He and my Great-Grandmother O'Halleran had eight children. Two died at birth, one died as a baby. The others—I'll just read it to you, all right?" And lovingly tracing the ancient inked handwriting with her finger, she read aloud.

Kiel McCrea O'Halleran born November 22, 1812, in Connemara, Ireland, married August 16, 1835, to Erynn Shayla Keenan born August 16, 1819, in Connemara, Ireland.

The children of Kiel and Erynn O'Halleran:

Ethan Ian O'Halleran born October 11, 1836, died in battle April 5, 1863

Erynn Eva O'Halleran born September 25, 1840, died September 30, 1840

William McCrea O'Halleran born July 10, 1842, died March 9, 1910

Sean Keenan O'Halleran born November 23, 1844, died November 24, 1912

Lauralynn O'Halleran (Masterson) born August 16, 1846, lost November 30, 1864

Carissa O'Halleran born June 20, 1847, died

John Kiel O'Halleran born February 4, 1851, died June 3, 1851

Virginia Anne O'Halleran born August 19, 1856

"So," Brant sighed, "everyone has died…except your Nana."

"Yes. And she was so young…the age Patrick is now," Lauryn reminded him.

"Do you suppose when Patrick is an old man, he'll remember being a boy and humiliating his sister one day when company came?" Brant smiled and winked.

Lauryn felt warm, delighted, and alive. "Probably not," she giggled. "If he does, he'll probably be like Sean and revel in the knowledge."

"Most likely," Brant agreed. Then he frowned pensively. "So the only person alive that was here when it all happened is Virginia." He drew in a deep breath and released it slowly. "Next, we ask your Nana about that blasted teacup," he stated. "It's driving me crazy."

"But what if it upsets her?" Lauryn argued. "She doesn't remember much about the whole thing, Brant…and she still carries so much guilt about being saved when poor Laura was lost."

"Do you want to figure this all out or not, Lauryn?" Brant asked, seeming rather puzzled suddenly. His patience appeared to be a bit thin. He massaged his temples and sighed in frustration. "Maybe that's the problem. Maybe you don't want to figure it all out. Maybe you like having the Captain all to yourself…at your beck and call day and night." He wasn't cruel in his accusation. He seemed completely in earnest at considering the possibility of its being true.

But hot tears stung Lauryn's eyes. She had not foreseen that he could imagine such a thing. Yet she had her own confusing thoughts and wonderings about Brant's true feelings for Laura. Regardless, she did feel concern for her grandmother was well founded.

"How dare you!" she scolded, standing up from her seat next to him and stomping her foot in irritation. "You know that's not true. Maybe you're so in love with Lauralynn that you don't want her found!" And even when his eyes narrowed angrily, she continued. "You're the one that was so hopeless when you knew…when you thought you'd never be able to see her again. Remember?"

Brant rose to his feet very slowly, his piercing eyes narrowed, searching her face. "There," he mumbled. "It's all been said, hasn't it?" Lauryn simply stood frowning up at him, her heart racing wildly as he looked at her. "I want her found. You want her found. Accusations aside, we both want the same thing. Agreed?"

"Yes," Lauryn whispered, though her heart still ached from the harsh words that hung between them.

"All right then. I'm sorry. I was just being…" he stammered.

"An idiot," Lauryn finished for him.

He grinned at her. "Yep. That's it exactly."

"I'm sorry too," she confessed. "It was wrong of me to—"

"Friends?" he interrupted, offering his hand to her. Lauryn felt like crying again. *Friends* was a disappointing term at that moment.

"Yes," she said, placing her hand in his. The contention and anger that had hung so heavily in the room dissipated instantly. Lauryn was relieved. It had been a terrible feeling, however short it may have lingered.

He shook her hand firmly before releasing it and saying, "What next then? My time here may be short. So let's make the most of it. Where do we go now that we know the family history?"

Lauryn drew in a deep breath. "When everyone returns from the cemetery, we pull Nana aside and ask her about the teacup," she said quietly.

Brant smiled and pinched her cheek. "That's my brave little sugar cube," he chuckled.

Lauryn couldn't help but smile with delight at his silly endearment, even if he had treated her more like a child than she would have preferred. Still, she liked his calling her endearing names. She would try to forgive him for loving Lauralynn and not her. After all, what a profoundly wonderful woman Laura must have been—must be—for men to dedicate their lives to her. In life and in death!

"I'll take you to the attic if you want," Lauryn suggested. If they were going to find Laura during Brant's visit, they needed every minute they could find to search.

"Sounds spooky," Brant whispered. "'I'll take you to the attic,'" he repeated in a deep, eerie voice. He was quite different than he had been those months before when he'd stayed for a short week at Connemara—and yet, somehow, the same. Apparently his injury had taken much more than his sight from him. Now it seemed far more than his eyes had healed. Lauryn found herself even more attracted to him because of it.

She smiled, amused by his teasing. "Laura's trunk is up there. Maybe if you look in it...if we go through it together..."

Brant frowned slightly. He seemed uncertain as to whether they it should do it. After a moment, he nodded. "All right. Lead the way."

They climbed the stairs together, pausing before the attic door. Slowly, Lauryn lifted the latch and opened it. Enough evening light remained that she could see her way to turn on the lightbulb hanging from the ceiling.

"Over here," Lauryn said, pointing to Laura's trunk. "I've been through it so many times. It helps me feel closer to her. Often the Captain comes up here too. We've gone through these things together." Lauryn knelt before the trunk. As she opened it, the slightest scent of wisteria blossoms danced through the room. Lauryn looked up at Brant, frowning down at her. "I'm certain it's all right, Brant. I...I wouldn't have brought you if I didn't think I should...that I needed to."

"I know," he mumbled.

What Brant didn't tell Lauryn was that, since returning to Connemara, his frustration with Laura's inability to rest was intensifying—and not just for her sake, but for his own! Each time he looked at Lauryn— looked at this girl before him, this little nutmeg-haired pixie—he could feel resentment rising in his chest. He wanted his own life. And, yes, he knew it was selfish. But he wanted it! Wanted his own adventure, his own love, his own family. He'd had the sharpest pang of jealousy rack his body when it occurred to him that Lauryn might love the Captain as a bit more than a ghostly friend. It angered him. And his quick temper concerning it was worrying.

She was distracting him. Every time he tried to concentrate on Laura, on clues that might be before him, all he could think about was how adorable Lauryn was—how sweet her lips were, how delicious a real kiss from her would taste. They had to find Laura, for Lauryn's happiness as well as his own. His little fairy needed to get on with her life. And he needed to get on with his.

"It's all right, sir," came a voice. Instantly, Brant recognized the voice as the one he'd heard before—the one who led him to Lauryn the last time he was at Connemara and they'd had a disagreement.

The smile on Lauryn's face as she looked past him told the tale, and Brant turned to see, for the first time, Captain Brandon Masterson.

"It's all right that you go through her things," the Captain repeated. He was as real as Laura, as real as any other person in the house. Brant marveled at the ancient uniform he wore and at the family resemblance.

"I can see you, sir," Brant spoke tentatively.

"Yes. For now." The Captain walked forward and offered his hand. Brant took it and shook it firmly.

Lauryn wasn't exactly certain that she was awake. As she gazed upon the unbelievable sight of the Captain and Brant standing across from one another and shaking hands, she pinched herself to make certain she was indeed conscious. Brant was much taller than the Captain. He was much more handsome—which was astounding, considering the good looks the Captain bore. And there they were, shaking hands. Smiling.

"How fares my lady?" the Captain asked.

Brant nodded and answered, "As well as can be expected, sir."

The Captain nodded. "Uncle Brand to you, sir." Brant smiled and nodded. Then the Captain's attention turned to Lauryn. "He will help you. The two of you together are so much stronger than you are alone."

"But I've tried for so long, Captain. I've failed so many times." Lauryn reminded him.

"You've never failed, my angel," he told her. "Now…I'll leave you two to your work. And, Lauryn—" He walked to her. She stood, taking his hand. "Do not be upset if you don't see me for a while."

"What? But what if—" she began to argue.

"I want you to concentrate on Laura now, not on me. I'm found. She's not." The Captain kissed her cheek tenderly and turned to Brant once more. "I understand the feelings in your heart, Brant. I appreciate your great sacrifice. It will be worth it in the end, you know."

Brant nodded humbly. "I know. Thank you, sir."

Then the Captain was gone.

Lauryn was silent for a long moment, confused, frightened at the Captain's revelation that he would not be appearing to her for some time. What would she do? She looked to Brant and felt guilty, felt as if her heart were betraying her beloved Captain—for she felt nothing but security, hope in having Brant there before her.

Suddenly she asked, "What are you thinkin'?" She couldn't help it. The question foremost in her mind just slipped out of her mouth.

"I'm thinking," Brant mumbled, "that I'm completely crazy. I stand around talking to ghosts like it were the most natural thing in the world."

Lauryn turned from him and knelt before the trunk again. "Well, if you're crazy, then I'm absolutely insane."

Gently, she lifted the ancient paper covering Lauralynn's wedding dress and set it aside. Brant sat down on the floor next to her, and she handed the wedding gown to him.

"See the wisteria on the bodice?" she asked.

Brant nodded but was silent. Lauryn assumed it must be a moving experience for him to actually hold these belongings of Laura's. She very gently handed him other items from the trunk—the sampler, the tintype, the doll. When she got to the bundles of letters—the letters she hadn't found that first day so long ago, the letters she'd found in the very bottom of the trunk sometime after, the letters that Brandon had written to Lauralynn during their courtship and his time away from her as a soldier in battle—it was then that Brant finally spoke.

"Have you read them all?" he asked.

"Well...no," Lauryn confessed. "I...I couldn't bring myself to do it. And anyway, Brand wasn't here the day she disappeared. What could the letters possibly tell me?" Laura's letters from Brand were separated into ten sets, each tied with a pink ribbon. Lauryn touched the soft ribbons with her fingers, wondering, as she always did, what intimate expressions of love they might secret.

"I don't know, but..." Brant paused and rubbed his temples with one hand. Immediately Lauryn was disturbed. She'd seen him do this before, when he was without his sight.

"Are you all right?" she asked desperately, placing her hand on his knee.

"I'm fine. I'm fine," he grumbled. "You should read these, Lauryn," he stated.

Lauryn frowned. "Why me? You read them."

"They're personal!"

"I know that, Brant! Why do you think I haven't read them before?"

"Well, you need to read them now."

"Maybe *you* need to read them now."

"I don't want to read them," Brant confessed.

"I don't want to read them either," Lauryn countered.

Brant grinned, and she was irritated. It was the kind of grin he had when he was amused.

"Very well," he conceded. "We won't read them. You're right. What good would it do? They're personal and don't pertain to the day in question." He chuckled and asked, "Were you this headstrong when I was here before?"

"Yes." Lauryn's response was quick and sure. "You just don't remember."

"Oh, I remember everything, Lauryn," he assured her with the familiar grin of mischief on his face.

Lauryn felt uncomfortable under his amused gaze. *What is he implying?* she wondered. She could hear the others talking downstairs and knew they had returned from the cemetery. Gently she began putting Laura's belongings back into the trunk. Brant hunkered down and helped her until everything was safe in its place once more. Then he offered her his hand. She accepted, and he helped her to her feet.

"Let's see if your Nana proves to be more help," he suggested, closing the attic door behind them.

"You'll be tender when you ask her, won't you?" Lauryn ventured.

"I'm sure that when *you* ask her, you'll be sensitive to her feelings," Brant countered.

Lauryn couldn't help smiling at his passing the responsibility back to her. "You are a carin' man." Lauryn giggled, delighted by their banter. "You'll not upset her more than necessary."

"Nope," he chuckled. "I'll be right there to comfort her after you've asked her."

Lauryn giggled. Brant was quite a wit. And yet in the back of her mind were the letters. Brand's letters to Lauralynn haunted her. Never before had they preyed on her mind. She'd all but forgotten them, having told herself they could not possibly help her. But now, for some reason, they lingered in her thoughts.

"Sir!" Sean greeted Brant as they entered the parlor. "You look as healthy as a bull. Completely healed, I see."

Brant smiled and struck hands with Sean. Aunt Felicity was cooing over Junie, a disgusted Patrick looking on, and Mindy was talking with Uncle Johnny and Nana.

"Yep," Brant assured Sean. "And it's nice to *see* you."

Sean chuckled and looked to Lauryn. "So have you managed to seduce my little sister into givin' up her dreams of Mr. Right in trade for you?"

"No. I'm afraid not," Brant said, grinning and obviously amused.

Immediately Lauryn's face turned crimson and burned with a terrible blush. Sometimes she was certain she hated Sean. He always, always humiliated her when she least wanted him to.

"Sean O'Halleran Kensington," Georgia scolded, arriving in time to hear him taunting his sister.

"Oh, go on, Mama," Sean argued. "If Lauryn thinks she can spend all these years goin' on to me about Mr. Perfectly Imperfect and not have to take some teasin' for it, she's wrong."

Lauryn's mother looked to her sympathetically and nodded to reassure her she shouldn't let Sean bother her. But being humiliated in front of everyone was hard to swallow. And furthermore, she loathed the way Sean always made fun of her romantic ideals.

"That's enough, Sean," Georgia reminded him.

"Who's this Mr. Perfect?" Brant's Aunt Felicity asked.

"Why, Lauryn's dream man, of course," Sean offered.

"Sean!" Georgia tried to halt her son's assault on his sister, but he was determined.

"Every girl should have her ideal in mind long before she's old enough to be looking," Aunt Felicity stated, going to Lauryn and taking her hand reassuringly. "Otherwise she'll end up with some devil that can never make her happy." Lauryn smiled, happy to have an advocate. But her relief was short-lived, for Aunt Felicity continued. "And I say there's no better man on earth than my dear nephew here. Don't you think so, Lauryn sweetie?"

Sean burst into a roar of laughter. And everyone in the room enjoyed their own giggles and snickers—everyone except Lauryn. Brant, though he didn't laugh, couldn't keep an amused grin from spreading across his handsome face. And even as Georgia scolded Sean again, she herself smiled with delight.

It was Brant who finally came to Lauryn's rescue just a moment before tears of humiliation escaped her eyes.

"Poor Lauryn," he sympathized with a smile. "Trapped in a room full of teasing fools." He went to her and put a comforting arm around her shoulders. "Don't you worry, sugar," he began. "Brothers always get theirs. Always." He squeezed her shoulders once more in his powerful arm and, releasing her, said with a chuckle, "I think Aunt Felicity is right, after all. If a girl isn't selective, she might end up with quite the devil. Isn't that right, Mindy?"

Everyone laughed again, including Sean, who suddenly embraced Lauryn affectionately. "You're a tough little dish, sweet sissy," he told her. "I do love you so."

Lauryn's heart softened, and she returned her brother's embrace. "I love you too. Even if you are a terrible tease," she confessed.

"Well, I am certain y'all must be tired after your trip. We'll have some cool lemonade and get everyone tucked in cozy, all right?" Georgia suggested.

"Indeed," Uncle Johnny confirmed.

"Um, Mrs. Kensington?" Brant began.

As both Georgia and Nana simultaneously answered, "Yes?" Brant specified, "Virginia."

"Yes, love?" Nana said, smiling.

"Lauryn and I were wondering if we could talk to you a moment."

"Yes," Lauryn added. "Brant has somethin' he'd like to ask you."

Brant winked at her, grinning.

"Why, of course, angels." Nana assured them. "Let's go out on the porch. It's such a lovely night."

Once settled in the comfortable wicker furniture on the porch, evening breezes heavy with the fragrance of the wisteria, it was Brant who did indeed pose the question.

"For most of my youth, Laura carried a small teacup with her," he said. "Although she hasn't had it with her for years, whenever I ask about it, she just responds, 'My sister,' and seems satisfied in knowing that you are well. Can you give…why would she have had a teacup with her, and where is it now? That's making me insane. It seems like a small thing, I know. But it just…it just…"

"It seems to me too that it would be important, Nana," Lauryn offered.

Virginia frowned and shook her head. "I don't know. I can't begin to imagine." She paused a moment and then asked, "Tell me what it looks like."

"It was small," Brant explained. "Too small to be a normal teacup."

"Maybe it's a demitasse," Lauryn offered.

"What pattern?" Nana asked.

Brant simply wrinkled his brow, clueless as to what she meant.

Lauryn smiled. After all, china patterns were almost always purely a feminine interest. She would've been quite astonished had he actually known what Nana was talking about.

"What color was it? Did it have flowers painted on it?" Lauryn explained.

Brant shook his head. "I don't know. It's a little teacup…thing. Small and white. Maybe it had flowers on it. Maybe I imagined that part."

"Well," Nana was thoughtful, "when I was very little, we used to have make-believe tea parties. We had a little table and a little set of china, a children's set. The pieces were white, embellished with tiny lavender flowers. We'd play for hours and hours, just us sisters. I cherished those moments, and even though the memory is faded…I cherish it. I was younger, after all, and it was a kind thing to do…to play with me like that."

"But why would Laura have a teacup with her?" Lauryn asked.

"I don't know," Nana mused. "I haven't seen that tea set for…" Then her face brightened. Her eyebrows rose, and her eyes widened as if she'd just seen a vision. "I haven't seen that tea set since before the battle, since before Laura disappeared."

Lauryn felt excitement rise within her. Brant had been right! She knew it! The teacup Laura carried with her was significant somehow.

"Where did you last see it?" Brant asked. Lauryn could sense the excitement in him as well.

Nana shook her head. "I don't know. It's been so long ago." She paused, seeming pensive. "I think…I think in the cellar."

"The old root cellar?" Lauryn asked.

"Yes. We used to play tea party in there," Nana answered.

"In the root cellar?" Lauryn exclaimed. "What a gloomy place to play."

"Oh, the cellar used to be different, Lauryn," Nana explained. "It wasn't as dirty and nasty as it is now. It used to be quite nice, the way I remember. And on a rainy day, when the house seemed too stuffy, the root cellar was a blessed escape."

"Well," Brant exclaimed, fairly leaping to his feet, "let's go."

"It's pitch black out!" Lauryn reminded him.

"That's what lanterns are for, sugar," he chuckled. "Are you coming along, Mrs. Kensington?"

"Not me," Nana laughed. "I'll leave the rootin' around in that spider- and mice-infested ol' cellar to you young people."

☙

"I hate that creepy ol' cellar," Lauryn mumbled as she and Brant walked through the grass toward the cellar. "Even in the daytime."

Brant held the lantern firmly in one hand to light their way. "Oh, come on," Brant urged. "I'll go with you. I can't believe you didn't show this to me before."

"It's hardly more than an ol' hole in the ground," she explained. "I've been there plenty of times, and there's nothin' special about it. It's crawlin' with spiders and mice, and I hate it. Anyway, you couldn't have…" Lauryn paused when she realized what she was about to say.

"I couldn't have seen it?" Brant finished for her, smiling. "I know that I couldn't see before, Lauryn. You don't have to be uncomfortable referring to it."

"I know." Lauryn smiled at him, noticing the way the moonlight made his teeth seem all the more perfectly white.

When they'd reached the door leading down into the cellar, Lauryn told him, "You'll have to be the one to open it. It never fails that somethin' comes a-scurryin' out of there and scares the waddin' out of me."

Brant chuckled. "All right. I'll play the knight in shining armor."

Lauryn smiled at him. How absolutely exciting it was to be outside in the dark, alone with him. Had the situation been different, had their intent been simply a leisurely stroll, it would have been quite romantic.

The old root cellar of Connemara was indeed a hole in the ground. And sure enough, as Brant lifted one side of the heavy door, a multitude of spiders scurried hither and thither, causing Lauryn's skin to crawl and a quiet squeal to escape her throat. Brant merely chuckled, as most men would have, no doubt, finding her being startled by a few of the earth's eight-legged creatures to be quite amusing.

"I told you," Lauryn reminded him, glad that she'd wound her hair into a tight knot at the back of her head before dinner. A spider in her hair was one of her worst reoccurring nightmares. "I hate it, I hate it, I hate it!"

As they descended the ancient and rotting wooden stairs into the dark, musty cellar, Lauryn's anxiety increased tenfold. She looked up, noting that, although her Great-Grandfather O'Halleran had lined the cellar walls with wooden planking, in many places the strong, winding roots of the wisteria trees above had pushed through the paneling, growing in odd tangles on the ceiling. Now the cellar was more frightening than even she remembered.

"You see, it's just a creepy ol' hole in the ground!" Lauryn exclaimed. "How on earth Nana could've thought this was a fun place to play—and especially tea party—is completely beyond me."

Brant grinned. Lauryn thought for a moment that the man seemed perpetually amused at her expense. But as long as he was smiling, she didn't seem to mind the reason.

Holding up the lantern, Brant mumbled, "There's nothing in here."

"Oh yes, there is!" Lauryn squealed as she felt something with eight legs crawling on her arm. Screeching hysterically, she began running in place and slapping at her arm. Brant quickly set the lantern down on the dirt floor and took hold of Lauryn's arm, flicking the spider from her body with one quick motion.

Lauryn stood trembling with residual horror, realizing that, in her mad dancing to try to brush off the spider, her wild mass of hair had come unpinned and hung in tangled ringlets down her back and over her shoulders—a perfectly luscious temptation for arachnids.

"Are you all right?" Brant asked, unable to halt the chuckle accompanying his question.

Lauryn scratched her arm where the spider had been, the sensation of its tiny legs still fresh upon her skin. "I hate it in here!" she reminded him.

"Yeah. I can see that," he told her. Calmly, he reached down and retrieved the lantern, holding it up once more as he peered into the darkness of the cellar. As he took several steps toward the furthest corner of the room, Lauryn reflexively reached out, taking hold of his arm for support and comfort.

"I know what you're thinkin'," she whispered. "Every time I come down here, I half expect to see a skeleton all dressed in a hooped skirt, propped up in that corner." As always, there was nothing there—only an empty barrel, no doubt a cozy hiding place for millions of things with eight legs. A small, child-sized chair, missing a leg and sadly forgotten, lay on the floor nearby.

"A piece of the past?" Brant asked.

"Maybe," Lauryn admitted. There were several other forgotten items in the cellar—an old potato planter, a bridle that hung on a hook on one wall, and several ancient-looking wooden buckets stacked up together. There was nothing to indicate Lauralynn had ever been there. Of course, Lauryn knew this already and soon grew impatient. Then, when a tiny shrew scurried across her right foot, she was completely undone.

Screeching like a mad banshee, she again began running in place frantically. "Brant Masterson! I'll not spend another horrible moment in this place unless you give me a darn good reason!"

Brant chuckled again. This time, however, instead of taking hold of Lauryn's arm, he placed a strong arm around her waist and lifted her up for a moment.

"Fine. Just stand on my feet."

Lauryn did as ordered. Her body completely flush with his, one of his powerful arms tightly around her, she placed her small feet one each on top of his. The situation demanded that she put her arms around his neck. There was no other way to balance herself on his feet. It was a completely inappropriate, fascinating, and fabulous predicament.

Obviously satisfied with his investigation of the cellar, Brant walked toward the door leading up and out. It seemed like having her standing on his feet didn't inconvenience him at all, for other than his legs being stiffer than usual, he walked as if she were not even there. Lauryn thought back briefly to the day her father had taught her the waltz. He'd had her stand on his feet in the same manner as he counted out the dance steps so that she could feel which way her feet would need to travel when being led. But this! This was much different!

First of all, their bodies, Brant's and her own, were completely together, tighter than any hug Lauryn had experienced with a man. Any man! Secondly, she could feel the solid definition of the muscles of his chest and legs against her own. It was completely improper. Completely! And it was entirely marvelous. Entirely!

But her zenith was short-lived. As soon as they reached the stairs and he released her, the intense guilt began. The moment Brant had taken her to him, the moment she had wrapped her arms around him, she'd forgotten their purpose for going to the cellar. Lauralynn had been driven from her mind by her attraction to Brant. It was a traitorous act on Lauryn's part.

Once out of the cellar, Brant closed the doors and turned to Lauryn, saying, "Well…you were right. Nothing there. Not one clue."

Lauryn brushed her hair back from her face and visually searched her limbs and dress for evidences of unwanted creatures that lived in webs. "I know. It's why I don't go down there. I—"

"You hate it," he finished for her with a smile. But then his eyes narrowed as he stepped toward her. "But you're so cute down there," he said.

Lauryn thought maybe he was all too well blessed with a gift of sarcasm. But the expression in his eyes said differently. "Cute?" she asked. "In the creepy ol' cellar, with spiders and rodents?"

He winked at her, and reaching out, he took her hand and began pulling her toward the house.

"Well, I guess the competition wasn't too thick down there, actually…when it comes to cuteness," she mused.

Brant's mind had already traveled back to the task at hand. "Why a teacup?" he grumbled. "She couldn't be holding onto a map or something. Just a teacup."

At that moment, Lauryn glanced up to the attic window. Light streamed through onto the grass below. There, as if framed in a painting, stood the Captain. Lauryn smiled up at him. He smiled, nodding his approval. Her heart lightened a bit. Brant would help her. Brant would free the Captain, the Captain and Lauralynn. And in the next moment, Lauryn thought, *Will Brant free me? Or has he already made my heart a captive?*

CHAPTER NINE

Having regained his sight, Brant wanted to investigate all of Connemara and the grounds again. This time, he would have a greater ability to link things together, should some kind of clues actually appear. The next day, Lauryn led him to the creek, the servants' house, and finally the springhouse. But nothing was found.

It had been a blessed time for Lauryn. She'd been alone with him. Patrick had taken to Uncle Johnny like a pig to mud and kept the elderly man too occupied with answering questions to give Patrick any time to visit with Lauryn and Brant. Lauryn's grandmother and mother were far too intrigued with Aunt Felicity's stories, opinions, and sense of humor to spend much time worrying over them.

As they approached Henry the statue on their way back to the house, Lauryn glanced and smiled at Brant. He paused and looked at Henry.

"I feel sorry for this man," Brant mumbled.

Lauryn giggled and asked, "Why? You don't even know him." If Brant knew just how well Lauryn and her friend Penny knew Henry, that would be another matter.

"He's so...so..." Brant mumbled.

"Broodin'?" Lauryn offered. "Lonely?" She smiled, caching away forever all her secrets where Henry was concerned. "I promise you, he's had his own adventures. Anyway, dark, broodin', interestin' men make the best..." She gasped, slightly horrified at what she'd almost revealed. She'd already said too much, and Brant hadn't missed it.

"What? They make the best what?" he prodded.

"Um…um…" Lauryn stammered. "They make the best…statues!" She tossed her head nonchalantly and began walking on.

"Wait a minute, sugar," Brant chuckled, catching her arm. "Tell me. What do they make? The best what?"

"Statues."

"Statues? I don't believe that's what you really had in mind." Brant was too observant. His sight restored, he had a strong sense to complement all of his others, and he was not going to be easy to fool.

"Statues. Truly. They make the best statues because…because…they're prideful enough to pose for them." It was all she would say, and with an indifferent smile, she pulled her arm from his grasp and walked on.

"Does Connemara have a basement?" Brant asked as they wandered back toward the house.

He seemed to be satisfied with her explanation about brooding, adventurous men being the best models for statues. In reality, she had meant to say they made the best imaginary lovers! What a narrow escape! Still, even though he appeared to let the subject go, she was suspicious. The basement was a different, safer topic of conversation.

"Oh yes," Lauryn moaned. "And it's even creepier than the ol' root cellar."

"Good." Brant chuckled. "Take me there."

"Brant! It's darker than anythin' in there and just crawlin' with critters and bugs," Lauryn argued.

"I'll go alone. No need to have you get upset again," he assured her.

But Lauryn didn't want him to go alone. What if he did find something she had missed in the past? So they went into the kitchen and opened the door to the basement.

"You ain't goin' down there, are you?" Patrick exclaimed as they started to descend the stairs. He and Uncle Johnny sat at the table immersed in a fiery game of cards.

"Your sister says this is her favorite part of the house," Brant teased.

"Well, she'll be squawkin' like a pinched hen halfway down, Brant. So plug up your ears!" With that, Patrick returned his attention to the game at hand.

"Basements are dark and cold, Brant, my boy," Uncle Johnny mumbled. "You be sure and make the most of it. You hear?" He winked impishly at Lauryn, who could do nothing to stop the blush from rising to her cheeks.

"You know me, Uncle Johnny," Brant assured him.

"Well, I hope so," the elderly man chuckled.

Lauryn simply brushed an escaped strand of her hair from her cheek and tried to appear unruffled. Yet her memory of being so closely held by Brant in the cellar the night before caused her blush to intensify and her heart to race. Who knew what flirtatious opportunities might await her in the basement?

The basement of Connemara, though cool, was unbearably stuffy. Brant coughed several times as he reached the bottom of the stairs; Lauryn was close at his heels, already looking anxiously around in the darkness for whatever creature might startle her next. The lantern that hung just inside the basement door was insufficient to illuminate the darkness. Lauryn's skin prickled as she imagined creepy, crawly things crawling in her hair.

"Great-Grandfather wouldn't have brought her down here," Lauryn said to Brant. "It wouldn't have been safe. The Union soldiers would have searched it."

"But he didn't think they'd find your grandmother and the others, and they were hidden right there in the house, right?" Brant reminded her.

"Yes, but...aahhh!"

Lauryn's shrill squeal startled Brant. He turned to see her dancing around frantically as a large, lethargic-looking rat waddled across her path. Brant chuckled and booted the rodent aside with his foot.

"Stay close, my lady," he teased. "This won't take too long." Indeed, after just a few minutes, Brant seemed convinced Laura had not died in the basement at Connemara.

"It's all brick...the basement. No allowance for secret doors or the like," Lauryn whispered.

Brant sighed with disappointment and held the lantern high to look up at the basement ceiling, which comprised the floors of Connemara House.

"What kind of wood is this?" he asked.

Lauryn looked at him in disbelief. "What kind of wood? How would I know that? All I know is it's crawlin' with livin' things I can't see down here and—"

"I've never seen a grain like that before. It looks…" Brant again held the lantern higher. He reached up and pressed the wood just above his head. "Where are we? I mean…what room is just above us?"

It seemed he was taking their conversation down an odd route, but Lauryn answered anyway. "The parlor. I think we should be just about…yep. Just under the parlor. Why?"

"Well, look at the wood up here. See how it's dark in some places and not in others. It's strange." Brant frowned and looked down at her.

"I'm sorry," was all she could think to say.

He smiled. "For what?"

"That Connemara's wood floors are…strange."

"I think just about everything at Connemara is strange," he chuckled.

Lauryn, about to scold him for teasing, instead sucked in her breath, horrified at the large eight-legged beast that was crawling along Brant's left shoulder.

"What's the matter, Lauryn? You're as pale as a sheet," Brant asked.

Somehow, though it was completely adverse to her normal behavior, Lauryn found the courage to reach up and brush the spider from Brant's shoulder; she stomped on it furiously and smashed it into nothing more than a large brown spot on the dirt beneath their feet, all the while screeching intermittently.

When she'd finished her frenzied mutilation of the beast, she stood before Brant, breathless with residual fear. Brant simply stood staring at her, eyebrows raised in astonishment.

"Well, one thing is for sure," he said. "That spider will never have the guts to do that again."

Lauryn laughed nervously at his humor. "I suppose he won't."

Then, with a devilish grin, Brant put his hand dramatically to his chest and breathed, "You saved my life."

Lauryn rolled her eyes, still too undone by her frightening experience to find easy mirth in the situation. "That'll be enough, Mr. Masterson," she scolded.

"But…but I'm sincerely grateful, ma'am," he chuckled. "I saw it all, my whole life, flashing before my eyes. And then, *whack!* I was back, safe in the arms of Connemara's basement."

"I'll have you know that it took every ounce of courage I had to kill that beast!" Lauryn snapped.

"I know. I know it did. And I thank you." Reaching out, he tucked a strand of hair behind her ear, which by now was completely free from its pins. He smiled. Lauryn, angry as she tried to be at him for mocking her, could only melt at the sight of him standing before her so handsome and strong, so amused and so approving. Brant Masterson was a living, breathing dream.

What a pistol she is, Brant noted as he studied Lauryn's flustered expression. Even in the low light of the lantern, he could see the remnant of absolute terror in her eyes. How perfectly sweet that she would protect him.

He relished the wild look of her just then—the way her hair escaped its proper pinning to stream down around her shoulders, naturally rebellious, the way her eyes flickered with residual determination in the face of fear. He half expected her to turn around and reveal a pair of gossamer fairy wings attached to her shoulders—half expected golden light to suddenly beam brilliantly from the tips of her fingers—half expected a radiant glow to appear like tiny threads of enchanted illumination woven in with every strand of her beautiful hair. She was too adorable to be safe. Too tempting. Too much an irresistible lure to a man like himself who had always possessed a great deal of self-control.

All his life, the females of the species had seemed drawn to him for some reason for which he had no explanation. When he was a boy, the girls were so silly in his presence that, at times, he had wondered if there were an intelligent one among them anywhere. He admitted that in his adolescence he had been somewhat conceited for a time. It was embarrassingly obvious that he was considered the boy to strive to win. He'd enjoyed the female attention he received and basked in his popularity none too humbly—but only for a short time. Laura herself had taught Brant to have a great respect for the tender, nurturing, romantic side of women. He'd never used his charms to beguile or mislead, never done any seriously damaging wooing or seducing. And as a man, he had at last found maturity, thank the heavens—not only physical, bodily maturity but maturity of mind and attitude. He'd read the hearts of many a young woman and learned to spare them greater heartache by being honest from the beginning of an acquaintance.

But this little pixie—Lauryn—this one was different! She intrigued him—her wit, the romantic daydreams he suspected she secreted, her way of thinking. All of it added up to nothing more than mortal danger to a man who boasted silently to himself about owning a profound self-control.

Again, Brant reminded himself that he'd come to help solve the infernal mystery that had plagued his life. He'd come to find Laura. Laura was why he'd come back. But he feared that Lauryn would prove to be too tempting, too perfectly adorable to resist for much longer.

"I hate the basement!" Lauryn exclaimed once they were in the kitchen again.

"I figured that," Brant chuckled as he hung the lantern on the hook just inside the basement door.

Lauryn brushed the dust from her shoulders. "I wonder where Patrick has dragged your uncle off to."

"Don't know," Brant mumbled. "But I'm sure Uncle Johnny will keep Patrick hopping."

"I'm certain one of them will keep the other hoppin', at the very least. Would you like some lemonade?" Lauryn asked.

"Sure," Brant agreed, pulling a chair out from the small kitchen table, turning it around, and straddling the seat as he sat down. "Well...you're right. Nothing notable in the basement," he remarked.

"Just another disappointment in a long line of them," Lauryn sighed, pouring each of them a glass of lemonade.

"So," he began as she handed him his drink and sat down across from him at the table, "what are your ambitions, Miss Kensington?"

"My ambitions?" she repeated. Lauryn had been fully prepared to converse further about the task at hand. The basement was unproductive, as were so many other places at Connemara. She was certain Brant would want to talk about where else they could look. His sudden change of subject caught her completely unprepared.

"Beyond finding your lost auntie, what do you plan to do? Will you seek higher education? Teaching perhaps? Become an actress? I mean, it's obvious you can dance well. I've seen you myself. That one in the cellar last night beat the one today though."

Lauryn sneered playfully at him. "I guess I don't have any ambitions," she answered.

"None?" he asked.

"Not unless you think—and most people don't—that being a good wife and mother is considered ambition."

"I think that's very ambitious. What harder job is there?"

Lauryn wasn't quite sure of his sincerity. Rather than continue the discussion about herself, she turned the tables.

"And you?" she asked. "What grand ambitions lurk in your mind and heart, Brant Masterson?"

He smiled, not at all bested. He answered anyway. "I like growing apples. Cattle too. Like my Dad. Only…not in Vermont. I want to be west. Before I left for the war, I purchased an apple orchard and farm in north New Mexico."

"You bought land in New Mexico? That's forever away!" Lauryn was very disturbed. Vermont was far, but New Mexico! It seemed so much farther. "It's so…so west!"

Brant chuckled. "It's marvelous out there, the way the land stretches out to the mountains. The mountains themselves are magnificent! At sunset, they're sort of…sort of watermelon-colored and…and purple. You've never seen anything like it. And the sky…perfectly blue."

"So you want to raise apples and grow cattle in New Mexico?" Lauryn asked.

Smiling, Brant corrected, "Raise cattle and grow apples, actually."

Lauryn smiled, realizing her mistake. "It sounds so…so secluded," she said.

Brant nodded. "Maybe. But it sounds fresh, challenging, and different to me."

"An escape," Lauryn muttered. He was looking for an escape. His life had been forever tremulous, not sweet and happy like Lauryn's had been. It was obvious that Brant wanted to find Laura and then leave it all behind him. She tried to understand it. She'd been happy at

Connemara. She had always felt that nothing would be worth leaving it. Nothing except maybe...

"Don't you want it?" he asked. "You act so...so content to be here, lingering with ghosts. Don't you want something completely different?"

Lauryn shrugged as Brant finished his lemonade. "I...I've never really considered on it too much, I suppose." Her answer, though she knew he might find it shallow, was honest. "To leave Connemara...my family. But then again...I suppose people *do* do that. It seems to me it would take a great deal of bravery."

"Maybe," he mused. "But it sounds great to me." He paused for a moment, lost in his own thoughts before he continued. "I almost had Dad sell the place for me—before I got home and they weren't certain I'd see again. But...I'm glad I hung onto it."

"It's good to hear that you have plans you're lookin' forward to...that make you happy, Brant." Lauryn was beginning to feel somewhat depressed. Where was her ambition? Where were her dreams? She knew what and where they were—sitting across from her, smiling handsomely as he thought on his own beautiful dreams of the west.

She'd always assumed she'd grow up, find her Mr. Perfectly Imperfect, all would go well, and they'd fall in love, smooth as syrup, and live happily ever after. It had never once occurred to her that maybe Mr. Perfectly Imperfect wouldn't be that easy to catch hold of after she found him. It had never occurred to her that maybe he wouldn't find her to be his own Mrs. Perfect.

"Lauryn! There you are!" Penny exclaimed, fairly bursting through the kitchen door, causing both Lauryn and Brant to jump. She was followed closely by her older brother, Jeffrey. "We saw your mama down in town. She said she thought you two would be here."

Lauryn was irritated that her time alone with Brant should be cut short by yet another set of intruders. But she smiled, for she did adore Penny.

"Well, hello again, Miss Penny," Brant said, standing and bowing slightly.

"Oh my stars! If you aren't all the prettier now, Mr. Masterson!" Penny exclaimed.

"And the angelic voice I heard so many weeks ago seems indeed to be owned by an angel," Brant flattered her in return. Lauryn swallowed the hot taste of jealousy that burned in her mouth.

"Hello," Jeffrey greeted, offering his hand to Brant. "I'm Jeffrey McGovern, Penny's brother."

Brant accepted Jeffrey's hand, shaking it firmly. "Nice to meet you."

"Hey there, Lauryn," Jeffrey greeted.

"Hello, Jeffrey," Lauryn answered, smiling. Lauryn had always liked Jeffrey. He'd been her first crush other than the Captain. But somehow, Jeffrey was never anything close to Mr. Perfectly Imperfect. She received her very first real kiss from him when she was thirteen. It had been quite disappointing. They each confessed to a feeling of having kissed a sibling or a cousin and enjoyed a friendly laugh. They remained friends and often attended the same social events. Jeffrey was very similar in feature to Penny, only a masculine version. He was a handsome man in his own right, with dark green eyes and blond hair a shade or two darker than his sister's.

"We've come to invite you to our house for a party next Saturday! Won't you stay over and attend, Mr. Masterson?" Penny begged. "I've invited your auntie and uncle. I met them in town just this mornin', and they said they'd love to."

"A party at the McGovern house is worth comin' all the way from Vermont just to attend, Brant. You won't want to miss it." Lauryn knew she was simply desperate to keep Brant in Franklin longer. Penny's parties were no more special than others, but maybe it would entice him into staying at least nearly two weeks.

"Well, if Aunt Felicity said we were going...I guess we are," Brant said.

Penny squealed and clapped her hands. "Fabulous! Come on, Lauryn." she ordered, taking Lauryn's hand and leading her out of the kitchen. "I need to borrow your mama's round, white linen tablecloths." Looking back to Jeffrey and Brant, she ordered, "You two gentlemen go on ahead and talk politics for a minute. All right?"

"As if you're givin' us a choice, Bossy Betty," Jeffrey scolded.

"That sister of yours is quite the little bullet," Brant noted as he offered Jeffrey a seat.

Jeffrey shook his head and chuckled. "Oh yeah. And you get them two together and…"

"It's like two magpies on a fence?" Brant finished.

Jeffrey chuckled and nodded in agreement. "So you're related to the man who's buried here at Connemara?"

"Yeah," Brant confirmed. "He was my Aunt Felicity's brother. You met her today."

"I did." Jeffrey studied Brant for a moment. Brant felt it was with disapproval. Unexpectedly, Jeffrey announced, "I was sweet on Lauryn for years and years and years."

"Really?" Brant stammered. He wondered if this southern gentleman's next move would be to slap him across the face with a glove and challenge him to a duel.

"Yep. She and I…well, I don't think I ever quite measured up to her ideal," Jeffrey admitted.

"Yeah. I've heard about that." Brant waited for Jeffrey's response.

"How about you?" he asked. "Do you think you might be him?"

Brant was only slightly stunned with the man's forthrightness. He didn't really think his own relationship with Lauryn, or lack thereof, was any of Jeffrey's business. Still, he must be friendly. No matter what the family history was, he was just a guest at Connemara.

"I'm pretty sure that I'm as far from being what that girl wants as any man," he muttered.

"Don't misunderstand me, sir," Jeffrey said. "I'm not jealous…not anymore. I just know…I just don't want her to be…"

"Hurt," Brant finished.

"Yeah. She's been a good friend for a long time. Penny and I both love her like a sister."

"Don't you worry. I'm not the heart-breaking type," Brant chuckled, feeling relieved that Jeffrey's concern was purely fraternal.

"So," Jeffrey sighed, seeming satisfied that Brant wasn't a malicious, lustful rounder. "Where did you fight in Europe?"

৫

"He is a walkin' dream, Lauryn!" Penny exclaimed in a whisper once the two girls reached the linen closet. "How are you keepin' your hands off him?"

"Penny!" Lauryn scolded. "He's here to help me find—"

"So what? That doesn't mean you can't have him after."

Lauryn shook her head. "I can't…I can't even dream those things, Pen. I've told you that."

"But he came back! You didn't think he would, and he did. Darlin', if you don't want him…then for Pete's sake, give him to me!"

Lauryn smiled. "I'm keepin' my head clear. I'll find Laura for him, and he'll go home and…and…"

"I thought you were findin' Laura for the Captain."

Lauryn looked to Penny, whose eyes twinkled with understanding. "I am. But for Brant too. Now…which tablecloths did you say you wanted?"

After retrieving the tablecloths and placing them safely on the gazebo bench, Penny and Lauryn linked arms and began to stroll about the grounds of Connemara. Jeffrey and Brant were still talking in the kitchen. Although Lauryn was still a bit irritated that their time together had been interrupted, she was more than happy for some light conversation with Penny.

"*He* is Adonis! That's all there is to it," Penny sighed.

"He is, isn't he?" Lauryn giggled.

"You've got to win him, Lauryn," Penny demanded. "By whatever means possible. Seduce him at every turn!"

"Penny McGovern! You're shameless!" Lauryn scolded.

"Of course! How else do you expect to get him? And he likes you, I can tell."

"He's occupyin' a great deal of my thinkin', that's for certain." Lauryn sighed in frustration. If only she had Penny's confidence where men were concerned.

"Well, I'm hopin' that all that time we spent learnin' on Henry will finally pay off," Penny confessed as they stopped directly in front of Henry, their special statue friend.

"How many real men have you kissed since Henry?" Lauryn asked with a mischievous smile.

"Not many," Penny giggled. "I'm havin' a hard time findin' any man who can give ol' Henry any competition." The girls giggled, delighted with their memories of practicing their kissing skills with Henry.

It had worked out so well when they were girls. Henry was the perfect height for them both. His arms were positioned just right, enabling either girl to be held in his embrace if they squiggled into it just right.

Lauryn, delighted by the memory, squeezed her way into Henry's granite embrace.

Penny laughed and clapped her hands. "A few more curves to work around since you last kissed our Henry, is it, Lauryn?"

Dramatically, Lauryn placed her hands on Henry's shoulders and gazed up adoringly into his slate-colored eyes.

"Oh, Henry! The times we've shared," she cooed. Slowly she let her hands travel the breadth of his shoulders, locking her arms around his neck. "Kiss me, you wicked, wicked man! It's been far too long. Don't you long for the petal softness of my lips?" Penny giggled as Lauryn continued. "What? You've missed me? I couldn't have returned from New Orleans soon enough had it been the moment after I left? You fool! Kiss me! Kiss me!" Then, quite dramatically, Lauryn raised herself on tiptoe and kissed Henry lingeringly on the mouth—kissed him until Penny's giggling ceased abruptly.

Turning to look at her friend, Lauryn tried to will herself to expire on the spot. Standing next to Penny, an amused expression on his face, strong arms folded across his chest, stood none other than the very man of her dreams.

Penny bit her lip, trying to stifle her amusement. Lauryn, crimson with the hot blush of humiliation, slid from Henry's embrace and smoothed her dress.

"So," Brant chuckled, "this is why Henry is so special to you."

There was nothing to be said. Caught in the act of kissing a statue was not to be dealt with by any other manner than humiliated silence.

"Thank you for the tablecloths, Lauryn. Um...bye," Penny mumbled, turning and almost running from the scene of the crime.

"When we were girls we used to..." Lauryn stammered.

Brant, still smiling, walked forward, stopping directly in front of her. Dropping his voice and bending to her ear, he said, "When you think you're ready for a real lover...you know where to find me, sugar." Then, with a wink, he turned and walked away, leaving Lauryn's mouth agape and her heart hammering.

CHAPTER TEN

Brant had gone with his aunt and uncle to the old Confederate cemetery just outside of town. Lauryn found herself pacing her room, waiting for him to return.

"You'll wear a hole in the floor, girl," the Captain chuckled.

Lauryn looked up to see him sitting on her bed, leaning back on one elbow and smiling at her in amusement.

"We're not gettin' anywhere!" she exclaimed. "He's been here a whole day, and so far, all we've discovered is that Laura and Nana used to play tea party in the old, smelly root cellar!"

"So…you're just impatient, is that it?" the Captain asked. "Ten years of helping me out, looking for hours every day, and you're just now getting impatient?"

"Well, yes!" Lauryn whined.

"Why are you so much more impatient now than you were, say, last year?" The Captain's eyes twinkled with mischief.

"Because…because…" Lauryn stammered. "Oh, I don't know! And where is Brant? He should be back by now. Doesn't he know we have work to do?"

The Captain chuckled.

"What's so funny?" Lauryn snapped.

"You could be looking on your own, you know."

"I've been lookin' on my own for ten years! What good has it done anyone? Besides, he came here to help me. Didn't he?"

"Did he?"

"What do you mean by that?" Lauryn was flustered and rather irritated with the Captain talking in riddles.

"Do you think he came back just to help you find Laura?"

"Of course! Why else would he have come back?" Lauryn tried to squelch the winged hope that rose in her bosom. She knew what the Captain was implying, and she knew it was pointless. Brant had come back to find Laura. That was it. Lauryn couldn't hope for anything else. It would only mean pain to her.

"You don't think you have anything to do with his being here?"

Lauryn buried her face in her hands then, relenting. "Have you seen him?" she asked in a tearful whisper. "Have you talked to him? Noticed his wit? His...he's perfect!"

"No man is perfect, darling," the Captain reminded her.

"I know," she admitted, sitting down beside him. "But he's...he's..."

"Perfect for you?"

"I can't feel this way for him, Captain! I can't!"

"Why not?"

"Because I think...I think if I feel any stronger—like him any more than I already do—I think...I don't think I can stand it! I think..."

"Don't think, sweetheart," the Captain said softly. "That's a mistake."

"He's so much older. So handsome and perfect. So experienced! What could I possibly offer him? What about me would be interestin' enough to keep his attention? Nope. It's best just to find Laura as quickly as possible and let him get on with his life. That's it. That's what's best. Where is he? There're things to do."

"Lauryn, just let everything—"

"I hardly know him!" Lauryn interrupted. "I've known him a few months, most of which—nearly all of which, except for a space of days—I've never even been with him!" Lauryn shook her head. "I'm insane. That's it. It's as simple as that. I've lost my mind."

The Captain chuckled again. "Well, I can see that anything I say when you're like this will mean absolutely nothing. So what do you say to a game of cards while you're waiting?"

Lauryn smiled and shook her head as she looked at her good friend. "You're no help at all."

"I know," he said, smiling.

Desperately, Lauryn tried to change the subject. "Did you see my roses this mornin'?" she asked. "I think they'll be quite lovely this year."

The Captain chuckled and didn't even have a chance to respond before his young friend began to ramble on once more.

"It's getting dark out! Nobody can read tombstones in the dark! Where are they? For Pete's sake, you'd think…" She stopped talking when she heard a knock on her bedroom door and simultaneously watched the Captain vanish.

"Who is it?" she asked. She knew it wasn't Patrick because he didn't even know what knocking was. He'd simply barge headlong into any room regardless of who might be changing clothes, bathing, or trying to find a moment's rest.

"It's me," came Brant's voice from the other side of the door. Lauryn's heart leapt in her chest at the knowledge that he had returned and was so close.

"Come in," she called before she could think to do otherwise.

Brant opened the door to Lauryn's bedroom and was immediately drenched with the sensation of walking into a dream. The evening light through the open windows and the gentle glow of the lamplight from one corner of the room, coupled with the flickering flames of numerous candles placed hither and thither, emphasized perfectly the impression of romantic femininity. Of sweet relaxation and haven.

Brant smiled, amused as Lauryn frantically tried to bind her mass of nutmeg locks into a tidy braid at the back of her head. She stood there enchantingly barefoot in her white dress, flustered and blushing as he looked at her. He smiled as he more thoroughly surveyed her bedroom. It was completely *Lauryn*.

The bed was small, covered in cozy handmade quilts, ruffled throw pillows, and a pair of stockings. It beckoned to him with an unusually inviting appearance. There was a simple wood chair next to it on which had been placed a doily and a large crystal bowl. The bowl was filled with water, numerous varieties of violets dreamily floating therein. Every imaginable shade of purple and lavender was represented in the tiny flowers. A few yellow blossoms splashed reflections of captured sunshine here and there. Brant noted that throughout the room were other small and large glass bowls all filled with water and a profusion of violets or small floating candles aflame. The room was small enough that the perfume of the tiny flowers was discernable if he breathed deeply.

There were framed photographs on the chest of drawers, another set or two of stockings draped haphazardly over a trunk in one corner. Books were stacked in another corner of the room, next to a bookshelf, oddly enough.

Brant smiled at Lauryn, again thinking, *This girl's a master seductress, and she's not even aware of it*, for he had an incredibly strong desire to lunge forward and...

"Are y'all back then?" Lauryn asked as she finished braiding her hair.

"Yeah," he affirmed. "And...and your mother is ready to serve dinner. She sent me up to get you," he said to her as he stepped into her bedroom and looked around curiously.

Lauryn was uncomfortable having him in her room. He'd been there once before, of course, but he'd been unable to see then. She rolled her eyes, irritated with herself as she remembered she'd tossed her stockings onto her bed instead of tucking them away properly.

"So this is your den of privacy," Brant remarked as he walked to the chest of drawers and looked at the framed photographs placed on top of it.

"Um...um...yes," was all she could say.

"I like it," he chuckled as he went to the pile of books next to her bookshelf. He looked at her with an amused grin. She immediately went to where the books lay opening to reveal the contents to him.

"I'm not as sloppy as you're thinkin'," she explained as she showed him the pressed violets, leaves, and tiny daffodils between the pages. "I like pressin' flowers." She peeled one of the tiny, paper-thin blossoms from its page and handed it to him. He accepted, twirling it between his thumb and forefinger as he looked at it.

"What do you do with them after you smash them?" he asked.

Lauryn shrugged. "Keep them," is all she could say.

He smiled, obviously amused by her answer. He stood up, went to her bed, and brazenly plopped down on it, stretching his legs out as he tucked his hands beneath his head.

"Ah," he sighed. "I like this bed. Very comfortable. And all the candles and floating flowers." He looked at her and winked. "I'd say you're quite the romantic, Miss Lauryn."

"A person's bedroom should be their haven. A place of relaxation and reflection…of retreat." Why did she feel so compelled to explain the appearance of her room to him? She had a nice room! She knew it. What did it matter if he thought it silly, the candles and flowers? She adored it.

"I guess I'm more like that about the barn," he mumbled. "Well…until I saw this room, that is." He turned his head to look at her and smiled. "I like it in here. It makes you want to…to stay."

Lauryn smiled back at him, pleased with the sincerity of his compliment. "Thank you."

"In fact, I think we should sit up at night talking in your room from now on instead of in my guestroom." His suggestion came as a complete surprise—a wonderful, dreamy, romantic, and tantalizing surprise!

"All right," she agreed with a delighted giggle.

"In fact," he continued. "After dinner—or at least before we go to bed—I think we should sit down and write some things. You know…put it all on paper. Sometimes when you can sit and actually look at the information you need, things jump out at you that normally wouldn't."

It was a good observation—a really good suggestion of something to do that might help their minds organize what they knew. "That's a perfect idea. It will help. It will help me if for no other reason than I've forgotten all the reasons that certain places or things aren't relevant."

"Exactly," he agreed. "But for now," he said, reaching out and taking her hand. He pulled her even closer to where he lay on the bed. "For now we better get downstairs to dinner. Aunt Felicity has had grand adventures in gardening today, and she'll want to tell us all about them."

Lauryn smiled. Her hand, held in his, was warm and tingling. His touch was like magic the way it caused her to burn with…yes, it was desire she was feeling. A desire to be even closer to him. To be in his arms.

"And your brother and Mindy and the baby are here too," Brant added as he rose from the bed, still holding her hand. "Uncle Johnny has already confiscated Junie from her parents. They'll be lucky to ever get her back."

Lauryn smiled, lighthearted and in awe that he still held her hand to speak. He reached up and wound his finger tightly in a strand of hair that she'd missed securing when she quickly braided it as he'd entered. He tugged on it teasingly. Turning and still holding her hand, he led her from the room.

"Come along, sugar," he chuckled. "Your mother will think I've succumbed to your charms and have compromised your good name."

His flirting with her caused Lauryn to shiver. The hand he held tingled. *This is dangerous*, she thought. He was distracting her. No. He was owning her, body, mind, and emotion! But she was enjoying it all too much to resist it. She let herself enjoy being led downstairs to dinner, his hand strong and capable as it clutched hers firmly.

When they entered the dining room, everyone else was seated. Mother and Nana sat together. Sean was at the head of the table, Mindy at his side and next to Aunt Felicity. Uncle Johnny and Patrick sat across from them. Junie was happily propped on Uncle Johnny's knee.

"Well, for Pete's sake, children," Georgia scolded playfully. "We've all been waiting on you."

"Sorry, Mama," Lauryn began. Brant had dropped her hand a moment before and now stood behind her chair, ready to seat her.

"You know how Lauryn is, Mama," Sean began. "She's up there in that flower-shrine she calls a room, and it's like pullin' hen's teeth to get her out. Isn't that right, Brant?"

Lauryn was vexed. She wasn't in the mood for Sean's teasing. She wanted to bask in the residual sensation of Brant's touch. She didn't feel like bantering with Sean.

"Actually," Brant said, "she had to kick me out of there. You'll have to go up, Aunt Felicity. Lauryn's a flower smasher just like you."

Gratefully Lauryn smiled at Brant as he sat down next to her. She'd been about to argue with Sean, angry that he would try to embarrass her in front of company. Brant rescued her from the need by complimenting her room when Sean could only make fun.

"I like Lauryn's room too," Patrick piped up. "You'll just have to get her to read you a story up there, Mr. Brant," he urged. "Stories are always, always better when she reads 'em in her room.'"

"I've no doubt," Brant chuckled.

"What do you do with all the flowers you press, sweet thing?" Aunt Felicity asked.

"I…I…" Lauryn stammered.

"She keeps them," Brant answered with an amused smile.

"Me too!" Aunt Felicity exclaimed. "Aren't we just two peas, angel?"

Lauryn smiled and nodded. She already adored Brant's Aunt Felicity and Uncle Johnny. Aunt Felicity had an insight that she admired and appreciated. Uncle Johnny was the kind of old tease her grandfather had been. It was a treat having them at Connemara.

Everyone at the table shared a pleasant dinner and retired to the parlor with very full stomachs, looking forward to traditional, evening conversation. Uncle Johnny had amused himself with Patrick and Junie nearly the entire dinner hour. Now the two children sat at his feet, and he watched them play, a perpetual smile on his face.

The subjects of conversation were the usual after-dinner kind—the war, the flu, the weather, the economy, the local gardens and babies, depending on which gender had the floor at any given moment. Lauryn sat listening and trying not to look at Brant every two seconds. Each time she did try to nonchalantly catch sight of him, he would be looking at her, smiling knowingly. It was quite unnerving.

Then, in the short space of one moment, Lauryn's happy world screeched to a sudden and uncomfortable halt. Sean decided to be the aggravating big brother.

"So, Brant," he began, "did Lauryn ever tell you about the time she and Penny got caught skinny-dippin' out at the old millpond?"

"Sean Kensington!" Georgia scolded immediately. She was too late, and Sean was bent on humiliating his little sister.

"Well, not that I can remember," Brant admitted, smiling and winking at Lauryn.

"Sean," Lauryn warned, "don't you dare do it."

"Oh, go on, Sean," Uncle Johnny urged. "Do it." Lauryn reconsidered for a moment her opinion of Uncle Johnny.

"Well," Sean began, "how old were you two, Lauryn?"

Lauryn glared at him and tried to halt the hot sting of tears rising in her throat.

"About fifteen? Just a few years back, right?"

"Sean…" Georgia tried to warn again.

But he was dauntless. "So Lauryn and Penny decide they need to go swimmin' one night. They'd been in town and didn't have their bathin' suits with them. But they *did* have their birthday suits along. Wasn't it old Mr. Jackson himself that warned the two of you that the entire population of the town was on its way to go canoein'?"

Lauryn stood up, angry, hurt, and completely humiliated. "We were entirely modest, Sean!" she shrieked at him.

"Modest? You were buck naked!" he laughed.

"We were not, and you know it! The only thing we took off was our shoes, stockin's, and dresses!"

"What else was there to take off, Lauryn?" he teased.

"Plenty!" Lauryn breathed The tears were brimming in her eyes, but she was determined not to let everyone see her cry. The incident at the millpond had been very embarrassing. Mr. Jackson had indeed called to Penny and Lauryn as they swam, warning them that several couples were on their way from town to go canoeing. The girls, though dressed in their underthings, were still quite mortified to have to wade out of the pond and allow Mr. Jackson to hand them their dresses. Someday Lauryn knew she would laugh at the memory. But not yet. It was still too fresh.

So with a polite, "Excuse me," she left the parlor and fled the house to the back gardens. Neither she nor Brant, who followed immediately, heard Sean's mother scold him. They didn't hear Sean laugh and tell his mother that someone in the family had to give those two some dramatics in order to let them have some privacy.

The night was warm and fragrant. The cricket's song and other bug noises created a soothing hum to accompany the sweet evening breezes. Still, Lauryn let her tears fall freely as she reached out and caressed the soft yellow petals of one of her early roses. She loved her roses, for they were hers. She'd planted them the year she was thirteen, and she'd nurtured them lovingly ever since. Her mother had insisted she plant something after she'd torn up a place in the gardens one year during her mad, frantic search for Laura's remains. Lauryn had chosen roses, yellow ones. She'd worked so hard that year and years since to make them flourish, and they would be beautiful again this year. Already they were blooming and fragrant.

"How can Sean be such a beast?" she mused aloud.

"It's the nature of brothers the world over," Brant answered from behind her.

Lauryn jumped and turned to face him, angrily wiping the tears from her cheeks—from insult to injury! Now, not only did he know about one of her deepest, darkest, and most embarrassing escapades, he had also caught her red-faced and crying like a child in the rose garden.

"Don't let him bother you so much, Lauryn," he counseled. "He's just teasing you."

"Well, some things take a while to get over," she mumbled.

Brant smiled. "Tell me the story—your version—why don't you," he suggested.

Lauryn shook her head and blushed.

"It'll make you feel better. I promise." His face was kind and concerned. She almost felt guilty, for she could see he felt bad, as if it were his fault she was feeling so attacked.

"It's true," she confessed, "what he said. Penny and I...we were hot. We'd been in town working in old Mrs. Robertson's gardens all day. We were dusty and hot and tired. When we passed the millpond...well, it was dark out, and the pond looked so cool and invitin', and so we..."

"Went skinny-dipping," he finished for her.

"But not really!" she insisted frantically. "We were still dressed. We had on our camisoles and our...our other underwear. It's just that...well, they're white and all. So, when we got out of the water..."

"Modesty was thrown to the wind?" he finished for her, dramatically.

"Yes," she admitted. Then sighing relievedly, she added, "I've always been so thankful to Mr. Jackson...that it was him that found us and helped us get dressed before everyone arrived. Besides, his sight isn't so wonderful anymore, and it was dark...so I've always lived in hope that...that..."

"He didn't get a really good look at you?"

Lauryn smiled. "Yes, exactly."

"Can I ask you something?" Brant inquired.

Lauryn's heart began to beat nervously. Did he want, perhaps, more details of that embarrassing moment in Lauryn's life?

"I suppose," she stammered.

"Why were you so horrified that Sean told us that story?" His question was simple but very unexpected.

"Because...because...it's not the most flatterin' thing to tell. Not the wisest thing I've ever done either. I don't want you to think...I don't want your family to think that..."

"That what?" he asked in low voice as he took a step closer to her. He was so close to her now that she had to tip her head back and look straight up in order to see his face and not be looking directly at his chest.

"That I'm an absolutely ridiculous little girl who is always and forever in a mess," she confessed. "The first glimpse your aunt and uncle had of me was when I was up a tree like a nine-year-old boy! I had a tear in the seat of my skirt, for pity's sake!"

Brant smiled, obviously amused at the memory. "That was my first glimpse of you too."

Again, the knife of humiliation twisted in Lauryn's stomach. It was true! She'd momentarily forgotten that Brant had never truly seen her before that moment. Lauryn felt her shoulders sag, felt her heart seem to fall with a thud into her stomach.

But Brant took her shoulders between his strong hands and told her, "And it was more perfect than I could ever have imagined." He chuckled for a moment. Then he brushed a strand of hair from her face and asked, "Are these your roses?"

Lauryn smiled. How chivalrous of him—first, to follow her out of the house, regardless of what anyone else in there might think, then to encourage her so, and finally to change the subject like a true gentleman would.

"Yes," she answered. "Mama made me plant them one day after I'd torn up the garden diggin' for..." she began.

"Laura's bones?" he finished for her. She kept forgetting that Brant seemed to have no trouble whatsoever discussing the fact that Laura's body was what they were looking for.

"Exactly," she giggled.

"All yellow, like this one?" he asked.

"Yes. I like yellow ones best."

"You'll need to show these to Aunt Felicity. You're beginning to understand what a love of flowers she has, aren't you?" he asked, winking at her.

"I believe I am," she admitted.

"All right then," he said with a heavy sigh. "I think it's time to make our list. My time here is short, and we've got a lot to figure out."

Lauryn's lighter mood darkened at his mentioning that he would be leaving soon. But he was right. Their time was short.

"Well, let's get busy." she agreed, plucking the lovely yellow rose blossom from its branch. She held the blossom out to him. "Thank you."

"For what?" he asked.

"For…for…" She couldn't just confess that it meant the world to her that he'd followed her from the parlor. "For helpin' me. With everythin'."

Brant accepted the rose and smelled it briefly before tucking its stem in his shirt pocket. "Any time, sugar," he chuckled. He placed his hand caressively on her cheek and smiled. Lauryn noticed the way his mouth twitched at one corner, almost indiscernibly. "Any time." When he bent and placed a soft, rather lingering kiss on her cheek near the corner of her mouth, Lauryn thought she might truly faint! It was exhilarating to receive such affection from him, and her cheek burned warm and delighted.

He took her hand then and began leading her back toward the house. "I think we should make our list in the attic," he suggested. Lauryn was a bit disappointed that he'd changed his mind from their having their discussion in the privacy of her room. "That way we'll have it right there at hand while you're reading the Captain's letters."

"Me?" she exclaimed. "I don't want to read them!"

"Well, I don't either," he chuckled as they approached the back porch of Connemara House. "Besides," he continued playfully, "I'm a guest. It would be bad manners to force me to read them. And anyhow…you know the Captain better than me."

"But you're a man," Lauryn reminded him. "You'd have more insight into his feelin's and such."

"Ah," he teased, "but you're a woman. You'll read a woman's letters from her lover with much more heart."

As they climbed the stairs to the attic, after having retrieved paper and pen from Lauryn's room, their playful banter continued, Lauryn saying, "But if you read them, I'll be able to listen as she would've listened to him speak and—"

"But she didn't hear him speak if she were reading a letter. So, you see, *you* need to read them." He still smiled devilishly as he pushed open the attic door and stepped aside for her to enter.

In the end, Lauryn would win out, and Brant would begin to read the letters. As they sat in the attic, night having fallen fully, Lauryn listened intently as he read. The deep intonation of his voice was intoxicating. Lauryn reached back and tugged at the ribbon that held her braid, releasing her hair and lying down on the floor in front of Brant, propped herself up on one elbow as she looked at him, and listened.

"*The fighting is brutal, my beauty,*" he read.

> *The dying men, the blood, the stench of rotting flesh. Sometimes at night—even when there's a breeze that blows the smell away—even then the stink of war seems to be branded into my nostrils, and I can't smell anything else. I try to imagine Connemara...you sitting out in the gazebo under the wisteria blossoms. I try and try to remember how it smelled, that beloved fragrance of your favorite bloom. But it eludes me, darling. Still, I can see you there...see your beauty. So at least my mind has beautiful visions to dream of.*

Brant paused in his reading, and Lauryn fancied there was excess moisture in his eyes. He blinked several times and then continued.

> *Tom Harper was lost today. They didn't get his leg sawed off fast enough, and he bled to death. I'll miss him sorely. It was such a great comfort having him here, a hometown boy, someone with such a close connection to the family, estranged though it was.*
>
> *Write to me, my angel. Let me feel your love for me through your words. I need you so much, every minute of every day. I fight for you, even if I am on the wrong side*

in some eyes. I'm fighting for you—to end this hell so that we can be together again. I'll try not to write such dreadful things next time. But it's hard to think of anything else to tell you. All that there is now is death, blood, mud, fire. Just remember that I love you, my Sweet Lauralynn. Soon we'll be together again. I'll hold you in my arms and let the sweet scent of your hair fill my lungs…let it make my mind forget the stench of war. I'll let the taste of your kiss free me from the bitterness of losing friends daily.

> *I love you,*
> *Brand*

Lauryn did not miss the deep understanding written across Brant's face. The Captain's description of the horrors of war were, no doubt, too fresh in Brand's own mind to be at all comfortable.

"It's hotter than hell up here," he swore under his breath as he began to unbutton his shirt. "Sorry," he apologized halfheartedly.

Lauryn didn't say anything. It wasn't hot in the attic at all. The evening breeze blew through the open window, giving a very cool environment to them. No doubt his blood was boiling because of the residue of war still in his mind.

"Let's stop for a while," Lauryn suggested. "Let's look at the list."

Brant sighed heavily, a frown still puckering his brow. He nodded rather indifferently, and Lauryn began to look over the list.

"All right. What do we know?" she began.

"We know that it's hotter than hell up here," he grumbled, taking off his shirt and rather angrily throwing it down on the floor. "Sorry."

Lauryn smiled, amused yet sympathetic, and continued. "She's not in the house. She's not in the springhouse. She's not in the servants' house. She's not in the cellar or the basement."

"And she ain't out waltzing around with that statue out by the cemetery," Brant spat.

Lauryn smiled, understandingly. "She was still alive the last time Nana and the others saw her. She had a child's teacup with her at some point—"

"Which reminds me," Brant interrupted, "your grandmother said she never saw that tea set again after that day. Does that mean it was looted away by soldiers? But why would soldiers have any interest in baby toys, and why would Laura have one of the cups with her?"

Lauryn shrugged. "I don't know."

"You read for a while," Brant demanded, tossing a packet of letters to Lauryn. He realized then his rude manner and added a sincere, "Please."

"Maybe we should take a rest from this for a while, Brant. After all, it's getting late, and we really haven't learned much."

"It's only midnight, and we've learned plenty. We've learned that the stink of war never changes." He was angry, hurting. But Lauryn did not argue with him. As he stretched out on his side next to her on the floor, Lauryn tried to ignore the thrill that traveled through her at the sight of his shirtlessness. The muscles in his arms and chest had been quite impressive when he'd been at Connemara months before. But it was now obvious that he'd been laboring hard the months he'd been at home, for his body was bigger, his muscles even more defined and impressive.

So clearing her throat and forcing her concentration to the letter in hands, she began to read.

My darling Laura,

I'm so sorry that I can't be with you just now. The turmoil at Connemara over this incident must be incredible. Just know that all will be well. Love continues even when someone is lost, and you will always have that.

"Who was lost?" Brant asked, yawning.

Lauryn shrugged. "This letter isn't dated, but I'm sure it must be her brother Ethan. He was killed in the war."

"That's right," Brant mumbled as he rolled over onto his back and tucked his hands beneath his head.

"And you'll always have me, my love. Forever," Lauryn continued. But when she looked to Brant, it was apparent that he was already sleeping. She smiled, thinking it amusing that he, who had just told her that midnight wasn't late, was unable to remain conscious a moment longer. But she would continue reading anyway. For one thing, it was far too wonderful to have him so near to her, and for another, maybe it would be better on his war-tortured mind for her to read through the Captain's experiences on her own. That way she could search for clues without having Brant further disturbed by his own memories.

She continued reading aloud, even though she was alone in her consciousness.

War is still war, my love. But I'm determined to write of something else. It cannot be good for you to only know of the terrible things I see. So…there's a young man here, my own age, and he's quite good at playing the guitar. His voice is fairly on key as well, and he's memorized 'Sweet Lauralynn' without even realizing how close he is to its root. He does a fair job of rendering it, and I tell him so. I've told him your name, though nothing else, and he says that when the war is over, he'd love to come and sing it to you in person. I carry your image, of course, and he said you were exactly the kind of woman that must have inspired the songwriter. How is that for irony, my sweet?

Lauryn's eyelids were feeling heavy, and she couldn't stifle the yawn that rose in her throat. One moment's rest of her eyes surely wouldn't hurt.

❧

Brant lay stretched out on the attic floor, his head propped up on one elbow as he watched her. Lauryn was next to him, sound asleep. He had awakened to find Lauryn asleep, her hair spread beneath her head like a blanket of soft, spun spice. In her hand, which lay at the side of her head, she still loosely held one of the Captain's letters. Her face was soft and at peace, the slightest of sweet smiles on her lips.

I am in so much trouble, he thought as he reached out and took some of her hair in his hand and raised it to his face, drinking in the essence of its natural perfume. The situation was inappropriate at best. If someone were to find them, he only half-clothed, she lying there, hair free, barefoot, and several of the buttons of her blouse undone—well, Georgia Kensington would have no choice but to throw him out on his behind.

And as far as his own self-control was concerned—he reached over and picked up his shirt, putting it on angrily and starting to button it. But again he was distracted by the way she bewitched him completely. He knew the feel of her lips. He'd kissed her twice before. Now his craving wanted the taste of her kiss again. There was not a doubt in his mind that it would be pure nectar, sweet and perfect.

He shook his head and rubbed at his temples. Time to retreat, he knew. But she stirred and sighed in her sleep, and the sigh left her lips parted ever so slightly. It was too much, even for a man of Brant Masterson's impeccable character. He felt the corner of his mouth twitch ever so slightly as he studied her. Carefully, he leaned over her, placing one of his powerful hands on either side of her small, curvaceous form. He shouldn't do it, and he knew it, but she'd bewitched him. Even in her sleep, she'd managed to bewitch him, and ever so carefully he bent and...didn't kiss her the way he wanted to, for he knew that the pressure from that kiss would wake her. Slowly, very carefully, he bent and slowly caressed her parted lips with the softest of his kisses. It was far more ambrosiatic—the taste of her—than he'd even imagined, and he was surprised and pleased when she smiled in her sleep, sighed heavily, and moistened her lips as if she'd tasted something delightful herself.

One more inhalation of her, the scent and feel of her hair, and he rose to his feet. He was weak and in a dangerous state of mind. He would leave her without even the courtesy of waking her. He feared if he lingered, even for a moment—if he woke her and she looked at him with that dreamy expression she sometimes had in his presence—he was an honorable man, but this fairy tempted him too deeply. Mustering every strength and resolve in self-control he could, Brant left the attic and retired, if somewhat fitfully, to his own room.

CHAPTER ELEVEN

Lauryn inhaled deeply of the fresh spring air sweetly scented with the perfume of every colorful flower imaginable that grew along Main Street. She was returning from posting a letter in town for her mother.

Brant and his aunt and uncle had been at Connemara for nearly a week. During that week, Lauryn and Brant spent days upon days searching, reading the Captain's letters to Laura, and talking. Amazingly enough, even with the seriousness of their search always looming, they did find time to laugh, go for walks, and talk of other things.

Still, Lauryn went to bed every night nearly sick to her stomach with anxiety, wondering how long she would have Brant. She knew he had agreed to stay at least until the McGoverns' party on Saturday. But that was only a few more days. Then what? He had to return home eventually, and she dreaded the day he would tell her he was going.

Brant went to play stickball with Patrick that morning, and Lauryn's mother, sensing her unrest, sent her to town to post a letter. She walked toward home now, along Main, admiring the loveliness of spring. It did give a body hope—hope in mystery solving, hope in love.

"The little rat," Lauryn mumbled as she saw Sean's automobile parked in the street in front of Connemara House. She was still furious with him for embarrassing her that evening at dinner nearly a week ago. She'd never forgive him for telling the skinny-dipping story to Brant. But she would exact her revenge, teach him not to do the like ever again.

Sean treasured that blasted auto of his. Even as Lauryn stood at his feet, listening to his carefree whistle as he worked, she knew how intent he was on making sure it was in perfect working order.

"Typical," she mumbled, putting her hands on her hips and looking down at his legs protruding from beneath the auto. "Always tinkerin' around with that blasted contraption," she muttered.

Sean hadn't heard her approach, she knew, for he did not pause in either his whistling or his tinkering. From just above the waist, Sean was wedged under the auto, and Lauryn could hear the familiar sounds of metal on metal as he fiddled with whatever gadget in the contraption that was giving him grief that day.

And then, oh, impish girl that she was, she felt an amused smile spread across her face as the perfect idea took shape in her clever mind. Yes! A brilliant idea! What a genius of prank she could be when given the opportunity. There he lay, completely unaware of her presence. His shoes, socks, and shirt lay in a heap nearby. There he was, his hands busy, his mind distracted, and in a position that left him unable to escape. He had made it too easy! He was losing his edge. Lauryn knew that once Sean began fiddling on his auto, he was oblivious to all else around him, completely vulnerable and unsuspecting.

Propriety could hang now, and he would catch what he more than deserved. It was one thing to tease her mercilessly in front of her family, but to do it in front of Brant and his family! Sean would pay. And Lauryn didn't care about the lecture that would no doubt follow from her mother—the one she'd heard a million times growing up when she and Sean were younger, the one about turning the other cheek and not letting Sean's teasing get under her skin. Poppycock! He'd really done it this time, and the perfect opportunity at vengeance was presenting itself at that very moment.

"You rat," Lauryn, mumbled, her smile broadening as she reached down and swiftly unfastened the waist of his trousers. She heard a thud and impishly delighted in realizing that Sean, startled and trying to sit up, had conked his head hard on that blasted machine. Then quick as a mouse, Lauryn stripped his trousers down as he squirmed and hollered. She nimbly yanked them completely from his body and then, trousers in hand, broke into a dead run for the house.

"That'll teach you, you little weasel!" she shouted over her shoulder as she ran, waving the trousers over her head like a victory banner. What a wit she was! And a proud one at that. It had been no easy task to strip Sean of his trousers quickly enough to get away before he could maneuver out from under the auto.

Racing across the front porch and into the entryway, she giggled as she saw her mother enter from the parlor.

"What is going on?" her mother demanded.

"Now, Mama," Lauryn began, knowing that she was about to receive a tongue-lashing, "he deserves it! He always does. You saw what he did to me the other night. Fair is fair, Mama. If Sean is gonna dish it out, then he's gonna have to take it!"

"Take what?" Sean asked as he stepped into the entryway from the parlor.

Lauryn's jaw dropped nearly to the floor. There he stood. Sean! Completely dressed, trousers and all!

"You didn't mess around with my auto, did you?" he asked, looking past his mother and out the window to the street.

"What on earth, Lauryn? And where did you get those trousers?" Georgia asked.

"Well, they're Sean's," Lauryn gasped.

"What's all the commotion?" Mindy asked as she too entered, Junie propped on one hip.

"Well, it looks like Lauryn has stripped someone of his trousers," Sean chuckled.

"Lauryn! What have you done?" Georgia shrieked.

"It was Sean! Out there workin' on his danged machine," she tried to explain. "I...I thought..."

Sean erupted into laughter, and at that very moment, the front door swung open, revealing Brant Masterson, trouserless. Already there was a bruise visible on his forehead, and as he tromped in wearing nothing but a scowl and his underwear, Lauryn thought she might indeed drop dead where she stood.

"Oh, Brant!" Georgia exclaimed in a horrified whisper.

Mindy looked the man up and down, smiling in delight, and Sean doubled over, clutching his stomach as his body was racked with overwhelming, delirious laughter.

Rubbing the goose egg on his forehead, Brant simply held out his hand to Lauryn and gestured for her to return the stolen trousers. Slowly, since she was greatly distracted by the sight of him in only his underwear, she held the trousers out to him. Everyone stood silent, save Sean, who still roared with laughter, enjoying his mirth.

"Lauryn, sugar," Brant mumbled, "the next time you want to get a good look at my manly shape…" He stepped into his trousers and fastened them up quickly. "Simply ask. It would save us both a great deal of…pain." He rubbed his forehead again, wincing as he did so.

"I thought…I thought…" Lauryn stammered.

"Well, now that the entire neighborhood has seen nearly all of me…" He frowned at Lauryn, the bump on his head obviously uncomfortable. "Tell me…is it safe to go back out and finish my work?" Lauryn felt the tears of hurt and humiliation welling up in her eyes. "Or is there something else you wanted?"

Shaking her head, Lauryn cast tear-filled eyes to the floor. Her humiliation was great. And yet there was some sort of devilish, secret delight in the knowledge of what she had done, and in the vision of Brant Masterson in his underwear. It was—yes—almost funny to her. But the embarrassment was stronger and won out.

"Wait 'til I tell the boys this one!" Sean laughed, rising to his feet again. "They won't believe me!"

Simultaneously Mindy and Lauryn's mother scolded, "Sean Kensington!"

"You'll do no such thing!" Georgia added. "Why, if such a thing should get around…"

"You yanked his trousers off, Lauryn! Do you realize that? You stripped a man nearly naked!" Sean teased, laughing boisterously again.

The shame was too much. Standing there in front of Brant, whom she'd embarrassed in front of everyone, it was too much. Reaching out, she shoved Sean with all her might, bursting into tears, and ran past them all, out the door, and around the house to the gardens.

She hated him! That Sean Kensington. Oh, he was so infuriating and heartless! When would he ever grow up? And how could she face Brant again? Pulling off his trousers! What had she been thinking? She'd been thinking that it was her devil of a brother under that confounded contraption, and he certainly would've deserved to be found nearly naked out in the middle of the street. But Brant! She wanted to hide forever. How could she ever face him again?

Sitting down hard on the ground near her happy yellow rose bushes, she wiped angrily at the tears on her face. It was too unreal. She'd actually, and publicly, pulled off his pants, right there in broad daylight! And yet the vision of him standing there—hair tousled, arms, chest, and most of his legs undressed for all the world to see—would not be a vision she could easily vanquish from her mind. Nor did she wish to, in all honesty. Still, how could she have done such a thing?

"It was a good prank," Brant admitted, chuckling as he sat down beside her.

Lauryn looked away quickly. Why did he always have to come after her when she was upset? Brant always sought her out. Always! She looked at him then, her heart swelling with the realization that he owned yet another quality that every woman wished for in a man—the quality of ever seeking her out and tending to her feelings when she was upset.

"It was a great idea. And he more than deserved it after teasing you so mercilessly the other night."

"But you didn't," Lauryn breathed, wiping at her tears again.

"Oh…I don't know," he corrected, reaching out and brushing a stray curl of hair from her forehead. "I've done enough terrible things to my own sisters over the years that…well, they'll be delighted with this, I'm sure." She dropped her gaze to the ground. He put a hand under her chin and forced her to look at him again. "Now, don't worry on it. It was funny."

Reaching out in a sort of panic, she took his arm. "I'm so sorry, Brant! I should've thought before I…I never think! I always just charge ahead and—"

"It's fine, Lauryn." He smiled at her then, an amused, rather sly grin. "I've never had a woman yank my trousers off before. I kind of liked it."

She smiled back at him, appreciative of his willingness to forgive her and making it all seem so trivial. He was so handsome, so considerate, and she reached out and put her hand to his cheek.

"You're a very forgivin' man," she told him, humbly.

He smiled. "Well, you're very easy to forgive." He stood and offered his hand to her. "Come on now. Let's go back. Your mother about has lunch ready."

Lauryn frowned. "Sean will be merciless," she told him.

Brant nodded and frowned a moment. Then with a mischievous grin, he suggested, "Well, we'll just have to distract him then, won't we?" And much to Lauryn's delight and astonishment, Brant stripped off his pants once more and flung them over his shoulder. "Come along, sugar. I'm starving."

Lauryn giggled. Taking his hand, she leapt to her feet.

"I ain't embarrassed about my body," Brant boasted dramatically. "Why, Sean can only wish he had the muscles I do, right?"

"Definitely," Lauryn confirmed. Though she hadn't thought it possible, she adored him all the more at that moment. For all the humiliation she'd heaped on him, his concern was for her happiness. His jesting and humor, he knew, were cheering her. Anyhow, he was right! Sean could only wish for such chiseled granite muscle definition as the like borne by Brant.

Lauryn's mother's jaw nearly hit the floor when her daughter walked into the kitchen with a pantsless man. But everyone at Connemara had a good sense of humor, including her mother.

Lauryn enjoyed sitting around the table with her family and Brant's. It was such a delight. The conversation was always interesting and humorous. Aunt Felicity and Uncle Johnny, being the entertaining characters they were, kept everyone amused.

The evening was spent pleasantly as well. Nana and Georgia sat on the front porch talking with Felicity and John while Brant and Lauryn sat in the cool grass below, trying to solve a puzzle that was seeming more and more an impossible challenge.

More often than not that evening, as it was every time Lauryn found herself alone with Brant, the conversation eventually left the subject of poor Laura and turned to other things. It was as if their minds needed escape. As if neither one of them could think clearly about the mystery anymore.

"So Nana asked me to go to New Orleans with her for a few months…and I went," Lauryn explained. Brant had asked her how she ended up spending such a long time in New Orleans. "And then the flu got so bad, and we didn't want to travel…and…" Lauryn paused, watching Patrick chasing fireflies here and there among the bushes.

"It's almost unendurable to lose a parent," Brant mumbled, seeming to have read Lauryn's thoughts. And she had indeed been thinking of her father.

"When my mother passed away," Brant continued, "I…I didn't think I would ever stop crying."

"How old were you?" Lauryn asked, carefully.

"Three."

"Three!" Lauryn gasped. "So young."

"And yet…Laura was only fourteen the first time she met Brandon," Brant reminded her, "and so young when she died. It's not right that such bad things should happen to people when they're so young."

"And I've decided," Lauryn began, "that girls must've looked older back then. Or been prettier. Or somethin'. So many of them married young, and so many of them married older men. I wonder why older men were attracted to younger girls?" Lauryn mused aloud.

"They still are," Brant chuckled.

"They are?" Lauryn asked, innocently looking over to him. Her heart fluttered at the sight of him stretched out in the grass next to her, smiling devilishly as he chewed on a long foxtail.

"Hell yes!" he exclaimed. "Sorry," he apologized then, shaking his head.

Lauryn giggled. It was one of his most adorable imperfections, his swearing. And he didn't swear excessively—not even often. Just on occasion and mostly just about hell. In actuality, Lauryn adored the way he swore and then apologized to her afterward. She secretly hoped he'd never really overcome it.

"It all works out anyway," he continued. "I mean, be honest with me, sugar…aren't girls almost always attracted to older men?"

"Well, I suppose you're right," she admitted.

"I mean, look at me and you. Perfect example."

Lauryn's eyes widened. Had he just implied that they were attracted to one another?

"Oh, don't put on that naive expression, Lauryn. I can admit it. I think you're—"

"I know, I know," Lauryn whined. "You think I'm *cute*." How she hated that he thought of her as merely cute. The word felt like dry straw on her tongue.

"Well, actually," he corrected her, lowering his voice, "I was thinking more…something like…tempting." As Lauryn looked at him, delightfully astonished, he winked, and her heart soared.

"Y'all come on in," Georgia called from just inside the entryway. "The skeeters will eat you alive if you don't."

Brant stood and offered a hand to Lauryn, helping her to her feet.

"We better hit the sack," he sighed. "Tomorrow I want to start again. I want us to write down absolutely everything this time."

But the next day was as fruitless as the one before. As fruitless as the two, three, and four before that. There was nothing, it seemed— simply nothing that pointed Brant or Lauryn to any kind of knowledge they didn't already own.

By that evening, Brant's temper was short, and Lauryn's hopes were nearly exhausted. And that's what she told the Captain.

"We've looked everywhere. Again! We've talked to Nana until I know she's sick to death of us. And I hate burdenin' her," Lauryn told the Captain. "We're missin' somethin'. I just don't know what."

"Read the letters in the trunk again," the Captain suggested. "Maybe there's something in them that you're missing."

"But you weren't even here when…the letters stopped days before she was lost. And they upset Brant so terribly. He doesn't say it, but the description of war…it distracts him from thinkin' of clues." Lauryn shook her head. Ten years of failure were beginning to take their toll on her—ten years of failure and the fact that her feelings for Brant were becoming more and more intense with each passing moment.

"We've missed somethin'," she mumbled again. "I just…I just can't…I'm so tired. I can't think anymore. And when I do think, all I can seem to think about is…" She stopped short, almost having revealed too much.

"Lauryn," the Captain said, sitting on the bed next to her, "it's all right to think about him. It's all right to love him."

"I don't love him," Lauryn nearly shouted. "For Pete's sake, Captain. I hardly even know him. He's a stranger, practically."

The Captain chuckled. "And it's okay to want to spend time with him, talk to him, be with him, help him…more than you want to be with me."

"But I don't. You're my dearest friend. I could never—" she began to argue.

"I have been your friend, angel. But you're all grown up now. You're ready for a different kind of friend…a best friend the way Laura is mine."

Lauryn was silent for a moment, thoughtful.

And the Captain continued, "Before now, our friendship, your desire to help me, was enough for you, wasn't it? But now guilt rises in you every time you're with Brant. You feel like you're betraying me and your promise to me. Lauryn…" He took her shoulders and turned her to face him. "I'm dead, Lauryn. Hadn't you noticed?" He grinned lovingly at her as she smiled back at him. "And I have a best friend of my own. You don't have to worry about me. Remember the reason I'm here, angel. To find my Laura…through you." He paused for a moment and then with tears in his eyes whispered, "I'm strong whenever I'm here with you, Lauryn. But when I'm not, I miss her. I long for her. I ache for her! I miss her so badly…so terribly that my tears could run forever." He caressed her cheek tenderly. "Now, don't try to tell me that you're not akin to me where those feelings are concerned. I know you too well, my peach."

Suddenly, Lauryn threw herself into the Captain's embrace, sobbing bitterly.

"You're right," she cried. "I…I care for him so much more than I should! More than I have a right to! And I do feel guilty for it. You've always, always talked with me and cared for me, listened to my ridiculous prattle. I owe you so much! I…"

"Lauryn, don't pass up your dream for want of helping me. You don't owe me anything. What are you talking about? I owe you everything. You've spent a lifetime trying to help me," he reminded her. "In fact," he mumbled. And then Lauryn tumbled to her bed as he instantly disappeared.

"What?" she whispered. It was so unlike the Captain to leave her in her moment of need. She was confused. What had she said to upset him so?

"Are you all right?" Brant asked a few moments later as he burst into the room, a look of deep concern on his face.

Lauryn looked up to him, wiping furiously at her tears. "What do you mean?"

"The Captain," he began, striding quickly to her, "he said you were upset." He dropped to his knees before her and, reaching up, took her face in his hands. The expression on his face was so sincerely one of worry that Lauryn felt her heart leap for a moment. "What's the matter, Lauryn?" he asked.

Lauryn understood then—something she never quite had before. And she understood why the Captain, for the first time since her eighth birthday when she'd been in the attic and turned to see him, had disappeared when she needed him most: because she didn't need the Captain most anymore. What she needed most, what she wanted more than anything she'd ever wanted in her life, was hunkered down on the floor before her asking what was wrong.

At that very moment, she felt a hand on her back—felt it shove her hard enough that she fell forward, throwing her arms around Brant's neck. When Brant's strong embrace enveloped her instantly, she wasn't angry that the Captain had pushed her into Brant's arms. She was glad. Once again the Captain had not failed her. He'd left her to fetch the one thing she really needed at that moment. She needed Brant. Brant was all she would ever need again.

"What's wrong, sugar?" Brant asked, rising to his feet and pulling Lauryn even more snuggly against him. "You have to tell me."

"I...I...we're never gonna find her, Brant," Lauryn sobbed. It was what she felt to be true. Lauryn wanted to find Laura now more than she ever had before. And she wanted to find her so that Brant would be free—to free herself. She wanted to find her so she could have her own chance of winning the only thing she wanted now. She wanted Brant. Yet it was impossible. If they hadn't found her by now, surely they never would.

"We'll find her," Brant growled. "We will. Together we'll find her." He released his embrace and held her face firmly in his hands as he spoke with determination. "I promise, Lauryn. We'll find her. We'll put them to rest...heal their souls. And our own." He wiped her tears from her cheeks with his thumbs as the corner of his mouth twitched slightly.

Lauryn was warmed by his conviction and smiled at him.

He smiled and hugged her once more. "You need to rest," he whispered. "We're both tired. Our brains are wrung out."

"I know," Lauryn admitted.

"Tomorrow," he began. "Tomorrow we're not searching. We're not thinking about it. We're not feeling guilty. Tomorrow we're escaping. Do you hear me?"

"What do you mean?" she asked.

"Tomorrow…I'll show you. Tomorrow." Then to her great astonishment and intense delight, he kissed her quickly on the lips. "Tomorrow we'll find peace…for a time, at least. Now get to bed. Sleep well." He left her rather abruptly considering he'd been holding her only a moment before—left her there in her room with every kind of emotion, good and bad, running through her veins—left her with the sweet tingle of his kiss still upon her lips. Left her wondering what the next day would bring.

ও

The millpond was calm and abandoned that next day when Lauryn and Brant arrived. Actually, the millpond was really a small lake, but everyone in Franklin called it the millpond. It was a lake that, in actuality, did have a mill on one side. There was a small, secluded island in the middle of it and plenty of room for canoeing. It was a popular retreat during the summer. The bees provided a comforting hum in the nearby dogwoods, and the sun was brilliant. A refreshing breeze cooled the morning.

When Lauryn came down for breakfast that morning, it was to find Brant explaining to Georgia that he was taking Lauryn out for a picnic and they would be gone the entire day. Being that everyone there, including his aunt and uncle, knew about the mystery of Laura and how hard Brant and Lauryn were searching, he told them their minds were tired, his and Lauryn's. They needed an escape, and he had planned it in the form of a picnic.

No one argued. In fact, Aunt Felicity giggled, "How divinely romantic!"

Lauryn's mother agreed. "You two will fare far better in your search if you take some time to clear your minds of it all."

And so it was that Lauryn found herself standing next to Brant on the millpond dock that morning. "I figure we'll paddle over to the other side and have lunch—completely free of any worry. Nothing over there will tax our minds," he told her.

Mr. Jackson, the man who took care of the dock and canoes, approached them. Lauryn had always, always loved Mr. Jackson—even more so since he'd helped her and Penny escape the embarrassment of being caught half-naked that night a few years back. He'd been a slave before freedom came to the black man and must've been, she guessed, near to ninety. His smile indicated he only had about seven teeth left in his entire head, and his hair was as white as the snow. His eyes twinkled with mirth whenever he talked to anyone, and he was the kindest fellow in Franklin, Tennessee. Lauryn was certain of it.

"Well, good mornin' to you, Miss Lauryn!" Mr. Jackson greeted as he neared them. "And to you, sir," he said to Brant, offering a hand.

"Good morning," Brant returned, shaking Mr. Jackson's hand firmly.

"What can I be doin' for y'all this fine mornin'?" the old man asked.

"Well," Brant began, "we're looking for an escape today, sir."

Mr. Jackson chuckled and slapped his leg. "I bet you is, sir! I bet you is!" He winked at Lauryn. "A bit a privacy?'"

"That would be exactly it," Brant agreed, chuckling.

"Well, I do believe I can help you with that, sir—as long as you promise me that you'll do right by our Miss Lauryn here."

"Oh, I promise, sir," Brant assured him.

"You only be kissin' her where nobody can see now. Hear me?" Mr. Jackson chuckled.

Lauryn gasped. Brant simply smiled and said, "I'll make sure of it."

"Well, this canoe over here is the best I got—most likely not to dump you in the water." The old man hobbled over to a canoe lying nearby on the shore. "I'll help you shove off too."

Brant set the picnic basket in the canoe and helped Lauryn in as he and Mr. Jackson sent it floating into the pond.

"Thank you, sir," Brant said.

"You sure is welcome, mister. And you take your time today. Ain't no hurry on my side." Mr. Jackson laughed and turned away, breaking into song to amuse himself.

"Now that man I like," Brant stated as he began to paddle into the lake.

"Me too." Lauryn was still pinching herself to make certain she was awake and not merely dreaming she was there with Brant and doing something other than searching for Laura. "Ever since I was a little girl, I've loved him. I used to come down here and sit on the dock and talk to him about the old days. He's a wise man. And he knows a lot." She paused and added, "He knew Laura and—"

Brant interrupted her. "That's nice, and we'll talk about it another day. Remember?"

Lauryn bit her lip in delight. Could it be that Brant truly wanted to spend the day with her? Alone and without any talk about Laura?

"All right," she agreed and looked up into the brilliant blue and clear skies. "I love days like this," she mused. She'd pulled her hair into a loose bun at the back of her head that day but secretly wished she could've worn it down. It was the kind of day she felt like being free. Wearing her hair up always restricted her confidence, her freedom of spirit. Still, as she watched Brant paddle the canoe out into the lake, she was glad she'd pinned it up. Otherwise, she might feel too free-willed and begin telling him her deepest secrets or some such thing that she might later regret.

"Penny's party is tomorrow, isn't it?" he asked, making casual conversation.

"Yes. I'm certain it will be a pleasant time. The McGoverns are wonderful people. And you'll get to meet Penny's parents. They're very sweet and hospitable—the ideal hosts for such an occasion."

"I bet," he said. "Penny's a sweet thing. And Jeffrey seems fairly nice."

"I adore Penny. I don't know what I would've done in my life without her," Lauryn sighed.

"Is Penny the one who introduced you to Henry?" he teased. "Or was it the other way around?" His smile was completely teasing—nothing malicious.

Lauryn giggled. "The other way around."

"Poor Henry," Brant sighed then, quite dramatically.

"What do you mean?"

"Well, someday you girls will leave him for other men, and he'll be abandoned—all alone." Brant was smiling.

But Lauryn's brow puckered. Henry? Alone? It seemed a rather heartless end to allow.

Brant obviously read her thoughts, for he added, "He's a statue, Lauryn. He's not real."

"He was very real to me for a good many years," Lauryn argued.

"Well, then you'll have to have another statue done—a woman…someone to keep him company," he suggested.

"That's a fine idea!" Lauryn exclaimed. Then she pretended to be genuinely overly concerned and said, "Goodness knows I could never be happy knowin' Henry was alone and forgotten."

Brant shook his head, amused, and paddled on.

After reaching the island in the middle of the lake and walking around it once, they spread the picnic blanket on the farthest bank and enjoyed their lunch of cold chicken, fruit, and muffins, talking all the while. Not once did Brant allow the conversation to turn to the Captain or Laura. He kept his word, which delighted Lauryn.

"It's nice here—peaceful, relaxing," Brant commented while he watched unique, snowy-white peacocks wandering about and eating muffin crumbs that he tossed to them.

"It is. I've always liked this place best in the spring—the peacocks and songbirds, the way the blossoms rain down from the dogwoods," Lauryn pointed out. It was a beautiful scene. Ten or twenty dogwoods, some with white blossoms, some with bright pink ones, surrounded the bank on which they picnicked. Each time the breeze sighed, scores of pink and white petals showered Brant and Lauryn with soft, fragrant petals, which lay on the grass, creating a carpet of pastel spring.

"There's so much that smells good here," Brant mentioned. He looked at her and winked. "A lot of stuff tastes good here too."

Lauryn wasn't certain what he was implying. But she said, "I'll let Mama know you liked the chicken when we get back," assuming he meant lunch had been delicious.

"You do that," he chuckled. Apparently she'd missed his meaning completely. He stood and strode to the water's edge, tossing a few muffin crumbs to the ducks and swans that frequented the millpond.

Lauryn looked away from him to two squirrels scampering among the trees. They were playful little creatures. They drove her mother nearly insane teasing the cat, but Lauryn always enjoyed watching their games.

"It's truly beautiful here, isn't it?" Brant mumbled. Instantly, Lauryn sensed a change in him. His voice was low and somewhat…was it anger she sensed?

"Yes," she affirmed. He appeared to be somewhat preoccupied with the beauties of nature. Perhaps it was an attribute inherited from his Aunt Felicity.

Then suddenly, without any warning, he stripped off his shirt and, slamming it to the ground, growled, "It's hotter than…it's hot out here." Dropping to his knees and leaning over toward the water's edge, he splashed the cool water on his face.

Lauryn found she was trembling. "Are…are you all right?" she asked. Something had changed suddenly. What had it been? Had she said something to upset him? He'd been commenting on the beauty of nature, on the delicious lunch they'd shared.

Again Brant doused his face with water. He seemed very disturbed! The muscles in his back and arms were tense as he paused and looked up to the clear blue of the sky. "It looks different to me now. It looks bluer than it did before. And still…it's the same sky, the same sun that lit the days over the trenches." He closed his eyes and inhaled deeply. "Same air I'm breathing in…taking into my body. Only…it's filled with the perfume of flowers and living things instead of thick with the stink of disease, mud, and death."

Lauryn said nothing. There were no words. She had suspected, all along, that their reading the Captain's letters had been bringing back vivid memories of the horrors of war for Brant. Death, loss, destruction. She'd worried that it would affect him aversely. And it seemed her fears had been well founded.

CHAPTER TWELVE

Since returning from Vermont, eyes healed and soul seemingly on the mend, Brant had not mentioned the war or his injuries very often. But a man could not keep such emotionally maiming experiences silently to himself forever, else they destroy him. She knew he needed to talk. It generated a deep and aching agony in her heart to know his mind was tortured the way a soldier's always was. Patrick had told Lauryn several things Brant had related to him during a conversation they had when Brant had been with them before. However, he'd never really said much of anything to Lauryn about it. She hadn't asked, thinking if he'd wanted to talk about it, he would have.

Lauryn had spent hours volunteering at the hospital listening to the wounded soldiers talking. It hadn't taken long before she realized that often the wounds a man suffers in such horrible circumstances were far more hurtful to their minds than their bodies. She sat silently, ready to listen to whatever Brant needed to say, if indeed he said anything further at all.

He returned to her and sat down in defeat in the grass. He squeezed his eyes shut for a moment. A tear traveled slowly down his cheek. Tears were silently trickling down Lauryn's cheeks at the sight of this man and his pain.

"Some of the boys," he whispered, "would get trench foot. It was so…bad. I never imagined anything like that before. I…I had to see so many of them lose their feet from it…or their lives. And the noise! It never stopped! The loud, sharp noises. The shouting, the screams. But then…when it did stop…it was almost worse because you knew it would only start again, and you'd have to drag some fine boy out with his blood all over you. Sometimes there was so much of him missing that you'd only drag half of him out…a piece of him and…"

His eyes were closed, and she silently begged him to open them, to look at her so the visions he was reliving would fade a bit. But he kept his eyes tightly shut as another tear revealed his pain. "And it was hard, almost impossible sometimes, to see in your mind everything back home—everything beautiful that you wanted to save…that you wanted to protect from the ugly things you were living. Some of the men, when they were dying, they'd call out for their mothers or scream apologies to their wives and children for failing…for abandoning them. They'd hand you a photograph of their girl…tell you how beautiful and sweet she was and ask you to keep fighting so that the war would never get past your trench and closer to her." Another tear trickled down his face from his closed eyes.

Lauryn thought her heart would break from the pain she felt for him. She wanted him to stop, to come back to the present and the beauty all around him—the soft green grasses, the dogwood blossoms that smelled so sweet, the sun glistening warmly on the pond's smooth surface.

"I used to wish, when I first went over, that I was still special to someone. That there was still a girl back home to write and tell me that I was all she thought about. But then…" He shook his head in disagreement with his own thoughts. "Then I saw the men dying, and I thought of the families…the girls they were leaving. I thought of the wives…widows at home—the girls who would have to wait to hear the news from the boy's mother. I thought of my aunt and my sisters how it would grieve them to lose me, and…and I was glad the only woman other than my family that I was special to…was already dead."

Lauryn swallowed hard, brushing the tears from her cheeks. "That's enough for now," she whispered softly, reaching out and taking his face gently in her hands. She'd learned too from volunteering that, just as there was a time to let a soldier talk, there was a time he needed to stop. They could talk themselves into the deepest despair if they weren't reminded that beauty had returned to them—beauty, love, hope, and good things. Many times Lauryn would sneak a sweet, playful puppy or kitten into the hospital. Always she was amazed at how the little bundles of fur and slobber would brighten the men's faces. She wished she had something up her sleeve now—something to bring Brant back to Tennessee and the beauty all around him. But all she had was herself. In the next moment, it seemed to be enough.

As he turned his face toward her, his eyes opened, and the tears in them, the pain, was almost too much to bear. Never had Lauryn seen such pain expressed in a man's eyes. But as he looked at her, the slightest of grins captured his lips, and he said, "You were the first thing I saw after my injury…after the fighting. After the darkness of war and blindness…the very first thing I saw, so light and bright and sweet, and for that moment I remembered why I went. What I was fighting for." Lauryn smiled at him, and her heart leapt at the knowledge he'd given her. Simultaneously, as she released his face and brushed at his still damp cheeks with the gentleness of her fingers, he raised one hand and wiped the tears from one of her cheeks with the back of his hand. The spontaneity of the simultaneous gesture broadened his grin, and Lauryn could sense Brant leaving Europe and coming back to Tennessee. "It's one reason I kissed you that day on the train."

Lauryn blushed and cast her eyes to the ground for an instant, not wanting him to read the pure delight she experienced each time the memory came to her. He stretched his arms over his head momentarily before lying back down on the picnic blanket with his hands at the back of his head.

"And it was so worth it…the chance I took in molesting you," he chuckled.

"You've never molested me," she giggled. "You're so funny about that."

"Oh, but I have," he assured her. "You just don't remember it because you were sleeping."

Instantly Lauryn began flipping through her mental pages of memory. Whatever was he referring to? Surely she'd remember being molested by Brant Masterson. Asleep even.

"You're teasin' again," she sighed.

"I'm not," he assured her.

"When then?" she demanded, shoving at his side.

He smiled, his mood lightening quickly. "Recently."

"How recently?" She had to know what he was teasing about.

"A few days ago," he confessed. "That night we were up late reading the Captain's letters in the attic."

Lauryn remembered that night well. How could she forget those moments alone with Brant? But she didn't remember ever being molested.

"What kind of 'molested' do you mean?" she asked him. "Do you mean *molested* as in…"

"As in making improper advances toward you," he answered.

"Oh," Lauryn said, still puzzled. "Improper advances…as in *improper advances* or simply improper advances?"

He laughed and sat up. "There's a difference?" he said, smiling. "You're nervous about it, huh?"

"No," she lied.

"You are too," he argued playfully.

"You tell me right now, Brant Masterson, what in the world you're talkin' about!" she demanded, jumping to her feet and stomping her foot.

"Oooo! I've got your dander up now, don't I?"

He was completely amused, and she was getting more and more upset with each passing moment. What could he possibly be talking about?

He stood up then, taking her shoulders between his strong hands. "Here," he instructed. "I'll show you. Close your eyes like you're asleep."

Lauryn raised one eyebrow distrustingly.

"Come on. Don't you trust me?"

"You've just confessed to making improper advances toward me in my sleep. Now you want me to trust you?" she reminded him.

"Come on now. Just close your eyes."

Lauryn closed her eyes. After all, she must know what it was that he did.

"Now," he continued in a low whisper, "sigh."

"Sigh?" Lauryn asked, her eyes popping open.

"Close your eyes, sugar," he demanded again, "and sigh."

Lauryn closed her eyes and sighed.

"No, no, no," he chuckled. "Close your eyes and sigh through your mouth."

Shrugging her shoulders in irritation, Lauryn did as she was instructed. But her eyes sprung open immediately when she felt the moisture of his mouth blend with her own for just an instant. She took a step back from him, completely thrilled and yet entirely surprised.

He smiled and winked at her. "You see," he mumbled, "I made improper advances toward you when you were sleeping the other night." Lauryn felt the blush rise to her cheeks. "I told you that certain things tasted great here. And I wasn't talking about your mama's chicken."

Lauryn was alarmed. Her mind and her body's reaction to Brant were telling her that she was not strong enough to have him! He was some all-powerful, perfect man that could completely control her if he ever chose to do so. Her heart raced madly, ached with the regret of not having been awake when he'd improperly advanced upon her in the attic. Her body hurt to be in his arms. Her mouth watered for want of his kiss. And yet, at the same time, she was afraid of him.

"I'll tell you what, sugar," he whispered as his hands went to her waist and pulled her closer to him once more. "I'll let you come into my room and make advances like that toward me anytime you want to. Okay? Then we'll be even." His smile was no less than entirely seductive. "Hell, I'll let you do it right here and now." He quickly sat down on the grass, pulling her down next to him. "Sorry," he whispered his usual insincere apology for swearing in front of her.

Lauryn was entranced, unable to argue or even comprehend immediately what was happening. Furthermore, she knew she was helpless in resisting him. She didn't want to resist him!

Taking hold of her wrist, he lay back in the grass, pulling her arm across his chest, forcing her to lie next to him. Lauryn tried to pull away from him, but the hypnotic quality of his gaze, his strength, and her desire to be close to him were clouding her ability to act rationally.

Brant's free hand went to her head, and he pulled her face toward his. "Come on, Lauryn," he whispered, smiling mischievously. "I've misbehaved. Molesting you in your sleep! What a cad I am. I deserve your revenge. An eye for an eye and all that."

She was frightened, his poor little pixie. He could more than just sense it. Hesitation and fearful inexperience were written across her blushing cheeks as clearly as if the words had actually been tattooed there. But Brant had noticed something about Lauryn Kensington, and he'd use it to his own advantage now. And to hers.

He had come to realize that Lauryn was not unlike Samson, in a manner. Her hair, the way she wore it, often determined her strength, her demeanor. Brant had noted the fact since he'd come back to Connemara. And now his theory would be put to the ultimate test.

Reaching out, he tugged at the pin holding Lauryn's hair in a loose knot at the back of her head. Immediately, her long, nutmeg ringlets cascaded down about his face and across his chest. He shuddered at their softness on his flesh, and the good man in him tried to argue the need for self-control with the devil in him who was nearly winning over. He knew he shouldn't be doing it, corrupting his sweet friend. But she was too beautiful, too compassionate and kind, too funny and caring, too delicious! He had to kiss her. *Really* kiss her. Just once he had to drink from her lips, savor her mouth, feel her body held tightly in his arms. He thought for a moment that perhaps his little Tennessee pixie was indeed just that—a fairy sprite with some magical power that was weaving a spell around him. Just once, he told himself. Just once he'd have a real kiss from her—something to fill his memory and dreams.

His theory did indeed prove accurate—for immediately after her hair was unpinned, Lauryn's eyes began to burn with a vixen's passion instead of an innocent's fear.

Lauryn smiled as Brant caught a strand of her hair in his mouth and tugged at it with his teeth for a moment. He couldn't be real, and she had to be dreaming. She'd heard of men like this before—men who could seduce a woman into acting completely out of her rational mind. But she never believed any really existed—at least not until she'd met Brant.

"Don't be afraid of me, Lauryn," he mumbled. "You've kissed me before."

Lauryn lost her balance as Brant took her face between his capable hands and pulled her closer. Her palms pressed against the warm, solid contours of his chest, and her heart beat so madly that she thought it might burst! Her face was so close to his that she could feel the warmth of his breath on her lips as he spoke.

"You see," he whispered, "all you have to do…" and he brushed her lips very lightly with his own for a moment. "Is that." Again he kissed her tenderly—kissed her so softly that, had it not been for the incredible thrill traveling through her being, she would not have been sure he actually had kissed her.

She was still frightened. He could sense it. Lauryn was uncertain of herself. No doubt she was very inexperienced, which only served to further fan Brant's devilish delight in ensnaring her. She needed tutoring, he knew. And he didn't want her to feel uncomfortable with him. He wanted her to trust him, know that he would calm her fears. He did not want her to feel in any way embarrassed for her sweet naïveté.

And so, without further pause, he rolled her onto her back and leaned over her dominantly. He wouldn't toy with her anymore. He'd simply kiss her.

Lauryn sighed when Brant buried his hands in her hair for a moment, gazing down into her face. His eyes were narrowed, his grin simply impish.

"Here," he mumbled. "I'll show you." He kissed her again, more lingering this time and far more firmly. It was heavenly, like floating in the most delightful of dreams.

"Are you afraid of me?" he asked unexpectedly.

Lauryn looked up at him, completely puzzled by his question. She didn't want to answer questions. She wanted him to kiss her. Of course, he *had* kissed her. But she knew with every thread of her existence that these kisses were only infantile compared with what he was capable of administering.

"How…how do you mean?" she stammered breathlessly.

"Are you scared of me?" he repeated.

How could she possibly answer? Of course she was scared of him! Scared nearly to death. After all, he was breaking her heart without even knowing it. He was intoxicating! He was powerfully intimidating. What woman on earth wouldn't be scared of him?

"I'm not scared of you," Lauryn insisted.

"Oh, really?" he mumbled. "Then stop trembling."

"I'm not," she managed to argue, in a whisper and knowing full well she trembled violently as he leaned over her.

"You are," he insisted. "Why?"

"I'm not scared of you," she told him. "It's just that you're...you're just very intimidatin' sometimes."

"Why?"

Lauryn had difficulty breathing for a moment. She found it hard to look at anything other than his seductive smile, his mouth. What should she answer him? The truth? That he was so perfect, so strong, handsome, clever? That she was afraid she'd never be able to find any sort of happiness in life without him? Of course she couldn't tell him the truth!

"You're...you're tall," she stammered.

He smiled. "I'm tall?" he repeated. "That's why you're scared of me?"

"I'm not scared of you," Lauryn insisted.

Brant brushed her lips lightly with his thumb, and Lauryn noticed the corner of his mouth twitching slightly.

"That's good," he mumbled. "I don't want you to be scared of me." Then he bent, caressing her cheek with his kiss.

Lauryn thought she would completely lose consciousness! Here was a man who was incredibly gifted in wooing a woman. Just the look in his eyes nearly melted her like butter in a hot skillet. And she feared she was powerless to resist him. Yet he was a gentleman, wasn't he? A man who thought that stealing some sort of a kiss while she was asleep had constituted molestation.

"Let's put it to the test, shall we?" he whispered. "Let's see if I can get past your being intimidated because...because I'm so tall," he chuckled. As he kissed her neck softly, Lauryn's body was covered in a delightful tingle, and she knew he was well aware of why she was scared of him.

"What?" she squeaked.

"We talk, you and me," he mumbled as he kissed her cheek once more. "We laugh. We discuss this miserable mystery until we're nearly sick. But you do all that with the Captain too, don't you?"

Lauryn didn't answer; she was too bewitched by him. He kissed her shoulder then, and even though her blouse covered her flesh, she could feel the warmth of his lips there, and she shuddered delightfully.

"We need…we need our own relationship, Lauryn—apart from them. We need a friendship…an association, a connection of our own making, if we're ever going to solve this miserable situation."

Lauryn's mouth was watering, her entire being trembling. She gasped as he kissed the corner of her mouth softly. She tried to focus on the pink petals floating down from the trees to land on Brant's back and in her hair.

"And the only thing I can think of at this point that you've never shared with him," he continued, "that you can share with me…" He kissed her, but very carefully, on the lips.

It was like someone lit a fuse that traveled down her spine and into her arms and legs! Her fingers and toes tingled, and she felt faint from not breathing normally.

"You may have been kissed before, sugar," Brant told her as his mouth hovered just above hers. "But nobody has ever kissed you the way I can." And his lips captured hers in a long, hard-pressed exchange.

Brant was finished with his boyish flirtations. The man in him was too dominant. Lauryn knew it assuredly as molten warmth seemed to course through every vein of her body, threatening to melt away her flesh and bone and leave only her soul to savor the euphoric delirium! His kiss spun a sort of hallucinative atmosphere about her. She felt weak and yet more vibrant than ever she had before.

His arms banded around her possessively, so powerfully that Lauryn wondered for a moment if he might simply pulverize her tender ribcage. His kiss was not sweet and soft, gentle and proper, any longer. It was hard and driven and exploding with passion. He broke from her for a moment and studied her intently. Lauryn could not take her eyes from his, which burned with an emotion that she could not quite identify. Still he held her face between his hands, and she was at his mercy, body and spirit. His thumbs caressed her lips for a moment.

"If I scared you before, sugar," he mumbled, "you're gonna be terrified by the time I'm finished." Lauryn couldn't stop the delighted grin that spread across her face. And when next he kissed her, his mouth seizing her own in a way she'd never dreamed of, she was astonished at her own response.

She entirely dissolved in his arms, her heart hammering so brutally within her chest that the ringing of it in her ears was almost deafening. Brant's hands released her face, traveling caressively the length of her arms, leaving her flesh stinging blissfully as they came to rest at her waist, holding her tightly and pulling her into an unyielding embrace. His embrace, coupled with the rapturous delirium evoked by his kiss, caused her to release some of her inhibitions, and her arms slid around his shoulders, savoring the strength of his muscles. His strength and powerfully passionate kisses fed the fire of her own ardor as she stood wrapped in his arms, the dogwood blossoms raining down upon them.

She tasted like the sweetest ambrosia, and Brant knew he could never satisfy his craving for her. Her body fit perfectly to his, and the sweet, ethereal fragrance clinging to her skin filled his senses with a fantastic satisfaction. He'd known she would be his undoing. He knew his desires for her would eat away at him, torture his body and mind. Why had he taken her to him? How would he now find the strength to give her up? To put her away from him when he so wanted to hold her, breathe her, own her? He kissed her harder, deeper, with an unquenchable thirst for her, suddenly feeling guilt rise within him in knowing that her tender lips had never before been so passionately assaulted. He tried lessening the demanding nature of their exchange, but the soft moisture of her mouth—alluring, accepting—it all bewitched him, provoking his passion for her, and with a low, regretful growl escaping his throat, he broke the seal of their mouths and held her to him for a moment, reveling in the scent of her hair in his nostrils, the silken texture of it against his face.

"I'm in a lot more trouble than I thought," he mumbled to himself.

Lauryn struggled to breathe calmly again. The flesh surrounding her lips prickled with the residual sensation that his roughly shaven face had caused there, and the moisture in her mouth continued to intensify, longing for his kiss again.

"What?" she breathed. He'd said something. But she hadn't heard him clearly.

Unexpectedly, he released her and stood, rubbing his chin. Anxiety immediately rose within Lauryn's bosom. Was he having some sort of violent regret?

"It's done," he mumbled, taking her hand and pulling her to her feet. "We crossed a certain bridge together, and things will never be the same again." He took her face in his hands and looked sternly into her eyes. "Do you regret it?"

"Never," she whispered. And as his smile returned, he took her mouth again with his—burying his fingers in her hair for a moment, kissing her thoroughly, forcefully, impassioned.

Her knees again weakened, but his arms were around her immediately, holding her close against him as he adored her, unlike anything her young, romantic mind had ever imagined. In her wildest dreams—and she'd enjoyed some wild ones where Brant was concerned—he'd never kissed her as perfectly as he did now, in an actual moment of reality. She'd never considered that maybe reality could be better than a dream. But it was! At least with Brant Masterson it was.

Eventually, their passion softened, and Lauryn found herself sitting in the grass, leaning back against a dogwood tree, Brant's head in her lap as he told her about his family back in Vermont. Still, it wasn't long before he sat up and kissed her again, softly on the lips, tucking his hand in her hair before scattering moist, gentle kisses up and down her neck.

"You'll be shy next time, you know," he told her.

"What do you mean?" she asked innocently, all the while thrilled that he had implied he would kiss her again, in some other circumstance.

"When we get back to Connemara…when we're surrounded by people and pressures again. We'll both feel this freedom slip away." He smiled and twisted a strand of her hair around his finger. "For one thing, your mother would have me tarred and feathered if she knew I'd paddled you out to an island to corrupt you."

"You haven't once corrupted me," Lauryn told him with a smile as she looked up into the blue of the sky.

"Maybe not," he chuckled. "But I've spent three hours kissing you—"

"Three hours?" Lauryn exclaimed. She fairly jumped to her feet. "What will people think?"

"About what?" Brant chuckled.

"About...about..." Lauryn stammered.

Brant shook his head, obviously amused. He stood slowly, rather unwillingly, and began gathering the picnic blanket. "Do you think the peacocks will rat us out to your mama and the rest of the town? All the same, I had better get you back to safety. Much more of this and I'll have to make an honest woman of you."

Lauryn's mouth dropped open in astonishment at his insinuation. She was speechless and could only stand before him, stunned.

Brant chuckled and then mumbled, "Lauryn! I thought you said three hours were shocking enough. But I'm not one to pass up an invitation like this one." He reached out quickly and pulled her head to his, savoring the flavor of her kiss one last time.

He smiled at her when their final embrace was over, held her cheek tenderly in one hand, and grinning said, "Oh, by the way...sorry—for molesting you in the attic, I mean."

Lauryn smiled, completely enslaved by his charms. "It's all right. I don't mind."

"You should," he chuckled as he bent over, retrieving the food basket and starting toward the canoe. "You should be spanking my behind pretty soundly for that."

Lauryn smiled, delighted at the knowledge he'd "molested" her, as he put it.

As she watched him put the picnic things in the canoe, as she studied him while he was paddling back to shore, she began to feel renewed, newly motivated about solving the miserable enigma that was before them. Finding Laura would free them all. And just maybe, with Laura at peace—well, maybe Brant would... Her heart soared for a moment as she tried to squelch her secret hope. For that present instant, she would thoroughly relish the memories of their time alone on the millpond island.

Brant Masterson had kissed her, Lauryn mused. No, no, no. Brant Masterson had far more than simply kissed her. He'd thoroughly kissed her, for hours upon hours! As Brant paddled for shore, each time she lingered on the memory of their...their...their liaison, she felt weak and tingly all over again. Each time she looked at him, watched his muscles work to move the canoe through the water, she thought of the way his kiss tasted, and the imaginary butterflies that dwell in every woman's stomach would take flight, causing a mad fluttering sensation in her bosom.

Her zenith met an abrupt end, however, when they reached the dock to find villainy at work. Two very dirty, villainous-looking men were harassing Mr. Jackson. Far more than harassing him! One of the men held Mr. Jackson's arms at his back while another prepared to bury his fist in the old man's stomach. Immediately, Brant realized what was happening and leapt from the canoe to shore.

"What are you doing?" Brant shouted as he strode over to the men and stepped between Mr. Jackson and the degenerate preparing to hit him.

"None of your business, purty boy," the stranger growled, grinning demonically and displaying a smile void of several teeth.

"Brant?" Lauryn called out. Brant shot Lauryn a warning look before turning his attention back to the matter at hand.

"It *is* my business!" Brant assured the men. Lauryn saw Brant's hands tighten into fists, saw the muscles of his chest and arms tense, and she knew the situation would not be remedied easily. "I'm gonna ask you again," Brant warned. "What the hell are you doing?"

Missing Teeth chuckled. "Well, this ol' piece a negra won't give over his gold money clip…and we're in far more need of it than he is."

"So," Brant said, frowning, "you're just a regular old piece of…" Brant glanced at Lauryn quickly, still a bit mindful that a lady was present and continued, "—lazy trash that's out robbing good people. Is that it?"

The man scowled. "You're half right, purty boy." He glanced at Lauryn, and her own stomach churned at his lustful appraisal of her. "But I ain't lazy…or trash," the man growled. "So I'll tell you what," he continued. Lauryn began to weep as she looked at Mr. Jackson, who had obviously been at the men's mercy for some time before she and Brant arrived. His lip was bleeding, and he looked otherwise near to collapsing. "Let's strike us up a deal, purty boy," the criminal continued. "I need me somethin' today. And I figure…it's either whatever money this ol' bag a bones has—you too, for that matter—or your little sweet bite there." He smiled at Lauryn again, nodding and licking his lips. "Yep. I figure we can strike us up a bargain."

Brant nodded and pretended to be thoughtful. Lauryn saw his jaw clench, his chest rise and fall with barely controlled rage. "Well," he began, "it's out of the question. You can't have the little sweet bite. And as far as my friend Mr. Jackson…well, I'm afraid I'm just gonna have to kill you."

Before Lauryn could blink, Brant buried his fist deep in the man's midsection. The man behind Brant released Mr. Jackson and took hold of Brant's arms, pulling them backward in an attempt to hold him. As the toothless degenerate recovered and aggressed, Brant braced himself against the man behind, raised one foot, and kicked the approaching attacker squarely in the chest, sending him stumbling backward. Brant threw his head back, brutally striking the forehead of the man behind. The man released his hold on Brant, who turned and planted a powerful fist on the villain's jaw.

"Brant!" Lauryn yelled, watching in helpless horror as the toothless villain recovered. He lunged at Brant with a knife he'd pulled from his waistband. Brant turned, receiving a severe cut in the chest as the man attacked him. Lauryn screamed as blood soaked his shirt. Brant didn't seem to notice the wound. He grabbed hold of the man's wrist and elbow. Swiftly raising his knee, he slammed the man's forearm across his thigh. Lauryn winced when she heard the crack of splitting bone and the man's shout as he dropped the knife and fell to his knees in agony.

Turning to the second man, Brant growled. "Come on! If you're gonna start something…you need to finish it!"

The villain looked from Brant to his injured cohort and back and sneered arrogantly. "You like pain then, purty boy?" the man asked.

"No," Brant growled. "But I sure like to hand it out."

The man lunged at him. Brant maneuvered swiftly, catching him by the shoulders and burying his knee in the man's midsection. The man doubled over, and Brant grabbed his hair, raised his face, and landed a brutal punch to his nose. He fell to the ground. Once more Brant hit him, rendering him unconscious. Turning to the first man, who was helpless and still writhing in pain and disbelief, Brant kicked him mercilessly in the jaw, giving him a reprieve from his pain as he too passed out.

Lauryn looked about slowly, stunned by what had transpired and how fast it all had happened. The two degenerates lay beaten and unconscious. Brant came to her, hunkering down and searching her face intently. Lauryn hadn't even realized until that moment that, at some point, her legs had given way beneath her, and she now sat in a heap on the ground.

"Are you all right?" he asked. His frown, his expression of complete concern, was genuine and selfless.

"Me?" Lauryn shrieked. "What are you worried about me for?" As she rose to her feet, he stood straight. "Look at this!" she whispered, reaching out and touching his bloodstained shirt. "How bad is it?" She reached up and began unbuttoning his shirt in order to better investigate the wound. Then, realizing the shirt was torn and soaked in blood, she simply tore it open and was horrified when she saw his damaged flesh. The wound was fairly deep and seven or eight inches in length.

"First my pants, now my shirt?" Brant teased. "I think I'm beginning to like the way you start stripping my clothes off every now and then."

Lauryn was too concerned to be embarrassed or amused. "Come on," she said, taking his hand. "We're gonna take you to the doctor and get that attended to." She looked past him to where Mr. Jackson struggled to stand. "Both of you!"

"We can't leave them here!" Brant argued. "What if they get away?"

Lauryn looked at the two unconscious men, bleeding and broken on the ground.

"I'm sure they'll be here when the police arrive, Brant," she said. "They look…they'll be here when we get back." She took hold of his hand and pulled him along as she went to Mr. Jackson.

"Mr. Jackson? Are you all right, sir?" she asked. He certainly didn't look all right, but she thought she might inquire just in case.

The elderly man shook his head and smiled. "I'm fine, Miss Lauryn. Just fine." He chuckled as Brant helped him to his feet. "And I thank you, sir. I was waitin' to meet St. Peter hisseff."

"You're sure you're all right?" Brant asked. "Maybe we better do what Lauryn says and get in to the doctor."

Lauryn was touched, knowing full well that she would've had a hard time getting Brant to seek medical attention had it not been for his own concern for Mr. Jackson.

Mr. Jackson chuckled. "Maybe, sir. Maybe."

CHAPTER THIRTEEN

Lauryn wiped angrily at the tears on her cheeks as the doctor inspected Brant's laceration. Of course, Brant insisted that Doctor Valance attend to Mr. Jackson first. And even though Lauryn knew that the old man was more feeble than Brant and probably needed treatment sooner, it seemed a long time that she sat there and stared at Brant holding his shirt wadded up against his wound, which continued to bleed.

"It's a nasty scratch, my boy," Doctor Valance mumbled as he cleaned the wound.

"Scratch?" Lauryn fairly shouted.

"Why don't you go on out and sit with ol' Jackson awhile, Miss Kensington?" Doctor Valance suggested kindly.

"Yeah," Brant nodded. "Go on out and check on him. I'll be right there."

Lauryn did as she was told, knowing her hysterics would not help either man to attend to Brant's wound.

Mr. Jackson sat on the sofa in the waiting room, looking incredibly old and tired. The light that normally glistened from his eyes was dulled.

Lauryn sat next to him and took one of his tired, weathered hands in her own. "You really should move in with Mariah, Mr. Jackson," she scolded. Mariah was Mr. Jackson's granddaughter, and for years she'd been trying to convince her aged grandfather to move in with her and let her care for him.

"I ain't gonna be a burden to my childr'n or my granchildr'n, Miss Lauryn. I won't do it," the old man growled.

"Well, then you're more selfish than I even thought you were," Lauryn scolded.

"Selfish?" Mr. Jackson squeaked. "How you come by that, Miss Lauryn?"

But Lauryn was a wise girl—a clever girl. "Children and grandchildren take and take and take from their parents…as they deserve to. You love them, raise them, care for them, teach them, and watchin' them become great people is your reward, right?"

Mr. Jackson nodded. "Hallelujah!" he agreed.

"Then, if your whole life is livin' for your children's happiness, why are you denyin' them the chance for more of it by givin' somethin' back to you, sir?" Lauryn patted Mr. Jackson's hand lovingly. "I can think of nothin' I'd rather do for my mama than to tuck her in at night, give her a good conversation, and make sure she's eatin' nicely when she's a little older and a little more tired—all the things she still does for me."

"I ain't no chil', Miss Lauryn," Mr. Jackson reminded her proudly.

"Of course not. That's why they still need you. Mariah worships the ground you walk on, Mr. Jackson, and well you know it." Lauryn smiled at him, understanding his pride. "Mariah still needs you more than you need her too. Still needs your wisdom, your life experience to teach her. Her children need you too. A grandparent is a valuable thing, Mr. Jackson. And how can all your grandbabies and great-grandbabies learn from you, absorb strength from you, if you're just too selfish to share it?"

Mr. Jackson's eyes narrowed, and a smile quirked one side of his mouth. "You're a sweet talker if ever I did see one," he chuckled. "Ain't that right, Mr. Brant?"

Lauryn looked around to see Brant standing there, bandaged like some sort of warrior, and smiling at her approvingly.

"Yes, she's a sweet little morsel," Brant agreed, winking at her. Lauryn felt warm at his approval—warm and proud at the knowledge of what he'd done to protect the helpless old man.

"Do you want me to drive you home, Mr. Jackson? Mr. Masterson, Miss Kensington?" Doctor Valance inquired.

"Not me!" Mr. Jackson said, struggling to his feet. "I'm just gonna stop me off at Mariah's house. Maybe I can talk her into feedin' me a good meal for a change."

He offered his hand to Lauryn, and she took it, smiling approvingly.

"Mr. Masterson?" Doctor Valance again inquired.

"No, thank you, sir," Brant said, shaking the man's hand. "But I do thank you for patching me up. I've sewn enough of my own cuts shut to know when my stitching won't do."

"I've sent my assistant, Luella, down to the police. I'm sure they'll get right out there and take care of that scum you left, sir," Doctor Valance said. "So you get on back to Connemara and rest up."

"I'll do that," Brant agreed, though Lauryn doubted he would rest at all.

Brant and Lauryn walked with Mr. Jackson to where his granddaughter lived just outside of town. Lauryn loved the old gentleman and could see Brant had taken an intense liking to him.

As they neared Mariah's house, Mr. Jackson suddenly asked, "Did you childr'n have fun on your picnic?" He chuckled quietly and winked at Brant.

"Oooohhhh yeah!" Brant assured him.

"Well, I'm glad to hear it," the old man said. "Miss Lauryn's great-granddaddy he'ped me out back durin' the war. He was a good man. A good man."

Lauryn smiled. She'd known for years and years that her great-grandfather Kiel O'Halleran and Mr. Jackson had a respect for one another. She'd always felt very proud of the fact that Kiel O'Halleran had recognized a good man when he saw one.

"Mmm-hmmmm," Mr. Jackson confirmed. "A good man he was. A good fambly. All famblies got their secrets…but nothin' could ever make your fambly bad in my eyes, Miss Lauryn."

"Thank you, Mr. Jackson." Lauryn's brow puckered for a moment, however. Had Mr. Jackson implied her family had secrets? Or had he just meant something else?

"Here's where I step off," Mr. Jackson said, shaking Brant's hand. "Thank you for what you done for me, Mr. Brant."

Brant smiled and winked at Lauryn as he said, "No, sir. I think I better be thanking you. That was the best canoe ride of my life."

Lauryn felt herself blush through and through, and Mr. Jackson chuckled understandingly.

"Glad to he'p you out, sir." He smiled at Lauryn. "Better braid up that hair 'gain, Miss Lauryn—else your grandmammy will have this boy's skin hung out to dry, I 'spect! Criminals a-fightin' or no!"

Lauryn blushed an even deeper shade of vermilion and immediately reached back to braid her hair. What a sight she must be! How embarrassingly obvious it was that she and Brant had been…that they had been…exchanging affections. All this time she'd been distracted by the wounded body of Brant, by Mr. Jackson's needs and ailing. She'd completely forgotten her own appearance.

Mariah met her granddaddy at the porch and waved to Lauryn, raising her eyebrows a bit as she studied Brant. Lauryn immediately decided that she and Brant would take the path less traveled back to Connemara. Brant's shirt had been left in a bloody heap at Dr. Valance's office. He wore only the bandages wrapped around his stomach from the waist up. And she must look a fright! Having braided her hair back and twisting a strand of hair around the end of the braid to hold it, she could only hope that her mother didn't remember she'd left the house that morning with a completely different hair dressing.

"What an adventure you've had today, Miss Kensington," Brant sighed as they followed the creek bed toward Connemara. "Canoeing, being molested, and, well…nearly being abducted by criminals."

"No wonder I'm so tuckered out," she mumbled. She could see the springhouse just ahead. Her adventure was almost over. Now it was back to reality—the reality of Brant's leaving, of the Captain and Laura's suffering. She sighed heavily as the burden of it all began to tax her mind once again. The knowledge of the intense wound Brant had received while defending Mr. Jackson was no help. It must be terribly painful, and it hurt her even more deeply to notice the way he didn't let on.

"Hey!" Brant exclaimed, startling her out of her rather depressing thoughts. "I can see Henry from here."

Lauryn looked up to see that indeed the old cemetery and Henry, the statue, were visible. Connemara rose out of the horizon like a great beacon of safety and strength.

Brant stopped for a moment. "Do you think…" He paused. He seemed so serious.

"What?" Lauryn urged. "What's the matter?"

Brant bit his lip and, frowning, asked, "Do you think I should tell him? Or would it be better coming from you?"

Lauryn frowned and shook her head. "What on earth are you talkin' about?" Tell who? Of course, everyone would be asking questions when Brant and Lauryn returned home in such states of dishevel, but whom did he mean specifically?

"Henry," Brant stated. "How can we lessen the blow for him? I mean, when he finds out you've taken another lover…it's best if you tell him first, Lauryn. A man's heart isn't granite, you know."

Lauryn smiled, delighted by his teasing. "Very amusing, Mr. Masterson. You shouldn't make fun of Henry. He's been very loyal and taught me much over the years," she said. As she turned to continue toward Connemara, Brant took hold of her elbow and spun her around to face him.

"We're almost home, sugar," he mumbled. His expression was tinged with something like regret. "What's say we have one more…moment of our own?" Brant reached out, gathering her against his body, stealing her breath with a heated kiss.

Lauryn sensed the finality of this kiss. They were home, facing reality, people, and frustration again. It was as if Brant were telling her things were back to normal—no more lying under the dogwood trees exchanging passionate affections as pink blossoms floated down around them. And so she let her arms go around him, let her hands caress his chest and shoulders, powerful arms, and strong back.

With a sigh of regret, he pulled away from her, smiling. "I feel bad for Henry," he mumbled.

"Why is that?" she asked, letting her arms drop to her sides.

"He was never able to taste you." And with that, Brant bent forward, tasting her kiss one last time.

৯

"You could've been killed!" Georgia exclaimed as everyone sat in the front parlor at Connemara listening to Brant relay the story of how he'd received his injury. "For Pete's sake! What's this town comin' to when men like that can just walk up in broad daylight and terrorize a sweet old man?"

"It's very unsettlin'," Sean mumbled, frowning. "I don't like it one bit! And I wish ol' Jackson would move in with Mariah."

"Maybe we ought to offer to have him live here again," Georgia mentioned.

"He won't do it, Mama," Sean reminded her. "He's a proud man, and he's gettin' too old to earn his keep the way he thinks he should."

"I think he'll consider livin' with Mariah, Mama," Lauryn assured her worried mother. "I had a long talk with him."

"Probably that, in itself, will do it. Once you've been on the receivin' end of one of Lauryn's lectures…a man's miserable enough to do anythin'." Sean chuckled and reached over to tweak Lauryn's nose affectionately.

"Can I see where the knife went in, Brant?" Patrick blurted out, unable to contain himself any longer.

"Patrick!" Georgia scolded. "We don't ask to see people's wounds."

"Why not?" the boy argued.

"Because it isn't proper," Georgia explained.

"I'd like to see it too" Uncle Johnny piped in.

"Same here," Sean agreed.

"Well, for Pete's sake, if this room isn't full of a bunch of morbid heathens," Georgia sighed. Lauryn smiled, knowing full well her mother's own curiosity issues. "Well, Brant, if you simply *must*…" she conceded.

Brant chuckled and began to unwind the bandages around his torso. "I'm supposed to have it changed before I turn in anyway. Now is as good a time as any."

Lauryn thought she was prepared for the sight of Brant's wound. But stitched shut, caked with drying blood, and with the bruising of his body, it looked much worse than it had fresh.

"Oh, Brant," Nana sighed, her eyes filling with tears.

"You're a hero, Brant," Patrick whispered, awed by the sight of the massive wound. "A hero, like you read about in books and such. I ain't never seen the like of that."

"Mr. Jackson's a hero, Patrick," Brant told the boy. "That man has more wounds, experience, and knowledge than you and I will ever have put together."

For a moment, Lauryn again remembered Mr. Jackson's words. *All famblies got their secrets…but nothin' could ever make your fambly bad in my eyes, Miss Lauryn.* Shaking her head, she returned her attention to her little brother, so mesmerized by the hero before him. So many years of mystery had caused her to be far too paranoid. She looked from Brant's wound to his face, the face that dominated her dreams, the smile that turned into kisses at times that would now govern her memory. A delightful tremor ran through her as he flirtatiously winked at her.

※

After such a day—a day of passion, excitement, danger, and emotion— Lauryn certainly could not find sleep that night. She wondered if she would ever be able to obtain a good night's sleep again! It seemed so long since she'd slept peacefully.

She listened to the clock striking midnight. It had been more than three hours since she'd carefully folded the dress she'd worn that day and put it away in the small chest in which she kept her treasures. She'd never wear it again. It was too valuable a keepsake, something to always remind her that their moments of dreamy passion had really happened.

It had been two hours since she had relayed the incident with Mr. Jackson at the millpond to the Captain—two hours since he'd told her that he indeed remembered Mr. Jackson, two hours since he'd assured her that it was well and good for her to have abandoned Connemara for an entire day of freedom. But still, her mind was alive though her body was tired. Something was…she couldn't put her finger on it. But something had changed. Not between her and Brant, though of course that was true, but something else. What was it?

The soft knock on the door startled her. "Who is it?" she whispered.

"Who else is up at this hour?" came Brant's curt reply.

Without a thought to her attire, or lack thereof, Lauryn whispered, "Come in."

Brant entered the room, shutting the door behind him. He looked tired, and a frown puckered his brow. His hand rested at his stomach in the vicinity of his wound, and Lauryn realized he must be uncomfortable.

"Are you all right?" she inquired.

"I'm fine." He wasn't, it was obvious by his terse answer. But Lauryn didn't press him. "I wonder if I'll ever be able to get a decent night's rest again," he mumbled. Lauryn smiled, completely sympathetic to his plight. Slightly irritated, he tossed a bundle of Laura's letters onto

Lauryn's bed. "Entertain me, wench," he demanded, attempting to be lighthearted and humorous.

Lauryn smiled. She rather liked his teasing her in such a manner. She thought she might like to be his wench.

"Very well," she agreed, sitting down on her bed and loosing the ribbon from the stack of letters. "Where shall I begin?"

"With the top one," Brant said with a sigh. He propped himself up against her headboard, wincing from the pain of his injury as he stretched his long legs out across the bed. Again he wore no shirt. As shockingly impressive as the sight of him half-dressed was, Lauryn was beginning to be more comfortable seeing him that way.

"Very well," Lauryn agreed. His grouchy mood was somewhat understandable.

> *My darling Laura,*
> *As is true of every moment that I live…I miss you! I am fine and healthy. Let me put your mind at ease in that regard first. Though your letters are slow in coming, I devour them when they do arrive. I am thirsting always to hear of your well being, to know that you are safe at Connemara. Your news of Moses Jackson was soothing to my very soul. He is a good man and deserves good things.*

Lauryn looked up to Brant, whose eyes had widened at the mention of the now familiar name.

"Come on now," Brant mumbled. "Surely we haven't picked up a letter that just happens to be about…"

When he didn't finish his sentence, Lauryn nodded her assurance. "Mr. Jackson—the very one whose life you saved just this afternoon—is named Moses. Moses Jackson."

"Well? Go on then," Brant urged. He let his head fall back against the headboard and closed his eyes. He seemed beaten down, somehow overwhelmed by such a prophetic occurrence. Still, he obviously knew, as did Lauryn, that the letter could not be ignored. Lauryn continued to read.

> *He has endured much, your Mr. Jackson. I guess someone as enduring and strong as he is has earned the right to be referred to as 'Mr.' and I am*

glad of it. I understand his daughter, Esther, has stayed on at Connemara. I'm sure she is a great comfort to your mother. My letter must be short today, my love. The fires are dying, and I am worn to the bone. I love you, Lauralynn.
    Brand

"Spooky," Brant mumbled when Lauryn finished reading the letter.

"What do you mean…exactly?" she asked, though she too felt a thread of odd uneasiness running through her.

"The whole thing," he explained as he yawned and stretched his arms for a moment. "The fact that we had such an experience with your Mr. Jackson today…then come home and end up finding him in Laura's letters."

"What do you think he meant today when he mentioned family secrets?" Lauryn asked. Mr. Jackson's remark had eaten at her all evening. She wondered if Brant felt the same way.

But he shrugged. "I don't know. Probably nothing specific." He leaned toward her and lowered his voice. "I have an aunt that threw herself into a mad love affair and ended up going crazy and being locked away in an institution." Lauryn's eyes widened, and Brant smiled at her interest. "So, you see, everyone has something…the proverbial 'skeleton in the closet.' I'm sure your family does too. For that matter, there's a *real* skeleton somewhere—but not in the closet or the basement or the cellar…"

Lauryn shook her head, smiling at his teasing.

He chuckled a moment before continuing, "But that doesn't mean there aren't other skeletons around here—" Brant stopped midsentence; shaking his head, he continued, "No, no, no. Your family secret is this whole mess with Laura and the Captain and the fact that a select two of their ancestry still see them." He ran his fingers through his hair and yawned again. "I'm too tired to think just now. Just keep reading to me."

"But if you're too tired—" Lauryn began.

"It will help me to get sleepy," he explained. "And maybe we'll discover something in the process, as well."

Lauryn continued, reading letter after letter until her eyes stung with dry fatigue—letter after letter about battles and people and the Captain's frustrations and losses. As she read, she began to feel selfish, selfish for all the years she'd spent complaining to the Captain about her petty little problems. What he'd endured, was still enduring, was far and away more horrid than anything she had ever experienced. It was humbling to read his letters.

Finally, after near an hour, Lauryn was too tired to read any longer. Refolding the last letter in the pile, she glanced over to see Brant slept soundly, propped awkwardly against her headboard. She smiled, glad he had found a bit of respite. Still, she hated to wake him once he'd finally fallen asleep. But what else was there to do? He certainly couldn't stay the night in her room. Could he?

She studied him for a long time—studied the peaceful look on his face, the calluses on his hands, the way his chest would rise and fall with each breath.

She could imagine Laura, lying next to the Captain in their bed before he'd left for battle, studying her gallant husband in the same manner. Only Laura had been free to hold the Captain, smooth the frown from his brow, kiss him as often and whenever she wanted to. She wondered if her ancestress would ever again be able to hold her husband, feel safe in his arms.

"Brant?" Lauryn whispered. "You must get to bed. It's so late." But he didn't stir. Not a breath. "Brant?" she tried again. She stood and walked to the head of her bed, leaning over him and softly calling his name. "Brant?" Her bed, unlike the one in the guestroom that Brant occupied, was big enough for both of them, and her fatigue and need to be close to him tempted her. But propriety was not to be sacrificed, she reminded herself. She thought, for a moment, of their time on the millpond island and the way Brant had teased her about needing to make an honest woman of her if they stayed any longer. For a brief instant, some impish impulse in her mind told her, *Lie down next to him. If someone found you, he'd be forced to marry you for propriety's sake.* But Lauryn didn't want Brant to feel obligated, forced toward her for any reason. So she tried again.

"Brant?" she whispered.

"Brant darling," he mumbled without opening his eyes. "Call me 'Brant darling,' and I'll move out of your way."

Lauryn smiled. His teasing manner had become one of her very favorite characteristics. "Brant darlin'," she whispered, "it's time you went to bed."

Again, without opening his eyes, Brant smiled and chuckled softly. Then he did open his eyes, though only narrowly, and looked at her, smiling. He was very tired. Lauryn could see the deep fatigue about him.

"Now kiss me good night, and I'll go," he said.

She smiled, shyly, hesitant.

"Come on. For old times' sake," he urged.

"Old times?" Lauryn giggled. "What do you mean 'old times'?"

"Come on now, sugar. Do you want to go to bed or not? I'm not moving until you kiss me good night."

Lauryn bit her lip and mustered all her courage. Bending forward, she placed a sweet kiss on his lips. Instantly, his arms banded around her like a steel vice as he pulled her down on the bed next to him.

"No matter what else happens, Lauryn," he whispered as he brushed the nutmeg locks of hair from her face, "whether we succeed in our search or not…no matter what…we had our day. Right?"

Lauryn could only nod. On the verge of tears—for his inference that their day of passion and peace had been an isolated moment in time never to happen again—she tried valiantly to hide her heartbreak from him.

Taking her mouth brutally, as if he had a thirst that could not be quenched, he let his hands caress the soft flesh of her arms and neck, shoulders and hands. He buried his face in her hair for a moment, kissing her throat, pulling her body against his one last time before he rather violently raised himself from her bed and stormed from the room, leaving Lauryn breathless and longing for the warmth of his arms around her.

Once in the privacy of his own room, Brant tore his trousers from his body and threw himself into bed. He knew his sleep would be restless now. He should never have gone to her room. Still, he reminded himself, there was that letter about Moses Jackson, and it intrigued him. But at what price? She'd been so vulnerable and willing to be in his arms. And in her nightgown with her hair down, for pity's sake!

No more kissing that little vixen, he told himself. It was dangerous. No more private moments like the one they'd just shared. He was weak when it came to Lauryn Kensington—weaker than he'd ever been in any situation in his life! She was dangerous to his self-control. He needed to solve the miserable mystery surrounding them. Needed to be free from Laura, the Captain, and Connemara. Free to own that little pixie in the room next door.

"Yep," he said out loud to himself. "Keep your head on straight." And with that, he would spend the next hour reminding himself of the danger he was in—a long hour before he would finally find sleep again.

CHAPTER FOURTEEN

Brant's Uncle Johnny wasn't himself the next morning. Lauryn noticed at once. He was quiet and somewhat withdrawn, lacking his usual life's luster. Perhaps Patrick were simply wearing him out, Lauryn wondered. Brant noticed the change as well, but when he asked his Aunt Felicity about it, she assured him his uncle was simply tired.

It still worried Lauryn as she prepared for Penny's party that afternoon. She felt nervous, worried that something would happen and Brant would have to leave her. Then she scolded herself for being so selfish and caring more for her own feelings than for the well-being of Uncle Johnny.

It was a beautiful night for a party. As the Kensington family and their guests drove to the McGovern home, Lauryn inhaled deeply of the warm evening air. She sat next to Brant in the auto. His arm rested on the seat behind her shoulders.

Brant had been as attentive as ever that day. It was obvious he was in pain from his injury, but he refused to acknowledge it in any way. He was as helpful, friendly, and teasing as usual, but Lauryn had known from the moment she'd seen him that morning that he'd put the day before out of his mind. He acted, in fact, as if it had never happened. And though it hurt her deeply, she'd known it would be that way. He'd implied it to her the day before, the night before. She had expected it, though she'd hoped for the opposite. She had expected it and was as emotionally prepared as possible.

She put on her smile and let her mind linger over the past to give her strength. At least Brant cared for her. Of that much she was certain. And his reason for returning to a less intimate relationship—Laura.

Laura still needed to be saved. Laura was still his focus. And though Lauryn was rather jealous, hurt, still she comprehended it all. Or tried to.

Therefore, when they arrived at the McGovern home to be met with the warmest of warm welcomes, Lauryn simply decided to enjoy being on Brant's arm. She did revel impishly in the delight of the shocked and admiring glances of the women in attendance as they saw Brant Masterson enter the room.

As any gentleman would, he asked Penny, his hostess, for the first dance. Lauryn smiled as she watched her friend blush. Someday she might tell Penny of her day on the island with Brant—tell her that it had been the most wonderful day of her life—tell her that Henry hadn't really helped them learn anything about kissing!

"You look ravishin' as usual, Lauryn," Jeffrey complimented as he came to stand beside her. Lauryn smiled at the flattering remark and giggled as he took her hand, raised it to his lips, and kissed it gallantly.

"Handsome charmer still, I see, Jeffrey," she said.

"I see your new beau is causin' quite a stir among the ladies this evenin'." Jeffrey smiled and winked.

"Is he?"

"Come now, Lauryn," he chuckled. "Don't play ignorant."

"The decorations are lovely," Lauryn commented, changing the subject. "Your mother is the perfect hostess."

"You know Mama," he replied. "Perfection! Everyone has to have the time of their lives or she feels she's failed."

"She puts too much pressure on herself. She always does a wonderful job, so she needn't worry," Lauryn assured him. She knew Mrs. McGovern needed to hear reassurances from every venue possible. And she knew Jeffrey would certainly deliver this one.

"May I?" Jeffrey asked, offering his hand to Lauryn.

Lauryn smiled. "Of course, sir."

Jeffrey led her to the dance, a quick fox-trot followed by a waltz. Mrs. McGovern always insisted on numerous waltzes at her parties. She referred to the waltz as "a beacon of classic hope, midst the ridiculous dances of the day that put one in mind of a cluster of recently beheaded chickens runnin' about!"

Jeffrey led Lauryn in the waltz, and as they finished he bowed to her chivalrously and led her from the floor. Immediately, Penny was upon them.

"Lauryn, you look beautiful! That lavender dress is simply a dream!" Penny exclaimed. "And I love this lace," she mumbled, touching the dainty lace at Lauryn's sleeve. Then lowering her voice, she added, "And your Prince Charmin' is too! My stars, Lauryn, if he doesn't send me into fits of delirium nearly!"

"I know it. Believe me, I do," Lauryn confessed as she looked across the room at Brant, who had Mrs. McGovern's captivated attention at that moment.

"You have to tell me," Penny begged, dropping her voice. "You have to, Lauryn. I mean, I haven't seen you for a week! Please tell me that it's because he's had you tied up at some secret rendezvous…your hand held at your back while he threatens to steal your virtue!"

Lauryn giggled. Penny was always so dramatic. And Lauryn had always confided everything in her. But dare she even imply that she had indeed spent time in Brant's arms? Penny's eyes were wide with excitement. And after all, what was a best friend for if not sharing secrets?

"Let's just say," Lauryn began, "Henry's not near the lover we thought him to be."

Penny squealed with delight, and Lauryn shushed her.

"You'll tell me all about it," Penny demanded, "in great detail, later. Won't you?"

"Shhh!" Lauryn warned. "He's comin' this way."

Lauryn watched Brant approach. He strode toward her with confidence and determination, not unlike a lion that had cornered his prey. He reached out and took her hand, placing it in the crook of his arm. "My turn, sugar," he said. "Sorry, Miss McGovern. But the next waltz will be starting shortly, and I need to have your friend here."

Penny giggled. "That's just fine, Mr. Masterson. You do whatever you want with her."

Brant's eyebrows raised, surprised at her comment. "Whatever I want, huh?"

Lauryn's heart was beating like a kettledrum.

"Anythin'," Penny assured him.

"Hmmm," Brant mumbled. "Anything I want, she says, sugar," he whispered in Lauryn's ear. Lauryn didn't even care about the shocked expressions on the faces of several of the older ladies who stood nearby and had caught the conversation between Brant and Penny. All she cared about was that Brant was now leading her to the dance. The music started, and he took her in his arms.

Brant's hand at her waist seemed to burn through Lauryn's clothing, sending a marvelous shiver along her flesh. She looked up to find him smiling down at her. It was the mischievousness in his smile that she loved most in that timeless instant. She fancied that, for all his avoiding mentioning what had happened between them the day before, it was still as fresh in his mind as it was in hers.

"You follow well," he said after a few moments.

"I was taught well," she explained.

He frowned. "Really? How well?"

"Quite well," she answered. Then to her dismay and delight, Brant began to lead into a crossover step—the very same step the Captain taught her years before. Lauryn followed him easily. He smiled and nodded his approval.

"He taught you well, your Captain," Brant noted.

"How did you know it was the Captain?" she asked.

"Who do you think taught me?" he whispered as he leaned toward her ear. Laura taught Brant the step? Lauryn's mouth dropped open in wonderment. "Don't try to tempt me into kissing you," Brant whispered. "My resolve where self-control is concerned is refortified today."

Lauryn shut her mouth quickly, simultaneously thrilled and disappointed.

"Now show me what you're made of. Can you keep up with me?" he asked.

Lauryn narrowed her eyes, accepting his challenge. He led her around the room in a flawless crossover waltz. Eventually, Brant returned to a normal step, and Lauryn triumphantly smiled up at him.

"You realize, of course," he whispered, "that there aren't two other people in this room our age who can pull that off."

"I do," she assured him. Almost instantly, an odd dizziness began to overtake her. It was as if she were looking through a thick fog.

Suddenly, it was the Captain's face she saw before her, the Captain's arms that held her—only for a moment—and then she could see Brant once more. She saw him saying her name, but she could not hear him.

Her dizziness increased as she realized what was happening. It was her vision—the one she'd had years past while dancing with the Captain in her bedroom, that odd, dreamy moment when the Captain seemed to change and she found herself looking through a veil of fog, searching for the identity of a stranger who held her in his arms. It had been Brant, the stranger in the fog! She knew it now! It was Brant who had been shown to her in that visionary dream. And now, that same moment, that blessed peek of the future, it was upon her again. Only it was reality!

"Lauryn?" Brant asked. "Are you all right?" The fog lifted, and the present was all around Lauryn once more. Brant, though still leading her in the waltz, studied her with concern.

"I'm…I'm fine," Lauryn lied. "Just a bit dizzy. You're quite a dancer, and I guess that I am not."

Brant's eyes narrowed suspiciously, but he seemed to let her fib pass. The music ended, and Brant escorted Lauryn to the refreshment table.

"You're sure you're all right?" he asked once more.

"I'm fine," she assured him. "Why don't you take Nana and Aunt Felicity some punch? I'm sure they're simply parched."

Again Brant looked at her, and she knew he was not as easily put off as she had hoped. He nodded. Filling two punch cups, he rather unwillingly left her in search of the two elderly ladies.

Once Brant was far enough away that he could not return too quickly, Lauryn escaped. As quietly and as unnoticeably as she could, she left the party and retreated out to the veranda. Breathing deeply, she tried to calm her frazzled state.

Her vision! The one she'd had years ago while waltzing with the Captain, the foggy vision of her Mr. Perfectly Imperfect—it was Brant! It wasn't as though she hadn't already been feeling he was the one she'd love forever. It wasn't as if she hadn't entertained ideas of belonging to him, being his wife. Of course she had—daily, almost hourly since the very moment she'd met him on the train months ago. But to have this…this…this vision come to her—it had flung her thoughts into complete turmoil, sent her heart aching far worse than it ever had before. She wanted to possess him with a greater urgency! She wanted to abandon everyone and everything else in her life in order to try and win him!

And had she won him? From the perspective of anyone who may have seen his behavior toward her—his attentiveness, their passionate moments under the dogwoods—Lauryn knew anyone witnessing the friendship they'd forged would surely think she had begun to secure him as her own. Of course, few living souls knew of their sleuthing together; few knew of Laura's incredible hold on Brant's loyalty and heart.

Lauryn's vision should've encouraged her, given her new hope. Instead, it depressed her, frightened her, allowed doubt into her soul somehow. Once more, in an unconscious, desperate attempt to shield herself from complete heartbreak, Lauryn tried to convince herself that it was impossible. She couldn't have Brant—not while Laura was still haunting him, not while Laura still occupied the loving space in his heart, maybe never! In her innocence and inability to believe herself worthy of such a man, Lauryn's uncertainties were very well founded in her own inexperienced mind. After everything that tried to tell her otherwise, could she still not believe she was capable of winning Brant for herself?

Looking up into the heavens, she pleaded in a soft whisper, "Please! Please stop this until we've found Laura. I can't take this." She clutched fiercely at the bodice of her blouse as if, somehow, she could squeeze the aching from her heart by doing so. She shook her head and brushed furiously at her tears, wondering how anyone could say that love was the ultimate happiness. She'd even said it herself, simple, naive, and untried fool that she was. How could anyone praise such a love as she owned for Brant when it caused such pain?

With each inhaled breath of air, her feelings for him grew. With every moment she lived, the invisible vine of her love for him wound more densely throughout her body, constricting her breath, stabbing at her heart, and heating her tears. They ran like hot rivulets down her face now as she struggled to calm herself, to steady her breathing and gain some shred of composure.

In those moments, Lauryn's chest began to fairly smolder with the ache of loving Brant. Her very breathing seemed to cause the excruciating pain to further intensify within her—the pain being caused from not being free to have him, his heart not being wholly free to have. He was perfect—perfectly imperfect! Perfect to her, for her. Every dream, every notion she'd ever had of the man she would lose her heart to, was embodied in Brant Masterson. It stung wickedly! For with Lauralynn still lost, the Captain so miserable without her, even despite the mystery that had brought Brant into her life, he seemed unattainable to her—a living, breathing dream never to be realized. And it was insufferable to Lauryn at that moment. She wanted Brant for her own, immediately! She didn't want to share him with Laura, with anyone, anymore!

"Lauryn?" Brant spoke quietly as he approached from behind her.

She released an audible and sorrowful moan of heartache. Always he followed her when she was upset. He never let her wallow in misery for long.

"Are you all right?" he asked, placing a strong hand on her shoulder, urging her to turn and face him.

She nodded silently and tried not to sniffle too loudly.

"What's wrong?" Brant turned her to face him, holding her firmly by the shoulders, and looked. Each time he bent toward her, Lauryn turned from him, embarrassed by her tears.

"Nothing," she lied. "I just…"

Unexpectedly, Brant pulled Lauryn into his arms and against the warm strength of his body. She could not help but return his embrace and sob into the freshness of his shirt.

"I think I understand," he whispered.

"You do?" she asked as fear washed over her. Did he really? Did he know she had fallen desperately in love with him?

As she tried to pull herself from his embrace, he held her tighter and whispered, "It was different when you were a child—exciting, maybe— this needful ghost. But you're an adult now. You want to live your own life. You don't want to have to worry…have the guilt that you have over their unhappiness."

Lauryn was silent. He was assuming their waltz spurred a melancholy over the Captain and Laura. She said nothing. Let him assume it. It was far safer than if he'd guessed at the truth.

He continued, "Then every time you're at a party or with loved ones—dancing, laughing, and just living—the guilt sets in and spoils it. Believe me, I understand. But it's all right, you know. I…I think it's only natural that we would want to leave it all behind and go forward. You don't need to feel bad about it. I mean…I know you do. But it is all right. We've talked about this before."

Lauryn remained silent. Brant, sweet, compassionate, and yet unsuspecting man that he was, still thought she was simply longing for the mystery to be over so she could go on. In a way, that was true, just not for the reasons he thought. And Lauryn was made all the more miserable because of the reality of her situation. If the mystery were solved and Lauralynn found, Brant would return to his home, far away, and be gone from her life. Lauryn's guilt was twofold—guilt at not being able to help the Captain and Lauralynn and guilt at not wanting to help the Captain and Lauralynn.

"I knew you were upset," Brant said, setting his chin on the top of her head as he held her. "When I looked at you just now, in there, the color had drained from you completely." He held her away from him and, using one strong hand tucked under her chin, tipped her face toward his. "I mean…for Pete's sake, Lauryn. You looked like you'd seen a ghost." With that he winked and grinned, amused with himself.

Lauryn smiled through her tears. It had been a witty remark, though Brant would never realize how completely true it had been.

"You're very sweet," she whispered, looking up into his narrowed eyes.

"Am I?" he muttered, and she noticed the way his gaze lingered on her mouth. No doubt her lips were red and slightly swollen from her crying. She noted the barely discernable twitching at the right corner of his smile. Was he withholding his laughter at her appearance or his own humorous remark? In any event, she pulled her face from his grasp and stepped back and out of his arms.

He took one of her hands in his and raised it to his lips, kissing the back of it chivalrously.

"Don't worry, Lauryn," he said, his voice low and soothing like hot cocoa on a cold, rainy night. "We *will* find her."

She forced a comforted smile. When Lauryn looked up at Brant once more, something in his eyes had changed. Again he kissed the back of her hand, and again she noticed the slight twitch at the corner of his mouth. Was it still only her imagination? Or had his lip twitched, ever so slightly, every time before he'd kissed her in the past?

"Will you stay until we find her?" she ventured. She had to ask him. She must know. She'd asked him before, and he'd always seemed to put her off or simply imply that he wouldn't. She needed to know finally and assuredly one way or the other.

Brant sighed and smiled rather sadly at her. "I'll stay as long as I can, Lauryn. And then—if we haven't found her in a reasonable amount of time—I have to go home. But I'll come back. And I'll keep coming back until we do find her."

"And…and after we find her?" Lauryn asked. It was a brave question, and she tried to prepare herself for his answer.

"After we find her?" he repeated, seeming at a loss of understanding.

"Yes. After we find Laura. Then what will you—"

"Oh, there you are!" Georgia exclaimed as she walked quickly toward them. "Brant! Your Uncle Johnny is havin'…well, your auntie called it a 'spell,' and she needs you right away."

"Oh no," Brant mumbled. Quickly, he kissed the back of Lauryn's hand once more. "It'll all be fine," he said firmly as he turned and hurried back into the house.

"Come along, Lauryn," her mother ordered. "We'll most certainly be callin' it an early night. I thought the poor man had passed away right there before me! He's as pale as a sheet, and I'm sure he's not all over it yet."

As she followed her mother back into the McGoverns' house, Lauryn scolded herself, as was her habit. Once again her selfish self-pity had been put to rest by the realization of truly desperate circumstances.

❦

"You'll put us on the train to home in the morning, Brant, and that's that!" Aunt Felicity stated.

Uncle Johnny was in a bad way, a condition he apparently slipped into now and again. Brant's Aunt Felicity explained to Lauryn's Nana and mother that the best thing to do was to get him back home to

Vermont. Brant agreed. He announced that he and his aunt and uncle would be leaving first thing in the morning.

Aunt Felicity argued with him. She had been insisting for near to half an hour that Brant should stay and finish what he'd come to do. Lauryn's guilt throbbed in her bosom. She hoped Brant would choose to stay at Connemara, though she knew he was too good a man to abandon his loved ones for his own purposes.

"Felicity—" Brant began to argue, his patience well past being spent.

"Aunt Felicity, young man!" Felicity snapped.

"Brant should go with you, Felicity," Nana interrupted finally. "You'll need assistance with John."

"I'll not have the boy ruining his fun just because—" Felicity argued.

"Fun?" Brant interrupted. "Auntie, what are you talking about? We've got to get Uncle Johnny home, and you can't possibly do it alone! I wouldn't let you even if you could. Besides…" He paused and looked at Lauryn with a frown. "I need to get back. There's…some things to be done."

Lauryn felt an uncomfortable chill envelop her heart. He was leaving her.

"Brant—" Aunt Felicity began to argue again.

"No more, Auntie," he growled. "We'll leave on the first train out in the morning." Then turning, and without even bidding anyone good night, he left the room and went up the stairs to retire.

ଛ

"He's leavin'," Lauryn told the Captain quietly as he stood next to her bed. "It's up to me again."

"You're very right to be upset that he's leaving, Lauryn. Don't try to make it sound like it's just because he won't be here to help you anymore." The Captain was too wise. Lauryn looked to him with tears in her eyes.

"Are you completely disappointed in me?" she whispered. It seemed she'd done nothing that day but disappoint the men she cherished.

"For loving him?" the Captain asked. He chuckled. "How could you even think that I would begin to begrudge you that?" He frowned at her. "I am disappointed, however, that you don't credit him more highly."

"What do you mean?" Lauryn asked.

"You think he won't come back."

"What reason does he have to come back to Connemara, Captain? There's nothin' more he can do to help me…or so he thinks."

"He's not here to help you, you rotten runt of a girl."

"Please, Captain. I—"

She was interrupted by a knock on the door. This time Brant didn't wait for her response and permission to enter her room. He simply opened the door and stepped in, securing the latch behind him.

"I've got to go back, Lauryn," Brant stated. "I've missed something at home. I want to look through the Captain's things again."

"What?" she breathed.

"I want to look through that old trunk at home, the Captain's belongings. There were things in the Captain's letters to Laura. We understood some of them, and others I don't think we did. Like…the one mentioning old Mr. Jackson. It can't simply be coincidence, Lauryn. And…and I think I need to look through his things. I don't remember seeing letters, but maybe I've just forgotten. I was pretty young when I went through it, and I didn't do a very thorough job. If there are letters…it's like a puzzle in my brain that I can't quite fit together."

"You'll let me know what you find?" she ventured.

He smiled encouragingly and assured her, "Of course." He stood towering above her. "I'll be back, you know."

Lauryn's heart leapt slightly. She wanted to believe him. "I'm sure you will," she whispered, holding back her tears.

His eyes narrowed. "You don't believe me."

"I…I…of course I do," she stammered.

Brant sighed, shaking his head. "You need some sleep, sugar."

"I suppose so," she admitted.

He knelt down by her bed and took her small hands in his. "What's the matter?" he asked. "What's wrong? And why won't you tell me?"

Should she confess? Tell him the truth? She settled for a part of the truth. It was all she could risk.

"I…I don't want you to leave," she sniffled.

He half smiled, half frowned. "I will come back, Lauryn."

Lauryn nodded and tried to believe him. "I know you will. I know."

The corner of his mouth twitched slightly as he looked at her, but he stood up. "Get some sleep now. You're tired."

"Good night," she said as he left.

"Good night, sugar," he responded before he left her room, closing the door behind him.

Brant had barely escaped her trap, he knew. As he ran his fingers through his hair and stripped his clothes off, he realized how close he'd come to faltering. He definitely had to quit going to her room at night. She was too soft, vulnerable, and willing to be in his arms at such hours and in such warm privacy.

It was good that he was taking his aunt and uncle home. He worried that he might take to ravishing Lauryn at any turn if he didn't get away for a while. Yet he did not want to leave her with the loneliness of searching on her own. No. It wasn't even that. He simply did not want to leave her.

As he climbed into the small bed of the guestroom, he wondered if he, in fact, would be able to leave her when the time came.

CHAPTER FIFTEEN

As Lauryn watched Brant help Aunt Felicity board the train, her heart seemed to physically ache at the thought of their leaving. No, at the thought of his leaving! She wanted to reach out and throw her arms around him, beg him not to go, beg him to take her with him. To never leave her side again! *How could it all have come to this so quickly?* she thought.

It seemed like only hours ago that she was on her way home from New Orleans with Nana—home to be with the rest of her family and the Captain. Nothing to that point had been more important to her than her family and helping the Captain. But now, if she could have Brant, if he would love her, want to spend his life with her, want to spend eternity with her, the wicked part in her heart, however small, would abandon the Captain and Lauralynn for the sake of belonging to Brant. Yet there would be no peace in her soul if she did that. But she *would* do it. She would! If it meant Brant would be hers.

But he *was* leaving. His baggage had been loaded onto the train, and Lauryn could see her mother helping Aunt Felicity and Uncle John settle comfortably in their seats.

Please don't leave me, her mind screamed at him. But she kept her mouth tightly closed. She watched him smiling at Nana and talking quietly with her as he held the elderly woman's hand affectionately in his own.

Lauryn heard the train engine begin to rumble a bit louder. With it, her breaking heart pounded harder. There were only mere moments remaining before he would be gone from her. Frantically, her mind began to conjure. How could she induce him to stay? Perhaps if she really did throw her arms about him and beg, surely then he would not leave her. She would faint. That was it! Faint, fall to the ground, and propriety and good manners alone would not allow him to leave an ill friend collapsed on the train station grounds.

"You come back as soon as you can, angel. You hear me?" Nana ordered Brant, gathering him into an affectionate embrace.

"Yes, ma'am," he chuckled as she reached up and pinched his cheek as though he were no more than a boy. Then turning to Patrick, Brant tousled his hair and patted his head. "You take care, Patrick. Stay out of too much trouble."

"Yes, sir," Patrick agreed, barely able to withhold his sweet tears of regret.

Then Brant turned to Lauryn. She could feel the color was gone from her cheeks. All at once, she feared that she really might faint and cause some dramatic episode. He took her hand in one of his; the thrill of his touch and the pain of losing him pounded throughout her whole body.

Reassuringly, he placed his other hand on top of her hand and pressed it firmly. "Lauryn…" he began. But he seemed uncertain as to what he should say.

Lauryn lowered her eyes for a moment. Then she looked up at him once again, trying to be strong. *If he loves me at all, for me, he'd kiss me*, she thought. *If he cared, he wouldn't mind that his aunt and uncle or Nana or the whole world might be watching. He'd kiss me good-bye if he loves me.*

And then, as if Brant read her mind, he let her hand drop. He took her face rather roughly between his powerful hands and kissed her hard on the mouth. Lauryn's heart both soared and broke in that moment. He was kissing her, insensible to whatever or whoever was around them! And he wasn't just giving her a tender, good-bye-at-the-train-station kiss. It was passionate, unbridled!

Instead of breaking from Lauryn immediately, Brant wrapped his arms around her waist, lifting her off her feet as he further ravished her before the public eye. His kiss deepened, in spite of the onlookers present, and Lauryn wrapped her arms around his neck and returned his kiss without restraint.

Patrick's astonished exclamation of, "Oh my hell!" was what finally brought them both to their senses.

"Patrick Kensington!" Nana scolded. "Wherever did you pick up such a thing?"

Brant released Lauryn and, smiling, winked at her guiltily.

Now this, Lauryn thought, was the perfect good-bye-at-the-train-station kiss. Shockingly dramatic enough to raise the eyebrows of every female onlooker and brutally masculine enough to cause every male onlooker to grin approvingly. Most important was the reassurance that it spoke to Lauryn. It was a confirmation of Brant's promise to return! And, oh, how she would miss the nectar of his kiss until he did! Would she starve to death from the lack of its nourishment? she wondered.

Brant stood straight and tall before Lauryn, still silent, as Nana continued scolding Patrick in hushed tones. Searching Lauryn's eyes, he frowned down at her.

Then, very unexpectedly, he took her hand and growled, "That's it." He fairly dragged her toward the train car and boosted her, quite indecorously, onto its boarding stairs. "Porter!" he shouted, retrieving his money clip from his coat pocket. "Porter!" he repeated, and a young man who stood nearby obediently trotted over.

"Mrs. Kensington," Brant addressed Nana as he began to count out a portion of money, "there is indeed someone your granddaughter must meet. My Aunt Felicity and Uncle John will be our chaperones, so you need not fret for propriety's sake. I realize Lauryn is without any belongings. I will remedy that as we go. Aunt Felicity can purchase whatever she may need."

Turning to a young porter, he said, "I need one more fare to match mine for the young lady. Now!" As Brant handed him a fistful of money, the porter understandingly smiled, nodded, and again trotted into the station.

Would not Nana argue against this highly peculiar situation? Lauryn wondered. And why didn't she question it herself?

Georgia stepped past Lauryn and to the ground. "They're both settled in and—"

Turning, Brant looked up, fairly glared at Lauryn, and commanded, "Take a seat near Aunt Felicity. I'll wait for your ticket."

Without a word, without a personal belonging, and even without proper traveling clothes, Lauryn turned and entered the car. Instantly upon entering, she could hear Auntie Felicity's delighted giggle.

"How romantic, my sweet! Kidnapped! And with such masculine determination," the elderly woman squealed gleefully.

It was then that Lauryn's own elation struck. As she sat down in a seat across from Aunt Felicity and gazed out the window, watching Brant explaining to her mother what he had ordered, it was only then she fully realized what had actually transpired in the past few seconds. Brant had, once again, proven himself the man of Lauryn's dreams. He had kissed her—in front of anyone and everyone—kissed her unashamedly, shamefully unashamedly! It had been a fulfillment of one of her many dreams. She would never have dared imagine more. And yet there she sat, ready to accompany him to his home. Without a personal belonging other than the clothes on her back, she was going home with him! To be with him, near him! Dared she hope to be in his arms on occasion there as she had been in Franklin? The thought sent goose bumps erupting over her entire body.

She would meet his family! And could it be that she would perhaps be able to glimpse Lauralynn the way Brant had been able to see the Captain?

Lauryn and Aunt Felicity both turned to look out the window as they heard a resounding, "All aboard!" The train lurched forward, and Lauryn gasped, seeing Brant still standing on the ground talking with her mother. The porter quickly trotted up to Brant and handed him something. Brant bent and quickly kissed Georgia on the cheek. Lauryn sighed with relief as he took hold of the stair bar and nimbly leapt aboard the moving train.

Lauryn smiled and waved to her mother, Nana, and Patrick, who all stood with expressions of shock as they waved back. Nana placed a kiss in her handkerchief and waved it at them as the train pulled away and Brant settled into his seat next to Lauryn.

"Being impulsive can get a man killed," he mumbled, straightening his collar.

"Being impulsive can win a man anything he wants," Auntie Felicity corrected. She then turned her attention to her husband, who was already asleep, though a frown puckered his brow. Felicity tenderly patted one of his hands and laid her head on his shoulder.

"Do you mind?" Brant asked Lauryn. "Coming home with us for a visit? It…it might help us…in our adventure," he explained, winking at her.

"Whatever is there to mind?" Lauryn responded.

"You don't even have a stitch of clothing other than what you've got on this minute," he reminded her.

Lauryn shrugged. "So?" She couldn't help reaching out and delightedly clinging to his powerful arm. He smiled, seeming not only relieved to find her happy but also amused at her excitement.

He raised an uncertain eyebrow and warned, "It's colder in Vermont."

"If you can take the warmth in Franklin, I can take the cool nights in Castledale," she assured him.

"Oh, I'm certain Brant will keep you toasty warm if he needs to, Lauryn," Aunt Felicity giggled.

Sighing heavily and looking out the window as the green of the south began to roll past, Brant thought, *I've lost my mind! I put her on a train bound for a houseful of strangers without an item of clothing or anything to her name…and why? Because I have a ghost haunting me, and she may be able to help me release it.* Then looking down to the beautiful young woman sitting next to him, the young woman who quickly turned her head when he caught her studying him at that same moment, he admitted the truth. *No*, he thought. *Because I've developed an obsession with her and could not leave her.*

He looked away from Lauryn and out the window lest his sudden desire for her again send him pulling her into his arms and ravishing her mouth with heated passion there before his aunt, uncle, and the world! He closed his eyes for a moment, trying to vanquish the desire to kiss her. But his mind only flashed visions of having her in his arms in a more private compartment of the train—of tasting her kiss, of losing his hands in the soft satin of her hair, unpinned by his own hand. Suddenly, he stood, excusing himself with the pretext of having to find the conductor and give him Lauryn's ticket.

What has she done to me? he wondered almost angrily as he made his way down the aisle. This sweet southern pixie? She'd bewitched him into thinking words like "love, marriage, babies!" All his life he'd had his own ghost, a woman lost and in pain without her lover. All his life he'd wanted nothing to do with a love that did such damage to people that it left them wandering for decades after they were dead in search of it. *And now*, he thought, after he'd delivered the ticket and explanation to the conductor and returned to his seat, *Now here I am on the brink of it.* The brink? *No*, he inwardly admitted. *I've already melted with it.*

"April or Rose will have something you can wear when we arrive, sweetheart," Aunt Felicity was assuring Lauryn as Brant maneuvered his way back into his seat by the window. "But Brant will have to hop into a station somewhere along the way and pick you up some necessities. Tooth powder and brush, in the least." Aunt Felicity smiled a she-devil's smile. "Of course, with that kiss back there…I suppose you two could share a toothbrush, and it wouldn't unsettle you in the least!" Lauryn blushed a deep vermilion as Aunt Felicity giggled.

"That's enough, Auntie," Brant grumbled. "The poor girl is about to detonate with embarrassment as it is."

"Oh, she's sturdier than you think, my boy," Aunt Felicity added.

"I know it," Brant admitted. And it was true. He knew Lauryn was up to the adventure. She wasn't worried. It was obvious by the expression on her face that she had complete faith in his ability to protect and provide for her. But he *was* worried about himself! Would he have the self-control necessary to keep his hands off of her long enough to focus on their shared responsibility to their spirit counterparts?

"I won't be much trouble or expense, Brant," Lauryn assured him. He seemed so unsettled suddenly. Lauryn wondered if he trusted her not to be a whining, needful traveler and guest in his father's home. "Truly."

He looked at her, frowning. "I never assumed that you would be, baby."

Lauryn's mouth dropped open, her heart fluttering at his calling her baby. She wanted to throw her arms around his neck and kiss him again. It was all too wonderful! Whether or not his intentions were merely to help further the search for Laura by taking her home to search the Captain's trunk with him, it was fantastic, the whole dream scenery of it all—the passionate kiss at the station, his forcing her onto the train and purchasing a ticket. All of it!

"Wake me for luncheon, darlings. Would you?" Aunt Felicity asked as she closed her eyes and let her head fall back against her seat.

"Yes, ma'am," Brant assured her.

"You can put me off this train and onto another returning at the next stop, Brant," Lauryn offered. She knew he would do no such thing, but she had to let him know she was willing.

"Sshh," he whispered. "Let's let them sleep awhile." Then raising her hand to his lips, he encouragingly kissed the back of it. Then he smiled and added, "Do you think I bucked your mama for nothing?"

Lauryn smiled. "Was she upset?"

Brant smiled too. "She tried to act like she was."

"Why did you bring me, Brant?" Lauryn whispered.

His eyes narrowed, and he paused, searching her face a moment before answering, "If we're going to get this thing solved, we need to keep at it…together."

Lauryn felt the disappointment sneak into her eyes, although she tried to veil it.

He must've seen it, however, for he added, "And besides, you tasted so good back at the station, I figured I'd bring you along…in case I need a snack later." He winked at her and then turned his attention to the passing scenery.

Lauryn thrilled at his teasing and tried to stay relaxed. It was a long trip to Vermont, and she'd have all that time to sit next to Brant, right up next to him, her arm touching his. So she might as well settle down and enjoy it.

Lunch was refreshingly simple, and Uncle Johnny drifted right back to sleep afterward. There were several station stops and dinner before Uncle Johnny and Aunt Felicity were settled in, Uncle Johnny snoring quietly.

Brant had spent a good deal of the trip gazing out the window, and Lauryn had let him keep to himself. He was very pensive, having much to consider. She guessed that he would talk when he was ready. As night fell and there was only darkness visible from the window, he did seem to seek out conversation.

"I really don't remember much of what was in the trunk. I was always a little uncomfortable about having gone through it anyway," Brant told Lauryn. "But even though I don't remember seeing any letters, I may just not remember. And if there are letters from Laura, maybe…maybe…"

"Maybe there'll be somethin' in them," Lauryn finished for him.

"Yeah," he said, smiling at her.

"What do you remember bein' in there?" she asked.

Brant shrugged. "I don't know. Clothes, a large knife, some photographs, a leather book with stuff written in it."

"A diary?" Lauryn was very interested in the possibility of such an item existing.

"A diary?" Brant sneered. "Men don't keep diaries."

Lauryn shook her head and giggled. "All right. A journal then?"

"Maybe," Brant mumbled. Then looking back at her with a deep frown and shaking his head, he grumbled, "A diary?"

Lauryn shrugged at her insignificant ignorance and asked, "What else?"

"That's just it. I don't remember."

"Well, I guess we'll find out, won't we?" she sighed.

"Yeah." Brant was quiet for a moment and then began, "Dad will be happy to meet you. I mean, after all those love letters you two exchanged when I was blind—who knows what the two of you really wrote?"

"He seems a very rare man," she admitted with a smile, "like someone else I know."

"You're not going to transfer your affections to my dad, are you?" Brant teased. "He's available too, you know."

Lauryn rolled her eyes at his ridiculous teasing. "You have to admit, he was kind to help you write to me…uh…us."

"He's a good man," Brant confirmed with an assuring wink. "April and Rose ought to dote on you like you were a new kitten too." He frowned playfully. "I think they always wanted a little sister instead of me."

"Why do you say that?" Lauryn asked. Her eyelids were beginning to feel heavy. In such a relaxed atmosphere, the low hum of the train rolling on the tracks, it would have been hard not to feel tired.

"They used to dress me up in their old dresses when I was a baby and call me Brandy," Brant admitted. "I didn't care much until I was about four. Then it made me mad."

"I think that's sweet," Lauryn whispered, letting her head rest back against the seat. "I used to dress Patrick up the same way. Until he got mad one day and kicked me hard in the shins." Brant's low chuckle was the last thing Lauryn remembered before sleep trapped her into unconsciousness.

Sleep while traveling is often uncomfortable and fitful, and Lauryn roused sometime later to find Brant's head resting against the window as he slept, and hers on his shoulder. She sensed in those moments of half waking that the train car lanterns had been dimmed in order to allow the passengers to rest, and she felt chilled. Wrapping her arms tightly about Brant's strong one against which she rested, she tried to make herself a more comfortable temperature for dozing.

In his light sleep, he seemed to sense her need. Slipping his arm from her grasp and shifting his body slightly, he turned and pulled her against his chest, enfolding her in his warm embrace. Lauryn felt herself smile, lost in a dreamlike bliss as she drifted to a light sleep again.

Sometime later, and there was no way she could truly know how long she'd been sleeping, Lauryn began to wake slowly when she felt the familiar sensation of her hair rebelling against her hairpin and falling down about her face and shoulders. She could feel Brant's warm breath at the top of her head, hear the rhythmic beat of his heart in his chest as her face rested against him. And she felt her hand in his, felt it being raised to his face, felt his lips lightly caressing the backs of her fingers.

Tipping her head upward and opening her weary eyes, Lauryn looked up to find him studying her as he kissed her fingers lightly.

"Go back to sleep," he whispered.

She opened her hand and placed it against his face while letting her thumb travel caressingly over his lips.

"Why?" she asked him. She gazed up at him, awed by his power over her senses, his incredibly handsome features.

"Because it's nighttime and the wolf in me is too close to prowling," he said. His voice was deep, his words insinuative.

"But I like the wolf in you," Lauryn admitted. She knew she was tired and wondered if she were really awake. Surely she hadn't really said that to him.

Brant grinned, his eyebrows raised in slight astonishment. "Really?" he asked, doubtful. Lauryn thrilled at the slight twitching at the corner of his mouth. He wanted to kiss her! He truly did! She knew it. But would he without urging? She wasn't certain.

"Oh yes," she whispered, turning in his arms so that he now cradled her, allowing for her to gaze up at him. She let her hands travel caressively up and over the contours of his chest to rest at his shoulders.

"Lauryn, you're playing with fire here, and I don't think—" he warned.

But some imp alighted on her shoulder and she ignored him. "You said you brought me along in case you needed a snack, Brant," she whispered softly. The look of astonishment on his face was delightful, and she giggled quietly. Brant's surprise was short-lived, however. In the next moment, he took her chin in hand and began an extensive enjoyment of her mouth.

❧

"So you're Lauryn," Darnell Masterson greeted, giving Lauryn a friendly kiss to the back of her hand.

"Yes, sir," she confirmed, recognizing instantly from whence Brant inherited his good looks. "And it's nice to meet you. Thank you so much for havin' me. I—"

"Having you? You mean harboring a kidnapper and his hostage," the man chuckled as he glanced at Brant, who had just returned from settling Uncle Johnny and Aunt Felicity into the house. Darnell Masterson was nearly as tall as Brant, with dark hair that had silvered at his temples.

"When I got Brant's telegram from your last stop, I thought, *I'm gonna turn that boy over my knee!* But now I see…I wouldn't have been able to leave you either."

"Lauryn's here to help me go through the Captain's things," Brant explained.

"Hell, I know that, Brant. You don't have to tell me," Darnell chuckled. Lauryn smiled, noting that Brant's father made no effort to apologize for his swearing. She was delighted by the fact that the apple hadn't fallen far from the tree where this father and son were concerned.

Just then, an auto in which were two beautiful, black-haired young women pulled up into the dirt drive in front of the Masterson home.

The two women alighted immediately, rushing forward in a flurry of raven locks and swaying skirts.

"Brant! Brant!" they called simultaneously, two sets of blue eyes flashing with excitement. "Our baby is home!"

Brant chuckled as the two females, obviously his sisters, Rose and April, captured him in loving embraces, smothering him with kisses.

"You handsome fool! What have you done?" one of the young ladies asked, nodding in Lauryn's direction. "He didn't molest you in any way, did he, Miss Kensington?" she asked.

Lauryn couldn't stop the heated blush that rose to her cheeks, and before she could answer, the other woman scolded her little brother. "Brant, you devil!"

"She's fine. She's fine. Aren't you, Lauryn?" Brant chuckled.

"Yes," Lauryn squeaked.

Instantly, the two sisters were upon her. "I love your hair!" one said. "Isn't this the most beautiful hair you've ever seen, Rose?"

"Oh my, yes!" Rose agreed. "Our little nieces-to-be will look so lovely with this in French braids."

"Rose," Brant scolded, "knock it off. Lauryn's not used to that kind of teasing."

The sisters looked to one another, skeptical, and then back to their little brother. "Is that right, Brant?"

"Welcome to Castledale, Lauryn," April greeted, taking Lauryn's hand in her own. "We're quite a herd of characters, you know. I hope you can stand us."

Lauryn could only smile and nod. It was like having Aunt Felicity twice over and younger standing before her. The teasing manner, even their features, were similar.

"Come on into the house, sweet thing," Rose said, putting a reassuring arm around Lauryn's shoulder. "You must be worn to a frazzle."

"Let's get you fed and rested," April suggested, taking Lauryn's hand and pulling her into the house. "Then you can tell us all about your trip."

As an afterthought, April looked back to her father and Brant. "We'll get some supper on, Daddy. Brant, be a dear and dig up Parker, will you? I think he's out in the orchards."

"Well, you're as bossy as ever," Brant said.

"And just as cute," April giggled. "So you still can't tell me no, can you?"

ଛ

"So," Rose continued as everyone sat around the table after dinner, "Brant comes downstairs one day and tells us he's got a ghost in his room. We, of course, just think he's fooling. I mean you know how he is, Lauryn. And he's been like that since he was born."

Parker was present, and April's and Rose's husbands and small babies. It had been quite a different dinner than Lauryn had been used to. The babies (there were three—two were April's, and one belonged to Rose) were toddling or crawling around merrily while the adults ate. Once in a while, Parker would toss a crumb to the oldest child, after whistling to him as though he were calling a dog. Lauryn, at first, wasn't certain whether she should be horrified at the treatment of the child or amused. But when everyone from Darnell on down broke into laughter and applause, delighting the child with admiration, she realized that it must be a special sort of "trick" shared by the family.

"Anyway," Rose raved on, "I was scared to go into Brant's room for months afterward!"

"You're scared to go in his room now, Rose," April reminded.

"And you're not?" Rose asked.

"Not if Brant goes with me," April defended herself.

Lauryn looked at Brant. He winked at her, obviously as amused as she was at the bantering of the two talkative sisters.

"And then Aunt Felicity talked your very own grandmother into coming up. I remember thinking she was the most beautiful woman I had ever seen next to Mother," Rose sighed.

"Yes. I can remember wishing I had been from the south so I could be so beautiful and refined," April agreed.

"We're going, Darnell," April's husband, Roy, said as he stood and offered a hand to his father-in-law.

"Roy isn't much for talking," Brant explained in a whisper to Lauryn. "Probably because he never has the chance." Lauryn stifled her own laughter, even though the very same thought had crossed her mind.

"Now, Roy? You can't be serious." April argued. Nevertheless, she reached down and picked up the toddler that had wearily laid his head on her lap.

"I'm certain Miss Kensington needs some rest. And there's no way in hell Felicity and John are getting any sleep with all this cackling going on," Anthony, Rose's husband, added, standing and also shaking Darnell's hand.

"You all have a good evening," Darnell said as he kissed his daughters and grandbabies affectionately.

"I cannot believe you are dragging us away like this," Rose protested as Anthony helped her gather the baby. "And you swore in front of Lauryn! I'm certain she isn't used to such language where she comes from."

"Hell no. They're refined southerners at Connemara," Brant exclaimed emphatically, sending all the men into triumphant laughter.

April and Rose gasped and turned to Lauryn. "If you get tired of all this...this barbaric nonsense," Rose told her, "you have Brant drive you on over to our place. You hear me?"

"Thank you. I will," Lauryn said, nodding, and realized it was the first thing she'd said since dinner ended.

Everyone stood on the front porch waving as Brant's sisters and their families drove away. Once they were out of sight, Lauryn giggled when Brant, Parker, and their father concurrently sighed with relief.

"Roy and Anthony will both be deaf before they're thirty," Parker mumbled.

Darnell chuckled and patted him on the back. "Well, your Violet is a quiet little thing, Park. Your ears shouldn't be in danger." Lauryn felt her nerves tighten when Darnell turned to her next. She couldn't relax in his presence, for inwardly, she longed for his approval. "And what about you, Lauryn?" he asked. "Are you a quiet one? It's hard for us to know. No one gets a word in edgewise when April and Rose are in the house."

Lauryn smiled. "I'm afraid I can talk a pretty mean streak when I have a mind to, sir."

Darnell chuckled. "I bet you can." He nodded his head approvingly and winked at her. "And why don't you call me Darnell instead of sir?"

"Why...I couldn't possibly," Lauryn argued.

"Well, how about Mr. Masterson at least? I'm not used to all this respect," Brant's father teased.

"All right," Lauryn agreed. "I'll try my best." Darnell chuckled again and then, turning to Brant, patted him firmly on the shoulder as he had Parker.

"Well, tuck her in tight, my boy. Felicity was done in and is probably sawing logs for the night." Brant nodded at his father, and Darnell turned to Lauryn once more. "Keep him in line, my girl," he added with a wink. "He's a bit too much like me to be trusted completely."

℞

"This was the girls' room when they were home," Brant explained as he spread an extra quilt over one of the two beds in the small, delicately decorated room where Lauryn would be staying. "I built a fire too. Figured you'd be cold."

Lauryn stood staring at Brant. He was so magnificent, and his home was so cozy, wonderful, and welcoming. He fluffed the pillow on her bed, and she smiled, pulling his jacket more tightly about her shoulders. He had draped his jacket around her shoulders early in the evening when she had been chilled. She loved wearing it. It smelled like him, was warm and large like he was.

Having been raised in the warmest of weather, and never having been further north in her life than Knoxville, Lauryn was quite chilly in Vermont. She wished Brant's arms were keeping her warm and not merely his jacket.

"Aunt Felicity laid out some things for you before she went to bed," Brant said, pointing to the nightdress lying on a nearby chair. "And if you need anything else," he added as he stood gazing down at her, "I'm right across the hall."

Lauryn could only nod her understanding. She feared if she spoke, she might simply ask him to ravish her with a good-night kiss.

"All right then," he sighed. "I'll leave you to your sweet dreams." He started to walk past her to the door but paused. Looking down at her, he grinned and asked, "What do you dream about, Lauryn?"

Lauryn smiled, trying to appear as if her heart weren't hammering nearly out of her chest because of his nearness. Shrugging, she answered, "I don't know. It mostly depends on what I've been thinkin' about before I go to sleep."

"Really?" he chuckled. "So…" He took her by the shoulders and turned her to face him. "So if I were to, say, be the last thing you saw before you fell asleep…do you think I might make an appearance?"

Lauryn cast her eyes down shyly. He probably suspected that all her dreams were built around him anyway. But she'd play his game. "Maybe," she admitted.

He took her chin in his hand and tilted her face to look up at him. "What would I have to do to be in your dreams, Lauryn?" he asked in the deep, provocative tone that made her mouth begin to water.

Exist, she thought. But she said, "Anythin'." He smiled triumphantly and pulled her against his body, burying his face in her hair for a moment before lingeringly kissing her neck. He kissed her cheek, her temple, and then her neck once more. Lauryn thought she might actually scream with frustration if he didn't kiss her fully on the mouth soon. And still his face lingered at her throat until, finally, the moisture in her mouth, her need for reassurance, pushed her beyond the limits of her own shyness. Taking his face in her hands, she directed his kiss to her lips. When at last he kissed her dominantly, demandingly, it was if the greatest thirst she'd ever known were being quenched, satisfied, but at the same time remaining unsatisfied.

He broke the seal of their lips and kissed her forehead as he whispered, "Good night, Lauryn. And if that doesn't get me into your dreams…I doubt that I can make it at all." With a wink, he left her alone, but much warmer than she'd been all evening.

※

The battle raged violent and mercilessly in the fields and streets of Franklin. Men were lying in the blood-soaked grasses of Tennessee; men were dying in the soft grasses of Tennessee. Men in uniform, gray uniforms with brass buttons. Buttons tarnished with blood and mud. Brass buttons with the letters "CSA" embossed on them. Young men. Men in gray—no. Men in a worn hue of green. Men in brown and green uniforms. Uniforms splattered with mud. Men lying in trenches, covered in mud and blood. No! Men lying in grass. Young men, very young men, lying in the Tennessee grass that was now stained blood-red. But…the men were in trenches! There were no brass buttons on these men. No buttons with the initials "CSA" on them. These men were in trenches in brown and green uniforms. But they were in…

"She's having a nightmare," came Brant's voice on the wind. "Wake her up, Laura."

The visions of dying men, whether in gray uniforms in the grass or brown ones in the trenches, began to fade. In their place were visions of home. Of beautiful, comforting, safe Connemara. Connemara, fragrant with spring's wisteria and Nana's cinnamon rolls. Connemara with the Captain sitting out by Henry, watching Patrick play, the small boy completely unaware of his audience. Connemara with its lace and velvets, its pansies and ghost.

Someone was stroking her hair. A soft hand, a woman's hand. Lauryn could feel a soothing touch smoothing her brow, and Connemara was there too—for the fragrance of Connemara's beautiful wisteria filled Lauryn's senses, and it comforted her. It vanquished the horrible dreams of war. And Lauryn opened her eyes. When she opened them and beheld the beauty of Connemara hovering above her, she was no longer frightened. She smiled. For the beauty of home, of Connemara, was there before her in the image—no, in the presence of Lauralynn.

"Brant," Lauryn whispered as she gazed at the beautiful spirit sitting on the edge of her bed, stroking her hair lovingly. "She's here."

"I know," Brant said from where he stood at the foot of her bed. "She couldn't wait to meet you. I told her you were tired. But you know how ill-tempered the Irish are. Especially the women." Lauralynn turned and playfully scowled at Brant before returning her attention to Lauryn.

"You're so beautiful, she says," Brant translated as Lauryn watched Laura's eyes fill with moisture. Her lips moved in silence again, and Brant added, "She says you put her in mind of Virginia."

Lauryn began to weep as Laura's own tears fell from her haunting eyes. Her great-aunt was so much more beautiful than she'd ever imagined. People never smiled in photographs in the past. It wasn't considered proper. Therefore, Lauryn had never seen Lauralynn's smile, and it was breathtaking. There was something else the old family photographs had never revealed—her hair! It was almost perfectly the color of fresh, summer-morning cream and hung in long, wavy ringlets, giving the ghostly vision the appearance of a fairy sprite. It was Lauryn's own hair, only cream-colored instead of sifted cinnamon and nutmeg. All these years, Lauryn had wondered from whence she'd inherited her wild tresses. And here was the answer sitting next to her!

Her eyes were brown, as brown as chocolate. They sparkled with a sadness that made Lauryn's tears flow even more profusely. She was there, Laura! She could feel her, smell her, see her as surely as she could the Captain.

"He loves you so much," Lauryn blurted out suddenly. "He's never given up. And I...I promise."

Lauralynn O'Halleran Masterson put one dainty index finger to her lips and smiled, nodding. Then she took Lauryn's face in her hands and kissed her cheeks sweetly. And somehow, even for her silence, Lauryn understood. There would be time to discuss it all, time for questions and searching. But Lauralynn had wanted to meet her grandniece. That was what she'd come for this time. Somehow, Lauryn understood that. And with one more gentle kiss placed on Lauryn's forehead, and a soft whisper of "Lauryn," she was gone, leaving only the lingering fragrance of wisteria.

"You loved her instantly, didn't you?" Brant asked in a whisper.

"I did," Lauryn admitted, wiping her tears from her cheeks.

Brant smiled, complete understanding evident in his expression. "I'll leave you then, to get some rest so that—"

"I can't possibly sleep now, Brant!" Lauryn exclaimed, fairly leaping from her bed and snatching the robe Aunt Felicity had left from a nearby chair. "Take me to the Captain's trunk."

"Now?" Brant asked, standing before her in nothing but his trousers.

"Well, of course. That's what we came to do, isn't it?"

Brant smiled and nodded. "We did."

The attic of Brant's family home wasn't nearly as inviting, or as well kept, as the attic at Connemara. Still, Lauryn found it somewhat charming in its own right, even though completely frigid. It was dark, except for the light of the lantern Brant brought with them, and smelled of dust that had been settling for years.

"It's pretty creepy up here," Brant mumbled as he tossed aside an old quilt covering several trunks.

"Are there spiders?" Lauryn ventured.

"Of course," Brant answered plainly.

Lauryn scratched the back of her neck as it prickled with anticipation of the possibility of seeing an eight-legged nemesis at any given moment.

"It's right here," Brant mumbled, setting the lantern on the floor next to where he hunkered. "Are you sure we should—"

"Open it," Lauryn demanded. She was curious, cold, and impatient.

"Bossy little thing when you're tired, aren't you?" Brant struggled with the trunk latch for a moment, and then, as Lauryn's eyes widened, he lifted the lid to reveal the ancient treasures within.

Reverently, Lauryn knelt next to Brant and peered into the trunk. A man's trunk was differently packed than a woman's, and no doubt the things he held valuable would be just as dissimilar.

"Go ahead," Brant whispered. "You first."

It struck Lauryn then how uncomfortable Brant was about the Captain. He hadn't known the Captain like she had. To him, the Captain was a stranger.

Reaching into the trunk, Lauryn blinked back the tears that welled into her eyes at the realization the Captain's possessions, tangible items that he had owned, were at her fingertips. The first thing she removed was a set of men's clothing, a suit. It was dark blue, woolen.

"Probably his wedding clothes," Brant mumbled.

Lauryn nodded and wiped the tears from her cheeks as she tenderly laid the suit aside. She shivered, chilled by the cold night air of Vermont.

"Come here," Brant demanded, sitting down on the floor. He pulled Lauryn into his lap and rubbed her arms for a moment to warm her.

Lauryn smiled, much warmer in Brant's protective grasp, and reached into the trunk again. A large knife, the handle engraved with the Captain's name, was the next item she found herself studying.

"It was a gift from his father," Brant explained, "on his twelfth birthday. A hunting knife."

"Seems a little lethal for a boy of twelve," Lauryn mused, trying to imagine Patrick in possession of such a knife in just a few years.

There was a stack of photographs within, photographs of Lauralynn and of ancestors unknown to Lauryn but familiar to Brant.

"There's Aunt Felicity." Brant pointed to a young girl posing stiffly in one group photo in which Lauryn also recognized a younger, less matured Brandon Masterson.

"She's adorable!" Lauryn exclaimed in delight upon identifying Brant's great-aunt as a girl of perhaps five or six, slathered in ringlets and lace.

Brant chuckled. "She looks very much the same in a way. Doesn't she?"

"And I'm certain she was just as saucy." Lauryn caressed the photograph, melancholy over the years that had passed between its creation and the time they now held it.

"I don't doubt it," Brant mumbled.

Setting aside the photographs, Lauryn retrieved other items from the trunk—an old bridle, a piece of cedar whittled into the shape of a pistol, and a tiny box marked *Lauralynn*, which held several locks of wavy, cream-colored hair. Last was the leather-bound book.

"The diary!" Lauryn exclaimed in awe.

"Journal," Brant corrected.

Lauryn looked over her shoulder and smiled up at him. "The journal," she corrected.

Her body began to tremble with the anticipation of secrets the book might contain. Would she and Brant find answers within? Would finding the answers they needed to reunite the Captain and Laura be that simple for them? As simple as cracking the spine of a book that had been at Brant's fingertips for nearly his entire life?

Immediately, Lauryn's hopes were dashed as she carefully turned the pages, realizing that it was merely a ledger of Brand's personal finances—money earned, obligations paid. Yet there were still interesting things to be noted.

"Look at this," Lauryn whispered. "It's a notation about a purchase from a jeweler. *One gold wedding band with, and including, three stones: one diamond (1/2 carat), two rubies (1/4 carat each).*"

"Laura's wedding ring from Brand," Brant mumbled. "It's a legendary story in our family. He spent six months' wages on it, or something like that."

Lauryn smiled and flipped through several more pages of the book. "And look at this," she muttered. "After they were married…almost six months later. *$10 United States Currency…sent to Laura to give to C.*"

"I'm sure he had to send her every cent he got," Brant offered. "Confederate money was worthless by then, and she was still in Franklin."

"I wonder what 'C' means," Lauryn mused. Still, the book, as interesting and as priceless a treasure that it was, didn't seem to hold any keys to the mystery of Laura's disappearance. "That's it," Lauryn sighed as she leaned over and looked into the empty trunk to ensure she'd removed everything.

Brant sighed. "I guess I kidnapped you for nothing." He leaned over, placing his hand in the bottom of the trunk and feeling around as if hoping to find some tiny clue. He sighed again, admitting their cause was lost—for the moment.

"Let's get back to bed," he grumbled, carefully pushing Lauryn from his lap and standing.

But Lauryn wasn't finished. These were the Captain's things, his earthly life.

"Would you…would you mind if I stayed a moment?" she asked. "Just to…just think on it all?"

Brant rubbed his tired eyes. "Of course not." And sensing she wanted to be alone, he asked, "Can you find your way back? Will you be careful on the stairs?"

Lauryn smiled up at him, "Yes, Brant. Thank you."

He nodded and left her to her own thoughts.

The moment he was gone, Lauryn burst into sobbing. However would they find Laura? There seemed no way. Brant and Lauryn had searched everywhere, taxed their brains until they were sore! And for what? For nothing! Nothing except frustration and something to keep them both from going on with life.

Heartbroken, defeated, and fatigued, Lauryn lay down on the dusty pile of quilts nearby and continued to sob. For a long time she cried— cried for the Captain, for his lost beauty, and for Brant. Cried for want of owning his heart, freely.

After a while, she began to feel a soothing warmth, a soft hand stroking her hair. She breathed in the fragrances of Connemara and home. She was not alone any longer. She could sense Laura at her side, and even though she could feel her hair moving as the ghostly beauty comforted her, even though she could just barely discern the beloved scent of the wisteria of Connemara, Lauralynn did not fully reveal herself. She stayed a whisper away from Lauryn's vision, and this prompted the tormented girl that lay on the quilts to close her eyes. To dream of home and of Brant. Of his smile and embrace. Of his kiss and protective nature. And she slept then—slept peacefully as one by one an unseen presence lovingly returned the Captain's things to the confines of the trunk nearby.

CHAPTER SIXTEEN

Brant pushed open the door to the attic. The sun hadn't quite risen yet. Still, the first rays of its arrival were peeking through the dusty attic windows and allowed just enough light for Brant to see through the darkness of the dusty room.

He had spent a fitful night, and for two very good reasons—the fact that he had the overwhelming feeling of having overlooked something important and the fact that he couldn't keep Lauryn out of his mind's eye.

She was distracting him, he knew, and this distraction was slowing their search. At the same time, he wanted the distraction. He wanted to concentrate on ways to make her cheeks burn with a delighted blush. He wanted to hold her, kiss her, talk to her about something besides the infernal problem before them.

Yes, she was distracting him to a dangerous level. He'd lain awake for some time after leaving her in the attic, wondering what he should do. Should he cut himself off from her completely, except to discuss the Captain and Laura's predicament? He'd almost convinced himself that he should, for he kept thinking of the expression on her face when he'd kissed her in the train, when he'd nearly ravished her under the dogwoods—the flash of her eyes, the pink in her beautiful cheeks.

Lauryn loved him. He was certain of it—and yet not certain. Surely not, he kept telling himself. But there were his own feelings to consider—the way he felt in her presence, the thoughts that traveled through his mind almost constantly. Those disturbing thoughts of wedding vows and spending six months of his own salary on some small but very significant piece of jewelry the way Brandon Masterson had.

But there was no freedom to feel, not while Laura was in such misery, not while she was lost. So he tried to bury his thoughts of Lauryn and weddings and babies. He tried to bury them, and he made up his mind about the distraction Lauryn proved to be. There must be some separation. He must keep himself from wanting her, from having her, from tasting her kisses. He had to put her away from him until the damnable mess was worked out.

And then it began to plague him again—intensely—the knowledge that there had to be something they'd missed. As he and Lauryn had been searching late into the night, he'd felt compelled, as he did now. They'd missed something. So intent was he on finding the "something" that he almost tripped and fell over Lauryn, who lay sleeping on the pile of old quilts. At once, all of Brant's compelling thoughts of searching out answers were gone—all his convictions at resisting her, gone. Lost to the overpowering scene before him.

Visions of Aunt Felicity's bedtime stories of forest fairies and sleeping beauties flashed through his mind. For there she was, indeed lying before him in peaceful slumber, the most beautiful girl he'd ever seen! It was like catching a leprechaun or finding a pixie asleep in the woods. He stood for a long time looking at her, studying the way her mass of wavy hair spread over the quilts on which she lay. The way her face, turned to one side, displayed the smooth soft surface of her neck. The way her hands lay, so relaxed, so lovely, one next to her face the other on her tummy.

Brant hunkered down, enthralled with the opportunity to again watch her so unguarded. It was impossible to study her at such length while she was awake and looking at him, talking to him. It would seem odd to her, he was certain, had he stared at her this way during one of their conversations. In a whisper, he thanked the heavens for the gift of letting him have his sight restored if for this moment only. Beholding before him such a sweet and beautiful vision as this, he was overwhelmingly thankful that he could see.

He let his hand feel the soft curls of her hair as they lay over the quilt. He could sense the corner of his mouth twitch as he gazed at her berry-red lips, parted gently as she slept. Closing his eyes for a moment, he tried to remind himself that she was his friend—a friend that had become far more than that but that he had only in the past few hours resolved must become merely his friend again—a friend who was trapped in a mystery with him, trapped by the past. A girl who…but his heart had started to beat faster, and the moisture in his mouth had increased until his sense of reason was all but gone. Gently, he slipped his hand beneath her head, grasping her carefully as he allowed himself to visually drink of her beauty—to taste the tender flesh of her neck with the softest of kisses. Closing his eyes, he remembered the moment in Franklin when she'd allowed him to smell her, and he noted her neck tasted far more delicious than even she had smelled. He was reminded then of their picnic when finally, blessedly finally, he'd been able to kiss her, drink warm fascination from her lips.

He'd meant to kiss her neck just once, to feel her skin beneath his lips and then leave her to her dreams, whatever or whomever they might be about. But she was like some strange potion causing a craving in him that he could hardly control, and he could not leave her. He let his mouth linger there, his lips pressed gently against her skin. And he was fairly strong, resistant to his desires, until he felt her small hand at the back of his head, her fingers sliding up his neck and into his hair. Then, when she fisted her hand, his hair clutched tightly in it, his strength was lost, and he collapsed beside her, wrapping his own powerful hand in her silken tresses. Pulling her head backward, he let his mouth travel to her throat, trailing kisses from the soft hollow of it upward to her chin.

As Brant's hands went to her face, his thumbs tracing her lips as he continued to place tender kisses on her neck and throat, Lauryn was afraid to open her eyes. Surely she was still dreaming! Allowing herself to awaken might instantly vanquish the bliss she was feeling. But she could not help his name slipping from her lips. "Brant," she whispered.

His kiss immediately stopped. So it was that she opened her eyes to see him, frowning, intent on her. Suddenly she was ashamed—ashamed of the passion she was feeling, ashamed of the blush that must be apparent on her face, the intoxicated light that, no doubt, burned in her eyes. She looked away, turning her face from him. She heard him curse angrily under his breath as he stood, fairly yanking her to her feet.

Clutching her hand tightly, he stomped toward the attic door, pulling her with him.

Lauryn felt tears rising in her throat as she followed him down the stairs, outside, and toward the orchards. He seemed to care nothing for the fact that she wore only a nightdress and a robe—care nothing for the fact that the sun was beginning to break over the hills to the east and everyone in the house would be rising at any moment. And why did he seem so angry when only moments before he'd been showering her with affection? She was confused, somewhat frightened, and very, very chilly.

Brant stopped abruptly beneath an ancient-looking apple tree bursting with fragrant spring blossoms.

"What, Brant? What is it?" she asked breathlessly.

How much was a man supposed to endure? How strong was he expected to be? She was adorable! Smart, witty, comical, beautiful! Soft, sweet, delicious, fragrant! What man could keep himself from such a woman? How did other men resist pouring out their heartfelt confessions of love to a woman like this the way he had, sincere or otherwise? Then he thought, *They don't! They write poetry, kill brothers, fight wars, cut off their ears with love in their blood and hearts.* He wanted her for himself. There! He'd admitted it. But he couldn't tell her—not now, not yet—for he feared that losing themselves in each other would keep them from freeing those tortured souls, and failure would somehow keep them from finding their own happiness. And so he answered her question. As a breeze blew through the secluded orchard, showering pink and white blossom petals over them, he answered her.

"We're friends, Lauryn," Brant mumbled as he tucked a wavy lock of cinnamon hair behind her ear and stepped toward her. Putting a hand gently to her throat, he pushed her backward, indicating she should walk, and thereby led her into further seclusion among the trees. The fire in his eyes told Lauryn of a tremendous passion lurking in him— unreleased, barely controlled. And a heat that began in her stomach, spreading out to her bosom and limbs, filling her cheeks with a rosy blush, permeated her being. There was a plush bed of grass, covered in blossoms in this secret part of the orchards, a place completely surrounded by the trees. Their sweet perfume was so different from the wisteria of Franklin, so strong and intoxicating, that Lauryn felt dizzy for a moment.

Brant sat down on the grass, seeming indifferent to the heavy morning dew. Pulling Lauryn to sit next to him and leaning back, stretching out his legs and propping his body up on one elbow, he looked up at her, his eyes narrowed and on fire with mischief.

"We're good friends," his voice mumbled, provocatively. Lauryn watched, mesmerized, as he unbuttoned his collar button and two more below that. "We're very good friends, Lauryn," he mumbled as he took her hand and coaxed her closer to him. Without pause, she leaned forward, looking down into his hypnotically handsome face.

"We're very good friends…who kiss." He reached up and caressed her cheek with the back of his hand. "And I intend to spend this sunrise kissing my very good friend."

Though the thought of his kisses was elating to Lauryn, his talk of friendship unsettled her somehow. There was something in his demeanor, a prophetic finality in his words. It frightened her.

"Friends don't…" Lauryn began breathlessly. It was not what she had wanted to hear. Friends? What she felt for him was so far and away beyond mere friendship, though that was part of it too. But there was more, for her. And yet his words were almost more seducing than had he confessed a mad, incurable love for her.

"Friends *do*, Lauryn," he mumbled.

Lauryn's heart was hammering so brutally in her chest that it was actually painful, torn between anxiety and the joyful anticipation of receiving his kiss. Lauryn gasped as he reached up, slid his hand around the back of her neck, and pulled her face downward toward his own. The first touch of his lips to hers was soft, barely discernable, so teasing yet so full of a promise. A promise of passion and more.

"Are you cold, baby?" he whispered into her ear as he pressed his whiskery cheek to hers.

"Yes," she admitted as her hands clutched the front of his shirt.

Brant pressed his forehead against Lauryn's, reveling in the sensation of her nutmeg tresses cascading down around his face and shoulders. Silently he apologized to Laura. But she would understand. She'd waited fifty years. Surely allowing himself a few more moments with such a beauty as this would not disappoint his spirit friend too much.

Indeed, he expected Laura would more than understand. And then he released his mind from its torment, and all there was to him was the girl that would soon be in his arms. He'd suffered much, and he would allow one more moment of beauty before denying it to himself until Laura was found.

Wrapping her tightly in his arms, Brant whispered, "I'll keep you warm." He kissed her forehead. Still, Lauryn resisted giving herself to him. She was frightened—frightened of something she couldn't see. There was a determination about him. A determination to...to what? And yet his arms were warm and inviting.

Reaching up, Brant took Lauryn's face in his hands as he laid her down in the grass next to him. He watched with delight as her hair fell in waves onto the green carpet woven by nature beneath them. Then he kissed her tenderly on the lips several times.

Brant's lips were warm, moist, as his kiss lingered on just her upper lip for a time. So wildly sensational was the gesture that Lauryn's entire body shivered involuntarily, breaking into goose bumps over every inch of flesh that held her together.

Lauryn looked at him for several long moments, seeing a deep regret burning with the passion in his eyes. Brant's hand, lost in her hair, his mouth whispering her own name in her ear, caused her coherent thoughts to be lost in a cloud of enchanted bliss. And when her mouth met with his, her heart understood what he was telling her. The message was deeper than his words. His hand at her waist, his mouth met with her own, hot, moist, reviving like some magical nectar—therein was his meaning unspoken. Her heart knew it, at last. He loved her! Truly loved her! For the moments spent in the orchard that day, apple blossoms falling about them like soft fragrant rain whenever the breeze intruded on their privacy, she lived the dream of his perfect kiss—of knowing that, though he could not speak it yet, Brant did love her. She knew with each caress he offered, the way he touched her face as they kissed. Let his hands caress her arms, her waist, tug on her hair. Let her catch her breath now and then as he kissed her neck, cheek, forehead, hands, shoulders. And as the sun rose higher, as its brilliant beams warmed the day, Lauryn held him, kissed him, cried for him.

Brant's shirt worked itself from being tucked in his trousers, and Lauryn's own palms tingled with the feel of his skin beneath her hands. In fact, the first time her bare palm met the exposed flesh of his back in her feminine caress, he shuddered, and she felt the goose bumps spring up on his skin beneath her hand. Felt his kisses intensify briefly. He was so warm and strong and capable. So intelligent, clever, protective, determined. So handsome, desirable.

Then, all too abruptly, Brant stood and pulled her to her feet. "Let's get you in the house before you catch a cold," he grumbled.

Lauryn paused. She tugged at his arm, and he turned to face her.

"You…you have somethin' to say to me, don't you, Brant?" she whispered. She knew he wouldn't confess anything to her—not yet, not while Laura was still in agony. But still she hoped—hoped to hear the words from his lips.

"We've missed something in the attic," he mumbled as he dropped his gaze and began tucking in his shirt.

"Oh," Lauryn muttered, beginning to shiver, for now her robe and nightdress were wet from having lain in the morning dew. And her heart, her heart was disappointed that he would not speak to her verbally what his soul had told her moments ago.

Brant looked away briefly, and Lauryn thought she caught the glisten of excess moisture in his eyes. She watched the lines of his face, able to see the clenching of his jaw.

"I want you, Lauryn," he mumbled. The confession was brutally masculine, strong, and unshakable. "I do. More than you will ever realize."

"But?" she offered.

"But…but…" he stammered.

"But that's all. I'm a friend…who has served as a diversion—"

"No!" he shouted, turning and taking her by the shoulders. "I mean, yes! You're my friend. And you're a diversion. But not in the way you're thinking."

"I understand, Brant," she told him, her voice breaking with emotion. "Truly. I do."

"No! You're misunderstanding!" he growled.

"I'm not," she said, placing a gentle hand to his cheek. "I do understand."

"Do you?" he asked, searching her face. "You are a distraction, Lauryn—a beautiful distraction that keeps me from…from concentrating. I can't think clearly when you're in my arms. I don't want to. I can't even remember Laura's name when I taste you. And if I can't get this—if I can't find her—it will destroy everything. If I can't find her, I'll be haunted…like no ghost could ever haunt me. Life will be…I can't live my life until…"

Lauryn nodded. "I know." Should she argue with him? No. She knew he spoke the truth. She asked herself then how much time she'd spent talking with the Captain and trying to glean clues from him since Brant had entered her life. Probably not more than a few hours. She asked herself how much time she'd spent in actually searching, in thinking of every venue possible. Even when she and Brant were talking about it, looking, searching, her mind wasn't truly focused.

"You're right," she whispered, wiping a tear from her cheek and shivering as her teeth began to chatter. "You're right. Let's go in," she suggested, walking past him and toward the house.

"Lauryn," Brant began. There was a tone of reconsidering his actions.

"No, Brant. Don't say anythin' else. Let's just get inside," Lauryn interrupted him as she hurried toward the house.

Once in her room, as she changed her wet nightclothes for dry day ones, she thought, *Lauralynn? Where did your father hide you?*

❧

"Did you sleep well, sweetie?" Aunt Felicity asked as Lauryn entered the kitchen later that morning.

"Yes, ma'am," Lauryn answered, pasting on a cheery smile. "And how is Mr. John?"

"He's much better, my darling. Much better." Aunt Felicity's smile softened. "I'm sorry John and I had to spoil Brant's visit to Connemara, sweet thing."

"You didn't spoil anything, Auntie," Brant corrected, appearing and kissing his aunt affectionately on the cheek. Lauryn was cautious when she looked at him, afraid she might rush to him, beg him to tell her what she so wanted him to—that he loved her and that they would be together once Laura was found. But she only smiled at him when he greeted, "Good morning."

"Good mornin', Brant," she did manage to say.

"Parker and your dad have already eaten like pigs and left for the orchards, Brant," Aunt Felicity stated. Lauryn's glance caught the stare of the older woman, who was looking at her quite suspiciously.

"I'll get out there too," Brant mumbled. "But…but I need to speak to Lauryn for a minute."

Lauryn felt instantly anxious. A small, nagging doubt, an uncertainty, rose within her bosom. Perhaps she had misread his actions that morning in the orchard.

Aunt Felicity's eyes twinkled. "Then I suggest you do it, boy," she told him. And, gracefully, she stood and left them to their privacy.

"Lauryn," Brant began, "this morning after we…after we talked…I thought of something."

"What do you mean?" It was her attempt at strength. She would hear whatever he had to say, good or bad.

Brant mischievously bit his lip and took her hand. "Come on. It's the trunk. I can't believe I didn't notice this before," he grumbled as he began pulling her toward the stairs that led to the attic. "I guess…I guess I was just too…" he stammered.

"Distracted," she finished for him as relief washed over her in realizing he had meant to talk to her about the trunk and not some sort of regret he may have had about their moments in the orchard.

"Yeah," he admitted.

"So…what did you think of?" she asked.

"The trunk," he answered as he led her up the stairs. "The Captain's trunk. It's not right."

"Not right?"

"Yeah. I'll show you." Brant opened the attic door. The attic window let in just enough sunlight to make the things within visible. "It's not right," Brant repeated as he hunkered down next to the Captain's trunk. "Look." He lifted the latch, propped open the lid, and began removing the familiar contents. "Here. Help me unload it."

Lauryn knew she and Brant hadn't packed the Captain's things back into the trunk. And she knew who had. Just as the Captain looked after Laura's things, she too must've seen to his.

A trembling traveled through Lauryn as she reached into the trunk and began removing the Captain's things. When it was completely empty, she looked at Brant and stated, "It's all here. Everythin' we looked at before."

"Yes, but look at this," Brant said, pointing to the trunk's floor. Lauryn watched as he put one hand inside the trunk and pressed at the bottom of it. The other palm he placed on the attic floor next to the trunk. "It's not right. It's got to be deeper than it appears. There's a false bottom here."

Lauryn looked at the noticeable difference in the position of Brant's hands. Indeed, the one inside the trunk was higher than the one on the floor—by two inches at least! At once her heart began to hammer excitedly, hopefully desperate.

"How does it open?" she asked. The excitement in her was welling to fantastic proportions. A false bottom! What was beneath it? Were she and Brant about to solve the mystery that had haunted so many for so long? Was his heart's freedom within the distance of a simple touch?

"I don't know," he mumbled as he felt around the edges inside the trunk. But it was tight, and he could not budge it. Finally, with a heavy sigh, he simply smashed his fist through the bottom of the precious trunk.

"Brant!" Lauryn exclaimed, horrified that he would attack it so. But in the next instant, she halted her scolding, for he pulled up the bottom, revealing the secrets beneath.

"Look at that," Brant whispered.

Lauryn swallowed hard as the tears rose to her eyes. There, in the true bottom of the trunk, were several stacks of letters, all tied with twine and addressed to "Captain Brandon Masterson."

"Laura's letters to the Captain?" Lauryn whispered.

Brant reached in and withdrew one of the tiny bundles. As he did, Lauryn's mind whirled. "Brant," she whispered, "Laura's trunk…in my grandma's attic. You don't suppose…"

"Let's not get too excited," he said, seemingly more to himself than to her as he gazed down at the ancient treasures in his hand. "I mean, these are private. Should we—"

"For pity's sake, Brant! We rummaged through all of Laura's from the Captain. Do you really think that—"

At that moment, Lauryn felt a breeze ruffle the sleeve of her dress. It breathed a familiar and beloved fragrance. The room was warm and airy and felt like early summer. Looking to Brant, Lauryn saw him smile but not at her. At someone behind her.

Slowly, Lauryn turned to see Laura standing in the attic. And being honest with herself at that moment, she was aware that she was indeed startled. The first time Laura had appeared to Lauryn had been when she was sleeping. Laura had sat on her bed just the night before. And Lauryn realized she hadn't seen her fully. For as she stood before her now, her hair still beautiful and soft, her face still as lovely as heaven, Lauryn was overcome with the realization that Laura had died violently.

The hem of her sky-blue dress was stained a dark brown. A large crimson stain showed at her abdomen where she had been wounded. The sight of her brought tears afresh to Lauryn's eyes. How selfish she had been, thinking of her own heartache when this beautiful young woman, her own blood, had been wandering in agony for so, so long.

"Laura," Brant began, walking to the ghost and handing her the bundle of letters he held in his hands, "are they important?"

Laura nodded her assurance. Although Lauryn couldn't hear Laura's voice, she did sense the faintest scent of wisteria as the spirit appeared to break into giggles.

"I know, I know," Brant chuckled then. "Stupid question, right?"

Laura nodded. Then smiling, she gazed down at the bundle of letters Brant had handed to her. When she raised her eyes again, it was to look upon Lauryn. Her expression was full of pleading as she offered the bundle to Lauryn.

Lauryn, taking the letters, asked, "Do you want us to read them? Is it…is it all right?"

With a look of sad melancholy, her amused giggle having ceased, Laura nodded. Then reaching up, she caressed Brant's face with her small hand for a moment before simply vanishing. With her went the warm breeze and the sweet fragrance, and the attic felt cold and lonely.

"Let's read them," Brant said. "Right now." Taking Lauryn's hand, he led her to the nearby corner where the quilts were still piled. He stretched out on the floor, resting his head on one of the quilts. Lauryn sat down next to him, tucking her legs under her as she handed him the bundle of letters.

Carefully, Brant untied the twine holding them and handed the top letter to Lauryn. "Here," he said, stretching his arms for a moment before tucking his hands under his head.

"You want *me* to read them?" Lauryn asked. "Out loud?"

"Of course," he answered, as if it were the most ridiculous question he'd ever heard. "We read all of the ones at Connemara that way." Lauryn looked around, wishing Laura would appear and read them. After all, she had written them. "Go on," Brant prodded.

"Exactly why *you* should be readin'," Lauryn argued, handing him the first letter. "A man read them originally. A man should be readin' now." Smiling, at him, she added, "And besides, fair is fair. I read all the others."

Brant accepted the letter humbly, his eyes locking with hers. For a moment, Lauryn saw a familiar pain in Brant's expression—the same one he'd had the day at the millpond when he'd been thinking back on the horrors and loss of war. But he seemed to mask it suddenly and simply began reading the letter.

"*July 17th, 1864. My Darling Brand,*" he began. Immediately, a lump formed in Lauryn's throat, and she wondered if she could indeed continue to listen. These were her letters, Laura's—a woman's letters to her beloved Captain. It seemed frightening and overwhelming with melancholy.

Brant seemed to sense her feelings. "She wants us to read them," he reassured her a moment before beginning again.

When will this all end? When will you be home again...safe in my arms? But, no! I will not write so black. You need bright things. Happy news of home and loved ones.

The weather is warm and fragrant in my Tennessee, Brand, darling. The wisteria at Connemara House has bloomed and faded, and the lovely blossoms that I love so are gone now until next spring. But that is fine. For there is every other manner of blossom to make my days lovely!

Father is forever storming about the house complaining about being too old to fight…not being able to find enough able-bodied men to do anything here in Franklin. But I'm sure you can imagine him. Remember how red his face gets! Redder than his hair even! Chuckle at his antics, my sweet. It will brighten your day, I am certain.

My sweet Virginia drew a likeness of you for me yesterday. It was rather good for a nine-year-old. Although…I had forgotten that your nose was crooked and your eyebrows so bushy! She is a dear little sister, and I am so glad to have her here to keep me company. I miss the other one too. But, as you know, that is not to be spoken of.

This is a short letter, my darling. For mother is calling me to get supper on. Remember that I love you. I love you beyond your ability to even understand. Beyond time and Heaven and Forever! Kiss me in your dreams, my love. And soon…soon you can hold me in your arms, and I will smooth the worry from your brow and keep you warm, safe, next to my heart. Your loving wife,

Laura

Lauryn wiped the tears from her cheeks and looked at Brant, who was staring at the letter in his hands, excess moisture apparent in his own eyes. "I can't listen to these," she sniffled.

Brant reached up and buried one strong hand in her hair just behind her ear. "They loved each other. That's a happy thing, Lauryn. It's what you always tell me."

"But they're lost and…" she stammered.

"And we'll find them."

The emotions—the frustration of being in love, being trapped by the mystery of death—were taking their toll on Lauryn. She felt despair, weak, and in that moment, she needed Brant's arms around her. Needed to be held warm and safe in his arms. Needed to feel him, the way Laura had not been able to feel her Captain when she'd penned the letter. So as he slowly pulled her down toward him, she did not resist. Rather she laid her body next to his, returning his embrace as his arms held her tightly.

He held her for a long time, whispering reassurances in her ear, stroking her hair tenderly until at last, her tears slowing their rush, he took her face in his hands and raised her face above his, saying, "We'll find her. I promise. We will find her!"

Brant shivered as Lauryn's hair brushed his face. As he held her tearstained face to his chest, he felt guilty for reveling in the sensation of euphoria he felt inhaling the fragrance of her being. Her dark, soft hair cascading down around her face tickled the flesh of his arms. She was so beautiful, so sweet, so unknowingly seductive. He had to taste her once. Just once. Then he would return them to their task. Return to his resolve to keep himself from her until…but no! He'd set the standard. Lauryn didn't truly understand the desires of a man—his inability to concentrate when he had such an obsession with a woman. He'd been unable to confess his feelings for her, though he had tried to convey them in the orchard. Still, with the words unspoken—as they must remain until Laura was found—he could not expect her to come rushing back to his kiss now. It would be weak and completely unfair.

And so, for Brant was a chivalrous man, he simply held her and let her tears soak into the soft cotton of his shirt. He thought of her instead of himself.

"Now," Brant mumbled finally and, Lauryn fancied, rather breathlessly, "let's go on." He opened another letter and at the same time asked, "Who is 'the other one' she spoke of?"

"What do you mean?" Lauryn asked, already having forgotten the details of Laura's letter for the bliss of being held in Brant's arms.

"She said, 'I miss the other one…that's not to be spoken of,'" he repeated.

"I don't know. Maybe…maybe…" Lauryn's mind worked to remember everything about her family's history.

"Hm," Brant mused. "Well…here's the next one," Brant sighed, brushing Lauryn's hair from her face.

July 30ᵗʰ, 1864
My Darling, Darling, Brand,
    Oh, I'm so angry! I know I shouldn't write to you concerning the trivial goings-on at Connemara House that disturb me, but, oh! I saw her today. There she was…watching me from across the street. At first, as

always, I felt so sad for her. Great pity nearly overwhelmed me as I looked at her dress, so worn and ill-fitting considering her—I pause to speak of it—her condition. She is my sister, dearest. I love her still. And yet, as I stood, feeling sorrow and pity and guilt, she smoothed the roundness of her belly and smiled at me with such a devil's smile that I nearly screamed! Right out loud! Right there in front of the mercantile!

What happened to Carissa, Brand? What would cause her to concoct such lies about the origin of the child she is expecting? Why would she strive to hurt me so? Her own sister?

Of course, I didn't dare to tell Mama or Daddy! Mama would've burst into tears, and Daddy would've lit out after Carissa with his pistol. And after all of this, Brand, my love…I still love her! My sister. I even miss her at times. What could make a person change so, as Carissa has?

And I think of the child, my niece or nephew, illegitimate though it may be. Still it is an innocent baby. Through no fault of its own, it will be born into poverty and disrespect. I can't bear it, Brand Darling! What will become of her? For all she has done, I can forgive her. But Daddy won't.

I'm glad, Brand. Glad that we gave her the money. It was the right thing to do. But ever I will be angry, I feel. The money, for food, I was thinking of the baby…and of her. But now, seeing her…perhaps she wasn't mocking me. Perhaps she is just happy to have the baby so that she won't be all alone. That is how I will think of it, darling. She is still good…somewhere inside. I know it.

Oh, Brand, end this war soon and come home to me. Maybe the two of us…together…maybe we could change Carissa's blackened heart.

I love you so, my Darling. My thoughts are of you every moment! My heart is with you…right there with you. I'm sending a kiss in this letter. Return to me soon!

Your Loving Wife,
Laura

Lauryn sat silent and astonished. What things had been revealed through this ancient letter?

"My hell, Lauryn," Brant mumbled as a thoughtful expression wrinkled his brow. "Sorry. But it would seem that we have begun to uncover another mystery in your family history."

"Carissa? Her sister?" Lauryn mumbled. "I've never heard such a thing. Carissa died as a baby. It's written right there in the family Bible. By my great-grandfather's own hand!"

"It's obvious she didn't die as an infant," Brant offered. "Are you sure the Bible said she died as an infant?"

Lauryn thought for a moment. "It says, '*Carissa O'Halleran born June 20, 1847, died.*' You read it yourself."

"No death date."

"No. Just 'died.' It's the way they wrote it when a baby died. Isn't it?" Lauryn's mind was a jumble of questions.

"It's apparent that there was some sort of falling out," Brant mumbled thoughtfully, almost to himself.

"But my Nana has never even mentioned another sister livin'. Surely she would've if…" Lauryn reminded him.

"You know how families were back then, Lauryn—especially in the south. If someone were disinherited, disowned…the family acted as if they had died. Or had never existed at all. And…" But he didn't finish.

"Go on," Lauryn prodded, though she knew before he spoke that his mind was concocting the same story hers was.

"An illegitimate child. Reason enough in the old South for your great-grandfather to have disowned a daughter," he stated. "But why would the child's origin hurt Laura?"

"I don't know!" Lauryn exclaimed. "This…this is too much to think through rationally, at least all in one moment."

"I know." Brant shook his head, still struggling to believe it all himself. "And your grandmother never spoke to you about any of this?"

Lauryn shook her head. "No. No. All I ever knew was that there were two baby girls that died. At least I always assumed they died as babies. In the family Bible…it does say her name, birth date, and then 'died.' You saw it. One has a death date; she was just a few days old. I just always thought the other died at birth. Actually…I never thought much about it."

He nodded.

"That's all I've ever known. I never thought to ask otherwise."

Brant stood up immediately. "We'll read more of these later. I want to ask Aunt Felicity about this. Maybe she'll remember something."

"My own Nana hasn't spoken of it. Why would you think your aunt would know?" Lauryn was still in a sort of shock over the circumstances the letter had revealed.

"Your Nana was a member of the family and probably instructed to never speak about all this," he explained. "My auntie wasn't." He smiled then. "And besides, she loves a good bit of gossip."

Lauryn smiled. His touch was magical—whether in mere friendship or otherwise—and it would be hard not to beg him for it.

CHAPTER SEVENTEEN

"Who was Carissa?" Brant asked bluntly.

"What, love?" Aunt Felicity mumbled, looking up to him. Brant and Lauryn had sought out Brant's aunt, finding her sitting in a rocking chair in the parlor working on her needlepoint. Brant had wasted no words of explanation, simply asked his question forthright.

"Carissa. Who was Carissa?" he repeated.

"Carissa?" Aunt Felicity asked.

"Laura O'Halleran's sister Carissa, Miss Felicity," Lauryn clarified.

An expression of sudden enlightenment passed across Aunt Felicity's face then. "Oh my!" she breathed. "I'd forgotten all about that."

"About Carissa O'Halleran, you mean," Brant prodded.

"No. Well, yes. I'd forgotten all about it…that whole mess. The scandal!"

Brant looked at Lauryn and she at him, and Lauryn knew his neck was prickling with an odd anticipation just as hers was. "What mess?" he asked.

Aunt Felicity dropped her voice and put a delicate hand to her bosom dramatically. "I don't know if I should say, dear. I'm not sure it's my place." Still, her eyes flashed with excitement.

"Please," Lauryn encouraged. "I think it may be important somehow."

Aunt Felicity looked about as if ensuring their privacy, and then bending her head toward Brant's and motioning for Lauryn to follow suit, she began.

"Well, as I remember, there were three O'Halleran girls—Lauralynn, Carissa, and Virginia. Lauralynn was the eldest…a mere year older than Carissa. Anyway, when my brother Brand went to work for their Daddy, Carissa fell in love with Brand too! But he only had eyes for Lauralynn. Oh, Carissa tried all manner of devious things to capture him away from Lauralynn, the way I remember it. But Brand loved Laura and only Laura. They were married in '63. Well, Carissa was furious—mad with fury! And showed up in her parents' parlor one day saying that she was with child." Aunt Felicity cleared her throat, actually blushed, and whispered, in an even softer tone, "And she said that the child was Brand's!"

Lauryn gasped audibly, and Brant's brows wrinkled into a frown. "What?" he said.

"That's the truth of it! She accused my own brother of…of such an atrocity. Well, we all knew it was a lie. A plain, ugly lie! And so did the O'Hallerans. Kiel O'Halleran was so furious that he disowned his daughter there on the spot—threw her out of the house, expecting and all, and told her he never wanted to set eyes on her again."

"And…what ever happened to her? To the baby?" Lauryn ventured, still trying to fully grasp what the woman had told them.

Felicity seemed thoughtful. She scowled pensively. "I don't know. I can't say for sure. I don't ever remember hearing of her…or of the baby, for that matter. All I know is no one ever saw her again."

Brant looked at Lauryn and mumbled, "No one but Laura."

"Oh, Brand and Laura…for all the pain Carissa caused, they were mighty benevolent, if you ask me," Felicity offered.

"What do you mean?" Brant pressed.

"Well, Brand once told me in a letter that, for all the pain Carissa had caused Laura, for all her lies…still Laura loved her and worried about the baby. There were several times that Brand sent money to Laura to secretly give to Carissa for food and clothing and things."

"There's an entry in his register. What did it say?" Lauryn mumbled.

"*$10 United States Currency…sent to Laura to give to C,*" Brant answered. He paused for a moment. "Even in her letter, with her anger at her sister, even for such a betrayal…Laura was worried for her."

"It was a sad end she met, I've no doubt," Aunt Felicity sighed.

"What now, Brant?" Lauryn asked. "All this…it's relevant. I feel it."

"We go back to Connemara," Brant mumbled. "There's something we've missed there too. I think we need to finish reading Laura's letters then. In a few days, we'll go back to Connemara and finish Brand's letters. We'll go back there and find out what happened to Carissa too." Leaning over, he placed an affectionate kiss on his aunt's sweet cheek. "Thanks, Auntie. You've been—"

"Invaluable. I know," she giggled.

"Really, Auntie," he assured her. "You have."

"Anything I can do to get you violating this girl out in the orchard again," she whispered, winking understandingly at Lauryn. Lauryn gasped, surprised by the woman's knowledge of what had transpired between her and Brant in the early hours that morning.

"Aunt Felicity, your spying and gossip will get you straight to hell," Brant grumbled as he turned and stormed from the room.

"Brant isn't the only one who likes to watch the sunrise from the orchard, Lauryn," Aunt Felicity whispered. Lauryn blushed as the woman's mischievously twinkling eyes burned into her own. "But don't you worry, sweet pea. He'll get over his knightly need to be gallant when he's slain the dragon. Yep. Mark my words…you'll be back in his arms soon enough."

"Thank you for your help," was all Lauryn could say. "All of it," she added with a smile as she left the room.

Brant had already climbed the stairs, and Lauryn could hear him heading for the attic. Was he serious? They'd only arrived the day before. He couldn't possibly intend to return to Connemara in such a short time—a few days, he'd said. Still, he was right. And her heart soared at the thought of his being back at Connemara with her.

"Brant?" Lauryn ventured as she stepped into the attic to find him angrily rummaging through the things that had been in the trunk. He'd already emptied the bottom of the trunk of its remaining bundles of letters and had the Captain's ledger tightly in one hand.

"First we'll talk to Laura," he growled. "Then we'll read the rest of these letters. We never finished Brand's letters. There's sure to be responses or something to these, the ones he sent the money in." Brant was incredibly angry, and Lauryn knew it had nothing to do with what they'd just discovered. "I want to stay a few more days…help Dad and

Parker start getting the orchards in shape. I've been gone too long, and they need the help."

"What's the matter, Brant?" Lauryn asked.

"What's the matter?" he nearly shouted. "Lauryn," he began then, trying to calm himself, "I'm a man. Do you understand? I'm a man!"

Lauryn simply nodded, trying not to smile. For some reason, there was something rather humorous about his sudden rage over his aunt's having spied on him.

"I'm…I'm not made to sit around reading love letters, keeping my hands off…" He paused, his jaw clenching tightly as he studied her quickly from head to toe. "I need work. Hard work. I need to be keeping my body busy, my mind empty of things I can't do anything about. I can't be running back and forth, sitting on a train, reading letters, spending every waking moment, and most of my sleepless nights, trying to figure all this out! Life needs to go on for me."

Lauryn said nothing. She recognized his mood. He was frustrated now, needing to release some of the aggravation somehow. Too many variables in the day had taken their toll on his patience. So she simply listened.

"A year ago, I was killing other men, Lauryn," he told her. "Carrying a gun and killing other human beings. Do you understand what that does to a man? I was protecting my country, watching my friends die horrible deaths. I was walking around in death and mud so thick that sometimes I wondered if I wouldn't just drown in it. And it's what I should've been doing. It *was* a righteous endeavor. Then I was wounded. Blinded. Stricken helpless. It gave me a lot of time to think on all of this mess." He motioned to the Captain's belongings lying around their feet. "Too much time. Then I met you, your family, I came home, talked with Laura, healed, had my family around me—all the while sitting around. It gives a man rise to appreciating what he has…well he should. It gives him over to wanting to make something of himself, wanting to live the good life in this good country that he fought to save."

"And ghosts and love letters and…and…" Lauryn dropped her eyes, overwhelmed for a moment—overwhelmed that she even dreamed of being able to fulfill his needs somehow—a man like this, so strong, so haunted, so wounded, and yet so ambitious. "And other things seem rather trivial after what you've been through," Lauryn offered.

"No!" he exclaimed, glaring at her. "That's just it. Family, friends, work…that's exactly what I fought for." Angrily, he tossed the letters and ledger into a heap at his feet. "But this, this…it has taken us so long to get anywhere! Don't you understand?" he asked, taking her shoulders in his hands and searching her eyes with his. "I need to work out in the sun, feel the sweat dripping down my face. I need to take my wife to bed and—"

It was Lauryn's astonished gasp that interrupted him, her eyes wide with surprise at the forthrightness of his speech. But he paused only for a moment.

"What? Do you want me to act like I don't think about all this, Lauryn? Do you think that I don't want babies to bounce on my knee and a wife to—"

Again, Lauryn gasped and clamped her hand over his mouth quickly. "Don't say it," she whispered.

"Don't say what?" he growled once he'd pushed her hand from his mouth. "Do you think it's never been said? How do you think you got here? How do you think I got here? Don't you think your perfect Captain and the lovely Lauralynn—" Again, Lauryn placed her hand over his mouth, and again he pushed her hand away. "And how do you suppose, sugar…that I'll ever get a wife, have babies, work my own land, if I can't get this mess all straightened out and behind me? How would any woman understand my relationship with the beautiful ghost that visits me at night? I'm not sure that you even understand it! Hm? Answer me that." He shook his head. "I can see it now. There we are, lying in our honeymoon bed, and in walks my beloved Laura. 'Oh, hello, Laura,' I say. 'Honey, this is Laura…my ghost. I couldn't help her out, so she'll be watching us every moment until—'"

"You and I both know that Laura would never intrude that way," Lauryn scolded.

"You're right. You're right," he admitted angrily. "But she'd be in my mind. And it's almost the same thing."

"You're bein' selfish," Lauryn accused. "All you're thinkin' about is yourself and—"

"Hell yes, I'm selfish!" he shouted, taking her chin in his hand and forcing her to look up at him.

"Quit swearin'," she told him.

"Quit pretending like it bothers you," he growled. "And quit pretending like you're not selfish too. You want to be in my arms as much as I want you there."

Lauryn was angry herself now—for being so blinded by her own misery that she'd neglected the knowledge of his. She stooped and picked up the letters and ledger that Brant had angrily discarded.

"I'll go back to Connemara," she told him. "I'll read through all the letters, alone. You're right. You do need a rest from it all," she encouraged him, looking up to find him sighing in defeat. "I'll find Laura for you, Brant." She reached up and touched his cheek with her hand, smiling before turning and leaving the attic.

She loved him—loved him desperately! And she desperately wanted to be the wife he'd spoken of wanting. If it took returning to Connemara alone, searching for Laura's body until she was nearly dead, she would do it! To save Brant's sanity and to have him for her own, she would do it.

"Don't say a word, Laura," Brant growled as Laura glided toward him, arms folded disapprovingly across her chest. "Don't say a word."

"*I don't have to*," came the softest of Laura's fragrant whispers.

"You don't understand!" he began to argue immediately, collapsing onto the pile of dusty quilts. "She lights this fire in me! I can't get her out of my mind! I can't concentrate on anything else." Looking to his spiritual companion, he added, "I can't find *you* for thinking about *her*."

"*And that's wrong?*" Laura asked.

"Do you really think I'd be able to be happy knowing you were still miserable?" he asked. "Honestly, Laura? Do you?"

Lauralynn Masterson shook her head compassionately and caressed Brant's cheek with her familiar and loving tenderness. "*No*," she admitted. "*And I don't think you would be happy findin' me and losin' her either, darlin'.*" She smiled. "*In fact, I think you'd be happier leavin' me and keepin' her.*"

Brant chuckled slightly. "I won't leave you."

"*Because you want her*," Laura finished for him.

"Exactly."

Laura sat down on the quilts next to Brant. "*Has it ever occurred to you, Brant…*" she began. The strain at trying to hear her voice was almost painful to Brant. Yet he listened, intently. She was wise. He'd learned that long ago. It was wisdom to listen to her. "*Has it ever occurred to you that this 'mess,' as you put it, is as much about your destiny as it is mine?*"

Brant bit his lip in frustration and nodded. "Yes. But I try not to think about it."

"*Why ever not, silly boy?*" Laura asked.

"First I'll find you," he told her. "Then I'll find me."

"*It's not meant to be that way, Brant. Findin' me…is findin' you.*"

"Sometimes you talk in riddles. Do you know that?" He shook his head, angry with himself for losing his temper and letting it go at Lauryn.

"*Yes,*" Laura giggled. "*I do know it.*"

"And where is that teacup you used to carry around?" Brant asked.

Laura began to fade. "*I don't know where the cup went. One day…it just wasn't with me anymore.*"

"But what…why did you have it?" Brant asked.

Laura shrugged, becoming even more transparent. "*I don't remember. But it comforted me…until you were old enough to.*" And she was gone.

ᘛ

"I'm sorry, Lauryn."

Lauryn startled at the sound of his voice but kept her posture, gazing out the window of her room.

"Look, I can be a real stinker sometimes. I need to have these…these…" he stammered.

"Temper tantrums," Lauryn finished for him.

"Yes," he admitted. "And…and I need to keep my hands off you, Lauryn."

Lauryn turned around. "By all means, Mr. Masterson," she agreed. "I never asked you to put them on me in the first place, now did I?" She quirked one eyebrow, adding, "Never asked you to keep them off me either, for that matter."

He smiled, his mood completely lightened. "You do understand, Lauryn," he began. "Don't you? I'm responsible for her. She's completely dependent on me. That kind of dependency is destructive to other things in my life."

"I do know," Lauryn reminded him.

"I know you know," he sighed. "I'm sorry, Lauryn," he said, quietly gathering her into a strong embrace. "I'm sorry that you always have to deal with my tantrums when I get frustrated." He smiled adoringly down at her. "We will do this together. It'll never get solved otherwise. We'll do a lot of things together," he mumbled insinuatively.

Lauryn recognized the roguish spark in his eye, the slight twitch at the corner of his mouth. It was in his mind to kiss her. But he was determined to focus on finding Laura before finding life. Still, she couldn't resist teasing him—tempting him—just a bit.

"We're friends. Remember? And you're responsible for what you do. Remember? And what you don't do. We don't want you to be too distracted now, do we?"

He smiled at her. "I remember," he admitted. "I'm responsible for letting myself be distracted. But if you endeavor to distract me…I'm not responsible for what you do. Isn't that right?"

Lauryn shook her head and smiled. What a witty, flirtatious devil he was. "I am responsible for what I do. You're right," she told him.

His expression softened even more as he understood her. "I guess…I guess I'm just a little too imperfect to be perfect, aren't I?" he chuckled.

Lauryn smiled, delighted at his implication that he was trying to live up to her dreamy ideal—which, of course, he embodied.

He continued. "I'm going out to the orchards to help Dad and Parker for a while. How about you read through some of these letters and…and we'll talk about it later?"

Lauryn nodded. She understood his need to work, to be distracted by something other than herself. "All right," she agreed.

"And you better telephone home. Let your mother know you're safe…if not the warmest you've ever been," he added as he turned to leave.

"I do understand you, Brant," she called after him.

He paused and looked back at her. "I know you understand my loyalty to Laura…my need to finish it," he told her. "But I think, sugar…that you don't understand, even a little, what I'm thinking where you're concerned." With a wink, he closed the door behind him as he left.

Lauryn felt the familiar leap in her bosom. Brant was dangerously attractive, powerful in that he could completely destroy her life, her ability to be happy or build her life and continue to be her happiness. Yet she knew he was right—that she didn't understand everything he was thinking. But was it all good or bad? She had no way of knowing. And whom could she talk to? Who knew him well enough to explain it to her?

"Lauralynn?" she called quietly. "Are you nearby? I certainly could use your insight where a certain man is concerned."

Like a refreshing spring breeze, fragrance filled the room as Lauryn called once more, "Laura?" And in the next moment, she was there, standing before Lauryn and smiling with compassion and understanding.

"*Lauryn*," she whispered. And Lauryn gasped, for she'd heard Laura's voice! She was nearly overwhelmed with the scent of wisteria. It was so strong that it was almost unpleasant. "*Lauryn*," the ghost figure repeated and motioned to the window where Lauryn had stood only minutes before. Looking out that same window now, Lauryn saw Brant striding determinedly toward the orchards.

"Tell me, Lauralynn," Lauryn whispered. "Tell me…what does he mean by all this? I can't…I can't bear to not have him any longer. And yet, when he's here and I know that I can't…I feel like I might die and…"

Lauryn was silent as Laura pressed the palm of her left had to Lauryn's right hand and laced their fingers.

"*Close your eyes.*" It was the tiniest, almost indiscernible whisper that Lauryn heard. She wasn't even certain she did hear it, for it was almost as if it were simply her own mind thinking it. Yet it was a woman's voice, and she knew it was Laura's. "*Close your eyes, and I'll show you somethin'.*" And so she did. Lauryn closed her eyes, and suddenly, it was as if she were dreaming while she was still conscious.

It was a memory she was seeing. It was she and Brant on the millpond island. She could feel his arms around her, feel the power of his kiss, feel the passion between them. Then it was as if she were watching a picture show, only with color. It was the Captain and

Lauralynn enfolded in each other's arms near the gazebo at Connemara. And although she didn't feel the passion in her own body as she had with the vision of her and Brant, she could see it. She knew it existed by the way they kissed, the way they held each other. Another moment came to her mind—she and Brant on the train to Vermont, the way his eyes burned as he gazed into her eyes, the way his mouth seized hers so wantonly. Again, the Captain then, lifting Laura's veil at their own wedding and kissing her tenderly before all the world. It was the Captain, lifting his bride, still wearing her wedding gown, and carrying her over the threshold of one of the bedrooms at Connemara. Gently, he let her feet fall to the floor. He removed her veil and kissed her sweetly at first. But as the moments wore on, Brand kissed Laura more demandingly, passion exploding between them as they embraced.

"He is only bein' careful with you," came Laura's voice as she spoke to Lauryn's mind—Lauryn's mind that now held visions of her moments with Brant in the orchard, both moments of passion and of heartache. *"Protectin' you like a tiny treasure. He's a strong man, full of ambition, guilt, hurt, love, desire. Trust him, Lauryn, for he only endeavors to bridle the love and desire until it is proper not to."*

Lauryn's eyes popped open to find Laura still standing before her smiling. *"Trust him,"* she heard the whisper. *"Trust him. Find me. And he won't be such a gentleman anymore."* Laura smiled as Lauryn's eyes widened. *"That naughty streak runs deep in the Masterson family, Lauryn. He's only tryin' to be worthy of you."*

As Laura began to fade, one more phrase came into Lauryn's mind—a startling revelation, accompanied by a vision. As Lauryn's mind witnessed Brand and Lauralynn, standing in the parlor in Connemara, Brand's head hung guiltily, Laura whispered to her mind, *"We have our own wicked ways to serve us, Lauryn."* And Lauryn saw then Laura—sweet, tiny, demure—as she took hold of Brand's shirt at his chest and kissed him hard on the mouth. In a moment, Brand's arms were around Laura's small waist, returning the affection, which blazed as furiously as each time Lauryn had basked in the delirium of Brant's kiss.

"Are you suggestin' that I...?" Lauryn stammered.

"Follow your heart, Lauryn," came the whisper as the beautiful Lauralynn vanished. *"Follow your heart."*

ਦ

"We're havin' the furniture out just this very minute," Georgia explained to Lauryn on the telephone sometime later.

"I can hardly hear you, Mama," Lauryn said, raising her voice and putting a finger in her other ear.

"Well, we decided to go ahead and get this done. The historical society is willin' to pay for the whole mess. So all it is to us is a bit of an inconvenience," Georgia explained.

"How long will it take them to strip the floors and all?" Lauryn asked.

"What, darlin'? I can hardly hear you," Georgia asked.

"How long will y'all be in with Sean?" Lauryn shouted.

"Oh, near to a week, I would think. More maybe. Why?" Georgia asked.

"We…we may need to come home right away. There's somethin' we've discovered and—"

"I'm losin' you, angel! I can hardly hear you. But we'll be at Sean's if you need us. I love you! And give Brant my love too. Bye now." And she was gone.

Lauryn certainly hadn't expected to find such goings-on at Connemara when she'd taken Brant's advice and telephoned home.

"They're restorin' Connemara," she explained to Brant when he sat down for lunch.

"What do you mean?" he asked.

"The historical society has offered to pay for the restoration if Mama will let it be toured a few days a week," Lauryn explained.

"Oh, how wonderful!" Aunt Felicity exclaimed. "It's such a beautiful example of architectural history."

"What all will they do to it?" Brant's father asked.

"Well," Lauryn began, "from what I gather, they're startin' with the floors. Grandmother O'Halleran had them painted over and carpets put down after the war. The society wants them stripped and varnished the way they would've been during the time of the Battle of Franklin. Then it's paint and wallpaper, any repair work from there."

"But it was redone just after the war, wasn't it?" Felicity asked.

"Yes, ma'am. It was. So there shouldn't be too awful much more than that." Lauryn glanced up to see Brant smiling approvingly at her.

She blushed for some reason, suddenly being drowned with visions of the passionate exchanges that they'd shared, suddenly thinking of his flirtatious words to her in her bedroom earlier. Had he indeed implied that were she to kiss him, being responsible for her own actions, it would then spur him on in the ways of affection toward her again?

Lauryn had thought about Brant's inference throughout the remainder of the morning. She'd considered it as she'd considered Laura's revelations to her. Had Laura been telling her that all Brant needed was a nudge in the right direction to let go of his feeling of being too distracted?

"Lauryn and I will have to go back to Tennessee within the week, Dad," Brant announced unexpectedly.

"What? You just got here!" Darnell exclaimed with disappointment.

"Ah, he's just selfish and don't like sharing Lauryn any longer," Parker chuckled.

"Well, that too," Brant chuckled. "But…this thing needs to get resolved. We found some things in the attic, and with what Aunt Felicity told us…well, we all know that Lauralynn Masterson isn't really here anyway."

Darnell Masterson put his fork down and studied Brant rather wistfully for a moment. "Getting on with your life, aren't you, Brant."

"Yeah," Brant admitted, returning his father's gaze. Lauryn sensed that something was being exchanged between them—an unspoken understanding.

"Cattle and orchards in New Mexico calling you bad, aren't they, boy?" Darnell mumbled.

"Among other things," Brant admitted with a wink.

Darnell chuckled and slapped the table victoriously. "Well, get on with it then, Brant. Life's too short to waste." He stood and winked at Lauryn. "You two get this thing worked out. It's time things went forward instead of always looking back."

Lauryn nodded and then looked to Brant, who was staring at her with an odd, rather hungry expression.

"Feel up to reading some old letters, sugar?" he asked.

"I suppose so," Lauryn sighed. But she thought, *I wish they were mine—letters from Brant to me.*

CHAPTER EIGHTEEN

There was work that needed doing—fences and buildings to be repaired, trees to inspect and spray, cattle to check on, daily chores, and more! Lauryn spent the time in Castledale trying to look busy. While Brant was out helping his father and Parker with the responsibilities of farm life in the spring, Lauryn listened to Aunt Felicity and a recovered Uncle John tell stories of life before the new century began.

April and Rose were kind, talkative women, with adorable children who proved to be weapons of beating boredom. Lauryn's time in the company of Brant's family was enjoyable; they included her in their work and activities.

Laura came to visit Lauryn often during those lonely days in unfamiliar surroundings. She showed Lauryn where the family photographs were kept, and she was able to gaze into the eyes of the boy Brant.

Lauryn assured Laura, time and again, of the Captain's well-being and infinite love for her. She told Laura of Connemara and its enduring beauty, of its inhabitants, of her sister Virginia, the lovely life she'd lived, and what a wonderful grandmother she was.

Something was missing, however. Brant was definitely keeping himself busy with working. He was so busy he seemed to have succeeded in distracting himself from her. He talked with her, laughed with her, even flirted with her, but he had not so much as taken her hand in his, even for a moment. Though his manner was friendly, his attentions to her encouraging, she was mournful for the loss of his affections, which had given her confidence in his caring for her.

Still, she managed to hang onto her perpetual hope of making the Captain and Laura eternally at peace, thereby finding her own happiness. Each evening after supper, Brant and Lauryn discussed what Lauryn had read in Laura's letters during his absence. It was true the information they gleaned from them was nothing short of fantastic.

Moses Jackson, for example, had indeed been freed as the Captain's letter to Laura at Connemara had implied—freed not by the plantation owners that claimed him but by the assistance of an unknown person and a secret chain of people and houses that were willing to help. Laura did not reveal in her letters exactly who had helped him, only that he had been made a free man.

There were other letters concerning Carissa. Apparently, Lauralynn aided her many times, sneaking baskets of food, clothing, and money to her. Lauryn found several more entries in the Captain's ledger pertaining to currency sent to Laura to give to "C."

In her letters, Laura expressed heartache over her sister's situation and yet heartache over her sister's betrayal as well. It was clear Laura eventually had been able to forgive Carissa for her lies and attempts to harm her. But she continued to struggle with understanding her sister's actions.

There were letters talking of Virginia that interested Lauryn. It was fun to read of her Nana being a little girl, scraping her knees up and horrifying her great-grandmother with her unladylike antics.

The more Brant and Lauryn read and the longer they talked, the more they were convinced that returning to Connemara and finding out what had happened to Carissa O'Halleran would prove a quintessential part of the mysterious enigma. Neither of them could explain to anyone their feelings of urgency where Carissa was concerned—just that it existed.

Furthermore, as Lauryn thought on everything that was happening in Vermont, she began to see Brant's decisions and actions as if they were a piece of a puzzle. And with Laura's help, she was starting to piece together that puzzle. She even had a plan, a plan to test the pieces of the puzzle and her ability to read them correctly. As each night brought nagging doubt, each new morning brought renewed optimism.

ᘊ

The train trip from Vermont back to Tennessee had been very different, indeed the reverse of the first trip. There was no warm embracing, no stolen kisses. Lauryn and Brant talked endlessly, perhaps rather nervously, about everything under the sun—except their personal feelings. So it happened that on a warm southern day, Lauryn found herself walking at Brant's side down Franklin's main street on her way home.

"You haven't forgiven me yet," Brant said as they walked slowly in the moist, southern heat.

"Forgiven you for what?" Lauryn asked, pretending ignorance. She knew what he was referring to, but she preferred not to think about it, still finding it too painful.

"For being a man. For being a man that's an idiot, like any other man," he explained.

"There's nothin' to forgive," Lauryn assured him.

Brant halted at once. Taking hold of her shoulders, he glared down into her face and growled, "You do forgive me, don't you?" There was a look of panic about him, and she wondered, as she had often over the past week, if truly he were hurting as much as he appeared to be.

"For what? For your tryin' to do what's right?" she asked compassionately.

He sighed in relief. "I'm just trying to…I'm just trying to…"

"To do the right thing. I know," Lauryn finished. She had, though not often consciously, noticed Brant's indecision growing since almost the very moment he made the decision to remain focused on finding Laura. She'd noticed and now allowed herself to concede that she wasn't just imagining each time the corner of his mouth twitched as she spoke to him. She had noticed the way his eyes traveled the length of her, his hands rolling into frustrated fists. At night she could hear him, pacing in his room and talking quietly to Laura—quietly, but with a tone of angry frustration. She had begun to understand that he was a man who realized when he was in danger of completely losing his focus and needed to bind himself. Still, it bothered her.

"But do you really know, Lauryn?" he pleaded. "I mean, do you truly understand why?"

"Probably not," she admitted. "I'm a girl, after all. We think differently than boys."

"You have no idea," he mumbled. Then he frowned and asked, "You do want me to do the right thing, don't you?"

Lauryn felt the swelling in her bosom that she did every time she spent too long gazing into his handsome face. She felt a mischievousness rise in her as well as she said, "Not necessarily."

"What?" he asked, his eyebrows shooting into arches with surprise. "What do you mean by that?"

"Look," Lauryn breathed with relief. "Connemara House." She was awed by its beauty, as always.

"Lauryn—" Brant began, but Lauryn had caught him off-guard, and she knew it. He was burning with curiosity at her remark.

"Brant, come on!" she called over her shoulder as she ran toward the front gates of Connemara.

"Lauryn! Wait a minute. You little brat." Brant chuckled, taking out after her. Lauryn knew she couldn't outrun him, but somehow returning home made her feel hopeful and free to be herself—free to release her own wicked ways, the ones Laura had referred to.

Lauryn had secreted her plan in her impish little imagination for several days now. She'd thought on it more and more. And she'd planned it out, knowing Brant and how he reacted to certain things. He hadn't lost interest in her, of course. He truly was trying to be gallant, trying to slay the dragon before kissing the enchanted princess in the tower. She was more certain of it now, with Connemara in sight and Brant hot at her heels.

Brant caught hold of Lauryn's arm as she ran up the front steps. Smiling, she turned to face him.

"You can't outrun me," he told her with a smile. "So don't even try it."

"Lauryn!" Georgia exclaimed from just inside the house. "Brant! Oh, I'm so glad you two have arrived safe and sound."

"Mama!" Lauryn sighed, hugging her mother tightly and basking in the fragrance of the lavender perfume she always wore.

Georgia's tears were instant and unexpected. The woman fairly threw herself into Brant's strong embrace, and he looked at Lauryn questioningly.

"Mama?" Lauryn ventured. "I was only gone a week."

"Oh, it's not even that, sweetheart," Georgia sniffled, pushing herself from Brant's arms and patting his cheek adoringly. "It's just that…well, we've just had somethin'…come into the house, darlin's."

A wave of insecurity washed over Lauryn as her mother dabbed at her eyes. She found herself reaching for Brant's hand for comfort. He grasped it without pause.

"I never knew," Georgia sniffled, "and I really don't think Nana remembered it all until…here—in the parlor. It's very bad in here."

"Mama…what are you goin' on about?" Lauryn asked. Lauryn had expected, even longed, to return home to Connemara with all her family's exuberance, love, and happiness. But to be met with tears, obvious tears of distress, it was far too unsettling, and Lauryn's mood of relief and joy of a moment before faded quickly.

Indeed, the furniture in the parlor was gone, as Lauryn had expected. Her mother had explained the restoration plans—the furniture being taken out and stored, the paint being stripped from the floors. Lauryn was rather taken aback to see the unfamiliar bare wood beneath her feet that had so long been hidden under carpets and paint. There was the smell of sawdust in the room, but Lauryn could not discern anything that would be the cause of so disturbing her mother.

"I'd forgotten about it all," Nana sighed heavily, entering the room. Lauryn turned to see her grandmother's face, ashen as she looked around the empty parlor. "Maybe I had never understood it, really. I was so young. But then they rolled up the carpets and began stripping the paint and—"

"Nana!" Lauryn pleaded. "Whatever is the matter with you two?"

"Your daddy always wanted to get the carpets out of here, remove the paint, and restore the wood floors beneath. That's one reason I talked with the historical society. But when they started removin' the paint several days ago…well, we realized exactly *why* Grandmother O'Halleran had the floors painted and the carpets put down."

"Why? And what does it matter, Mama? Everythin' will be back in place soon enough and…" Lauryn tried to console her mother.

But Georgia's tears seemed only more prolific. "When they stripped the paint…" she began, her voice cracking with emotion.

"Blood," Brant stated flatly.

"What?" Lauryn exclaimed, turning toward him. She followed his gaze as he nodded toward one corner of the parlor. There the floor was marred—blackened with a large dark stain. At first, it only appeared as if the wood were a different color, as if someone had accidentally poured out a bucket of something there. But as Lauryn looked more closely, she noted the oblong, oval shape of the stain—exactly as if someone had been propped up in the corner and bled out on the wood planking.

"This house was used as a makeshift hospital during the Battle of Franklin, wasn't it?" Brant asked.

Nana nodded and dabbed at her own tears. "The stains are everywhere throughout the house," she told him.

"Yes," Georgia agreed. "They're much worse on this side, however."

"The sun came in stronger through these windows on the east. It made for better lightin' for the surgeons," Nana whispered as tears streamed down her face. Lauryn felt her body begin to tremble as she looked about. "See there." Nana pointed to a place before the large front window in the parlor. "You can see where the surgeon's table was. And the buckets they used to…durin' their work."

Lauryn did look and was overwhelmed with sorrow to see the dark rings left by buckets and the small circular stains made by the pressure of table legs. In fact, as she looked around the parlor, she could see other dark stains on the floor. And turning, she noted similar ones in the entryway.

"Patrick's room is terrible," Georgia sniffled. "Just awful!"

"I remember them leavin' the boys that were beyond savin' in that room until they died and someone could take them out for burial."

Tears were streaming down Lauryn's face as she thought of the wounded men, waiting in such miserable pain and agony to be tended while the battle raged outside. Brant too stood silent, his eyes filled with moisture as he stared at the large stain in the corner. No doubt his particular visions were far more vivid than Lauryn's. She clutched his arm, trying to draw strength from him and yet give him comfort at the same time.

"The historical society has been in to see this." Nana added quietly, "They want the house restored anyway—I might even say *especially*. They think it will serve to remind generations to come of what this country endured durin' that horrible war." She dabbed at her tears again. "I think they're right."

"But, Nana, Connemara House…it's our home!" Lauryn cried out.

"But how can we live here now, Lauryn?" Georgia asked. "Even if we covered it all up with carpet again, we'd know it was there. And besides…it's history. Sad though it may be, men died here fightin' to preserve this town. They should be remembered, and this house and the stories here cannot easily be ignored."

"Nana?" Lauryn pleaded. "You'd give up our home?"

But Virginia Anne Kensington was elsewhere. Her mind floated through time to the past, remembering what she'd tried so long to forget.

"I was only a child—Patrick's age," she said quietly as she stared out through the window into the yard. "The battle had been horrible! I was so frightened. It seemed like it would never end. And the doctors and surgeons needed our help. There were so many men, hurt, bleedin', dyin' in our house and only Daddy, Mama, Sean, Lauralynn, and I here to help them. Everyone else was gone, except the doctors and two or three nurses. Everyone had left because of the battle. But Daddy knew how to help. And Connemara House was protection of sorts. So we stayed."

Lauryn looked to her mother, who sniffled and tried to hold back her sobs. She looked up to Brant, still staring at the stains on the floor. And she looked to her Nana, trying to imagine what a horrible experience the war had been for a young girl.

"Laura would talk to the men, try to soothe their minds, ease their pain however she could. I remember the hem of her dress—it was drenched with their blood. Three or four inches up around the entire hem…a dark stain all the way around it. She'd bend down to tend the dyin' soldiers, and they'd bleed out on her dress.

"The surgeons would amputate limbs—arms, legs—and toss them out this window onto the front porch. Sean would gather them up, and…and…I would go around givin' sips of water to the soldiers waitin' their turn to be tended to.

"I'll never forget their faces—so sad and tired and defeated. Whenever one would pass away, I'd tell Daddy or Sean, and they'd take him out back and lay him in the grass until there was time to tend to them proper. The bedroom in the back was filled with soldiers who were so close to death you could smell it. But there weren't very many cots there. Still, we tried to make them as comfortable as possible until they went."

"Oh, Nana," Lauryn whispered through her sobs.

"Laura was like an angel of mercy. Her beautiful smile was the last thing on earth some of those men ever saw. And I remember thinkin' that there wasn't anythin' closer to heaven for their eyes to behold before they rose up to it," Nana whispered. She shook her head and wiped furiously at her tears before continuing. "Then Daddy was shot and Lauralynn...and we had to hide. And when we returned to Connemara, so much later, there was a new porch, painted floors, and large carpets throughout the house...and I never again wondered why. All I ever wondered about was Laura."

"The carpenters have sanded 'til their arms are raw, " Georgia told them. "The stains are soaked all the way through the wood—clear through 'til you can see them when you go down in the basement and look up. And it wouldn't be right to tear these floors up and destroy such a visual lesson in history."

"But, Mama," Lauryn argued, "everyone is buried here—Daddy and Grandpa and the Captain. And what about Laura?"

"My beautiful, beautiful sister," Nana whispered to herself. "Still lost." Nana turned to Lauryn. "I've told the historical society that we need time. I've had the furniture stored, except for the things in the attic—they still need to be taken—and we've been stayin' with Sean and Mindy. I guess we'll all just stay there until we've decided what to do." Nana reached out. Taking Lauryn's hand in one of hers and Brant's in the other, she pleaded, "Time is short now, my angels. You must find her. Soon!"

Patrick came running in through the front door. "Lauryn!" he yelled, throwing his arms around his sister's waist. "Oh, brother! You're sobbin' like the rest of these fool women," he grumbled.

"Patrick, you don't understand all this," Lauryn began to explain tenderly.

"I do so!" he argued. His bright eyes immediately filled with tears as he hurried over to the corner with the largest stain. "I understand that the soldier who died here, in this spot...he found peace. He stepped into heaven in our house! And though it was a terrible thing to happen, he's in heaven where he can't hurt no more. Maybe Daddy knows him, and they're sittin' around talkin' about Franklin and Connemara House right now. Maybe they're talkin' about how warm, loved, and at home they felt here. Just like we do."

Lauryn smiled. Her little brother had indeed found his own peace with the house's history.

"You're right, boy," Brant offered, tousling Patrick's hair as he passed him on his way to the entryway. "They found peace—one way or the other." Brant stepped into the adjoining room and began looking around at the floor there. He returned quickly, however, and embraced Virginia comfortingly. The elderly woman smiled up at him and winked.

"Come along, Patrick," Nana said, brightening suddenly. "You're good for a body's soul. Why don't you take your Nana for a walk, hm?"

"Sure thing, Nana," the boy said, taking his grandmother's hand and wiping angrily at a tear that had escaped his eye. He paused before leaving through the front door, however, and looked to Lauryn. "Think about it hard, Lauryn. It's all right. They were helped here—helped or they found heaven. Connemara ain't a bad place at all. It's home. It's a part of heaven."

Lauryn smiled and nodded at her brother. He was right. For all the horror and tragedy of war, for all the death and pain, his heartfelt explanation was right. The soldiers who had died in Connemara House had died with Lauralynn at their side. They'd found their peace—found help, compassion, and love. Connemara was, as ever, a beacon—a symbol of hope and beauty.

"Here I am an utter mess again, sweet pea," Georgia sighed, taking the handkerchief Brant pulled from his pocket and offered her. She smiled at her daughter. "I'm sorry you've come home to find...all this."

"It's all right, Mama." Lauryn couldn't take her eyes from the bucket rings on the floor. "Everythin' will be fine."

Then Georgia lowered her voice. "We need to be happy for Nana's sake, and I've done a very poor job of it. This has upset her terribly." Then, in even a lower whisper, she added, "And you keep an eye on Brant, darlin'. This kind of thing may bring his own memories back all too vividly, you hear?" She squeezed Lauryn's hand and wiped at her cheeks. "Now I had better splash some water on my mess of a face before Mr. DuMonde with the historical society arrives. We're meetin' to talk things out a bit."

Lauryn turned to Brant, who stood looking at her with the saddest of expressions. "I…I can't believe all of this," she cried. "We were only gone for a week."

"It's disturbing," he mumbled as he walked to the dark stain in the corner. Hunkering down, he pressed a hand to the floor, the place where some poor soldier had bled so terribly fifty years before. "I'm glad your family has decided to preserve all this…allow the public to see it." He stood and turned toward her once more. "I know it's your home, Lauryn. I don't mean to sound heartless. But this is a very important part of history and—"

"I know," Lauryn interrupted. "I just feel…strange now, knowin' that we lived here all these years…walked these floors…never realizing what was under the carpets."

"What a day that must've been," Brant mused. "Can you imagine it? The O'Halleran family, so used to the lovely southern life, suddenly finding themselves in the middle of a battle, their home turned into a hospital…a morgue." He paused for a moment and looked around the room. "Exactly where was Laura when she was wounded?"

"Right there. Near where you stand now. She was assistin' my great-grandfather with the wounded soldiers here in the parlor," Lauryn reminded him.

"She was helping. And this room is fairly covered in bloodstains," Brant mumbled, frowning thoughtfully. "And to think, all these years that Laura's been telling me about the blood on her dress…she wasn't referring to her own wound."

Lauryn gasped slightly as the realization fully struck her as well. "The hem of her skirt," she whispered.

Brant nodded. "The dark stains that I always thought were mud." He shook his head in irritation. "Blood! From the soldiers that were brought in here…wounded. Just like your Nana said." He pointed to the large stain on the floor at his feet. "Do you know how much a man would have to bleed to leave a stain like this one?"

Lauryn shuddered, horrified at the thought. "No. And I don't even want to imagine."

"Laura's dress would've easily been saturated at the hem, simply from walking around in this room while she was helping the men." He ran his fingers through his hair in discouragement, disappointed in himself. "I thought it was mud. That's why I was so curious about the springhouse when you first took me there."

Suddenly, a great anxiety began to rise within Lauryn's chest. The room began to spin, and she knew that if she did not leave it, she would faint. "I have to get out of here for a moment," she whispered as she fled the house. Once outside, she stumbled down the front porch steps and onto the grass.

"Are you all right?" Brant asked, taking hold of her arm in support. Lauryn was so thankful he had followed her out—for his sake, as well as her own.

She nodded. "I will be. It was just so warm in there. I felt as if I couldn't breathe." Suddenly tears burst from her eyes, and she looked up at him. "This is my home, Brant! I've lived in this beautiful house my whole life! And now…it will never, never, never be the same—turned into a museum, empty of laughter and love, and all that people will see is the ugliness!"

Brant reached out and gathered her into his arms. "Well, let me tell you something," he began in a low, soothing tone. "This is a beautiful place, even still. Think of it the way Patrick does. I think he's right. Maybe…maybe you need to let it go, for a lot of reasons. But you need to remember that it was your home—your beautiful, warm home, filled with love and memories. And what better thing to happen to poor Connemara House, who endured so much, than to be appreciated, admired for her beauty and benevolence? To let people stand in awe of her experience, always the beauty of the South…still after that horrible day so long ago. Like your Nana, it healed. But I do think now…now might be the time for your family to let it go. Let it help remind others of what happened here, a tribute to all of those who bled for it."

Lauryn hugged him tightly. Her beautiful Connemara—even now, as she looked to the vine-covered home she'd loved so much, it was still magnificent. Perhaps it had healed, like a soldier who comes home from battle with scars on his body but his soul still in him. Beautiful—like the soldier who held her in his strong arms now.

"Nana is right then," Lauryn whispered. "Our time to find Lauralynn just ran out." Forcing herself to release Brant, Lauryn stepped back and looked up at him as she wiped at her tears. "Let's ask Nana about Carissa."

"Now?" Brant questioned. Lauryn knew how little either of them wanted to upset Virginia further. But Nana herself had told them time was short.

"She won't mind, Brant," she assured him. "Let's do it. Now! As soon as she gets back from her walk with Patrick."

Brant nodded at Lauryn. He could feel it—the end—as if it were lurking around the next corner. And he wasn't sad or afraid. Rather he was glad—for so many reasons too. Glad for Lauralynn and the Captain. He could feel it, the fact that he and Lauryn would find her. But mostly, he was selfish in his gladness. Keeping himself from Lauryn—no, keeping himself from loving Lauryn completely and entirely like she was meant to be loved by him—was near to driving him insane!

He'd struggled with guilt, ever since the morning in the orchard when he'd told her he wouldn't touch her again—struggled with guilt and yet fury that he'd made such a ridiculous statement, struggled with anger and self-loathing for hurting her in such an inane way. Keeping himself from her hadn't helped him to stay any more focused on finding Laura. In fact, it had made it all the worse! For now, instead of the sweet feel of Lauryn next to him, instead of the delicious taste of her mouth as they kissed being his distraction, it was the lack of those things that burdened his mind—the lack of owning her trust that caused him to nearly break into fits of angry swearing.

And so Brant was glad for the ominous feeling in his soul—the feeling that things were about to change, forever.

CHAPTER NINETEEN

"Nana?" Lauryn began as she and Brant sat with her grandmother on the front porch. "We…we've discovered somethin', and we need to ask you about it."

Instantly, Virginia's eyes widened with hope. "What, darlin'? What have you found?"

"In Vermont, we found letters in the Captain's trunk. We…we were readin' some of the letters Laura wrote to Brand while he was away at war. There's a reference to…why didn't you ever tell us? We think it might be important."

"What, dear?" Nana asked, confused at Lauryn's rambling.

"Your sister Carissa," Brant stated. "Why didn't anyone ever talk about her?"

Lauryn felt guilty instantly when she saw the rosiness drain from her grandmother's face. Nana had been through too much miserable memory in the past few days to be emotionally healthy.

Quickly, Lauryn tried to soothe her. "We don't want to upset you, Nana. But in one of the letters—and maybe we should've just gone through the Captain's again—but…but Laura mentioned havin' seen Carissa and—"

"I saw her too," Virginia confessed in a barely audible whisper. "The day of the battle. I saw her. Here at Connemara House."

"What?" Lauryn exclaimed. It was unbelievable! First of all that her Nana could have a sister that she never, ever spoke of. And now this?

"The day of the battle, I saw her. Carissa was here. But I was too afraid to tell anyone. And besides…whenever was there time with a war ragin' on our own property?"

"Why was she here?" Brant asked.

Nana daintily wiped a tear from her cheek with the handkerchief she produced from the waistband of her dress. "She…she was alone. So alone. And she was…she was…"

"Expecting a baby?" Brant finished for her.

Nana nodded and sniffled. "She had come in search of safety and…and maybe to find Daddy's heart had softened. But she made me promise not to tell that I had seen her. She wanted to speak to Daddy herself because she didn't want to upset Mama further…or Lauralynn. So she kissed me on the cheek, asked my forgiveness for the sinful things she'd done to herself and the family, and…and I never saw her again."

"Never?" Lauryn asked.

"No. Never," her grandmother confirmed. "Sometimes I'd think I saw her…on a street corner or by a tree. Even as I'm older, I sometimes think that…but it's always someone else. Not her."

"Laura had seen her too, on other occasions," Brant mentioned.

"I know," Virginia Kensington admitted. "She told me. It had upset her terribly. She felt as if Carissa was mockin' her—still tryin' to ruin the love she and Brand had. But nothin' ever could've. Nothin'! And Carissa knew that. And besides, Laura helped her. I think Carissa's heart did change. Truly. And Laura was able to forgive her. And she helped her, though Daddy never knew."

"So Carissa was here that day," Brant mumbled pensively, more to himself than anyone.

"I'm sorry, children," Nana sighed suddenly. "This day has been too much for me. I'll talk with you about it later…but I just feel that I can't take another moment of it just now. I need some rest."

"Of course, Nana," Lauryn soothed. "You just sit here in the rocker and rest your eyes awhile."

Nana nodded. "Oh, Carissa," she sighed. "How I loved her! And she was good to me. Always played tea party with Lauralynn and me. Always helped me and looked after me. Always…until Brand and Lauralynn…"

"Rest now, Nana," Lauryn soothed. "Put it from your mind."

"Thank you, darlin'," Virginia said as she sighed a breath of letting go.

ॐ

Lauryn stood in the barren room that had been hers for her entire life—the room that now stood empty, lonely. The soft, lovingly stitched quilts were gone, the soft bed, the crystal bowls of floating flowers and candles. Everything was gone—everything except the gruesome bloodstains on the floor. There was a particularly massive one directly in the center of the room, and it was disturbing beyond description to Lauryn. Her beautiful haven of privacy, gone forever.

Brant had gone for a walk. He'd said he'd needed to think. So with her Nana resting in the rocker on the porch, her mother on the back porch with Mr. DuMonde from the historical society, and Patrick off getting into who knew what kind of mischief, Lauryn found herself completely, and somewhat unwillingly, alone.

"They're at peace," he said from behind her. Instantly, at the sound of the Captain's familiar voice, Lauryn felt comforted. She turned to face him. "The men who died here…they're happy, peacefully that way."

Lauryn nodded and tried to smile at him. "And…and do you think it's right, Captain…to let Connemara become…become…"

"Yes. I do," he stated, stepping forward and gathering her into his consoling embrace. "Without tangible and dramatic tokens of history, people forget what went before, why they have freedom, how their ancestors made their lives possible."

"But Connemara…it's my life! Every childhood memory I have is here! How can I ever leave it behind and…" Lauryn sobbed.

"Connemara will stand forever, Lauryn," the Captain reminded her. "And it is, after all, a *thing*. People have been born here, loved here, and had to leave it behind for generations now. Isn't that so? Connemara protected and warmed you, and you will always love her. But you would've left soon enough to live your life out somewhere else." The Captain took her face in his hands and gazed adoringly into her eyes. "But you'll never lose Connemara. She's part of your soul."

Lauryn smiled and snuggled tighter into his embrace. "I know. I suppose that secretly I'm more worried that…that Connemara is what has kept Brant…that Connemara is the magic that…"

"That kept him coming back to you," he finished for her.

"Yes," she admitted.

"No, sweet angel. You did that on your own."

"Lauryn! We're losin' our minds," Brant growled as he entered the room.

"What?" Lauryn exclaimed, pushing herself from the Captain's arms immediately.

"Excuse me, sir." Brant nodded at the Captain as he took hold of Lauryn's hand and began fairly dragging her from the room. "But time's a-wastin', and all this mess with the house nearly made me forget why we rushed back." Glancing back at the Captain, he added, "You might want to come along, sir." The Captain nodded and followed them out of the room.

"What are you goin' on about?" Lauryn asked, trying to hitch her skirt up enough to enable her to keep up with his furious pace toward the attic.

"The false bottom…in Laura's trunk. Remember?" he mumbled, undaunted.

Lauryn gasped, suddenly remembering their purpose and rather horrified that she'd allowed herself to forget it. As they rushed up the stairs toward the attic, Lauryn's heart began to pound madly. Her skin prickled, and she knew. She knew they would find something, something that would change their lives—hers and Brant's, Laura's and the Captain's—forever.

※

"I knew it," Brant mumbled as he set the last treasure of Lauralynn's trunk aside and put his hand flat on the trunk bottom. Lauryn's heart began to beat madly with anticipation. It was important! Her very soul knew it.

Careless of the trunk's condition or end, Brant drove his fist through the planking that was the false bottom. "I knew it," he repeated. "It is just like yours, isn't it, Captain?"

"Yes," was all the Captain said. Lauryn noticed momentarily again that the Captain didn't seem as…as vivid as he had before. But as Brant reached into the trunk, removing a small bundle of letters, her thoughts turned to their task once more.

Setting the letters aside quickly, he reached in again and withdrew an ancient piece of sheet music and a photograph perhaps fourteen inches in width and twelve inches high.

"Oh my goodness," Lauryn whispered as she gazed at the photograph Brant held. "Brant?" Lauryn breathed as he held up the photograph for her to see better. "Brant…are you seein' here what I'm seein'?"

The photograph obviously had been taken on Brandon and Lauralynn's wedding day, for there they stood, the Captain and his lady, at the center of focus, surrounded by other people. Lauryn recognized her Great-Grandfather and Great-Grandmother O'Halleran. She'd seen them in other photographs in the family albums, knowing them at once in the one Brant now held. There were two young men she recognized as well, Lauralynn's brothers. And there was her grandmother, Virginia Anne O'Halleran, a small girl of eight, standing to Lauralynn's right and holding a china doll. But the other person in the photograph astonished Lauryn the most! The person standing directly to Laura's left sent a shiver up Lauryn's spine and caused the hair on the back of her neck to bristle.

"It's Brandon and Laura," Brant mumbled. "But…but…if I didn't know better…and I *do* know better," Brant stammered, "that girl next to the Captain is the spittin' image of…of your friend Penny McGovern."

Carefully, Lauryn took the photograph from Brant's trembling grasp. Turning it over to see if there were anything written on the back, she read aloud. "*August 16, 1863. The wedding of Brandon Masterson and Lauralynn O'Halleran.*"

Lauryn caressed the ancient-looking penmanship with her fingers as she continued to read, "*Keil McCrea and Erynn Shayla O'Halleran. William O'Halleran, Sean O'Halleran. Virginia Anne O'Halleran, aged 8 years, Carissa O'Halleran, aged 15 years.*"

As she looked at the photograph again, Lauryn felt as if she couldn't breathe. "Brant, it can't be. The similarity…it's a coincidence, right?" She looked to the Captain. "Captain? It's just coincidence, isn't it?"

But the Captain was fading. "I'll leave that to you."

"But, Captain?" Lauryn called. He was gone. Odd, Lauryn thought, that he should leave when they had just found…

"Similarity?" Brant exclaimed. "They could be twins, Lauryn."

And it was true! As much as Lauryn's mind fought the reality, it was true. Carissa O'Halleran was the exact image of Penny McGovern.

"And would you look at that," Brant breathed in an awed whisper. Lauryn was stunned by their discovery, yes. But not too stunned to be even further astonished when she looked to the piece of sheet music he handed to her.

In a hushed, disbelieving tone, she read the title of the music, " '*Sweet Lauralynn.*' *By Brandon Carmichael Masterson. July 11th, 1863.* The Captain wrote this song?"

"No wonder that old Union soldier song was so important to Laura. I used to wonder why she was so determined that I memorize it," Brant whispered.

"Now you know," Lauryn whispered. Then, looking to the photograph again, she said, "Brant..."

"I know," he agreed, reading her thoughts. "I think we better make a trip over to see your friend Penny."

જ

"This is insane, Brant," Lauryn whispered as Brant knocked on the large oak door of the McGovern house. "What are we doin' here? It's just a coincidence. That's all it is. I'm certain it can't possibly be anythin'." But even as she tried to convince herself that Penny's resemblance to her great-aunt Carissa was purely mischief of nature, she knew, as surely as Brant had told her he knew. Carissa and Penny were somehow related.

"You know as well as I do that it isn't a mere coincidence, Lauryn," Brant mumbled, seeming to read her thoughts.

Lauryn could hear approaching footsteps emanating from inside Penny's home. A moment later, the door opened to reveal none other than Penny McGovern standing before them.

"Lauryn! Mr. Masterson," she greeted in her delighted, friendly manner. "Whatever brings the two of you to be knockin' on our door?"

"Um...um..." Lauryn stammered. She felt Brant's hand at the small of her back encouraging her.

"May we come in for a moment, Miss McGovern?" Brant asked.

"Well, of course, silly ducks! Come on in." Penny smiled, obviously very pleased at a visit. "Mama's out just now, and Daddy and Jeffrey are down sellin' horses…so I do hope it was me that the two of you were hopin' to find at home."

"Actually," Brant began, taking the seat in the parlor Penny gestured for him, "we do want to talk to you."

Penny raised an eyebrow. "My. This does sound serious! And dear Lauryn…you look like you've seen a ghost."

Brant chuckled and shook his head at the irony. It was Lauryn who finally held the old photograph out for Penny to see. Penny cocked her head to one side, clearly puzzled, and took the photograph.

"This is a beautiful photograph, Lauryn!" she exclaimed. "Why, wherever did you…" She stopped, and Lauryn held her breath. "Would you look at that," Penny giggled with delight. "Do you know how very few photographs we have of Granny McGovern when she was young? Where did y'all come across this?"

Lauryn was overcome and put a hand to her temple. "You mean…you mean you recognize someone in that photograph, Penny?" she whispered.

"For pity's sake! Of course I do!" Penny held up the photograph and pointed directly to the image of Carissa O'Halleran. "That's my Granny Carry. Don't tell me y'all don't see the resemblance she and I share."

"Oh, we see it, all right," Brant mumbled.

"My stars!" Penny sighed, looking at the photo once more. "Just look at her! As young as springtime." She smiled and studied the photograph a moment longer. Then she asked, "Who are these other people? I had no idea Granny stood in a weddin'!" Penny quirked an eyebrow. "Still, they look familiar. As if I've seen them somewhere before."

"The little girl…there…" Brant said, pointing to Virginia. "That's Virginia O'Halleran Kensington, Lauryn's Nana."

Lauryn couldn't speak. She felt as if she might swoon, if the truth be told. Carissa had lived! Obviously she had married and had a family. That would make Penny her cousin!

"What?" Penny gasped. "You mean your Nana and my granny knew each other way back? Why, that's wonderful, Lauryn!" Penny giggled with delight and squeezed Lauryn's hand affectionately.

"Actually, Penny," Lauryn whispered, "Carissa O'Halleran…was my Nana's older sister."

"Her sister?" Penny repeated. "But…that can't be, Lauryn. I would certainly have known that."

"Are you sure that's your grandmother?" Brant pressed. "Are you positive?"

"Yes! I know this is her!" Penny insisted. "And anyway, look there, at her wrist. She still wears that same bracelet to this very day. Why didn't I know any of this? I don't think anyone knows of it." Penny continued to stare at the photograph, as if it would speak back to her and explain.

"What do you know about your grandmother?" Lauryn asked. "Will you tell us about her?"

"Why?" Penny seemed suddenly very defensive. "I can tell there is more to this than y'all are tellin' me." She inhaled deeply and then looked directly at Lauryn. "You tell me what you want to know about her…why you don't already know about her…and what I don't already know about her."

Brant, however, was impatient. He snatched the photograph from Penny. "This is Virginia O'Halleran," he began to explain rather roughly, pointing to Lauryn's Nana. "This is Carissa O'Halleran." Again, he pointed to the image of the young woman in the photograph. "And this," he said, lowering his voice, "this is their sister, Lauralynn O'Halleran."

Penny frowned for a moment, but then her face brightened, revealing her sudden understanding. "Lauralynn? *The* Lauralynn? The one they never found? I thought she looked familiar."

"Yes," Brant sighed, tossing the photograph onto the sofa in frustration.

"We're thinkin' that maybe your granny knows somethin' about her…about that day she disappeared," Lauryn confessed.

Penny frowned. "Why would Granny know?"

"They were sisters, weren't they?" Brant growled.

"I never knew that before now. And I'm sure there's a reason for it." Penny was close to tears. Lauryn could see the moisture heavy in her eyes. "Would you like to tell me what that reason was?"

"Are you certain you want to know?" Brant asked gruffly.

"Brant, be patient," Lauryn said softly. Brant sighed with impatience.

"Tell me," Penny demanded. "Just tell me what you know, Lauryn."

"It's not…it's not a very flatterin' story, Penny," Lauryn warned. She adored Penny! They had been friends as long as Lauryn could remember. It upset her that she would have to tell her longtime friend such a tale.

Once again, Brant buffered the pain for Lauryn by telling the tale himself. "Lauralynn fell in love and married a man from Knoxville," he began, suddenly patient and in a very compassionate manner. "Brandon Masterson…my great-uncle. Carissa had fallen in love with Brandon as well and was apparently very envious. She…she tried to put a wedge between Brandon and Lauralynn." Lauryn looked to Brant lovingly, grateful for his tact and sensitivity to Penny's feelings for her grandmother. "It was bad enough that old Kiel O'Halleran disowned Carissa…banished her from the family. The old O'Halleran family Bible has an entry—*Carissa O'Halleran born June 20, 1847, died.* It had been assumed all these years that she died at birth. But Lauryn and I have been going through letters and talking to people, and we know she lived. It's obvious in just looking at you."

Penny was silent, frowning. "What…what did she do to cause her father to disown her?" she asked simply. Again Lauryn felt a lump in her throat and was unable to answer. She didn't like the fact that her beautiful, joyously natured friend was distressed.

"She became pregnant and insisted that it was Lauralynn's husband who was the baby's father." Brant had a way of just saying things plainly.

Lauryn felt physically ill when she saw the tears escape Penny's eyes and begin traveling down her cheeks.

"Penny, I don't mean to cause you pain or to upset you or make you sad," Lauryn assured her. "It's just that…we have to find out what happened to Lauralynn. And we know, from these letters we found, that Lauralynn had seen Carissa a short time before the battle when she was lost. We just…we were just hopin' that somebody in your family knew somethin' to help."

Penny wiped at her tears and sniffled. "I suppose…the one to ask would be…Granny Carry."

"She's still alive then?" Brant asked. "Where? Can we talk to her?"

Lauryn sat in stunned astonishment, unable to speak. Her grandmother's sister, alive still?

Penny shook her head and rose from her seat, going toward the window. "She…she lives in Memphis with my Uncle Nathan. She's not well at all. She's been bedridden for months and months." Penny stood, wringing her hands nervously. Then suddenly, and unexpectedly, she turned back to face Brant and Lauryn. "She's a good, good woman. Always loving and kind and…and…honest. This is so hard to take in."

Lauryn rose to her feet and rushed to Penny, enveloping her in a loving and friendly embrace. "It's all right, Penny. It's fine."

"Think of it this way, Miss McGovern," Brant offered. "You and Lauryn…you're cousins."

"What's all this about?" Jeffrey asked, entering the room.

Immediately, Penny released Lauryn and answered, "Wonder— wonderful news, Jeffrey."

Brant dropped his head for a moment, uncomfortable.

"Brant and Lauryn…Brant and Lauryn have discovered a family connection."

Lauryn fancied for a moment that Jeffrey's smile of greeting faded slightly. "How so?" he asked. "Good to see you again, Brant." Jeffrey offered a handshake, and Brant accepted.

"Well," Lauryn began, for Penny shook her head, clearly too unsettled to tell the tale to her brother, "it seems that your nana and my Nana were…were sisters."

"What?" Jeffrey exclaimed, smiling and obviously in disbelief. "What nonsense have you two girls cooked up this time? And, Brant, how did they lure you into such a game?"

"It's no game," Brant stated, retrieving the photograph from its place on the sofa nearby and handing it to Jeffrey.

Jeffrey studied the photograph for a moment, frowning. He turned it over, reading the information written on the back of it. "Well, I'll be dipped in…in batter," he stammered.

"It seems true enough," Lauryn began. "Isn't it…isn't it marvelous, Jeffrey?"

But Jeffrey frowned, apparently skeptical. "If it's so *marvelous*, why does Penny look like she's goin' to vomit, Brant looks like he's ready to beat the waddin' out of the devil, and you, Lauryn—" His eyes narrowed as he continued "—you look like you been seein' one too many ghosts these days?"

It was Penny who came to their rescue. Lauryn was grateful because Brant had inhaled deeply, straightening his shoulders and clenching his jaw tightly shut as if preparing for battle.

"Dear Jeffrey," Penny began, "it's all…it's all quite lewd, actually." Penny swallowed hard. "It seems that Lauryn's great-grandfather—I guess we can call him great-grandpappy now too—it seems he had Granny McGovern…um…disowned when she was younger."

Now it was Jeffrey's turn to appear indignant and defensive. He inhaled a deep breath and curtly said, "Really? And you believe that, Pen? That Granny could do anythin' to warrant her own father disowning her?"

"It's true, Jeffrey," Brant nearly growled. "I'm not saying that your grandmother isn't the most wonderful of women. By the look of your family, your sister, she must be a great person. But even great people make mistakes in their past, perhaps mistakes that have been paid for dearly…not to be talked about later on. And—"

But Jeffrey put a hand up to quiet Brant's explanation. He hung his head guiltily for a moment and then said, "I know all about it."

"What?" Penny and Lauryn exclaimed simultaneously.

"Granny told me…last month when I was in Memphis. She…she was afraid she was goin' to pass on without any of us knowin'. Daddy didn't even know. He thought Grandpa McGovern was his real father. But…but he's not." Jeffrey reached out, taking Penny's hand and squeezing it reassuringly.

"Did…did she tell you who was his father, Jeffrey?" Lauryn ventured.

Jeffrey swallowed hard. The defensive expression gone from his face, replaced by the relief of truth-telling, he said, "Yes."

"And…" Brant prodded.

"A young man named James Nettles—a Franklin boy that left soon after…soon after she…" Jeffrey stammered.

"It's irrelevant, Jeffrey," Brant told him. "Your father was your grandfather's son. And that's that."

"That's what I told Granny," Jeffrey admitted. "That's what I kept telling her. But...but she wanted someone to know the truth."

"Why didn't you tell me, Jeffrey?" Penny asked. It was obvious that the secret Penny and Jeffrey's grandmother revealed to Jeffrey had weighed heavily on his mind.

Jeffrey shrugged. "What good would it have done?"

"What good would it have done?" Lauryn suddenly exclaimed. "Jeffrey," she began as tears flooded her cheeks, "you know the tiniest bit about what...about what I've gone through in my life because of my Nana's sister's disappearance that day durin' the war! Did it not occur to you that your grandmother may have been able to help me? Didn't you once think that maybe...maybe she knew somethin' that would give me a hope gettin' on with my life and...and..."

"No, Lauryn. I...I honestly didn't," he confessed.

As Lauryn buried her face in her hands for a moment, suddenly overwhelmed with anger, resentment, and anxiety, she felt Brant gather her into his arms, softly stroking her hair as she cried against his shoulder.

"It's all right, Lauryn," Penny offered. "We'll...we'll go now. The four of us! We'll go to Memphis and talk to Granny."

"No," Jeffrey demanded. "She's suffered enough."

Lauryn was suddenly furious—mad and out of her sensible mind. Pushing herself from Brant's embrace, from the strong arms she only wanted to linger in, she turned to Jeffrey, outraged. "She's suffered enough? What about those who still suffer, Jeffrey? What about the Captain? What about Lauralynn and Brant and me? What about the fact that I'll never have Br—never have what I want, not a chance at it, until your granny's sister is found? If she's as wonderful as you say, then she'll be glad to help us! Right? Won't such a wonderful woman, repentant of her sins that caused such devastation to her family...won't such a profoundly wonderful woman be glad to help her family now?"

Jeffrey stood silent, attempting to control his own anger. It was Penny who offered hope.

"Jeffrey, has it occurred to you that...that maybe Granny needed this to happen?" Penny reached out and took hold of her brother's arm. "That, in order to live...or die...in peace, that maybe she needs to—"

"I'm going to Memphis," Brant suddenly growled, "with or without the rest of you." With that, he nodded to Penny, turned, and left by way of the front door, slamming it violently.

"So am I," Lauryn said, leaving the room almost as dramatically as Brant. She didn't hear Penny tell her brother she was going too, and he could join them or not.

☙

"Carissa? Alive?" Nana breathed as she sat in the rocker on the front porch of Connemara. She was listening to Brant reveal what they'd discovered about the McGovern family.

"You never noticed the resemblance, Nana?" Lauryn asked. "Truly?"

Nana shook her head, still disbelieving. "I…I thought I had imagined it." The elderly woman closed her eyes for a moment and inhaled deeply the warm, fragrant air of Tennessee. "I have a sister," she whispered, "livin'."

"Yes, Nana. Yes," Lauryn soothed.

"I was so much younger than my sisters," Virginia began. Lauryn knew she was in the past—as surely she knew it as she knew that Brant was somewhere other than the front porch in his mind. He stared off into the grass of Connemara's front lawn, silent and as brooding as a man could ever be.

Her attention was quickly drawn back to her Nana as she said, "Their childhoods were over by the time I was a toddler. But they used to dote on me like I was their favorite dolly. They'd play games with me, dress up their old china dolls for me, give me the prettiest tea parties you ever saw. They had secret places they played in. They always said they'd show me…but they never did. Always just played with me on the porch here, under the gazebo, in the cellar when days were too hot to stand the sunshine out."

"Pardon me, Miss Virginia." It was Penny. All three Connemara residents were startled from their private thoughts as Penny spoke.

"Penny," Nana greeted, her eyes filling with tears, "you are the image of her, child."

"Oh, Penny," Lauryn began, standing and suddenly feeling awkward. This girl, this sweet girl that had been her dearest friend for so long, now things were strange between them. "Penny...I...I..."

"I've reserved tickets for all of us on the mornin' train to Memphis—even you, Miss Virginia," she said. "Jeffrey wants to go too. We'll all go together." Penny was frightened, nervous, uncomfortable. It was painfully apparent.

Lauryn watched as Nana smiled at her and held her arms open to hug her. "Angel girl, Penny McGovern," Nana chuckled through her tears. "And to think...all these years wasted when you should've been callin' me Great-Auntie Virginia."

With a heavy sigh of relief at acceptance, Penny threw herself into Nana's arms and hugged her tightly.

Lauryn wiped the tear from her cheek, feeling an overwhelming love and attachment to her dear friend. She glanced at Brant, who was standing now, smiling in relief. He winked and nodded his encouragement.

After Penny and Nana wiped their tears from their cheeks, Penny turned to Brant. "I...I don't know exactly how this all affects you, Mr. Masterson," she admitted. "I don't know if your own childhood was disrupted as Lauryn's was. I don't know if you simply care because you love Lauryn." Lauryn winced, expecting Brant to offer an immediate argument at Penny's inference. When he did not, she glanced at him carefully, in time to see him smile. "But it's important to me that you understand that I will do anythin' to help. Anythin'."

Brant smiled at Penny and pulled her into one of his powerful embraces, kissing her cheek softly. "Thank you, Penny," he chuckled, and Lauryn tried to squelch the twinge of jealousy in her throat.

Then Penny turned to Lauryn. "I...I love you, Lauryn," she said. "You have been my best friend...my whole life. And...and when this is all over...I know we'll be closer than ever."

Lauryn felt guilty for once again letting jealousy enter her heart where Penny was concerned. "Nothin' could change the way we love each other, Pen," Lauryn told her, and they giggled and tightly hugged. Lauryn glanced at Brant over Penny's shoulder as they embraced. He winked again, assuring her all was well.

"Oh!" Penny exclaimed, suddenly releasing Lauryn. "I almost forgot!" Quickly, she reached down and picked up a small wooden box sitting on the front porch step. Lauryn was puzzled, for she hadn't noticed Penny carrying anything when she arrived.

"I want to share this with you, Lauryn," Penny explained. "And with you, Miss Virginia—I mean Auntie Virginia," she giggled excitedly. "My granny gave these to me when I was just six or seven. She said they belonged to her when she was a little girl and that she wanted me to have them always." Penny removed the lid from the box to reveal a good amount of crumpled paper within. "I got to thinkin'…that it would be wonderful for us to split the pieces up now—some for me, some for Lauryn, some for you, Auntie Virginia—and we can take a piece or two to Granny when we go."

Lauryn gasped and her Nana clutched at her chest, her own breath lost to her, as Penny reached into the box and produced a small, child-sized white china cup embellished with the tiniest of lavender flowers.

"It's a child's tea set," Penny said, completely unaware that even Brant held his breath and had paled. "Granny said she adored it when she was a little girl, and every piece is here except for one of the cups. I suppose it was broken or lost or somethin' and…Lauryn? Are you all right, Lauryn?"

It was the last thing Lauryn heard for several long, long moments. The next thing she knew, she was aware of the soft green lawn of Connemara beneath her, of Penny's frantic voice calling to her to wake up, and of Brant's hand at her cheek as he gently patted it.

She opened her eyes to behold Brant's worried face just a breath above her own. "The cup, Brant," she breathed. "Laura's cup…"

"I know, sugar," he mumbled. "I know. Are you all right?" He helped her to sit up. He looked to her Nana, still sitting in the rocker, leaning anxiously forward. "She's fine, Mrs. Kensington. She's fine."

☙

"All this time," Lauryn said as she sat at Henry's feet caressing the soft petals of one of the pansies that grew there, "all this time, just down the street." She couldn't put her thoughts into words. Her mind was still whirling with the events of the day. "This seems to be the longest day of my entire life," she said finally, leaning back against Henry's legs, overwhelmingly tired all at once.

"Tomorrow…tomorrow we'll know more," Brant assured her. "I know it." He looked at Lauryn from where he sat in front of her. "This will all begin to unravel tomorrow. It has to." He smiled at her, and she noted the way the corner of his mouth twitched slightly.

It was time, she told herself. The events of the day had been far too emotionally overwhelming. She needed Brant—needed to be in his arms, needed reassurance that he needed her. And she was tired—too tired to think clearly, to remember her plan to test him.

So with every ounce of the remaining physical and mental strength she could muster, Lauryn reached out and took hold of the front of Brant's shirt. Clutching the fabric tightly in her fists, she pulled him forward and captured his mouth with her own in a very intimate, very impassioned kiss. His surprise was not long-lived, however, for he had her face cupped firmly in his hands as he returned her kiss just as furiously.

His kiss was so deep, so driven, that she could not breathe and finally had to break from him to find one saving breath before she would have slipped into another faint.

Her time to catch her breath was not long, however. Before she'd even gotten control of her senses enough to open her eyes, Brant fairly flung her onto her back in the pansy beds at Henry's feet.

"My hell, Lauryn," he breathed, a delighted grin spreading across his face. "I thought I was going to explode before you found the guts to break that damned promise I made to you."

"Don't swear, Brant," Lauryn whispered breathlessly, smiling up at him.

"Don't talk," Brant ordered, his mouth finding hers again in the brutal passion ignited by the power of lovers kept apart too long.

He'd kept himself from her too long! Lauryn knew it by his manner of kissing her. His kisses were driven, thirsting. There were moments he seemed to forget she was a tender young woman whose face, lips, arms, waist, and shoulders were not used to such ravaging, however careful he was of respecting her virtue. Brant was barely in control of himself, and Lauryn secretly thrilled in the knowledge.

After a long while, and Lauryn had no way of gauging how long, Brant drew a deep breath, kissed her once more very tenderly on the mouth, and, raising his head, studied her for a moment. His thumbs caressed her tender lips, and the back of his hand stroked her cheek as he gazed down into her eyes, which Lauryn knew were sparkling with emotion.

"Lauryn," he mumbled. "Lauryn…you know I love…I love…"

Though her heart sunk at Brant's inability to confess his heart to her, she was not fully disappointed. And she understood. There was still too much keeping them apart—too much to be done for them to be completely happy in one another.

So, understanding, she finished for him, "You love to kiss me." She reached up, caressing his whiskery jawline with her palm. How she loved to touch him, ensuring that he was real and living.

He sighed, obviously delighted by her soft caress and disappointed in himself for not being able to finish his own sentence. But he smiled and nodded. "Yeah," he whispered, in defeat, brushing a wild curl from her forehead.

"I love…to kiss you too," she whispered.

He grinned and kissed her gently several more times before helping her to a sitting position. As he pulled several violets from her hair, he glanced up at Henry, who had been watching them the entire time. "Sorry, man," he said to the statue. "But…you just aren't man enough to handle a woman like this."

Lauryn smiled and, strangely enough, felt rather sorry for Henry, the mateless statue. Brant looked at her again, pulling another petal from her hair.

"Don't let me make any stupid statements about never touching you again, Lauryn," he told her. "You're lucky you weren't…compromised before now."

"You would never compromise me," she reminded him.

He shook his head as he stood and helped her to her feet. "Don't be too sure, sugar. My blood is hot enough to boil the devil out of hell."

"Quit that swearin'," she giggled.

"It's not swearing when you use it in a biblical way," he argued, adorably. "Now come along, baby. We have another trip to take tomorrow." He took her hand and led her toward the house.

"Glory be, Patrick," David McGovern, Patrick's cohort in mischief that day, exclaimed in a whisper from his hiding place behind Captain Brandon Masterson's tombstone. "You ever seen the likes of that before?"

Patrick Kensington shook his head, still in awe of the goings-on he'd just witnessed between his sister and Brant.

"Heck no!" he admitted in a whisper. "And I hope not to see the likes of it again until I'm old enough for my own blood to boil the devil out!"

⁊

"We're goin' tomorrow," Lauryn explained to the Captain late that night in her bedroom. "All of us—Nana, Penny, Jeffrey, Brant, and me. We'll talk to Carissa, and...and I feel that—"

"Don't speak it yet, Lauryn. Please," he whispered. The fear was evident in his voice, in the grimace of painful hope on his face. "I...I can't hope too much. I'm...I'm..."

"I understand." Lauryn reached out, taking the Captain's hand reassuringly in hers. "When I get back, when I've talked to Carissa..." The Captain nodded, forcing a smile. He was trying to be hopeful, she could tell. "This is it, my Captain—the event, the person that will help us."

The Captain reached out and brushed a lock of hair from Lauryn's cheek. Smiling, he bent and kissed her forehead softly. "You are an angel on earth, Sweet Lauryn." And he was gone.

Lauryn sighed heavily. The nearly painful throbbing of melancholia that washed over Lauryn at that moment caused tears to spring to her eyes. She would miss her Captain. How greatly she would miss him. And in her soul, Lauryn knew he would be gone soon. She had seen less and less of him since Brant entered her life, since they'd begun to get closer to solving the mystery of Laura. She wondered—was it because more of her attention had transferred to Brant? Or had it something to do with actually getting closer to finding Laura? Were they closer to finding her? And did that make it less necessary for the Captain to appear to her?

CHAPTER TWENTY

The train rumbled along rhythmically, the scenery outside rolling by at a relaxing pace. Lauryn had related to Jeffrey and Penny, in greater detail, her experience with the Captain. But they had paled all the more when they had learned of Brant's experience with Laura. In fact, Lauryn had been astounded by the pallid state of their faces when Brant explained why Lauryn had fainted upon seeing the child's tea set Penny had shown them, the one with the missing cup. Naturally, Penny had been very curious about Laura's possessing one of the cups when Brant was a child. And like Lauryn and Brant, she was also bothered by not knowing why it no longer appeared with her.

Now, as Nana related the entire story of Lauralynn and Brandon, Brant was oddly silent, frowning out the window, obviously lost in his own deep thoughts. Lauryn could read his frustration, his hidden resentment toward the fact that help had been so close at hand and unseen for so long. However, she tried to focus intently as Nana finished relating her experiences the day of Laura's disappearance to Penny and Jeffrey.

"I saw Carissa that day," Nana said, almost reverently. "She smiled at me and blew me a kiss, and I knew I had seen her for the very last time." Then Nana seemed to brighten. "But now," she sighed, "now she's found to me. And I can't wait to see her!"

"She's very old, Mrs. Kensington," Jeffrey reminded.

"Darling, I realize that," Nana chuckled. "She is older than me, and I can tell you, young man, that I am quite well aware of my own ancient state."

Suddenly, Brant rose from his seat. Without a word, he made his way to the aisle. As he began striding rather angrily toward the back of the train car, Lauryn did not pause in following him. His stride was so long and so determined she had to rush to catch up to him. Reaching the back door of the car, he opened it and stepped out onto the small landing.

"Brant?" she asked, instantly revitalized by the cool air outside. "I'm sure they don't want the passengers out here. It's not exactly safe," she said, taking hold of the ladder leading to the top of the car.

"Then you should go back," he growled softly. "No need for both of us to be in trouble."

"What's wrong, Brant?" she asked. It was obvious he was very, very upset—more so than she had sensed at first.

"I hate her," he stated bluntly. "How could she not come forward? How could she not help in the search for Laura, after all Laura did for her? After forgiving her, helping her, and loving her so unconditionally?"

"She's an old woman, Brant—" Lauryn began.

"And how could she do that to them?" he interrupted. "How could she lie about a thing like that? About who the father of her baby was? How could they forgive her, Brandon and Laura? And why do we have to be reduced to seeking her out for help?" He was enraged, and Lauryn felt it best to let him vent for a moment. "And what's Jeffrey's hitch? He's so protective of her…a lying, deceptive, heartless—"

"I…I can't say—" Lauryn whispered.

"Yeah, I've noticed," he growled, turning to her. "You've been pretty accepting of all this. At first, I was so blinded by the possibility this might lead us to Laura that I enjoyed a few hours of elation too. But now…" He shook his head and continued, "Now I hate her. Somehow, this is all…all of it…somehow this is her fault. I feel it! Everything you've endured, I've endured…everything our counterparts have endured! It could've been resolved long ago if one person had come forward. How can she truly claim regret when she's hidden it all for this long? It's not like she hasn't had decades to resolve it, Lauryn!"

Lauryn gasped as he turned and slammed his fist into the steel train car several times, overcome with uncontrollable anger and frustration.

"She should've come forward, Lauryn!" he shouted. "It should never have come this far."

Lauryn watched, frowning with sympathy for the fist he now regretfully rubbed. She would not be surprised if his outburst had caused him some broken bones.

"Brant," she said calmly, reaching out and placing a hand on his arm soothingly, "you're right." He looked at her, still frowning from anger or pain, she couldn't tell which—possibly from both. "She was wrong to keep silent, to hide. But…but had she come forward earlier, had she contacted the family, it doesn't mean Laura would've been found. And…and what if she had? Then…then…" She paused, afraid of his reaction to what she was about to say. Did she want to see in his eyes what she might? If there were disagreement—which she knew there wouldn't be, but if there were—what then? "If she had come forward…if Laura had been found by someone other than you or me…then you and I…" She felt the tears welling up in her eyes. "You and I would never have…" She couldn't finish. She couldn't confess to him that she was glad, sinfully glad, that Carissa had never appeared before! If she had, Brant would've had no reason to come to Connemara. Lauryn was glad that the mystery had continued for so long. Whether admittedly conscious of it before that moment or not, she was glad that Laura had not been found before—for if it had not been just the way it was, she would not have known her heart's desire, her dreams come true in Brant.

Brant looked at the beauty standing before him, her eyes filled with tears. He watched for a moment as the wind blew spiced-colored ringlets around her face, awed by the meaning of her unspoken words. It was at that very moment that he realized his emotion toward Carissa McGovern shouldn't be that of resentment, of hatred, but rather of thanks—for Lauryn was right. Had the mystery been solved before now, he would perhaps never have met his beautiful Lauryn—might never have known the ecstasy of her kiss, the rapture induced by her caress, the joy in his heart at her wit, sweetness, and inner loveliness.

He could see then the doubt, the questioning of his sincerity, as she asked, "You *are* glad that we…that we know each other, aren't you, Brant?"

He loathed the fact that he could not speak it to her, that he wasn't able to just take her in his arms and whisper all the things his heart felt into the softness of her hair. But until things were settled—until life could be about him, about her—it hurt him to see her self-doubt, her doubt in his true feelings for her. She had so much more courage than he did. Where would he be? he wondered. Who would he be without having been led to her?

"Will you come and visit me in hell, Lauryn?" he asked quietly.

"What?" she whispered, completely puzzled by his sudden change of demeanor.

"When I'm roasting on a spit for eternity…for being thankful that the Captain and Laura were wandering in pain, searching for each other aimlessly for fifty years…grateful to Carissa for keeping silent when she shouldn't have, so that I could know you, hold you…will you come down from heaven, my own angel, and visit me?"

As Lauryn felt the tears escape her eyes and trickle down her face, Brant reached out and gathered her into his arms. She nuzzled her cheek against the soft freshness of his shirt and let her arms slide around his waist, returning his embrace.

"Brant," she began, "I…I…"

"I'm sorry, Lauryn," he interrupted. She had nearly spoken of her love aloud to him, but his apology had silenced her. "I'm a weak-minded fool," he told her. "Not like you. No. You're strong, brave. You see the deeper meaning in things. I thank you for your wisdom."

She looked up at him, thrilled at the tiny twitching at the corner of his mouth, because she knew what it foretold. In the next moments, as his mouth worked a delicious spell of passion with her own, she wondered if she might burn in eternal flames as well. Her delight in the feel of the faultless sculpture of his body as he held her, her wicked pride in the uncommonly handsome features of his face as her hand caressed his cheek, and her ecstasy at being lost in his perfect kiss seemed too heavenly to be right.

ℛ

The elderly woman's eyes were closed as Jeffrey led everyone into her room. Tears were already rolling down Nana's cheeks, and Lauryn couldn't cease her nervous trembling. She watched as Penny went to her granny's bedside and bent, kissing her on the cheek. The old woman stirred, opened her eyes, and smiled at her granddaughter.

"Penny, sweet," Carissa O'Halleran McGovern spoke quietly, "what brings you round to see your old granny?"

Penny glanced over her shoulder at Lauryn, smiling uncertainly. "I've…I've brought visitors, Gran," she explained. Lauryn held her breath as the old woman looked past her granddaughter to the strangers standing in the room.

Carissa's eyes were a brilliant green, her hair perfectly white and twisted into a long braid that hung over one shoulder. Instantly, Lauryn saw the resemblance to her own Nana, and she wondered if Laura might look the same had she lived to be elderly.

"Um…Gran…this is…this is…" Penny stumbled over her words, obviously afraid somehow to tell her grandmother who the visitors were. It was Lauryn's Nana that stepped forward.

Lauryn watched anxiously as her Nana made her way carefully to the side of the old woman's bed. Reaching out, she took Carissa's hand and smiled down at her.

"Carissa?" Nana ventured.

"Yes?" the old woman responded. Lauryn noted the way an expression of near recognition crossed her face momentarily.

"It's me, dearest. Virginia," Nana revealed.

Instantly, Carissa's eyes filled with tears. "'Ginny?" she whispered. "Our little Ginny-Bean?"

"Yes, dearest," Virginia confirmed, tears running down her face. "Ginny-Bean."

Carissa closed her eyes, her brow puckering with emotion as her own tears streamed down her cheeks. "I'm sorry, Ginny," she whispered. "I'm sorry…for everythin'. For leavin' you, for Brand and Laura, and…and all of it."

"Sssshhh," Nana soothed. "It was forgiven long ago, Rissy. Forgiven long ago." Nana raised Carissa's hand to her lips and kissed the back of it lovingly. "I'm only glad we've found you, dear. At last, I have my sister again." Carissa sniffled and opened her eyes, smiling as Penny brushed a tear from her own cheek and handed a handkerchief to her grandmother.

"Who else has come to see the sinner?" Carissa asked.

"Gran...I'll have none of that," Jeffrey scolded, striding to his grandmother's bedside and kissing her forehead lovingly.

"Jeffrey, angel," Carissa greeted, "I see you've been out to save my soul."

"Though I would do anythin' for you, Gran...it wasn't me." Jeffrey turned and motioned for Lauryn and Brant to come forward. But Lauryn found she was frozen, unable to move at first. Brant took her hand and pulled her with him as he went to stand next to the bed.

At once, Lauryn saw the look of startled awe as Carissa looked first to Brant and then to her. "Have I passed on, Jeffrey? The man is so akin to...to..."

Brant nodded at the woman and spoke. "I'm Brant Masterson, Mrs. McGovern. Brandon was my great-uncle."

The woman's eyes then rested on Lauryn. But Lauryn couldn't find her voice. She could only stare down at her great-aunt in stunned silence.

"And this is Lauryn, Rissy," Nana explained. "My own granddaughter. She and Penny have been the best of friends since before they could walk."

"You must hate me," Carissa cried out suddenly, looking directly at Brant. "You must think me the most vile of women."

"No, ma'am," Brant assured her. "Not at all." Lauryn's heart swelled with adoration for Brant, his having overcome the feelings toward Carissa that he'd experienced for a time before their conversation on the train.

"I was so young," Carissa began. "I was so young and so foolish and so jealous. And he loved her instead of me, and I...I...couldn't accept it! I was certain that...that if..."

"Don't upset yourself, Gran," Jeffrey interrupted. "It's in the past. It's over."

But the elderly woman was far too upset to be settled so easily. "Wouldn't you do anythin', angel?" she said, looking directly at Lauryn. "If you were younger, less wits about you...wouldn't you do anythin' to have him?" Carissa pointed to Brant and continued, "Anythin' you had to do to make him your own? If you were a weak person, a weak-minded fool, if the devil had you in his clutches with a jealousy in your heart that you thought would kill you? Penny?" Carissa looked to her granddaughter. "Penny, I'm wicked, I know, but—"

"It's in the past, Aunt Carissa," Lauryn offered suddenly. "That is not why we came."

"But...but, Ginny-Bean, I..." Carissa stammered. Nana kissed the back of Carissa's hand once more, smiled, and caressed her cheek.

"I understand, ma'am," Brant told her. He reached out and took Carissa's hand from Nana's grasp. Then Lauryn watched in awe as he leaned over the old woman, kissing her upturned palm. "I think I do understand how a person could lose their way when they love someone so much."

"Do you?" Carissa whispered. Brant nodded and leaned over, whispering something in the woman's ear. Lauryn could not hear what Brant was saying, but when Carissa's eyes fixed on her as Brant spoke, she knew that whatever he told her had helped, for her weathered face softened, the pain fading a bit from her eyes.

"Thank you, love," Carissa whispered, stroking Brant's face gratefully. "Thank you for that."

"Gran, I think this is too much for you today," Jeffrey began.

"No, Jeffrey. But...but may I have some time alone with Ginny?" Carissa asked in a whisper. "Just me and Ginny. I'm very tired and need to rest soon...but my sister is near me, and I want to speak with her. Alone."

"Of course, Gran," Jeffrey said, taking Penny's hand and pulling her away from the bed. "Everyone out. Now." His manner was too demanding and final, but Lauryn understood a person's desire to protect his grandparent. So she followed Jeffrey and Penny out of the room, and so did Brant.

"I don't want you two drudgin' all this up for her," Jeffrey stated when they'd all settled in the parlor. "She's old. She's beaten herself her entire life over her mistakes. It's not right to torture her like this."

"We're far from torturin' her, Jeffrey," Penny argued. "And she's delighted to have her sister back."

"I'll thank you for whatever you said to her, Brant," Jeffrey said, attempting gratitude. "But I won't let you—"

"Jeffrey," Brant began. Lauryn saw his jaw tighten for a moment and knew he was struggling to control his temper. "I understand your concern. But we're here to ask some questions. And we'll ask them. And you'll let us. Your grandmother isn't the only person that has suffered…or is still suffering."

"I don't know who you think you are," Jeffrey growled at Brant, "but don't think you can come into this house and start orderin' everyone around!"

"I know who I am," Brant stated angrily. "And believe me, I have a right to talk to that woman."

"Jeffrey," Penny intervened. She stepped in front of her brother, between him and Brant. "Gran needs this to be resolved too. Lauralynn was her sister. We need to let it—" Her attempt at soothing her brother was interrupted as he shoved her aside to step closer to Brant in a threatening manner.

Lauryn's breathing quickened, nervously. She could sense that both men were ready to throw far more than merely threatening words at one another. "Brant?" she ventured. "How about a walk?" Brant continued to glare at Jeffrey. "What do you say?" she urged again, tugging on his arm. Brant glanced down at her then, and it must have been just enough to distract him from whatever thoughts of violence he was having toward Jeffrey, because he smiled and nodded.

Lauryn linked her arm around Brant's, sighing with relief. "Good. We'll be back in a little while," she said to Penny.

"I'll keep an eye out for the grannies," Penny assured them, "in case they need anythin'." Jeffrey remained silent, glaring past Penny toward his grandmother's bedroom.

Once outside the house, Lauryn exclaimed, "Whew! I was worried there for a minute. Thought you two were goin' to go at each other's throats."

"We were," Brant admitted.

They began walking leisurely along the street, passing white picket fences as they went. The summer had brought bounteous beauty to Memphis. All the lawns were plush, the flowerbeds bursting with color. The air was light that day, the sun brilliant.

"She knows more than she's told Jeffrey," Brant said finally. "Or Jeffrey knows more than he's telling us. He's awfully protective of her."

"She is his grandmother. But…I think you're right," Lauryn agreed. She hadn't planned to tell him that she felt Jeffrey was hiding something. But she *had* felt it and was glad to know he had as well. "What exactly do you think we're not bein' told?"

Brant shrugged. "I can't say. It's just a feeling I have."

"Imagine it," Lauryn exclaimed quietly. "All these years...Carissa's been alive and leading a perfectly normal life. All this time Penny has been my cousin! It's just so strange to soak up."

"Would you do anything, Lauryn?" Brant asked suddenly. Lauryn looked up to him, puzzled by his question. He gazed straight ahead, a thoughtful pucker wrinkling his brow.

"What do you mean?" she asked.

"Would you do anything to keep...to try and..." He shook his head and shrugged his shoulders as if trying to dismiss his thoughts. "Nevermind."

"What?" Lauryn prodded. "Tell me. Would I do anythin' to what?"

Brant inhaled deeply and glanced at her, smiling. "She made it sound so desperate, like she would've dropped dead if she couldn't make him love her."

"Oh," Lauryn breathed, realizing to what he referred. Carissa had asked her and Penny both if they could imagine feeling so desperate to make a man love them that they would resort to any means necessary. "You mean would I...would I ever consider..."

"Would a regular girl—any girl I grew up with or know now, for instance—I wonder what pushes a girl to be that frantic. So desperate that she would—"

"She was in love with him," Lauryn answered simply.

"But..." Brant seemed unconvinced. "I mean, I can see how a man...we have so much less self-control, in general. So directed by physical..." He shook his head again. "I guess I'm just comparing her to my sisters." He paused and smiled down at Lauryn. "Or to you." Chuckling, he added, "You'd never be so desperate as to do anything like she did to try and catch a man. You're too good and honest...and smart."

"I'm smart enough to know that you can't force someone to love you. They do or they don't. And if they don't...your dreams are shattered anyway. So why make so many lives miserable?" Secretly, Lauryn could somewhat understand how a woman could be so in love with a man that she would do almost anything to have him. Still, she kept the information quietly to herself and looked up to him to find him staring thoughtfully ahead. "What are you thinkin'?"

"I think I'd at least consider it."

"What?" Lauryn exclaimed, aghast.

"I think I would." He glanced at her. Lauryn's mouth gaped open, shocked at Brant's revelation. "I mean, say you want to marry this girl, and her father won't hear of it. But even these days, most families prefer a shotgun wedding to scandal and fatherless children. And knowing that...maybe I'd truly consider seducing the girl and getting her father to demand that I marry her."

"You would not!" Lauryn corrected him. She knew Brant would never do such a thing. Didn't she? "You wouldn't do that!"

"I said I might *consider* it, Lauryn," he reminded her. "I think anyone would consider it. It's just a matter of how strong you really are."

"Well, I like to think that I'm stronger than Carissa was. It was her own sister's husband she coveted. Remember?"

"You're right there," Brant relented. "What she did was much worse because of who she hurt."

"Is that what you told her in there?" Lauryn asked. "Carissa, when you whispered to her—is that what you told her? That you could understand her desperation?"

"Pretty much," Brant chuckled. He winked mischievously at Lauryn, and she smiled, charmed with the impish side of his nature.

"Lauryn! Brant!"

Lauryn and Brant turned to see Penny hurrying after them.

"She wants to talk to y'all! Right now! Granny says she has somethin' to say," Penny panted, short of breath from her sprint.

❧

"I went to Connemara that day," Carissa admitted quietly. As Lauryn and Brant sat at the foot of her bed, Nana sat next to her, encouragingly holding her hand. "The battle was...it was horrid. I was frightened. My time was so close. The baby was so near to bein' born, and I was entirely destitute. Laura had been givin' me money." The old woman paused, her lower lip trembling, tears sliding down her cheeks. "After all I had done...she still helped me." She paused and dabbed at her eyes with a handkerchief and then continued. "I needed more money...since

I had lost all hope of Daddy ever takin' me in again. So I went to Connemara. I waited until Laura came out to help a wounded soldier into the house, and then I called to her. She came to me, told me that she loved me no matter what I had done and that she wanted to see my baby born in safety. But I knew Daddy wouldn't have it. So she gave me all the money she had, kissed my cheek, and…and then I saw Ginny-Bean and…and…"

"You never saw her again," Jeffrey stated, ending the story rather abruptly. Penny glared at him, obviously irritated with his interference.

"She was lost that day. I've missed her every moment since," Carissa sniffled. "I've missed everyone since that day. I never returned to Connemara. I left…went north for a time and met my darling husband. But eventually we came back south, and…and here I end up."

Lauryn's disappointment was so great that she thought she might scream. It seemed the one hope of finally finding Laura was for naught.

"That's all you remember, ma'am?" Brant urged.

Carissa smiled at him for a moment and then looked away. She nodded and dabbed at her tears.

Brant sighted heavily. "May I ask just one more thing, Mrs. McGovern?"

"Gran is completely worn out, and I think—" Jeffrey began.

But Carissa held up her hand to signal that Brant should continue.

"How…how did you come by that little tea set? The one you gave to Penny? And do you know whatever happened to the piece…the cup that's missing from it?" Brant's question was gentle but very forthright. Lauryn felt the hair on the back of her neck prickle as an expression of surprise crossed Carissa's face for a moment.

"The little white set with the lavender flowers?" Carissa asked in a near whisper.

"Yes," Brant urged.

"I…I…" Carissa glanced at Jeffrey for a moment, and Lauryn wondered why—for Jeffrey's eyes narrowed as he nodded to his grandmother. "I…I…took it from Connemara that day, that last day I was there. It had been left in the cellar…in a little basket. And when I saw it, I took it. I wanted something to remember my family by. To remember who I really was."

"Why were you in the cellar?" Brant asked.

"It's where Laura and I spoke…that last time. In the cellar. Just like when we were little girls and used to play tea party with our dolls. It was cool in the cellar on hot days and—" Carissa explained.

"She needs her rest now," Jeffrey demanded, taking hold of Lauryn's arm and tugging at her. "Thank you for your help, Gran."

"The cup, Mrs. McGovern," Brant prodded, "what happened to the cup that's missing from the tea set?"

Carissa closed her eyes and laid her head back against her pillows. "It's lost. Just like Laura," came her answer.

"We'll let you rest now, dearest," Lauryn's Nana whispered, kissing Carissa's forehead tenderly.

"Thank you, Aunt Carissa," Lauryn said.

Carissa opened her eyes. A single tear trickled down her wrinkled cheek as she smiled sadly at her sister's granddaughter.

Once everyone left the bedroom, it was Nana who spoke first. "Well, I'm afraid you children are right back where you started," she said to Brant and Lauryn.

Sighing heavily, Brant announced, "Well, I, for one, am going right back to where I started. I'm not waiting for the morning train back to Franklin. There's a train in an hour, and I plan to be on it. Any other takers?" Lauryn could see the frustration in Brant's eyes. Now that their hopes of ending the mystery had been upset, he was ready to move on—or rather, go back.

"I can't leave Rissy so soon. Now that I've found her again…I just don't want to leave. Penny has agreed to stay on with me here for a few days," Nana told them. "But I'm certain Lauryn wants to go back with you."

"She can't go back alone with him," Jeffrey interjected. Lauryn noted the way he looked from Nana to her and Brant and back again. He was obviously befuddled at what appropriate measures he should take. "I intended stayin' on, as well. But, Mrs. Kensington, you're not truly considerin' lettin' Brant escort Lauryn home…alone. Are you?"

Brant took an angry step toward Jeffrey, obviously intent on another confrontation. But it was Nana who intervened this time. Shaking her head to discourage Brant from any rash action, she turned to Jeffrey herself and said, "Jeffrey…there is no one on this earth more capable of seein' Lauryn home safely than Brant."

"I've no doubt he can see her home," Jeffrey grumbled. "But what about seein' her virtue home with her?"

Before Lauryn or Brant could act in defense, the air rang with the sound of a swift slap delivered to Jeffrey's face by Nana's small hand. "Don't you ever disrespect Lauryn again, boy. Or me or Brant, for that matter. I won't have it! You're my nephew now, and I have a mind to treat you a little less like a neighbor and more like family. I expect the same from you." Nana turned to Brant then, whose eyebrows were still raised in surprise. "You see Lauryn home for me, Brant."

"Yes, ma'am," Brant promised, grinning delightedly.

"Oh, Lauryn!" Penny exclaimed, hugging her friend. "I know y'all expected more. All of us did. But let's just be glad we know what we know. All right?"

"Of course," Lauryn told her, kissing her cheek affectionately. "When y'all get back…we'll have lots of talk and laughter again. Promise me?"

"Promise," Penny agreed, returning Lauryn's kiss.

"Let your mother know that I'm fine, sweet pea," Nana said as she hugged Lauryn. "And I'll be home in a few days. She'll be in a complete tizzy over the house with all that's goin' on. Y'all help her, you hear?"

"I will," Lauryn promised.

Then Nana took hold of Brant's shirt, tugging at it until he bent and kissed her cheek. "And you get Lauryn home safely," Nana told him. Lauryn watched as her Nana then whispered into Brant's ear, "Virtue and all."

Brant chuckled. "I'll try."

"You'll *do*," Nana stated, winking at him.

Brant did offer a hand to Jeffrey, who shook it politely. Penny, however, hugged Brant, kissing him sweetly on the cheek. Then she too put her lips to his ear and whispered, yet loudly enough for Lauryn to hear, "I think it wouldn't hurt if you tainted Lauryn's virtue just a tich on the way home."

Lauryn felt herself blush when Brant chuckled and winked at her. "Thank you for the advice, Miss McGovern." He turned to Lauryn. "Let's go then. I'll get your bag."

While Brant went toward the front of the house to retrieve the small bag Lauryn had brought in anticipation of a longer visit, Jeffrey spoke. "I know you understand, Lauryn," he said.

Lauryn looked at him, still a bit miffed at his uncooperative behavior. "Understand your desire to make things easy on your gran? Yes," she admitted. "Understand your completely vile behavior toward Brant? No."

Jeffrey sighed and nodded. "Jealousy does rear its ugly head from time to time, Lauryn," he told her, "even in Tennessee." He reached out and took her hand, raising it to his lips and kissing the back of it softly. "I knew you first, remember."

Lauryn blushed, flattered by the compliment yet somehow doubtful of its sincerity.

&

It seemed strange to Lauryn, she and Brant leaving everyone else behind—especially her Nana and especially when it seemed that she and Brant had been the most hopeful about the trip. And now they sat, side by side, on the train home, as far from settling things as when they arrived.

It was very dark outside, so the scenery wasn't a venue of entertainment. Still, Brant was quiet as they traveled on. The only indications to Lauryn that he was even awake, in fact, were his eyes being open and the way his thumb would caress her fingers now and again as he held her hand.

"Whatever are you thinkin' about, Brant? The silence is deafenin' in here," Lauryn whispered at last. Many of the travelers were sleeping as the passenger car lanterns were now dimmed. Lauryn could not find one fragment of her body that wished for unconsciousness.

"What am I always thinking about?" Brant mumbled.

Lauryn sighed with discouragement and squeezed his arm reassuringly. "I know. It seems there will never be anythin' else to life until—"

"What happened to that teacup?" he growled suddenly. "It sticks in my mind like a parasite!" He shook his head with frustration. "And she didn't tell us everything. I still think she knows more."

"She's very old, Brant," Lauryn reminded him. "So much more even than Nana. Maybe…maybe she doesn't remember. Or maybe…maybe it isn't important…the cup."

"Or maybe we should just give up and go on with life, Lauryn." He smiled, if somewhat defeatedly, and said, "Maybe I should be spending more time tainting your virtue and less time chasing ghosts."

"Oh, don't play the rounder to me, Brant Masterson," Lauryn giggled, thrilled by his flirting. "I know there's no safer place on earth for me than with you."

Brant chuckled and kissed the top of her head. "Oh, is that so?"

"Yes. Of course," Lauryn sighed, laying her head against his shoulder.

"Well…I suppose there's no better way to keep a demon lover righteous than to profess a sure knowledge—however innocent that knowledge might be—of his devotion to chivalry, now is there?"

"A demon lover," Lauryn whispered, smiling. "I like that."

"Which?" Brant asked, the intonation in his voice dropping to a deep, seductively rich level. "The demon part or the lover part?"

Lauryn looked up into his eyes to see them smoldering with mischief and desire. "Both…together," she admitted in a whisper.

"You're asking for trouble, sugar," Brant mumbled as the corner of his mouth twitched slightly.

"I hope so," Lauryn breathed a moment before he kissed her.

☙

"The Trills, just down the road, have put their house and property for sale," Georgia explained as Lauryn and Brant sat in Sean and Mindy's parlor with her. "It's a good price, and you know Nana has always admired the place." Georgia's lower lip quivered slightly, and her eyes filled with moisture. She inhaled a breath of resolve and continued. "And…and it's close to Connemara, at least. I feel I need to telephone Nana first…before deciding. But Sean thinks it's a wise investment, and…well, we do need a place to live. I think it's important to Patrick to stay near his friends and…and…" Georgia looked to Brant then. "What do you think, Brant dear?"

Lauryn felt nauseated. Each time she thought of permanently abandoning Connemara, her stomach churned, and her heart felt as if it had been pierced by a hundred tiny needles.

Brant took Lauryn's hand in his own, squeezing it encouragingly as he answered, "It sounds like a good choice. If Sean thinks it's a good choice, then I'm sure it is. I...I would like to know, Mrs. Kensington—though I understand that it's not my place to ask..." Brant paused, seeming uncertain whether he should continue with his intended questions. Lauryn looked up to him, interested in what he had to say.

"Go on, Brant," Georgia urged him.

"Well," Brant began, "what is your agreement with the historical society as far as your...well, I guess rights to visit the grounds, tend to the cemetery, or take anything you would want for sentimental value?"

Georgia smiled at Brant, understandingly. Reaching out, she placed a hand caressively to his cheek for a moment. "We take everythin' in the house with us, darlin'. They would like for us to loan them some family portraits and furniture pieces to add to the authenticity of the period and family lineage. But at any time we wish it, our things will be returned to us. As far as the grounds...the historical society will maintain the cemetery and grounds, but we will always be allowed to return whenever we want. In fact, Mr. DuMonde has promised that a key to Connemara's front door will always remain in the possession of a member of our family."

Brant nodded, and Lauryn's very soul loved him even more for his concern over Connemara's changing hands. She knew he was thinking as she did; the nagging possibility was in his mind that they might never find Laura now. Their hopes were becoming fewer and fewer, and he wanted to know whether Connemara would always be accessible, just in case hope in finding her were renewed one day.

Lauryn had agonized over the Captain's fate as well. Because of her failure, the Captain was doomed to roam Connemara alone, and she was sickened at the thought. Since returning from Memphis three days prior, Lauryn had sensed Brant's growing discouragement. Her own defeated emotions were growing, and she knew his were as well.

"Is there anythin' *you* would want from Connemara, Brant?" Georgia asked unexpectedly. "Anythin' specific? Nana and I had some ideas of our own of things we would like to give to you…but if there's somethin' special you'd like to have, please tell me."

Brant dropped his eyes for a moment. Then looking to Georgia, he answered, "There is something, Mrs. Kensington. But…but I'd rather not say…just yet."

Lauryn's curiosity was immediately piqued. What could Brant want from Connemara? Laura's trunk perhaps? Her portrait? Her mind burned with wanting to know, but she knew Brant well enough to understand that he would not tell anyone until he was ready.

"All right, sweetheart. I won't press you yet. There is still some time." Georgia turned to Lauryn. "And what about you, sweet thing? What shall I save aside for you? Sean has asked for Daddy's old desk, the one that belonged to Grandfather O'Halleran. We'll leave it at Connemara because it has such an historical value, but you need to—"

Lauryn interrupted her mother by standing quite abruptly and saying, "I need some fresh air, Mama. I…I…think I'll just take a walk." As Brant moved to join her, Lauryn shook her head at him, smiling. "You don't have to chase after me, Brant. I'm fine. Just needin' a bit of activity."

"How about I drive you over to Connemara?" he offered, smiling. He knew her so well. "I'm sure your mother won't mind lending me the auto to do that."

"Of course not," Georgia confirmed.

Lauryn smiled at him, loving him so much more at that moment for knowing her so thoroughly. He had read her thoughts and knew she had a particular destination in mind.

"All right," Lauryn agreed, smiling at him.

Just then, Mindy entered the parlor. "Nana has just telephoned," she said to Georgia. "She's at the train station."

"What?" Georgia exclaimed. "She left Memphis and didn't even tell us?"

"Apparently," Mindy said, smiling. "You know Nana. When she gets a mind to do somethin'…"

Georgia laughed. "Oh yes! I know Nana." Then turning to Brant, she suggested, "Why don't you let Lauryn off at Connemara and fetch Nana from the station for me, dear boy?"

"Of course," Brant said.

CHAPTER TWENTY-ONE

It was beautiful. Still. Even when empty, and with the painters, carpenters, and all other manner of strangers in and out of her as they refreshed her appearance, Connemara House stood strong, beckoning, and beautiful as Lauryn stood just inside the vine-covered front gate of Connemara.

Brant helped her out of the auto and, leaving her to her melancholy thoughts, drove off to pick up Nana at the train station. And now she stood gazing at Connemara, wondering how she would ever live anywhere else and be completely happy.

She studied the wisteria vines, though void of blossoms now, yet stunning still with the intense green of inexhaustible leaves. She studied the windows and thought of the years she'd spent gazing out them into the blue of the sky, dreaming of what life might hold for her. She thought of Nana's rocking chair, gone from the porch now, and how much she had learned sitting at the grand lady's feet on warm summer nights.

"She'll stand forever," the Captain said.

Lauryn looked to where he stood next to her and smiled. "I hope so. She deserves to."

He took Lauryn's hand and led her as they walked. "You'll have to be sure the gardeners keep up the wisteria. And your roses," he remarked.

"You left us…when we found the family photo in Laura's trunk. When we found your music," Lauryn reminded him. "And…and you've been so…so distant. I've not even seen you since—"

"You mean I seem so…ghostly now," he corrected her.

345

Lauryn dropped her gaze in sadness. "Yes," she admitted. "I can almost see right through you today. And you haven't been to see me since—"

"It's time, Lauryn," he stated. "Life has to go on for you."

"But we haven't found her!" Lauryn began to panic. The realization was upon her that for reasons of which she had no comprehension, she was losing the Captain.

"Your family must leave Connemara, Lauryn," he told her. "And you must go on." He smiled and placed a loving hand on her cheek. "And you must go on without regret."

"I can't!" she cried. "I can't be happy knowin' you and Laura aren't happy!"

"Shh," he soothed. "There's time a bit, still." Then he smiled and said, "You found Carissa, didn't you?"

Lauryn nodded and wiped the tears from her cheeks, attempting to be brave for the Captain's sake. "We did," she admitted. Then looking at him, she asked, "Did you know? You had watched Penny grow up with me. You must've wondered."

The Captain shook his head. "Blinded by another woman's vision in my mind, I guess."

"We did speak with Carissa." It was all Lauryn could bring herself to say for a moment. And then she added, "She says she doesn't know anythin'."

The Captain sighed and smiled regrettably. "At least she has her family again."

"But we're movin' from Connemara, Captain! Permanently! What…what am I to do?" Lauryn buried her face in her hands and cried quietly for a moment. Then with a deep breath and a brave resolve, she answered herself. "I'll still live nearby…and the family has unlimited visitin' rights to the property and—"

"Carissa said nothing? Nothing to help?" the Captain interrupted.

Lauryn shook her head. "No. But…but I have hope still. Someday…" Lauryn looked at him then. His face was grave, hope draining from his handsome countenance. Lauryn knew he needed to know.

"She saw Laura…the day she disappeared. They met, one last time, in the cellar to…" Lauryn stopped. Something had made the tiny hairs on the back of her neck prickle. "It's the last place anyone alive saw her," Lauryn mumbled. Her mind told her that she'd checked the cellar a thousand times over the years, never to find a clue, any evidence at all that Lauralynn's life had ended there. But something urged her on now—something in her memory of the way Carissa had spoken of the cellar, of the last moments she and Laura had spent together there. Suddenly, a flood of more recent memories enveloped her mind.

When Brant had asked Carissa how she came to possess the tiny tea set, her answer had been, *I…I…took it from Connemara that day. It had been left in the cellar…in a little basket.* And Carissa had said she and Laura had played with the tea set in the cellar.

And there was something her Nana had said—something about having played with the tea set in the cellar with her older sister. Then there was the fact that Laura had always been so adamant that Brant play tea party when he was a little boy! She'd always thought that it seemed against Laura's loving, nurturing nature to torture a little boy so by insisting he play at tea party.

Lauryn's mind began to smolder with thoughts and emotions coming together like storm clouds, pointing to one item and one place: the missing teacup from the set Carissa had given to Penny and then the cellar.

"Come along, my Captain!" she said, taking his hand and racing toward the cellar.

⅋

The root cellar was as dark and as musty as ever. And as always, it caused Lauryn to sniffle several times until fresh air entered through the open door. Standing just inside, Lauryn paused, looking up at the cellar's dirt ceiling covered in wisteria roots. She thought that it had been some time since anyone had cut them back. She wondered, if the historical society left them unattended, would they perhaps fill the cellar one day, obliterating the ancient part of Connemara? Had other things been hidden in the cellar, covered by some sort of camouflage the way the roots had disguised the ceiling?

The air being somewhat fresher, Lauryn bent down and lit the kerosene lamp sitting just inside. This was it—the very last place Carissa had seen Laura. The cellar itself seemed more intriguing, more important, than it ever had to Lauryn at that moment. There had been too many references to the cellar in recent months, too many hours spent by Brant agonizing over the existence and then unexplained disappearance of the teacup Laura had carried when he was a child.

She thought of how she and Penny had spent hours of their girlhood each summer, having pretend games of knights and princesses, secret lovers who were reformed highwaymen, and such things that are the imaginative dreams of young girls. And now, now it was easier for her to imagine the O'Halleran girls at play in the cellar. It was even possible for her to visualize Carissa and Laura's last moments together, there in the cellar that they had played in as children.

As she made her way into the belly of the cellar, stepping over various kinds of rubble, Lauryn was even further overwhelmed with sentiment. She was reminded of the excursion she and Brant had first taken together into the cellar, which now seemed so long in the past. And she thought of all the other times she had hoped to find Lauralynn hidden in there. She smiled at herself, remembering how, as a young adolescent, she'd found the courage to finally peer into each and every barrel, afraid of being startled by the sudden discovery of a skeleton. That was before she realized the barrels were placed in the cellar long after Lauralynn had disappeared. Even now, as always before, there was an impression of mystery in the cellar—a sense of something hidden.

"Ow!" Lauryn exclaimed as she stubbed her foot on something. The toes on her left foot were stinging. Bracing herself against the planked wall, she looked down to see that she had tripped on an old ax handle. Upon further inspection, she found her foot was unharmed other than the uncomfortable throbbing from her stubbed toe. Brushing her hand on her dress, for the planks of the wall were filthy, she gasped as a tiny mouse popped out of a knothole near her head and plopped to the ground, scurrying off.

"For pity's sake!" she exclaimed, her heart hammering madly. "You scared the syrup out of me, you little rat!" She glared at the knothole in the planking from whence the mouse had appeared. It was only the size of a nickel, just big enough for a mouse to pop through. Lauryn frowned, knowing her father had sealed up the knotholes in the planking years before. Apparently the rodents had worked diligently at undoing his hard work.

It angered her momentarily that her father's hard work should be destroyed. Bracing herself against the planking with her hands, Lauryn started to peer into the knothole. She caught herself quickly, for what woman in her right mind would want to peer into a dark hole in some rotting plank when a mouse had only just popped out? Where there was one mouse, there were hundreds of others. Shaking her head at her stupidity of even considering looking in the hole, Lauryn looked back into the throat of the cellar, intent on completing another investigation of it.

However, she paused an instant later, her attention arrested by something else. Just where her right hand pressed against the planking, she could see something—a mark or an odd grain in the wood perhaps. It wasn't anything she hadn't seen before, but it was something she hadn't noticed—hadn't really pondered or had the knowledge that she did now, only recently, to use to determine exactly what the thing might be.

A cold chill ran the length of her spine, and the hairs on her arms and the back of her neck stood erect as she looked at the darkened area on the wood planking. There, just near the knothole where her own hand now pressed, was indeed an oddity—a marking of some sort, several in fact, but one particular mark catching her attention. Brushing at the dirt and years of dust on the planking, she endeavored to uncover the darkened area. Frustrated, she lifted the hem of her dress and rubbed frantically at the spot, even spitting on the fabric and rubbing harder. When she succeeded in somewhat cleaning the area, she stepped back, her hands going to her mouth in horror as she whispered, "Oh no!"

Lauryn could not believe what she was seeing. Surely her mind was playing tricks on her! There, next to the knothole from which the mouse appeared, were several dark stains. One was almost the exact shape of a hand. Not an entire hand, perhaps, but definitely a palm mark with four fingers and a thumbprint at appropriate distances to perfectly match the placement of a small hand—just as if someone had leaned against the planking, as she had just done herself. Someone whose hand was covered in blood! The discolorations were dark and eerie, exactly like the bloodstains in Connemara House, except these had been hidden under decades of dust and dirt. They simply were not as discernable as the ones in the house because neglect had caused harsher deterioration. No one had painted carefully over these stains or refinished these seemingly worthless wood planks. And as Lauryn reached out, matching her palm and fingertips to those on the ancient paneling, she knew. She knew whose hand had pressed there long ago.

Frantically, Lauryn turned and ran up the cellar stairs and into the light. "Brant!" she screamed. "Brant! Come quickly!" In the next moment, she remembered he had just left her at Connemara to fetch her Nana home. "Captain? Captain!" Where had he gone? She'd left him just outside the cellar doors. She was alone at Connemara, and she was frantic! A sort of panic set in. What should she do? She'd found a clue—the most important of her life! Then a warm calm begin to wash over her as she thought she had touched Laura's hand in a manner. There was hope renewed that the mystery, the tragedy of Laura, would be solved.

Again she called, "Captain. Captain?" Where was he? Why did he not appear to her? Had her neglect of him caused him to be unable or unwanting to appear to her? "Captain? Please!" After long moments, she heard his voice from behind her and turned to face him.

"You've found something," he said. It was a statement, not a question.

"I…I think so," she answered.

The Captain was even less visibly tangible than he had been only minutes before. Was it the afternoon sun? "What have you found, Lauryn?"

"I…I…think it's a bloodstain. A handprint. There, in the cellar. It's small like a woman's, just the size of my own," she told him excitedly.

"Then…you think Laura was there?" he asked. His face looked so hopeful suddenly, so pleading! It broke Lauryn's heart, for although she had found a clue, and it surely was an important one, she had not yet found Lauralynn. She did not want to give him false hope.

"I…I don't know. But it seems that…it seems possible. Don't you think?" she asked.

The Captain smiled, a sad sort of smile—a smile that Lauryn had seen many times over the years. It told her he was not convinced her discovery was important.

"Here!" she said, reaching out, taking his hand and urging him toward the cellar. "Let me show you. Once you see it, you'll believe me."

But as they reached the cellar door, the Captain stopped. "I can't enter there, Lauryn."

Lauryn turned to him, tugging at his hand. Then she remembered. Long ago, as a child, she had begged the Captain to search the cellar with her. It had been such a place of mystery to her, and she wanted to share it with him. But he had been unable to enter.

"The earth," she whispered.

The Captain nodded. "You remember now that I cannot enter the earth. My body...the earthly part of me is already there, and I—"

"Cannot return into the earth," Lauryn finished for him. "But it's there!" she exclaimed suddenly. "I swear it! I'm not imagining it! A stain in the wood, just like those that are in the house. And it's a handprint! It makes sense, doesn't it? That if Lauralynn were wounded in the stomach, she would've clutched at it with her hand? And then, being weakened, would've used her hands to support herself against a wall."

The Captain's eyes filled with tears. His face grimaced in pain. "My Laura," he whispered. "And I wasn't there! I wasn't...I should've been here. I..."

It was only then—after ten years of knowing him, sharing his deepest hopes—only then did Lauryn realize that all the while the Captain had felt guilt as well as deep heartache over Lauralynn's disappearance.

"You were a soldier, Captain, doing your duty, fighting for a just cause. That was your place," she said.

"My place was here! At her side! Protecting her! Had I been here, she may not have—" he raged.

"You may have had to watch her die," Lauryn finished. "Could you have endured watching her die? Would that have been easier?"

"No," he admitted. "But it would've been an end. None of this roaming—her lost, me searching...you and Brant, your young lives destroyed by ghosts and worry."

"Our lives have not been destroyed! Don't you see?" she pleaded. "You...you and Lauralynn have given us each other!"

"Perhaps," he said, forcing a smile.

Lauryn dropped his hand and turned toward the cellar. "There's something here. I know it," she called to him.

"Wait for Brant to return. He'll help you. He'll know where to look from here perhaps," the Captain suggested. "Wait for Brant."

But Lauryn paid him no heed. She was close! She felt it! If she were close—if she could somehow find Laura's body, find an end to the torture that both lost spirits had endured—then would Brant be hers? She felt that he would. During their moments on the train home from Memphis, something had changed. Brant seemed to have been letting go of Laura somehow, looking toward the future and his own life.

"I couldn't leave you upset like that, Lauryn," Brant said as he stepped into the cellar behind her.

"Brant!" Lauryn exclaimed, throwing her arms around his neck and hugging him tightly. "You perfect, perfect man!"

"Well, I doubt that. But your Nana will just have to wait at the station a little longer until I'm certain that you're—"

"Look! Look what I've found!" Lauryn released him and, taking his hand, led him to the place where the wood was stained. "I was talking with the Captain, thinking about things, and I realized...Carissa said she took the tea set from the cellar that last day she saw Laura! Nana said they all used to play tea party down here. And you! Why do you think Laura would torture you so as a child, making you play at dolls and tea parties?" Carefully she pointed to the bloodstains on the paneling. "Look. It's a handprint. Just the size of mine."

Immediately, Brant put his eye to the knothole nearby.

"Do you think that's wise?" Lauryn asked, taking a step backward, lest another mouse come popping out of the hole. "I mean, I've already seen one mouse jump out of there."

Brant looked at her. "A mouse? You mean there's not just dirt behind these planks?"

Lauryn shrugged. "I don't know. What else would there be?"

Brant's face paled slightly. "Lauryn...you said your great-grandfather didn't believe in slavery."

"That's right," she confirmed. "But what would that—"

"Remember what Mr. Jackson said to us...that day after we had been over to the see the doctor? He said your great-grandfather was a good man and that..."

"That all families had their secrets," Lauryn finished for him.

Brant glanced about the cellar quickly, finally picking up the ax handle Lauryn had tripped over when she'd entered the first time. Sticking his index finger into the knothole, he said, "Anybody around here ever been linked to helping slaves escape?" he asked. Lauryn shrugged. "There's no dirt wall behind these planks." And shoving his shoulder hard against the plank that contained the knothole, he worked to insert the ax handle into the space created between the bowed plank and the one next to it.

The wood split, cracking noisily. Brant began tearing away at the dry, brittle wood. "Here," he said, handing Lauryn a piece of broken wood. Lauryn hadn't time to set the wood aside before Brant simply went crashing through two broken planks and into another room. Lauryn's heart hammered fiercely within her chest as she handed the lantern to Brant and stepped over the broken planks into the secret room with him.

Brant coughed. Lauryn covered her nose and mouth with her hand while the stale air in the hidden room began to freshen by the air entering from without. Brant held the lantern up, and Lauryn followed his gaze to the room's ceiling. Like the cellar, the dirt ceiling of this secret room was covered in wisteria roots. Large roots lined the walls and part of the floor.

"I think your great-grandfather took more than one secret with him to his grave, Lauryn," Brant said, pointing to an ancient iron collar lying on the floor at their feet. Stooping and picking it up, Brant held it out to her. "A slave collar. And it's been cut off someone." Lauryn shivered as she looked at the device of human misery. To think that such things had actually existed made her heart ache.

"The Underground Railroad?" Lauryn whispered. "At Connemara?" Somehow the knowledge made her proud, all the more loving of her special, beautiful home.

"Come on," Brant said, reaching back and grasping her hand tightly as he held the lantern up and began to move forward. "I think we've…" And his words stopped as, at the same instant, Lauryn gasped.

There in one far corner of the dark, forgotten room…

"Laura," Brant breathed.

Reverently Brant led Lauryn to the surreal scene before them. There, on an ancient, broken bed, the remains of a feather tick beneath her, lay a young woman's skeleton, still dressed in the manner of the past.

One skeletal hand hung off one side of the bed. On the floor, just at the tips of its fingers, lay a small, child's teacup—white and embellished with lavender blossoms. Laura's other hand lay at her stomach; the fabric of her dress beneath her fingers, though faded and spotted with holes (no doubt from tiny creatures of the earth or other means of decay), was still dark with bloodstains—bloodstains that, like those in Connemara House, were over fifty years old. Her tiny shoes were still on her feet and there, on her left ring finger, the ring the Captain had saved so diligently to purchase.

"Brant," Lauryn breathed as she looked on the sight. The wisteria roots had grown around the skeleton. But they had grown tenderly, softly cradling Laura's arms and body as it lay on the bed. Lauryn watched as Brant reached out and took a cream-colored curl between his fingers. Miraculously, an unusual amount of Laura's beautiful hair still cascaded from her skull down, over her shoulders. The hair was as bright and as silky in appearance as that owned by her spirit. Reaching out, Lauryn lifted the tarnished golden locket at the skeleton's throat— the one Brandon had given Laura before he'd left for war.

"You can't tell."

The voice so startled Lauryn that she screamed as she spun around.

Brant turned too, shouting angrily as he glared at Jeffrey. "What are you doing here?"

"You can't tell that you've found her here," Jeffrey growled.

"Jeffrey?" Lauryn breathed. Her mind spun, wondering why it would be Jeffrey that should intrude upon Laura's secreted tomb.

"She's an old woman, Lauryn," Jeffery said, meeting Brant toe-to-toe threateningly. He paused, looking down at the strangely peaceful sight. "It was so long ago, and she was young. Frightened."

"What are you talking about?" Brant demanded.

Lauryn was confused as well. She couldn't fathom what he was babbling about. They had found Laura! After so many years, Laura was found! And Jeffrey didn't want anyone to know?

"Granny Carry," he explained. "Whatever she did…it's in the past, and she's suffered enough for it."

"Jeffrey," Lauryn began, "I don't understand. Why would findin' Lauralynn hurt your nana?"

Jeffrey swallowed hard, and tears brimmed in his eyes.

"Carissa killed Lauralynn. Didn't she?" Brant said flatly. "That day she came to Connemara…either she wounded her further, killing her, or she left her here to die. Didn't she?" Brant reached out, grabbing the front of Jeffrey's shirt in one powerful fist. "Tell me! Or else I'll beat the—"

"Last year," Jeffrey interrupted in a whisper, "Gran was really sick. I was stayin' down in Memphis with her, takin' care of her one night, and she told me. She told me that her name was Carissa O'Halleran and that the O'Hallerans living in Connemara House were her family. She told me that she hid her sister durin' the war—the sister that everyone in town knew about…the one that had disappeared during the battle."

"She told you? All this time? You've known all this time?" Lauryn cried. She was furious with him! She knew she felt as Brant did—that she wanted to hit him. To hit something!

"She only told me last year. I asked her…about Lauralynn…because I knew the story. Everyone in Franklin does. And she told me. She told me that she hid Lauralynn."

"Why didn't she ever tell anyone else, Jeffrey?" Lauryn was nearly hysterical. The Captain and Laura had been tortured, unsettled for over fifty years! And all the time, Carissa O'Halleran had been alive and known where Laura was. It was too much to bear! She began furiously beating Jeffrey's chest. "How could you? How could you not tell us? You've known where she was! Carissa knew! And you never told us. Do you know the torture they've been through? What Brant and I have been through? Do you realize—" Lauryn struggled when Brant pulled her back and away from Jeffrey.

"She killed her. And he's been protecting her. Isn't that it, Jeffrey?" Brant accused calmly.

"She didn't kill her! She didn't. She tried to help her. She hid her. I…I didn't know where she had hidden her," Jeffrey told them. "I only knew that they were sisters. I think Gran…I think…it was a long time ago, Lauryn. Gran is an old woman. Her mind has been tortured by this her entire life, I'm sure."

"Even *you* think she left her here to die, don't you?" Brant asked him as Lauryn sobbed. "Carissa…she was jealous. She left Laura here to die, didn't she?"

"No," came a weak voice. Lauryn turned to see Carissa step into the room, assisted by her own Nana and Penny. "She died while I was here with her."

"Gran," Jeffrey began, "you don't have to say anythin'. No one blames you for anythin'."

"Hush, Jeffrey," Carissa said softly. Then looking to Brant and Lauryn, she began. "I *was* jealous, for a long, long time. It ate at me…destroyed me, as jealousy and hate always do. But…but I loved Lauralynn. And…and I came here that day, afraid that somethin' would happen to them…to me…to her. I came to Connemara that day to see her. But everythin' was…horrible! Death was everywhere!" She swallowed as tears streaked her face. "I came into the parlor, just as my brother Sean was hidin' Mama and Virginia. I saw Daddy sittin' at the desk. Laura helped him to sit, even though she was bleedin' and hurt so badly herself. He didn't live long. Laura and I were both there. He saw me. He forgave me…told me he loved me. Told me that I owed Laura my help. Told me to hide her in the secret room in the cellar…the room she and I had known he hid escaped slaves in. And I did. I took her there."

The old woman looked to the bed, her face contorting with the painful memories as she gazed on her sister's remains. "I stayed with her. The battle was so fierce. I even heard the soldiers come into the cellar lookin' for people. I was so afraid they'd find us, so afraid of what they'd do to us if they did! I found the tea set, the one we had played with as children. Laura told me that Daddy had brought the little tea set in here once when he was helpin' a family escape. I took one of the teacups and gave it to Laura…reminded her of happier days between us…when there wasn't a war. When we had been sisters and friends and played together at Connemara. And then…then she told me that she loved me…forever. And…and her breath stopped, and she was gone. She simply quit breathin'. And I…I never told anyone."

"But, Gran," Penny asked in a whisper, "why didn't you tell anyone? Why?"

"I was afraid. Everyone knew what had happened—how horrid I had been! How miserable I was. About my shame. I knew...I knew that if I told anyone, anyone at all, I knew they'd think I killed her. I knew they would. They'd all think I killed her to try and win Brandon...or to make him miserable. So I kept my secret. I left. I went north and then to Memphis after the war and married my Mr. McGovern...a wonderful man who loved me in spite of my sins. And every day of my life, I've been afraid...afraid to tell. And I've loved Lauralynn too. Every moment."

The resentment, the hurt, the near hate were draining from Lauryn. And as Brant gathered her in his arms, stroking her hair soothingly, she could feel the harmful pain leaving him too. As she looked to where Laura had spent her last moments, suddenly there was only relief and love in Lauryn's heart.

"Carissa?" Virginia asked. "Are you all right, love?" Lauryn smiled, warmed through her entire being as she watched her Nana place a loving arm around Carissa's shoulders.

"She's here, Ginny," Carissa whispered. "She's still here." Carissa buried her face in her hands and sobbed bitterly.

"No, Carissa," Lauryn heard her grandmother say. She watched as Nana took Carissa's hand. "That's not our Lauralynn anymore. And it hasn't been for many, many, many years."

"Will you look at that?" Patrick gasped as he came charging into the room, his mother close behind him.

"You hush, Patrick," Nana warned. "This is an important moment. And it's to be joyous."

Lauryn looked up into the warmth of Brant's eyes. "It's over," he mumbled.

&

Two days later, the former resident family of Connemara gathered at the old family cemetery for a quiet service held to, at long last, lay to rest the earthly remains of Lauralynn O'Halleran Masterson. Brant and Sean had quietly removed Lauralynn's skeleton from the secret cellar room and placed it in a simple pine coffin. Lauryn, her grandmother, and Aunt

Carissa then placed the small teacup in with the remains and covered them gently with a soft white sheet as Georgia and Mindy dabbed at the moisture on their cheeks. Patrick sat uncommonly quiet near the gravesite, Junie on his lap playing with the buttons on his shirt. Every few moments, Lauryn would see her little brother kiss his niece tenderly on the head, and she knew it was his way of expressing his young but very deep feelings.

As Lauryn stood watching Sean and Brant fill in Laura's grave with the rich soil of Connemara, she wondered why the Captain hadn't come to her, to let her know that all was well. It had been two days since she and Brant had found Laura. And in those two days, no amount of wishing or calling for the Captain had brought him to her.

She wondered what was in Brant's mind too, for he'd barely spoken to anyone since finding Laura. She looked to her Nana and Aunt Carissa, standing with their arms linked, tears upon the cheeks of their beautiful elderly faces. She looked at her cousins Penny and Jeffrey, again amazed that they were indeed her cousins.

And Mr. Jackson was there. "I always thought the fambly knowed about that Underground Railroad room, Miss Lauryn. Never occurred to me that ol' Mr. O'Halleran had kept the secret all to hisself," he told her before the service.

Already the historical society was fantastically excited. Not only was Connemara House of such historical value, but now that it was known its cellar had served as part of the Underground Railroad, Lauryn knew that Connemara was meant for another adventure. One that it would travel alone, without Lauryn and her family.

As everyone stood looking at the now-finished grave, Lauryn looked again to Brant. Her body ached to be in his arms! Her lips longed for his kiss! Just a glance from him would have been enough at the moment. But he stood solemn before the grave. Even after everyone else had gone, he stood, pensive and seemingly oblivious to everything and everyone else around him.

One by one, everyone left. Mr. Jackson said he had to get "on home to supper at Mariah's 'fore she skins me alive." Sean and Mindy took baby Junie and Patrick and started for their own home, and Lauryn's mother said she wanted to walk through the rose gardens for a moment.

Even Penny and Jeffrey, after hugging Lauryn tightly, took their leave. Lauryn felt oddly alone as she stood watching her Nana and Carissa dab at their tears with their lace hankies. Brant still stood staring at the fresh grave, and Lauryn was lost. For the first time in her life, she felt lost—lost to her family, lost to the Captain, lost to Connemara, and, most of all, lost to Brant, who still remained so silent and brooding.

Burying her face in her hands for a moment, overwhelmed with conflicting emotions, it wasn't until she sensed the soft fragrance of wisteria, heard her Nana's startled gasp, that she raised her head. Standing at the edge of Laura's grave was the Captain. At his side, on his arm, as beautiful as the day she died, was Laura.

"Laura?" Carissa breathed. Instantly, Lauralynn rushed forward, throwing her arms around first one sister and then the other in a loving embrace.

"All is well, my darlin's," Lauralynn said. Lauryn felt her mouth gape open at the beautiful and very audible sound of Laura's voice. "All is well."

"But, Laura—" Carissa began.

Lauralynn O'Halleran Masterson shook her head and smiled. "All is well," she repeated.

And as Lauryn watched the Captain coming toward her, she noticed that Brant's eyes were filled with moisture as Laura approached him.

"Thank you, my angel," the Captain said, taking Lauryn in his arms and kissing her forehead tenderly. "Thank you."

Lauryn looked up at him, tears streaming down her face. "You're goin', aren't you?" she choked.

"We are. And you're to be happy," he said. "I promise we'll never be far…that we'll watch you be happy. Never too far away."

Lauryn turned as Laura approached, leading Brant by the hand.

"Thank you, Lauryn," she spoke. The melody of her voice was soothing to Lauryn's soul. Yet Lauryn's tears increased, for she knew this was a good-bye that would haunt her always.

"You see," Laura said, taking one of Brant's hands and one of Lauryn's in her other, "the family had two lost members, angels. Not just one. Not just me."

"Carissa," Brant mumbled.

Laura smiled at him. "Yes. Carissa. She needed peace. She deserves it. And I couldn't rest until she and I, both of us, were found. I didn't even know myself why, couldn't tell Brant why…until…until you found me and everything became clear."

"You couldn't talk to me because—" Brant began.

"Because I was bound. By bein' lost to Brand…to Connemara. All I knew was where Brand *might* be…near you, Brant. Near *his* home and family, and that is where I lingered. I'm sorry for your hardship, my sweet boy."

Brant shook his head and smiled. "What would my life have been without you?"

Lauryn felt a pang of heartache. What a bittersweet reality it was to have found Laura—and in finding her, lose her—lose the Captain.

"I love you, sweet Lauryn," the Captain whispered, caressing Lauryn's cheek softly. "Thank you, Brant." His voice seemed quiet, far away somehow.

"And I love you…both of you," Laura whispered, her voice slowly vanishing to nothing more than a fragrance. "Have peace now…and life," her mouth moved. Then she turned to the Captain, and Lauryn watched with wonder as they kissed, passionately, joyously. And then, as if they'd never been, they were gone.

"They're gone, aren't they?" Lauryn said. There was a sweet sort of peaceful longing in her, as if two spaces were now empty in her heart—voids left by the Captain and Laura. And yet she wasn't sad for the loss of them. Their journey of over fifty years was finally, blessedly, at an end. They were together. Happy. Forever.

But as she watched Brant, standing very still and looking off into the distance, his eyes narrowed and full of tears, a trembling began to overtake her—a trembling so strong that she wondered if her knees would indeed give way beneath her. What would be their lives now? For so long, both she and Brant had longed to live free of the mystery. But now that it was upon them…

"Yes," he mumbled. "They're gone. I can feel it." He put a hand to his chest just over his heart and closed his eyes a moment. "They're gone." He looked to her then and added, "And we're both free." He turned and looked at her, his eyes narrow, emotion blazing from them. Lauryn felt her breath shorten, her heart begin to pound furiously, as he strode toward her with an aggression she'd never seen in him before, a determination in his eyes that was almost frightening.

Upon reaching her, he didn't pause even for an instant but took hold of her face and kissed her almost brutally. His mouth demanded response from her! His kiss was so driven and deep that she could hardly catch her breath.

"Lauryn," he breathed as he kissed her, let his hands be lost in her hair. He kissed her neck, her face, her mouth, and after long moments that found Lauryn crying in his arms, the salt of her joyous tears mingling with their kiss, he paused, looking at her with a longing, an emotion that was too profound to describe.

"I love you, Lauryn," he said, his voice low and intensely passionate. "From the very first instant I touched you…heard your voice. I swear it. I loved you from that moment."

"Brant," Lauryn sobbed as he held her face in his hands, forcing her to look at him through her tears. She felt as if her heart might burst from her chest with the sudden ecstasy she felt because of his confession.

"And I don't care. I don't care about anything else! I'd rather die and wander around forever…than to live another minute without owning you!" he added.

"I love *you*," she stammered through her sobbing. "In my dreams, before I met you…I loved you. I've loved you my whole life!"

"I couldn't have you, you know," he mumbled, his own eyes filled with tears. "Not wholly…not when we both were bound by the past. You understand that I had to keep myself controlled…disciplined. I would've failed otherwise…because so many times I simply wanted to leave—to take you away from here…and selfishly live my own life."

Lauryn smiled and caressed his face with her hands. He was hers! Truly and finally. She could touch him whenever she wanted, ask for his arms around her, feel his magnificent kiss whenever she needed him. Which, she knew, was every minute, eternally. The freedom she felt was rapturous, as if she'd begun to breathe easily for the first time in her life.

"I'm ready now," he began, kissing her quickly. "I'm ready to ask your mama for the thing I want from Connemara."

Lauryn smiled, understanding. "And what would that thing be?"

Brant smiled, chuckled, and hugged her. "And we'll stay here," he added, kissing her forehead lovingly. "If that's what you want…we'll stay here. As long as I can have you, that land in New Mexico doesn't…"

"No," she interrupted. "That's where I want to be…with you. Everythin' is…is different now. There's too much of the past here. And all I want is the future. I want every tomorrow, every moment yet to come, to be *our* moments. I don't want to belong to the past anymore, Brant. I only want to belong to you."

Lauryn felt weakened with love, at the same time powerful with it, as Brant smiled lovingly down at her. Brushing a stray curl of nutmeg from her cheek, he took her face in his hands and kissed her again.

"I won't be able to stop now, you know," he mumbled into her ear as he held her to him. "You'll have to marry me soon."

"When?" Lauryn giggled.

"Tomorrow," Brant determined, kissing her again.

"Where?" Lauryn sighed between kisses.

"Here…at Connemara House," Brant answered. And then they were lost, but only to the world, for in each other's arms they were found—found in their love.

Virginia Anne O'Halleran Kensington sighed as she watched the young lovers, now oblivious to all else around them. "A love like no other, that one," she said.

Carissa O'Halleran McGovern smiled. "Oh, maybe like *one* other, dear sister. Maybe like one other."

EPILOGUE

Lauryn Masterson slid her hand to the back of her neck and lifted her braid as she brushed the hair from her forehead. The evening breezes were cool, and she was very glad, for the summer days in New Mexico were hot and dry. Still, as she gazed at the mountain, turned a brilliant shade of watermelon pink by the setting sun, she was happy to look forward to another day filled with the brilliance of blue sky, the space of the pastures, and love of her family.

She closed her eyes, breathing the freshness of the air scented with cedar, pine, sagebrush, and wildflowers. She could hear the windmill busily spinning to fill the water troughs, hear the breeze dancing through the cottonwoods down by the riverbank. A calf bawled, and Kitty, her pregnant and very lovable tabby cat, purred at her feet.

"Mama!" Ginny called. Lauryn opened her eyes to see Ginny, now almost five years old, rushing toward her, dragging a dusty three-year-old brother behind. "Mama, there is bird mess all over Henry again!"

Lauryn giggled. Ever since Ginny was born, it seemed, she had worried over Henry. "Well, we'll just have Daddy wash him off again, sweet pea."

"But, Mama, it's all down he's face and he's shirt…and there's a big ol' wad of it on he's foot, and Michael sticked his finger right in it and wiped it all over his face and…" Ginny babbled excitedly.

Kneeling down, Lauryn gathered her two children into her arms, hugging them lovingly. "Oh, I'd be willing to bet that Henry's had bird mess on him most of his life, Ginny. Don't worry about him so."

"But, Mama!" the child whined, stamping her foot. "He's all messy!"

Brushing a curl of ebony hair from Ginny's cheek, Lauryn smiled. "Well? What about May Belle? Did the birds get May Belle?"

When Sean and Patrick shipped Henry, the statue, from Connemara to New Mexico several years before, Brant commissioned a sculptor in Santa Fe to create a statue of a woman to keep Henry company. He affectionately dubbed the female statue, which was sculpted with attire true to the same time period as Henry, as May Belle. Brant explained that the statue reminded him of an old schoolteacher he had as a child, Miss May Belle Bomgardner.

"May Belle is fine, as always, Mama." Ginny sneered. "Them birds never mess on May Belle."

"That's because May Belle is a lady, and they know it," Lauryn told her daughter. Lifting her apron and moistening its edge with her tongue, Lauryn proceeded to clean Michael's face. "There's Mama's big boy. Now you quit playin' in that bird mess, Michael! I swear, you put me in mind of your Uncle Patrick."

The thunder of approaching hooves captured Lauryn's and the children's attention. She looked up, enchanted by the sight of Brant and Keil riding toward them. Though only nine, Keil had already become a good rider under his father's guidance. Both riders reined up, smiling contentedly.

"Mama!" Keil exclaimed. "You should see the writhin' maggots livin' on that ol' cow that died last week! It's amazin'!"

"I'm certain it is," Lauryn commented. "And where's your shirt, boy? You're goin' to be burnt through and through," she scolded. "Brant...he's gonna be browner than a bean, just like you."

"Hell, Lauryn, ain't nothing wrong with brown beans. Is there, Keil?" Brant chuckled.

"Brant!" Lauryn scolded. "For pity's sake, quit that swearin'."

But Brant only chuckled and looked to Ginny, who was tugging on his pant leg.

"What's the matter, kitten?" he asked.

"Daddy, them birds have been at Henry again. You've got to do somethin' about it!" Ginny whined.

Brant laughed. "Henry's fine, Ginny. You have Keil help you water that wisteria out by Henry." Brant held a hand out to Lauryn. "And you two watch Michael. I'm stealing your mama away for a bit." Winking flirtatiously at Lauryn, he asked, "Up for a ride, sugar?"

Lauryn smiled and tugged at the ribbon holding her braid a moment before mounting up behind Brant. She hugged him tightly around the waist, letting her face rest against his bare back. His skin was warm from work in the sun, and he smelled like leather and dust.

"Hang on, baby," Brant told her. At his signal, the horse broke into a comfortable pace. Lauryn smiled as she tipped her head back, letting the breeze cool her cheeks and blow through her hair. She waved to the children as they stood watching their parents ride away, grateful for the blessing of their happy faces.

Riding with Brant was always exhilarating. It always had been one of Lauryn's favorite pastimes. Ever since she and Brant had moved to New Mexico, they had ridden together. Riding with him was something of a romantic notion to Lauryn, and she reveled in it.

"The sunset is beautiful today," Brant sighed as he sat next to Lauryn atop the giant rock in the west pasture. "Look at that mountain!" he exclaimed.

But Lauryn was too distracted by a much larger beauty in the world. As she studied her husband, she smiled, thinking how much more handsome and attractive he was now even than he had been when they first met all those years ago. Reaching up, she twisted a dainty finger in his hair at the back of his neck.

"You need a hair trim, Mr. Masterson," she said.

Taking the piece of straw he'd been chewing out of his mouth and flicking it aside, Brant smiled at Lauryn and said, "You need a kiss, Mrs. Masterson."

Lauryn giggled, delighted, as always, by his teasing nature. "I do," she admitted. In an instant, she was in his arms, his skillful kisses sending her heart soaring with love and passion for him. It had always amazed Lauryn, the fact that she never tired of Brant's kisses. She still craved them as strongly as she had from the first time he'd kissed her.

His lips left hers, and she lay in his arms looking up at him as he gazed down into her face. The pink of the sunset washed over them like a painter's dream.

"I love you, Brant. I love you so much more than ever I did. And I never knew that I could," she said.

"I love you, Lauryn," he told her. "Thank you for finding Laura all those years ago. For finding me…for loving me." And as Brant gathered her into his arms once more, as she lay in the bliss of knowing his love, watching the sun set, as it sent violet-pink color to kiss the clouds, Lauryn fancied she sensed a familiar fragrance for a moment— the fragrance of home, of history, of dreams come true. The fragrance of sweet wisteria, the very fragrance of Connemara and enduring, eternal love.

ଛ

"Do you think we should tell Mama and Daddy?" Ginny asked. Tenderly, she kissed Michael on the forehead and wiped a smudge of dust from his face.

Keil Masterson stood looking at the giant arbor their father had built to support the wisteria that came from his mother's family home in Tennessee. He studied the two statues that stood under the arbor protected by the splendid vine that covered it. No one in the valley could ever explain how the Masterson family had been able to nurture wisteria to grow so healthy and so prolific in the dry desert heat of New Mexico. But Keil thought he knew, and so did Ginny, and even young Michael.

"Well? Do you, Keil?" Ginny repeated. "Do you think we should tell them?"

"Tell Daddy and Mama that we haven't watered Mama's wisteria in months and months? That we saw a man in a uniform and a lady with sunshine hair cleanin' bird mess off Henry the other day?" Keil shook his head again. "They'd never believe us." He looked to his little sister. "Would they?"

To my husband, Kevin…
"Mr. Perfectly Imperfect" Personified!

ABOUT THE AUTHOR

Marcia Lynn McClure's intoxicating succession of novels, novellas, and e-books—including *Shackles of Honor*, *The Windswept Flame*, *The Haunting of Autumn Lake*, and *Beneath the Honeysuckle Vine*—has established her as one of the most favored and engaging authors of true romance. Her unprecedented forte in weaving captivating stories of western, medieval, regency, and contemporary amour void of brusque intimacy has earned her the title "The Queen of Kissing."

Marcia, who was born in Albuquerque, New Mexico, has spent her life intrigued with people, history, love, and romance. A wife, mother, grandmother, family historian, poet, and author, Marcia Lynn McClure spins her tales of splendor for the sake of offering respite through the beauty, mirth, and delight of a worthwhile and wonderful story.

BIBLIOGRAPHY

Beneath the Honeysuckle Vine
A Better Reason to Fall in Love
The Bewitching of Amoretta Ipswich
Born for Thorton's Sake
The Chimney Sweep Charm
A Crimson Frost
Daydreams
Desert Fire
Divine Deception
Dusty Britches
The Fragrance of Her Name
The Haunting of Autumn Lake
The Heavenly Surrender
The Highwayman of Tanglewood
Kiss in the Dark
Kissing Cousins
The Light of the Lovers' Moon
Love Me
The McCall Trilogy
Midnight Masquerade
An Old-Fashioned Romance
One Classic Latin Lover, Please
The Pirate Ruse
The Prairie Prince
The Rogue Knight
Romantic Vignettes—The Anthology of Premiere Novellas
Saphyre Snow
Shackles of Honor
Sudden Storms
Sweet Cherry Ray
Take a Walk With Me
The Tide of the Mermaid Tears
The Time of Aspen Falls
To Echo the Past
The Touch of Sage

www.ingramcontent.com/pod-product-compliance
Lightning Source LLC
Chambersburg PA
CBHW070621260626

47161CB00007B/2533